DAWN
TO
DEADLY
NIGHTSHADE

Shelagh Mazey

With thanks to Mr and Mrs George and Mary Smith
for kindly allowing their home to be photographed
for the front cover

Matador
9 Priory Business Park,
Wistow Road, Kibworth Beauchamp,
Leicestershire. LE8 0RX
Tel: (+44) 116 279 2299
Fax: (+44) 116 279 2277
Email: books@troubador.co.uk
Web: www.troubador.co.uk/matador

ISBN 978 1783060 238

British Library Cataloguing in Publication Data.
A catalogue record for this book is available from the British Library.

Typeset by Troubador Publishing Ltd, Leicester, UK

Matador is an imprint of Troubador Publishing Ltd

Printed and bound in the UK by TJ International, Padstow, Cornwall

*For my family
with all my love*

TABLE OF CONTENTS

LIST OF CHARACTERS

PORTLANDERS FEATURED IN BRANDY ROW

JOSHUA DRYER (1832) *Heir to Alvington Manor*
REBECCA STONE (1838) *Sister*
VIOLET STONE (1814) *Mother*
MATTHEW STONE (1811) *Stepfather*
BENJAMIN STONE (1832) *Cousin*
ANNIE STONE (1810) *Ben's mother*

ALVINGTON MANOR STAFF

GARETH WILLIAMS (1798) *Butler/House steward*
MICHAEL PORTER (1800) *Footman*
JOHN MOORE (1827) *Groom*
BILLY RIDDICK (1832) *Stable boy*
PERCY SANDFORD (1810) *Gardener*
THOMAS HAWKINS (1831) *Gardener*
HENRY HODINOTT (1820) *Handyman*
MRS ABBOTT (1802) *Housekeeper*
FLORA BOUCHER (1810) *Cook*
ROSA PRICE (1825) *Parlour maid*
LOUISA ELIZABETH BONFIELD (1833) *Chambermaid*
EMILY POTTS (1837) *Housemaid*
ELSIE HALL (1833) *Kitchen/Scullery maid*
CHARLOTTE HODINOTT (1827) *Laundress*

THE WARREN FAMILY
HOME FARM

GRANNY WARREN (1768)
JACK (1792) & ELIZABETH (1795) WARREN
SIBLINGS: MALACHI (1825), JACOB (1830),
LUCY (1836) & BEATRICE (BUNNY) (1844)

THE BOUCHER FAMILY
KEEPER'S COTTAGE, POUND LANE

JOHN (1809) & FLORA (1810) BOUCHER
SIBLINGS: LETTIE (1838) & TOBY (1846)

CAMP ROAD FAMILIES – ESTATE WORKERS

BERT (1773) & ROSE (1783) SMITH *(Retired)*
MICHAEL (1800) & MAUD (1802) PORTER
HENRY (1820) & CHARLOTTE (1827) HODINOTT
JOHN (1827) & SUSAN (1831) MOORE
SIBLINGS: LUKE (1851) & LILLY (1853)
PERCY (1810) & MARY (1812) SANDFORD

SIBLINGS: ROBERT (1830) & HARRY (1833)
JACK (1805) & MOLLY (1802) HAWKINS
SIBLINGS: FRANK (1823) & THOMAS (1831)

THE BONFIELD FAMILY
KNAPP COTTAGE, PRESTON PLUCKNET

ARTHUR (1808) & MARTHA (1813) BONFIELD
SIBLINGS: MILLIE (1834) & LOUISA (1833)
GRANDDAUGHTER: AURORA (September 1851)

THE FAIRWAY FAMILY

AMBROSE FAIRWAY (1804) *Solicitor's Clerk*
DAUGHTER: CLARA (1834)

THE HAWKINS FAMILY
COBB COTTAGE, DRAY ROAD, ODCOMBE

GABRIEL (1802) & ESTHER (1805) HAWKINS
SIBLINGS: RAYMOND (1832) & JEAN (1831)

THE MEAKINS FAMILY
SUMMERVILLE HOUSE

SIR OLIVER MEAKINS (1793) & LADY ANNABEL (1797)
SIBLINGS: NATHAN (1818) & OLIVIA (1813)
ALISTAIR MCNAB (1802) *Scottish steward*
WADMAN (1818) *First Footman*
APSEY (1823) *Olivia Meakins' Ladies maid*
MRS FAVERSHAM (1799) *Housekeeper*
MORTON (1813) *Butler*
MRS CHUBB (1807) *Cook*
RAYMOND HAWKINS (1832) *Poacher & beater*
JEAN HAWKINS (1831) *Housemaid*
AMY PROCTOR (1838) *Kitchen maid*
BOBBY TOMKINS (1835) *Butcher boy*

THE BRIDEWELL FAMILY
CLIFTON MAYBANK MANOR

SAMUEL BRIDEWELL (1791) & EDITH BRIDEWELL
(1795)
*SIBLINGS: ALICIA (1824), KEZIAH (1822) & SERENA
(1820)*

SUPPORTING CHARACTERS

CONSTABLE GUNDRY
DR GILLINGHAM
LORD AND LADY HELYAR *of Coker Court*
COLONEL AND MRS SEYMOUR *of Sutton Bingham Manor*
SIBLINGS: RUPERT (28) & ASHLEIGH (24)
MR & MRS STOURTON *of Abbey Farm, Preston Plucknett*
MR JONATHAN BIRCH – *Magistrates Court Prosecutor*
LORD HARVEY-GOLDSMITH – *Crown Court Judge*
MR ABLE MORRISON – *Crown Court Prosecutor*
REVEREND DAVID PHELPS (1802) *Local Vicar & JP,
Chairman of Quarter Session*

MENAGERIE

Hercules, Perseus – *Shire horses (brown)*
Capricorn – *Josh's Horse (black stallion)*
Andromeda *(brown)* Cassiopeia *(grey)* & Capella *(bay)*
Honey – *John Boucher's springer spaniel.*

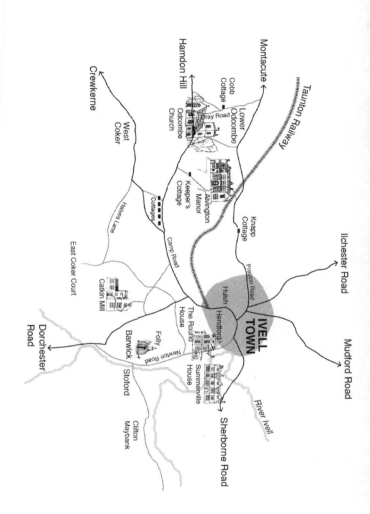

THE PROLOGUE *(June 1851)*

Joshua Dryer looks back and waves to his proud parents, his sister Rebecca and his cousin Ben with an overwhelming mixture of excitement and sadness, as he leaves Portland behind him. He has his few possessions packed in a haversack on his back and he sits tall in the saddle on a hired horse. He is following the route that leads to the ferry bridge, and he is filled with apprehension at his new role as lord of the manor at Alvington, near Ivell in south Somerset.

He hopes there will be enough of interest in Somerset to keep him happy there. He has been brought up in a small cottage in Chiswell on Portland and in all his twenty years he never imagined leading the life of an aristocrat. But that was his father's background and he at least has to try to live up to his name.

He found life rather mundane as a young man living on such a small island and at the age of sixteen he was itching for adventure. He knew his mother would never allow him to go off to sea and so he ran away to join the crew of the Methodist missionary brig, sailing off to New Guinea with Captain Buck. What an adventure he had! He soon recovered from his seasickness and had much enjoyed the camaraderie of the sailors. He gained satisfaction from watching the Methodist missionaries teaching the heathens they encountered the principles of Christianity, and they influenced him in his decision to try his utmost to always lead a good and moral life. If it had not been for the news he received on his return, of his inheritance, he would have gone with them again on their next voyage, but how could he turn his back on this fortune?

As he reaches the ferry bridge he passes a young couple. The man raises his hat to him and the young woman curtseys and he is reminded of the story his mother told him, of how she and his father first met. His father was the new preventive man and his mother was in the process of conveying illicit spirits, hidden in pockets stitched on the underside of her petticoats. Although unaware of his purpose, she was immediately struck by this stranger's handsome appearance. His deep brown eyes had been very intense as he looked at her and he was meticulously dressed, with dark, wavy hair touching his neck from underneath his tall hat. However, at the time she had been terrified he might detect the sound of the bottles clinking against the pebbles, as she dipped in a curtsey to him. Little did she know she was destined to marry this striking stranger and bear him a son.

He has few recollections of his father, as he died when Joshua was only three years old, but he still remembers the exhilaration of being carried high up on his shoulders as they walked along the shoreline, burying his face in his soft, black hair as he clung with both hands around his father's neck. As he grew up his mother told him he looked more and more like his father every day. He remembers loving him above all else and missing him dreadfully after he was killed by those lawless smugglers.

He is curious to know what his grandfather had been like, for his father had turned his back on him and his fortune. *Will he be able to fill those boots*, he wonders, as he continues on his journey to Ivell? He plans to meet Mr Fairway, his solicitor, who is escorting him to the manor and introducing him to his staff. He is uneasy at having to take command of domestic employees, all far more experienced than he is himself and some of them far more advanced in years, but all he can do is his best.

It has been many years since Alvington has witnessed such enthusiastic endeavours from the staff. When the crippled Christian Dryer died in January 1850 there was much conjecture among the estate workers as to what was to become of them. It takes the lawyers six months to trace Joshua Dryer to the Fiji Islands, by which time he is on his return journey to Portland.

At the beginning of June, Gareth Williams, the steward, orders that all rooms should be made ready for his imminent arrival. This is no small task, as the house has been shut up for so long. Diagonal shafts of sunlight pour in when the shutters are thrown open, glistening through mites of dust as the sheets are ripped off the long enshrouded furniture.

The staff have only been told of his age and his bachelor status and, the female workers in particular, are eagerly awaiting their first glimpse of the young master. The sound of a carriage pulling up outside has them all in a quandary. There is still much to be done; surely it is not possible that the young master has arrived so prematurely? Rosa, the parlour maid, runs to the front window. "No need to panic, it is only Mr Fairway."

Mr Fairway walks importantly up the gravel drive to the main entrance and pulls on the bell rope. Gareth Williams strides to the door.

"Good day to you, sir. Please do come in."

"Thank you, Williams," says Mr Fairway, removing his hat as he steps over the threshold. "How are things progressing?"

"I am afraid there is still much to be done, Mr Fairway. When do you expect young Mr Dryer to arrive?"

"I understand he has some business to attend to in the town tomorrow, but he has indicated that he should be finished around midday and I will bring him here immediately afterwards. He requests refreshments to be prepared for our arrival and dinner at seven."

"Very well, sir."

Mr Fairway cannot help smiling at the hive of industry within the house. He has no intention of suggesting that the young master will not expect such tremendous efforts on their part, simply because he is not used to such a lifestyle. The less they knew about that, the better. Even the tailor with whom tomorrow's business is to be conducted will not guess that the expensive suit of clothes that Joshua will be wearing is the only one to his name.

Mr Fairway is quite sure that the young master will indeed be able to keep all such information a closely guarded secret. *He has the air of a gentleman and has travelled to foreign parts with the Methodists, converting the heathens to Christianity. He has walked the streets of London and most of the folk on the estate have travelled no further afield than the market town of Ivell. For all his tender years he has the look of a mature man about him. An ambitious man at that*, thinks Mr Fairway, with a grin. He cannot help feeling excited that he is the agent of the law who has brought this man into Ivellian society. That he is the one who has, well and truly, put the cat among the pigeons. *All the enterprising females in the vicinity will be having attacks of the vapours over this, the most eligible male for miles around.*

Gareth Williams strides through the main entrance; three maids are polishing the oak treads and balustrading of the staircase. "I have prepared the main bedroom for the young master, Mr Fairway."

"I think, Williams, that you will have to get used to calling him by his correct title. He is after all, the Lord of the Manor of Alvington and entitled to be suitably addressed."

"Of course, Mr Fairway, forgive me, but it is how we have been referring to him below stairs."

"I understand that Williams, but it is your responsibility to instil respect for the young gentleman in the minds of the rest of the servants. I want nothing or no-one to make this transition any more difficult than necessary for his lordship."

They walk on through the south facing rooms. The massive casement windows have been thrown open and a fresh August breeze flutters those of the curtains that have been re-hung, after their brisk beating at the hands of the maids. Mr Fairway looks out onto an expanse of lawn, the ornamental lake and the fields beyond. The gardeners are below the terrace working on the herbaceous border.

As they pass on through the ground floor rooms, Mr Fairway can see why the household is in such a frenzy of activity; the place is in utter turmoil as many of the rooms have been shut up for so long.

"Williams, I can see you are going to have to concentrate on the main living rooms at present. There is no virtue in opening up rooms that are unnecessary."

"That has been our intention, Mr Fairway, but it is difficult to judge how many of the rooms his lordship will consider essential to his needs."

"I should suggest that the kitchen facilities, the dining room, the drawing room, the library, the gun room, the dressing room, the master bedroom and two guest rooms should be immaculate. The ballroom, the upper west wing and the remaining bedrooms can be set aside for the time being until such time as his lordship shall see fit to entertain."

They reach the top of the main stairs and Williams opens the door to the master bedroom. It looks magnificent: the mahogany furniture shines with beeswax, the four-poster bed looks fresh and clean with crisp, white linen folded over a wine coloured, monogrammed eiderdown.

In the corner of the room is an exquisite Japanese six-leaf screen covered in figured silk, behind which is a commode and washstand with jug and bowl. Everything is in pristine condition and Mr Fairway is suitably impressed.

"Well, Williams, I can see everyone is doing their best and I cannot ask for more than that. I'd just like to see the kitchen before I leave."

They make their way back down the stairs and turn left, down the corridor and left again into the kitchen. The smell of baking immediately taunts Mr Fairway and his mouth starts to water uncontrollably. His wife, bless her, had been a wonderful pastry cook and he had lost pounds in weight when she had sadly died giving birth to his Clara. It was some considerable time before his little daughter was as accomplished a cook as her dear mama had been, but he is proud to boast that she is as perfect as he could wish in all respects.

Flora Boucher is a lady of ample proportions, as one would imagine a capable cook to be, and she is certainly a good advertisement for her profession. "I hope you ain't bringin' dirty boots onto my scrubbed flag floor, Mr Williams? Emily's got enouf on 'er 'ands without 'avin to do things twice."

"Have no fear, Mrs Boucher, we have been right through the house without making a mark, I can assure you." Mr Fairway beams at her.

Mrs Boucher immediately loses her composure, "God bless my soul, Mr Fairway. I didn't see 'twas you there." She is flustered and her face has a rosy glow, she wipes her brow with the back of her hand.

"I am pleased to see the kitchen so productive, Mrs Boucher, and I am sure his lordship will be most impressed at the standard of your cuisine."

She is in the process of taking a tray of baking out of the oven.

"My, that smells so good, my dear lady. How do you do it?"

"Oh, 'tis years of practice, Mr Fairway. Would you like a small helping of honey cake? I 'ave some that 'ave cooled by now in the larder."

His flattery has had the desired effect and the little man beams with pleasure. "Are you sure you can spare some?" he asks politely.

"I wouldn't give none to just anyone you know, sir, but as it is yourself, it pleases me to know just how much you do like my cookin'." She turns to the steward begrudgingly, "There is enough for you too, Mr Williams, if you are still hungry after that big breakfast you 'ad this morning."

Gareth Williams is getting impatient. "No thank you, Mrs Boucher." He turns to Mr Fairway. "As I have several duties to attend to, Mr Fairway, would you please excuse me?"

"Certainly, I will just sample Mrs Boucher's delightful cake and then I too must return to my office. I shall see myself out." He stands up and holds out his hand to the steward. "I am entirely satisfied with the progress made so far, and I am much obliged to you. I will see you all tomorrow at around noon, when I shall hopefully deliver the new lord of the manor into your capable hands."

"Good day to you, sir."

Mr Fairway insisted that he should not spend his first night in Somerset alone at an hotel, however,

Joshua cannot help feeling ill at ease imposing on the good nature of his self-appointed advisor in this way. His instructions had been to follow the road from Hendford, past the junctions with South Street, the borough and Church Lane, continuing along the cattle market road to the junction right into Sheep Lane. Their cottage is at the bottom of Sheep Lane, where it turns the corner to Stairs Hill. It overlooks the Sheep Fair Ground and backs onto Church Cottages.

Joshua has no difficulty finding the place and having passed through the dirt and dust of the main thoroughfare is impressed with the neat and tidy appearance of the little building, set above the sloping road of Stairs Hill. However, before he can tend to his own needs he has to see to those of his hired horse. He makes his way to the horse pool, where he was told he would find the horse keeper. He hands over the animal and pays the man the remainder of the hiring fee. The horse pool is well used as a watering place and resembles a quagmire. Thus he is very tired and a little muddy when he eventually knocks on the door of the little cottage. He is scraping his long, leather riding boots on the metal provided when his knock is answered by a young lady in mop cap and apron.

"Would you be so kind as to inform the master of the house that Joshua Dryer hast come, of Portland."

The girl offers a charming smile but, before she can answer, a voice calls out from within. "Come in; come in, my dear sir." Mr Fairway jumps up from his armchair to greet his honoured guest. He bows, "I am your servant, my Lord."

"Come now, Fairway. Do not ridicule me in this way."

"You mistake me, my Lord. I am in earnest."

He looks offended that he has been misconstrued. "I wish you to consider me completely at your disposal."

"Forgive me, sir, I am not used to the lifestyle just yet. It will take some time for me to adjust to the conventions and proprieties of the upper classes."

"Fear not, dear boy. I will be your counsel in such legal affairs that you are not trained to comprehend and in matters of social etiquette, I will be your guide." He indicates a comfortable chair. "Please sit down, remove those boots and make use of the foot stool."

Joshua does as he is bid gratefully. Mr Fairway relieves him of his tall hat, placing it on the stand in the hallway. The boots he places beneath, on the flag floor.

He turns to the young maid, "Clara, my dear, have we refreshments ready for his lordship?"

"Of course, Papa. I shall serve you shortly." She leaves the room hastily.

"I am sorry, my Lord. I should have introduced you to my daughter, Clara."

"Please Mr Fairway, I should be much obliged if you would call me 'Joshua'. I feel decidedly uncomfortable with our relationship on its present standing, and as I have no one I can call a friend in this county, I would very much value your looking upon me as a friend."

"It is decidedly unconventional, my Lord, but as it is your wish, I am honoured to be considered your friend. I must, however, insist on proper address in public."

"Agreed; but you have omitted to tell me your Christian name in return, Mr Fairway."

He laughs, "I am embarrassed to say that it is 'Ambrose', my Lord."

"Ah," he shakes his finger in mock admonition "No more 'my Lord', remember?"

Clara enters with a tray of cutlery and proceeds to lay out the table in the corner of the room. The silver knives and forks glisten against the clean, white cloth and in the centre a bowl of yellow roses look as if they have only just been picked. Clara moves them to a sideboard and Joshua cannot help noticing how shy Fairway's daughter is, who, for the most part, keeps her eyes downcast.

"Clara, my dear, I would like to introduce you formally to our guest, Mr Joshua Dryer, Lord of the Manor of Alvington. My Lord, this is my daughter, Clara."

Joshua stands up, "I am delighted to make your acquaintance, Miss Fairway." He takes her hand and bows, touching his lips to her soft skin. He is surprised at the silky texture, for surely it is she who is responsible for the domestic duties of the household.

She smiles as she dips in a curtsey, "I am pleased to meet you, my Lord, but please forgive me, I am in haste not to spoil your supper."

He releases her hand hastily. "I am so sorry, I would not dream of delaying you when I can already smell the savoury aroma of a tasty meal."

The meal proves to be a culinary delight and his hosts are excellent company. After the lamps have been lit and the curtains are drawn, they relax. Clara joins them after the dishes are done, all the time quietly working on her embroidery. Joshua learns a lot about Ivell and its people, about the gloving industry for which it is renowned and about the local landowners and their estates, including his own.

Later Clara shows him into the little box room that is their guest room. Although tiny, it is equipped with everything he requires. In no time at all he is abed and mulling over the day's events. It has been an exhausting journey, after he had said his farewells to his mother and Matthew and to Rebecca and Ben. It seems like another world, this place that is, after all, only five and twenty miles from Portland and the sea. He is already missing the sound of the breaking waves and the cry of the sea birds. *Will I ever settle to this new way of life?* he wonders. Ambrose has given him all kinds of advice from domestic to financial investments, and he is now quite exhausted.

He hears the rumpus of the folk leaving the Half Moon Hotel a little way up the street and later he hears the church clock chime at midnight. Then he hears no more until dawn.

Early the following morning Joshua joins the Fairways for breakfast. He is impatient to get to Alvington as soon as he can, but his trip to the tailors is unavoidable. Mr Fairway is to accompany him as far as his office and direct him from there. This proves to be quite simple as the shop in Middle Street can be seen from the borough and, as they part company, they arrange to meet again at noon before leaving for the estate.

Mr Solomon, the tailor, is eager to please his esteemed client and apart from measuring him up for three new winter weight suits of clothes he is also able to supply him with two lightweight outfits, already made. These had been made for a young man who was intending to get married, but his fiancée had unfortunately run off with his best friend and he no longer required them. One set is in mainly blues and the other is a dark green; both are, amazingly, a perfect fit and Mr Solomon wraps them in a brown paper parcel for him.

Joshua spends some time in choosing the correct blend of fabric and colours for his winter wardrobe: a soft though hard-wearing material for the trousers, elaborate cream and lemon waistcoats and rich, dark coloured dress coats. He also wants a lounge suit made, similar to the one that is displayed on the dummy in the window. He chooses several silk shirts, cravats and wider neck-cloths. The time flies by and he has not even considered the need for new undergarments. "How soon do you think the winter suits will be ready?" Joshua asks. "I would appreciate delivery as soon as possible. If you could treat the order as urgent, I would be much obliged."

"Have no fear, my Lord, they will be with you before the October chills, I can assure you."

"I would be grateful if you could make it sooner, if possible, as many of my possessions were lost in transit from London and one has to keep up appearances." He passes Mr Solomon a generous tip.

"I will endeavour to do my best, my Lord." He quickly pockets the gold sovereign.

"I wonder if in the meantime you would also mind sending round a selection of your best winter underwear, Mr Solomon."

"Certainly, sir." He makes a note of this on his order pad.

"Thank you so much for your thorough attention to my needs, Mr Solomon. I shall doubtless be calling on you again. Until such time I shall leave my requirements in your capable hands." He holds out his hand to seal the bargain. "Good morning, sir."

"Thank you, my Lord, for your valued custom. Good day to you, sir."

Joshua is relieved to leave the cluttered little shop and step outside into the sunshine, with his parcels tucked under his arm. He strides quickly up the hill to the borough, knowing that the church must be about to strike midday. As he turns into the churchyard he sees Mr Fairway leaving his office building and he hails him. Now the last stage of his journey is in sight.

CHAPTER 1 *(June – September 1851)*

ALVINGTON MANOR

Millie Bonfield is waiting anxiously beside a copse at the summit of a small knoll. The late afternoon sunlight is catching her thick, red hair as she perches on a gate and scans the pastures for the first sight of Nathan Meakins. As soon as she spots him she can tell that he is angry, as he spurs his horse across the fields towards her. He wastes no time with pleasantries.

"What the devil do you think you are up to, Millie, dragging me all the way over here?" He flicks the reins from side to side, agitating the horse.

His anger makes her heart thump anxiously and feeling wretched she stammers, "I… I am sorry, but I had to see you privately, away from Summerville House."

"*You* had to see *me* did you, Millie? I am afraid I am not used to being given orders by my domestic staff, who the dickens do you think you are?"

She steps down from the gate and moves closer to him, causing the horse to lower its head and shake it from side to side. "Please don't be angry with me, I am so scared and I need your help." She looks down at the ground dejectedly and when she looks back up she is looking through a mist of tears. "I thought you had feelings of love for me."

"I did have, until you got yourself in the pudden club. That has changed everything."

She pleads with him, unwilling to believe he can

be so cruel and detached. "But I need your advice, time is going on. What am I to do?"

"That is your problem," he says sharply, "I told you to get rid of it."

"I cannot, it is too late." She brushes the tears from her eyes. "I didn't realise there was a baby, I am too far gone and now it would be dangerous." She coaxes, "Can you not see it in your heart to take care of me and your child? I would make you a good wife, I could bear you lots more babies and I am not so unattractive… you told me I was beautiful once."

Meakins laughs at this and the sound is brittle and callous, "Well, no woman looks so wonderful with a huge, swollen belly."

She flinches at his unkind words. "But it will disappear when the baby is born, I will make sure that it doesn't spoil my figure. I am still young and it will soon recover and then in a couple of months, after my confinement, you could buy me some pretty gowns."

Meakins shifts in the saddle and the animal nudges its rear against her, pushing her to one side. "I don't care to; I have better things to spend my money on."

He is arrogant and heartless and anger rises in her. "You couldn't keep your hands off me a few months back," she retorts bitterly.

"Don't delude yourself, Millie. Why would I want to lumber myself with a penniless wife and child when I have the pick of the gentility here about? Someone who would bring with them a nice fat dowry is what I need, not a brood of scruffy urchins from the local hovel."

She gasps, his words stabbing through her heart like a dagger. She is stunned that he could be so merciless after all his wheedling to get her into his bed. *He was never going to truly care for me, baby or not. What a fool I have been to believe anything to the contrary.* She is ruined. Bitter tears of anger spike her eyes and she finds her tongue, "You are a vile, selfish, arrogant pig! You have used me for your own ends and nothing more and I never want to set eyes on you ever again. I hope you get what you deserve, Nathan Meakins, and I hope you rot in hell." She turns from him and runs as fast as she can across the rough ground, blindly stumbling across thick, grassy tussocks, the tears running down her face as she goes and her unruly red hair flying wildly in her wake.

Joshua is excited as he travels along the Preston Plucknett road beside Mr Fairway. He is eager to see the estate and manor house that he has inherited from his grandfather. As they go he looks from side to side at the lush green Somerset countryside and the small cottages interspersed in clusters along the roadside, where barefooted children are skipping and playing.

"You say that the estate has been in good hands since my grandfather's death?"

"Yes, it has, it really runs like clockwork. You will obviously want to make some changes, but I would recommend letting things run on for a while whilst you adjust to your new position."

"I agree, I am most anxious not to prove wanting in the eyes of the staff. Due to my youth and inexperience I know I have a lot to learn, but I do need something else to challenge me in the meantime. I have led a very active life, whilst at sea, and I should hate to be bored."

Mr Fairway looks thoughtful. "Well, you know the old manorial courtroom is in the east wing of

Alvington Manor and your grandfather was a Justice of the Peace, which I am sure you would find both interesting and challenging. It would also give you some standing in the community and as a member of the gentry you should be able to get nominated quite easily."

"Do you know, Ambrose, I think you may have something there. That would be very interesting and maybe Captain Buck from the missionary ship would support me in that. He got to know me very well on the long trip to New Guinea, but am I not rather young?"

"I believe you have to be at least twenty-one to serve, but you will need to do a bit of studying first, so you could use the next year for that," replies Mr Fairway. "I have some volumes that I can bring for you next time I visit and I am sure that, once you get to know Reverend Phelps, he will also sponsor you. He is your local vicar, who takes services in the estate chapel at Alvington Manor, but he is also the chairman of the quarter sessions," continues Mr Fairway.

"I would be most grateful, Ambrose, thank you."

As the wheels clatter on Joshua notices out of the corner of his eye a pretty young red head running from the opposite direction, parallel with the road, through the fields on his right. Her hair is thick and flying wild and her eyes are stormy. She seems to be very distressed and Joshua is concerned, but they are passing by and Mr Fairway is talking to him again. Whilst listening to him, Joshua observes on the high ground in the distance a rather aristocratic looking gentleman astride a dappled-grey horse, standing hard and looking down at the young girl. He relaxes a little; it must have been a lover's tiff. No need for him to get involved and his attention turns back to Mr Fairway.

Mr Fairway is pointing out landmarks like the old Abbey Farm and the pond, before they come to the crossroads and take a left towards Odcombe. A short way along the road they arrive at the imposing entrance to Alvington Manor and their carriage passes through the piers of the great gateway and along a meandering driveway. On reaching yet another set of impressive pillars, Joshua is stunned at the beauty and magnificence of the mansion before him. The manor house itself faces him, with the other buildings arranged so that together they form a square. On the left are what appear to be a coach house, stables and a clock tower, and on the right is a smaller dwelling house with a little chapel behind it. On either side of the driveway are perfectly manicured lawns, with herbaceous flowerbeds all around, set against the bordering walls. The driveway terminates in a turning circle and the carriage is drawn to a halt. The whole effect takes his breath away − surely it cannot be that he is the new owner of all this! He feels a shiver of excitement and apprehension as he braces himself before meeting his staff.

As the carriage pulls up a young man, who looks to be the same age as Joshua, runs up to lead the horses into the stable yard. Mr Fairway and Joshua disembark and the lad introduces himself as Billy Riddick, the stable boy. They shake hands with him and then turn towards the front door. Mr Fairway leads the way. As they approach the door is opened and they are greeted by Gareth Williams, the steward and butler.

"Good day to you, my Lord," he says in a lyrical Welsh brogue as he bows his head.

On entering the hall, Joshua is astonished at the immense height of the ceilings. He looks around the handsome wainscoted room, but he soon realises that all the household staff are lined up to greet him and, as Mr Fairway stands aside, Joshua shakes hands with each of them and Gareth tells him who they are and each of their duties.

"May I present to you firstly Mrs Abbott, who is our housekeeper." Joshua makes an effort to remember that Mrs Abbott is tall and slim with her greying hair pulled back off her face and fixed in a bun and that she is wearing a mourning brooch and a chatelaine's chain.

She dips a curtsey as Joshua takes her hand. "Good morning, my Lord."

Joshua smiles. "Good morning, Mrs Abbott."

"Next we have Mrs Boucher, who is our cook." Noting that Mrs Boucher is a typical cook, plump and jolly with curly brown hair, Joshua takes her hand and again she dips a curtsey. "I'm very pleased to meet you, my Lord; we 'ave been very much looking forward to this day."

"Me too, Mrs Boucher, me too," says Joshua, as he shakes her hand sincerely.

"Our footman is Michael Porter."

Mr Porter is impressively tall, clean shaven with sideburns and good looking. He bows and then takes Joshua's proffered hand. "Good morning, my Lord, I hope we all come up to expectations."

"I am impressed so far, Mr Porter, so it bodes well."

Gareth continues: "This is Rosa Price, our parlour maid." Joshua cannot help but notice her rounded, well-developed figure and he smiles appreciatively as she dips to curtsey.

"Good morning, Rosa."

"Good morning, my Lord."

"Moving on, this is Louisa Bonfield our chambermaid."

Louisa has the most amazing eyes; they are neither

green nor blue, but a strange mixture of the two, giving them a fluid depth that is quite startling. She has a mass of red hair the colour of burnt copper. *She is charming*, thinks Joshua, as he takes her hand in his and she smiles, looking right into his eyes as she curtseys for him. "I am pleased to meet you, my Lord."

"The pleasure is all mine, Louisa," he says, smiling warmly down at her.

"This is Emily Potts, the housemaid." Emily is a little dumpling of a girl with dimples and she gives a pretty smile as she curtseys. Her curly hair is held in place under her cap with a hairnet, which is clipped to the back of her head with an ivory comb.

"Hello, my Lord."

"Hello, Emily."

"Here we have Elsie Hall, the scullery maid." Gareth frowns at her, "Stand up straight, Elsie, and stop fidgeting."

Elsie is a scrawny little thing, who looks to be the youngest, but Joshua thinks she probably hasn't stopped growing yet. She gives him a warm, shy smile as he takes her hand and she dips. "I am sorry, my Lord, I didn't mean to fidget."

"Don't worry, Elsie, I don't intend to keep you here long."

"And lastly," continues Gareth, "Charlotte Hodinott, the laundry maid." Charlotte is a tidy young woman who has long blonde hair, which is plaited, wound into a heavy coil and pinned neatly against the nape of her neck.

"Last but not least I am sure, Charlotte."

"They call me Lottie, my Lord. My hubby is Henry Hodinott, the handy man."

"I am pleased to meet you, Lottie."

"The outside workers will be here first thing tomorrow morning to be introduced to you then," says Gareth.

All the staff are cheerful, friendly and well turned out and Joshua is suitably impressed. "Well, this is a fine welcome and I am very pleased indeed to be introduced to everyone after all this time. I am sorry that you have been rather rudderless, so to speak, over the last few months, but I am assured that you have all worked extremely hard keeping the ship afloat." *Oh dear,* he thinks, *whatever am I babbling about! I had better shut up before I make an even bigger fool of myself.* "I will take the time over the next few days to get to know each of you individually, but for now please all go on back about your business. I would, however, be grateful if Mr Fairway and I might be served some refreshments, if that is not too much trouble."

"Of course, my Lord, please come this way." Rosa steps forward and leads the way through into the drawing room.

On reaching her home Millie is distraught. She goes straight up to the attic room that she shares with her sister and flings herself onto her bed, crying as if her heart is breaking. Her parents and her sister Louisa are all out at work and the cottage is silent, apart from the sound of her weeping. She can see no way out of her troubles; her parents will be ashamed of her and her father will want to kill him.

Eventually she hears the gate creaking and sees Louisa coming up the garden path and she decides that she has to confide in someone. She wipes away her tears, brushes her hair and tidies up her appearance, but cannot dispel the fear coursing through her.

Louisa immediately notices her red eyes. "Whatever is wrong, Millie? You look dreadful."

It is no use; she has to tell her sister, no matter what she may think of her. "Oh, Louisa, I am in a terrible fix," her tears brim over again and she slumps down on the bed.

"It cannot be that bad, Millie."

"It is, Lou, it is awful."

Louisa sits down next to her and puts her arm around her younger sister, "Tell me what is troubling you."

She takes a deep breath, "I am with child," she whispers.

"What did you say?" Louisa pulls away from her to look her in the face. "I couldn't have heard right."

"I am carrying a baby, Lou."

"But how can that be? You are not seeing anyone."

"It is Nathan Meakins' child."

"What!" Louisa stares at her in disbelief. "Oh, Millie. How could you, with that arrogant man?"

"He was kind to me, Lou. He singled me out with his flattery. I know now that he was insincere, but I believed him, Lou, I thought he really liked me." Her mouth quivers and she wipes away the tears with the back of her hand.

Louisa feels a shiver of distaste go through her. "Have you told him of your condition?"

"Yes, and he told me to get rid, but I have already felt it move inside me and I don't feel I can kill my own baby. Besides, I don't know how to, Lou, I might just harm it, and then what?"

Louisa nods towards her sister's stomach. "How much longer do you have before the baby comes?"

"I don't know for sure, but my curse stopped back in January."

"Christ, Millie, you must be about six months gone already!"

9

"That would mean September time, then," she says dejectedly. "He is not going to help me, Lou… what am I going to do?" she bursts out crying again.

"Well, you have managed to hide it from everyone so far, but it will get more and more difficult as time goes on."

"Maybe when it comes we could leave it by the door of the sanatorium and some kind person will care for it and no-one need ever find out that it was mine."

"Do you think that you could bear to do that, Millie? You may never see your child again."

"What choice do I have? I cannot face Ma and Pa with this, I am so ashamed, Lou, and I am afraid of what Pa will do to Meakins if I tell them the truth." She wipes away her tears and gives a sad sigh. "That he seduced me to start with… but then, when he got me alone, he wouldn't take no for an answer and he… he forced me."

"The evil scoundrel! I could kill him myself."

"That is just bold talk, Lou; you know you don't mean it, but thank you for comforting me, I have never felt so alone, not being able to tell anyone." She blows her nose in her handkerchief.

Louisa puts her arm around her sister and holds her close. "You should have confided in me before now, Millie, then maybe you wouldn't be in this mess."

"You know, even though he was so rough with me at the time, I thought that it was passion that had a hold on him and I forgave him. I convinced myself that he must desire me very much."

"Oh, I am sure he desired you, Millie, but he used you all the same and now you and his baby are discarded like old boots."

"Don't go on, Lou. I never want to hear his name again. I am not going back there to work, either. I shall ask Ma to bring back work for me from the glove factory and I can work from home. I shall say that I miss you all and I have decided to come back home… that I find the work tiring and would rather be stitching gloves.

"That is a passable plan and you can wear a pinny over your clothes, which should hide your bump for now at least."

"I don't know, Lou, sometimes I feel it might be a blessing if the poor little mite was stillborn."

"Don't say that, Millie, I am sure it will all be all right in the end."

Joshua and Mr Fairway have enjoyed their refreshments and now Mr Fairway is giving him a guided tour of the house. Joshua is trying to take in all the stylish rooms, the beautiful furniture and classic old master paintings that now belong to him. He could never have imagined in his wildest dreams a more impressive and attractive home. He looks out of the windows in the master bedroom at the colourful herbaceous borders, immaculate lawns and the picturesque duck pond with the green fields beyond.

"This duck pond looks to me more like a modest lake, Ambrose. Do you think that it might take a boat?"

Mr Fairway joins him at the window. "I don't see why not, perhaps you should have a word with Mr Hodinott, your handyman, when you meet him tomorrow."

"I think I may, Ambrose, I think I very well may."

They go downstairs and along to the well-equipped kitchen. The aromatic smells of a meat casserole gently simmering on the range fills the air as they open the door, accompanied by the mouth watering aroma of potatoes roasting in the oven.

"Wow, that smells so good!" Joshua exclaims as he lifts the lid to see what is cooking. "Are you going to stay for supper, Ambrose?"

"Well, I must say that smells very tempting."

Flora Boucher enters from the back door and jumps at the sight of them. "Oh my goodness, my Lord, you frightened the life out of me."

"I am sorry, Flora, but Mr Fairway has been showing me around and we were just savouring the smells of your cooking."

"Of course you were, my Lord, I don't mean to complain. I just didn't expect anyone to be 'ere that is all, my Lord."

"Is there enough for Mr Fairway to join me tonight?"

"Of course there is, my Lord, there's plenty there."

"Then you shall stay, Ambrose, and no arguments."

"Thank you, I am most grateful."

Together they enjoy a stroll around the garden before supper is served. Both eat heartily and Joshua realises that he is going to be very well looked after here, by all the staff and in all respects. As he says farewell to Mr Fairway he cannot help thanking him for all his hard work in tracking him down, for, if it had not been for him, he may never have realised his inheritance. "I am very grateful to you for your vigilance and resolve in tracing my family and thus opening up to me all of this." He opens his arms wide and turns on the spot to encompass all around him. "I feel that I must be the luckiest man alive at this moment."

"This has been the most rewarding duty that I have ever had the honour to perform and I am truly happy for you, my boy. I hope it brings all you deserve and you will always be content here."

"I think that I shall be. I have a very good feeling about it." They shake hands and Mr Fairway climbs aboard his gig. Joshua calls goodbye as the carriage rolls off down the drive. He turns wearily back into the house. It has been a long day and he plans to retire early.

The following morning all the estate workers are on parade and Joshua steps out to meet them. Billy Riddick immediately removes his cap.

"Good morning, Billy, how are you this morning?"

The lad looks up with his cheeky smile. "I am well, my Lord,"

"You look well, Billy," Joshua smiles back. "Tell me, Billy, I know that you live above the stables, but do your family live far from here?"

The smile fades. "I have no family, my Lord; I come from the Coker Poor House."

"Oh I am sorry, Billy, I did not know that. Well I hope that you will think of us as your family now, lad." He pats Billy reassuringly on the back.

His smile returns. "I will. Thank you, my Lord."

Joshua moves on. "And this is…?"

"Robert," says Robert Sandford.

"And Harry, my Lord," responds his brother.

The two lads look alike, with identical quiffs of sandy brown hair falling across to the right of their foreheads and the same blue eyes. "You two must be related?"

"Yes, my Lord, we are brothers and we both work on the land, hedging, ditching and fencing," replies Harry.

Robert points down the line. "The head gardener, Percy, is our father, my Lord, and we live up Camp Road."

"I see, well I am pleased to meet you both, you three may as well carry on with your duties."

Along the row is Isaac Warren and his two sons, Malachi and Jacob, who run the Home Farm. Isaac holds out his hand and introduces his two sons. Joshua shakes each man's proffered hand in turn. "I am very pleased to meet you all and as soon as I can I would very much like to visit the farm and meet the rest of your family."

"We would be honoured to see you, my Lord. My Beth will put on a fine spread if you let us know in advance when it will be convenient."

"I will take pleasure in the anticipation of it. In the meantime don't let me detain you any longer; I am sure you have much to occupy you."

Next in line is Henry Hodinott and he doffs his cap. "I am Henry Hodinott, the groundsman and indoor handyman, my Lord."

"I am pleased to meet you, Henry; you must be Lottie's husband."

"Yes, my Lord."

"And where do you live?"

"I also live along Camp Road, my Lord; number six."

"I should like to have a quick word with you after all the introductions, if you would not mind waiting."

"Of course not, my Lord."

John Moore steps forward as Joshua approaches him. "John Moore, groom, my Lord. I live at number three Camp Road with my wife Susan and young son Luke, my Lord."

"Good morning John, Do you enjoy working here?"

"I do, my Lord, very much. Billy and I get along very well together."

"That is good. Well, I don't think I need to keep

you just now, I will come along to the stables later and we can discuss my mount."

As John Moore leaves, Joshua moves along to the next man. "Ah, Percy, our head gardener and father of Robert and Harry."

Percy doffs his cap, "Yes, my Lord, pleased to meet you, my Lord. As you can see I got me hands full with those two lads and this here is my under gardener, Thomas Hawkins."

The lad takes a step forward. "And my Pa is the ploughman," interjects Thomas in a rather over eager way, then he removes his cap and holds out his hand. "How do ee do, my Lord."

Joshua shakes hands with his two gardeners and compliments them on their hard work. "The gardens are superb, you both obviously work very hard and I am impressed. I will not delay you any further, thank you for introducing yourselves to me."

As the gardeners return to their work Joshua moves along to the boy's father. Jack Hawkins holds out his hand and Joshua shakes it, "Good day, my Lord, I am the ploughman. I live up Camp Road with my wife Molly, who takes in gloving and my two sons, Frank, who works at Home Farm, and Thomas, who you just met. I am afraid my Molly had difficulty birthing Tommy and he is a bit on the slow side, but he is big and very strong and he tries his hardest to please. You will not find a lad more loyal."

"Don't worry, Mr Hawkins, I will not prejudge the lad. Besides, I can see just by looking around me how hard they both work. I am sure Percy would not be able to manage without him."

"That is very fair of you, my Lord. Do you mind if I wait for John, because I need to show him a badger set over by the beech trees?"

John Boucher is the last man in line. He has a

gun slung over his shoulder and a springer spaniel at his feet. The dog wags its tail as Joshua draws near. "Let me guess, you must be the gamekeeper?"

"John Boucher, my Lord, at your service."

"Flora's husband?"

"Yes, my Lord, and this here is Honey." He strokes the head of the spaniel, who nuzzles him for more fuss, "We live in Keeper's Cottage just off Pound Lane with our two little uns, Lettie and Toby."

"Well, I am very pleased to meet you and if either you, or you, Jack," he turns to Jack Hawkins, "require any help or instruction then please don't hesitate to come and find me. I want everyone to feel that they are able to approach me whatever their problems. I am here to help. Right, off you go and find your badgers."

He turns then back to his handyman – "Now then. Henry, wasn't it?"

"Yes, my Lord."

"I wanted to talk to you about the pond; well, it is really a mini lake isn't it? Only I wondered if it is deep enough to launch a small boat?"

"I don't see why not, my Lord, I think it would be fine if she had a shallow enough draught."

"Well, in that case I wonder if you would set to work constructing a jetty, because I know just the person to build us a boat."

"Right you are, my Lord, where would you like it situated?"

"I don't mind, either to the right side, or the left side of the lake, as if you were looking down from the terrace. Perhaps you could ascertain which would be the most suitable site according to the stability of the land? It may be prudent to get some idea of the depth of the water overall."

"I will make a start today, my Lord, it will be

quite a challenge and I will enjoy that."

"In that case, once she is surveyed, I will be able to correspond with my step-father on Portland and commission a small vessel."

Thus, the next few months are filled. Henry constructs a raft and ropes it across the lake and on fine weather days, with Joshua's help, they survey the water and discover that it is eight feet deep at the southern centre, varying to seven feet towards the north shore and ideal for a small boating lake. Joshua writes to his father and asks him to start work on a suitable vessel.

Early in September Mr and Mrs Bonfield are outside Knapp Cottage one evening when Louisa arrives home. She admires the flowerbed that her mother has been weeding, full of lavender, herbs, daisies and chrysanthemums. "That looks nice and tidy, Ma."

"Well, your father and I just thought we would make the most of what is left of these shorter evenings before the sun goes down."

The musky lavender and chrysanthemum smells mingle with the mint that her father has disturbed as he digs over their vegetable plot and lifts out the last of their potato crop. He looks up. "It is nice to be out in the fresh air after suffocating in that stuffy, smelly factory all day."

"I'm sure it is, Pa."

"There is some lamb stew and dumplings on the trivet for your tea," says her mother, "I don't think Millie has eaten yet either."

"Oh that sounds perfect, I am famished." She rubs some mint fresh from the plant between her fingertips and puts it to her nose. "Mmm, that is mouth watering."

Louisa goes inside and can smell the lamb stew as it simmers gently. She then runs upstairs to find Millie. As she opens the door to the attic she can see that Millie is doubled up on the bed and groaning in pain. She runs to her. "Millie, what is it?"

Millie grabs her hand. "Oh, Lou, I am so scared; I think the baby is coming."

Louisa feels the panic rising inside her. "What, right now?"

"I think it will be a little while yet, but I have been having pains since midday."

Louisa looks horrified. "And Ma and Pa haven't suspected anything?"

"No, nothing."

"Well, we had better get fully organised before they come in for the night. I will get some towels and some water for you." She grabs the ewer from the washstand and rushes downstairs to the pump. She fills the ewer and the kettle and hangs the kettle above the fire to warm through, snatches two towels from the airing rack and the scissors and string from the scullery, then rushes back upstairs with her arms full.

"It is lucky that Ma and Pa are still outside, is there anything else we will need before they come in?"

"A midwife would be nice," Millie cries through her pain.

"I am here and I will do my best, Mill." Louisa smiles kindly at her sister and pours out some of the water for her. "Have a sip of water."

Millie drinks from the beaker.

"I am going to go back down to bring us up a bowl of stew each and the hot water. It will probably be cold by the time we need it, but hopefully it will have taken the chill off it."

"I don't want any stew, Lou." Millie makes a face of disgust.

"A little bit of the gravy won't do you any harm, but if not I will eat two bowls. I am really hungry and then Ma and Pa will think you have eaten too."

Moments later Louisa is back and she sits down to eat her food. It seems that every five minutes Millie is stifling her cries of pain in the pillow and Louisa tries to ignore it for a while, in order to eat.

In between Millie's periods of pain Louisa spoons some of the stew into her mouth. "It will give you energy," she whispers.

"It is actually very tasty, thank you, Lou." Minutes later, she is doubled up again.

Louisa finishes her meal and feeds Millie some more until she refuses and Louisa finishes what is left. Then she takes the empty kettle and two bowls back downstairs.

On her return she wipes Millie's face with a dampened flannel and then rubs her back to ease her tension. "Is that better?" she asks.

"Yes, thank you, it does help."

As the sun sets the room grows dark and Louisa, her hands shaking, lights their two chamber-sticks, which flicker soothingly against the sloping ceilings of the small room. Millie is dosing between her pains.

Louisa decides to go back downstairs to see their parents, so that they have no need to venture upstairs to their room.

"Where is Millie?" asks her mother.

"She is lying down as she has her monthly pains, Ma. I thought I would read to her."

"That is thoughtful of you, Lou. Do you think a drop of cowslip wine might help her?"

"That's a good idea; I will take some up with me." She fetches the cowslip wine and a glass. "I just thought I would come down and say goodnight."

She kisses the top of her mother's head and she responds, "Goodnight dear, sleep tight."

"Goodnight, Ma." She kisses her father on his cheek. "Night Pa."

"Goodnight, Lou Lou, God bless. Say goodnight to Millie for us."

"I will."

Back upstairs her sister is hanging onto the brass bedstead, her face contorted in agony. She has one of the towels in her mouth and she bites down on it. As the wave passes she pulls herself up and swings her legs around to the floor.

"I am afraid my waters will break and go all over the bed. Pass me up the chamber-pot just in case."

"I doubt you will have enough warning for that. I'll put some rags under you, on top of the towel, Millie."

They spend many hours with Millie alternately hanging on to the bedstead in pain then quietly pacing the room as it eases, and Louisa giving her a drop of wine. Her waters break and Louisa clears away the wet rags from under her. They hear their parents retiring for the night and dowse their candles until all goes quiet again.

It is about 2am when Louisa thinks she can see the baby's head and she holds her sister's hand. She whispers, "Push as hard as you can, Millie."

Millie shoves the towel in her mouth again to muffle the sound and gives an almighty push. Minutes later, the head pops out. Louisa clears the mucous from its nose and mouth and the baby gives a little protest, then with one more push the shoulders follow and the baby slithers out onto the towel. The cord is a strange purple colour and is pulsing with blood and Louisa expertly ties it off in two places then plucks up the courage to cut between the two.

"What is it Lou Lou? Is it all right?" asks Millie breathlessly.

"Oh, Millie, you've got a little girl and she is beautiful."

Millie bursts into tears of relief that it is all over.

Louisa picks the little mite up, washes the baby gently in the tepid water and then rubs her tiny, bony little back gently and she starts to cry.

"Quick, put her on your breast, Millie, to stop her from crying." She wraps her in the spare towel and lays her in her sister's arms. The baby tries to suckle and then falls asleep in the warmth of her mother's embrace.

Louisa notes her sister looking down regretfully at her child as she cuddles it, possibly for the one and only time. She clears away the afterbirth and gently wipes her sister clean. She is very relieved that it is all over, so many things could have gone wrong. She sighs, "You have a beautiful baby girl, Millie. What are you going to call her?"

"I cannot name her, Lou, because I cannot keep her. We must keep to the plan and take her and leave her somewhere where she will be quickly found and she will be well looked after."

Louisa sees the anguish in her sister's eyes as she tries to put on a brave face, and her heart breaks for her. She is uncertain, and she feels the tears welling up at the thought of giving her dear little niece away. What would their mother think if she only knew? "This is not right, Millie, her father should take responsibility for her and you."

"No, Lou," her sister is defiant, "I don't want him anywhere near me or her, but you have to do it tonight. Much as I would like to, we cannot delay.

We will never be able to keep her hidden from Ma and Pa once the dawn breaks and I cannot bear to do it myself, besides I am too exhausted."

Her voice breaks and with tears running down her face, Millie plants a tender kiss on her sleeping baby's forehead. "Bye my precious little one, may God watch over you." She passes her to Louisa. "Please Lou, you must take her for me now, or I will never be able to part with her."

Louisa sorrowfully wraps the baby in Millie's dark green woollen shawl and, placing her on an embroidered pillow in a basket, she gives Millie one last peek at her. Sobbing silently Millie turns away, burying her head in her pillow. The lump in her throat is painful as Louisa asks for the last time, "Are you sure Millie?"

Millie replies huskily, "Yes, please go, I cannot bear it."

She has to respect Millie's wishes and so with tears running down her face Louisa sadly picks up the basket and holding her breath she quietly sneaks down the stairs. She pulls back the bolts on their front door and steps out into the night. She decides on Alvington Manor, because it is not too far away and, because she works there, she will be able to see for herself the outcome. She also knows the perfect place to leave her, so that she is sheltered from the weather.

Her sister is right; she does not want that devil Nathan Meakins to have anything to do with this dear little baby, who deserves all the advantages of living in a big house like her father's. She wraps another old shawl around the basket and ties it round her neck to help balance the weight, for she needs her other hand for the lantern, it is so dark and murky outside.

It is a typical foggy autumnal night and she can

hear her own footsteps echoing behind her. She holds up her lantern; following the roadway with difficulty and has to stop and listen every now and then to be sure she is not being followed, for she fears being discovered with the child.

As she finally reaches the courtyard in the front of Alvington Manor the baby starts to whimper. She rocks the basket gently from side to side. There is no time to lose, or she will be discovered. Heart thumping and with a huge painful lump in her throat, she quickly places the basket in the covered opening underneath the clock tower. She places the other shawl over the top for extra warmth and then she hides from sight just outside the gate, to keep watch for a while through the tears running unchecked down her face. The child cries with more urgency and the sound echoes in the foggy atmosphere. If she stays any longer she may be discovered; she will be missed at home and she needs to check that Millie is all right. Besides, if no-one else discovers the poor little mite, she can do so when she returns to work at 8 o'clock. Reluctantly, she abandons the tiny baby to her fate.

CHAPTER 2 *(September 1851)*

THE BABY IN THE CLOCK TOWER

In the Dower House, Rosa Price, the parlour maid, fixes her cap in place and then steps out into the damp autumnal weather. Her first task will be to lay some fires, as there is a definite chill today. As she turns and closes the front door of the Dower House behind her, she hears a cat mewing. The sound is coming from the clock tower. There is it again. It is a pitiful sound echoing on the foggy air, almost like a baby crying. Poor little thing, it will be cold out here; maybe she should get it some milk. She decides to investigate and walks over to the clock tower to see if she can spot it and then it cries out again.

Her heart leaps; *my goodness surely it is a baby, crying like that?* She hurries towards the sound. There in the shelter of the archway, underneath the clock tower, she spies a basket and tucked inside is the tiny baby, all wrapped up against the cold. "Oh my goodness whatever are you doing here? There, there, poppet, don't cry." Gently she lifts the basket and takes it into the main house. The movement seems to calm the child and she closes her eyes trustingly. Rosa goes straight down to the kitchen.

"Flora, come quickly, look what I have found, hidden under the clock tower."

Flora Boucher appears from the larder and looks into the basket, "Oh my God Almighty, wherever 'as that come from?" She is absolutely flabbergasted.

"I don't know but it is tiny, must be a newborn," says Rosa.

"Oh, poor little mite; put it down there by the warmth of the range, Rosa. Someone 'ad better tell the master."

"I'll go, Flora." Rosa rushes off to tell Joshua.

Flora calls after her, "Tell 'im that Susan Moore up at Camp Road 'as a young un and maybe she can spare some milk for it."

"Good thinking, Flora." She replies, as she runs down the corridor.

Minutes later, having bumped into Rosa and hearing the news, Elsie and Emily rush in. "Oh he's beautiful," cries Emily.

"Can I hold him?" asks Elsie excitedly.

"How do you know it is an 'im?" asks Flora Boucher, amused.

"Well, we don't, shall I have a look?" asks Elsie.

"I don't see why not, but be very gentle won't you."

"Of course I will." Carefully Elsie lifts the first shawl and then she unwraps the soft, green, woollen shawl and the linen towelling. "She is a little girl and she is perfect." The handling wakes the baby up and she starts to whimper, so Elsie wraps her back up and rocks her gently to and fro, until she closes her eyes and goes back to sleep. She returns her to the basket.

"She seems very content," says Flora Boucher.

Joshua then arrives with Rosa in tow. He lifts the basket up to see what all the commotion has been about and there, snuggled up in the green shawl, is the sleeping child.

"Well, this is not an everyday occurrence, is it?" says Joshua, looking flummoxed. "What a perfect little face. How could anyone bring themselves to abandon her to a fate unknown?"

"Where do you think she has come from, my Lord?" asks Rosa

"I don't know. She could be anyone's, but I would not have thought she was born very far from here, would you?" says Joshua thoughtfully. "Someone has taken great care to keep her warm and they have chosen here for a reason."

"Do you think we will be able to keep her, my Lord?" asks Emily.

"Well, in all my imaginings with regard to running this estate I never once dreamt that I would be making decisions about an abandoned baby!" Although this is a judgement not to be taken lightly, he does not want to appear heartless to these women, all of whom were either looking at the child tenderly, or looking directly up at him appealingly. "I would have said that it was not possible, but I am told that we have a nursing mother here on the estate and allowing that the good Lord has entrusted her to us, I think that, until such time as we find out who her family are, or if they are able to claim her, we should consider giving her a home."

"Oh my Lord, that is wonderful and so kind," says Flora appreciatively.

"I will send Billy up to Camp Road to ask Susan if she will be the child's wet nurse. If she agrees, then I don't see any reason why she cannot stay here with us."

"What should we call her, my Lord?" asks Flora.

"That is a good question and I think you should all give it some thought. If we are able to keep her, we will decide upon the best suggestion."

Louisa arrives moments later. All the women are calling out possible names and when they see Louisa they proudly introduce her to their new little infant. The look of feigned amazement on Louisa's face makes them all laugh, including Joshua. She did not realise that she was such a good actress, but she is thankful that they all fell for her subterfuge.

He explains to her, "We are waiting for Susan Moore to turn up in the hope that she will be able to feed our little foundling, as well as her own little boy, Luke."

"That is a good idea." Louisa smiles down on the child and tenderly strokes her downy cheeks. She looks up to find Joshua watching her intently and, fearing that he might read her mind, she says, "Do you think we should allocate a room to serve as a nursery, if Susan is in agreement, my Lord?"

"That seems sensible, Louisa."

"May I go and discuss this with Mrs Abbott? I met her on my way in and she is in the drawing room."

"Of course, by all means make a plan, but don't make too many changes until we have agreement from Susan Moore."

"I won't, my Lord." Louisa goes off to find Mrs Abbott. *Things seem to be working out nicely; Millie will be so relieved.*

After about half an hour Susan Moore arrives with Luke tied close against her body with a large shawl and she is shown into Joshua's study by Mrs Abbott.

"Has Billy explained our dilemma to you, Susan?"

"Yes, my Lord, he has, and I have brought some swaddling that was our Luke's, some towelling napkins and some of Luke's baby clothes."

"And are you prepared to share your milk with our little waif?"

"I am prepared to give it a go, my Lord, but if I

don't produce enough then I may not be able to continue."

"I understand, of course, we are very grateful for your help for however long you are able to offer it." He turns to Mrs Abbott. "Mrs Abbott, would you mind showing Susan and the baby up to the room you have allocated as the nursing room? And please, get her anything that she needs to be made comfortable there."

"Of course, my Lord; please come this way, Mrs Moore."

Susan follows Mrs Abbott upstairs to the smallest of the bedrooms where there is an old wooden rocking cradle that Louisa has made up with a large pillow as a mattress and some aired linen and a blanket folded over a few times for warmth. In the corner is an old nursing chair that must have been used once upon a time by Joshua's grandmother.

Susan releases her own child from the wrappings and passes him to Mrs Abbott, who lays him in the cradle. Then she makes herself comfortable in the chair. Mrs Abbott fetches her a cushion on which to rest the new baby in her arms and then she passes her the baby from the basket.

"What a dear little mite," she murmurs. "I hope she takes to my milk, Mrs Abbott."

"Well, we shall soon see."

There is a knock on the door and as Mrs Abbott opens it she puts her finger up to her mouth for quiet. Louisa stands there and they converse softly. "I just wondered if you needed anything for Susan or the baby, Mrs Abbott?"

"If you wish you can stay here and keep an eye on Luke for us, only I have the dinner menu to sort out with cook."

"Of course, Mrs Abbott, it will be my pleasure to do so."

As Louisa enters the room and Mrs Abbott leaves she is rewarded by the sight of her little niece suckling contentedly on Susan's ample bosom. "She seems to have taken to it," she whispers.

"Yes, she is doing really well for a newborn. I will try to express some more milk for her for the night times," replies Susan quietly.

"That is going to be a problem isn't it? Maybe it would be better for all three of you if you stayed down here for a few months until she is weaned."

"I don't think that my John would be happy with that. I could stay down here for a few days, now that I am here, if you wish, but we have not been married that long and John would miss us dreadfully. She could come back up to the cottage with me though, just until she is sleeping through the night."

"That is very kind of you; I will suggest that to his lordship if you like, because I agree it would be better for all of you, Luke included."

"Thank you, Louisa."

Louisa sits down between the cradle, where Luke is soundly sleeping, and his mother. Gently she rocks him to and fro while watching the little one contentedly feeding. *It is all going to turn out fine. I can go home and tell Millie that her baby is being well looked after by Susan Moore, until she sleeps through the night and then she will return to Alvington Manor and from then on I will be able to keep her informed daily.*

Louisa goes home that night, eager to tell Millie what has transpired and she is pleased to see the relief in her sister's eyes.

"Thank you, Lou, for all that you have done. I don't know what I would have done without you."

"She will be fine, Millie, don't you fret, there are

a lot of people now who all want the best for her and I will be your spy. Ma and Pa are oblivious as to what we have done and that nasty piece of work Meakins will never find out, as long as I have anything to do with it."

"I feel so lost without her, Lou, like a part of me is missing. My breasts are full of her milk still and I feel so sad all the time. I wish it was me working at Alvington Manor, but then I don't think I could bear to see someone else feeding my precious child."

"It will get better, Millie, with time. His lordship has asked the staff to come up with a name for her and I have had an idea, unless you have chosen something yourself."

"No, Lou, I avoided it because I would never be able to keep her, and therefore will never be able to call out for her."

"Well, you remember the fairystory book that Ma used to read to us at bedtimes when we were little? One of the stories in it was *Sleeping Beauty* and we both loved that story."

"Yes."

"Well the princess was called 'Aurora' and I thought that if you liked it, I could suggest it and they may choose that name for her."

"I do like it, Lou, and she could be called 'Aura' or 'Rora' for short while she is little."

"Shall I suggest that then, or do you want to choose something else?"

"No, that is rather pretty and a name fit for a princess." She surreptitiously wipes away her tears, but Louisa notices all the same.

"Don't be sad, Millie. You will, in time, find yourself a nice, kind man who will give you other babies I am sure, and at least she hasn't been taken to the poor house."

"Don't think I am not grateful for all you have

done, and I haven't changed my mind, Lou. I had no choice, though, did I? Given the choice I would prefer to have been able to keep my baby, but I could not bring shame on the family and I could not risk Pa's reaction."

Several days later Joshua is presented with the list of possible names. The younger girls had suggested names like Esther, Victoria (after the queen) and Elizabeth. Flora suggested biblical names like Rachael, Naomi, Ruth and Hannah. Thisbe, Zinnia and Rose were all suggested by Mrs Abbott because they were the flowers blooming in the garden at the time.

"There is also the connection with the biblical story of Pyramus and Thisbe, Pyramus being the most handsome youth and Thisbe the loveliest girl for miles around and the baby being found in the hole in the wall beneath the clock tower."

"It is a lovely name, Mrs Abbott, but wasn't that a tragedy?" asks Louisa.

"Well, yes it was."

"It would be a shame to jinx her any further, don't you think? She has not had a very auspicious start so far, has she?" suggests Joshua.

"Well, I wondered about Aurora," ventures Louisa. "It was the name of the princess in *Sleeping Beauty* and it means 'new dawn', which seems rather appropriate as she was found at dawn."

"And maybe someday she will find her prince," says Flora Boucher.

"I like that," says Rosa.

"Well done, Louisa, that is very pretty and very unusual," says Joshua.

"So it is decided?" asks Rosa.

"If everyone agrees," says Joshua. They all say, "Yes."

"In that case I shall go upstairs and tell Susan, because she is planning to take Aurora home with her tomorrow."

Louisa goes home that night and tells Millie that their suggestion was the favourite and that she is to be called Aurora from that day on.

The following day is warm and sunny and Mr Fairway visits, bringing his daughter Clara with him and two volumes of books for the guidance of Justices of the Peace. As they enter the large, oak panelled hall, Clara is looking all around her with admiration.

Her father hands the books to Joshua, "I was right, Joshua, you have to be at least twenty-one to become a Justice of the Peace and you need two nominators, as we discussed."

"Well, I will have known David Phelps for a year by then and I can contact Captain Buck nearer the time. Thank you very much for these, I will enjoy getting stuck into some legal matters for a few months."

Joshua looks across at the slender young girl accompanying Fairway, her straight flaxen hair twisted into a chignon at the nape of her neck. "I am pleased to see, Ambrose, that you have your lovely daughter Clara with you today."

"Ah yes, my Lord, we are going on later to visit friends."

Clara dips a curtsey. "Hello, my Lord, I am pleased to see you again."

"Likewise, my dear. Have you visited Alvington before?"

"No my Lord, but I think it is a wonderful building." Clara smiles self-consciously, as they follow Joshua into the drawing room and he rings to summon the afternoon tea trolley.

"Rosa, would you mind asking Louisa to come into the drawing room presently? There is no immediate hurry, ask her to finish what she is doing first."

After passing around the dish of sandwiches and sweetmeats he pours the tea and they chat amiably. They have all eaten their fill when there is a gentle tap at the door; he calls, "Come in." Louisa enters. Her eyes are downcast as if she has been remiss in some way and he is going to chastise her.

He immediately puts her at ease. "Louisa, as it is such a beautiful afternoon, I wondered if you might care to take Clara outside and show her around the garden?"

Louisa is thrilled. "Of course, my Lord, it will be my pleasure."

"Well, you are both about the same age and I thought you might enjoy each others company."

Clara jumps up, happy to leave the men to their mannish talk and they go off together.

"That was very thoughtful of him, wasn't it?" says Clara. Louisa agrees as she takes her arm and they both step out into the garden. "Yes, he is very kind and so young to be taking on all this responsibility," adds Louisa.

"My papa would agree with you, he says Lord Dryer is planning to become a Justice of the Peace, which is why we came today to bring him the legal books."

"Well, you have to admire him; he doesn't mean to idle his time away like so many toffs, and he's not uneasy on the eye either."

"No, I would say very handsome actually," and they both laugh at Clara's enthusiasm.

The warmth of the summer sun is lovely and relaxing and the scent of the flowers wafts towards them as they stroll along the balustraded terrace, down the wide steps to the large lawn and the south front of the manor. In front of them is the duck pond, where most of the ducks are dosing in the sun with their heads tucked under their wings.

"This is a magnificent house and a beautiful garden, it must be lovely to be able to enjoy this every day."

"Yes, it is, we are very lucky and the new master is such an improvement on the last. I was so surprised he asked me to show you around; it makes such a difference not to be treated as a servant. It was a dour place when it was run by his old grandfather, but now it is light and happy again." Louisa is warming to her guest as they stroll together arm in arm and she decides to confide in her. "We are even going to be having a little baby girl living here soon. That would never have happened in his grandfather's day."

"How did that come about?" asks Clara.

"Well, she was abandoned in the clock tower and Lord Dryer is so kind that he says he will give her a home here."

"Where is she now then?"

"She is with a wet nurse up on Camp Road until she is weaned," Louisa points southwards up the hill, towards the ridge above their valley and in the direction of the Camp Road cottages.

"He seems to be very kind indeed," says Clara.

They stroll on around the lake in silent companionship, listening to the birds singing merrily, and across to the east of the garden, into a woodland area where there is a scattering of autumn flowering crocus. Louisa can smell a bonfire and see the spiral of smoke as it curls above the trees. Soon they are passing Percy Sandford, who is trimming back a buddleia bush, and then they spot Thomas Hawkins, who is brushing up some fallen leaves and wheeling them to the small bonfire over near the boundary wall. They both smile and wave as they pass.

They continue following the path under the trees, chatting away frivolously. Then turn back around and along a stunning herbaceous border, which is a riot of colour; the last of the butterflies flutter among the red, yellow and mauve dahlias and bright orange rudbeckias. Louisa recognises, among the many species that are still in flower, the tall, pink-flushed cleome and the low growing French lavender, clumps of pink and orange nerine and tall white and pink Japanese anemones, chrysanthemums of all colours, Michaelmas daisies, helenium, echinacea and sedums, all intermingled with beautiful ferns and tall, frail grasses.

"I know I work here, Clara, but I don't often have the opportunity to stroll around the grounds like this and I have really enjoyed your company today."

"Me too. Maybe if I accompany Papa in the future, Lord Dryer will let us do it again."

"I would like that, but perhaps we had better return now, as I expect your papa will be wondering where we are."

The herbaceous border runs all along the edge of the balustraded terrace and through an archway beside the dower house, to the main west front of the house. They exit the archway, as Billie Riddick is bringing their carriage around to the front of the house, and Joshua and Clara's father come through the front door. Both girls dip in a curtsey.

"We were just thinking of sending out a search party," Mr Fairway jokes. "Have you enjoyed your stroll?"

"Yes, very much thank you, Papa. It has been lovely and Louisa is a charming companion."

Ambrose Fairway notes the healthy flush in his

daughter's cheeks as he hands her up into the carriage. "I am pleased my dear. It is good to get you out in the fresh air. Thank you very much, Louisa, for entertaining her."

"You are welcome, sir, I very much enjoyed our jaunt myself. Goodbye Clara, I hope we see each other again soon." She drops a curtsey. "Goodbye, sir," and she returns to her domestic work.

Mr Fairway turns to shake hands with Joshua. "Good to see you again, dear boy, and let me know if I can be of any further help with your studying."

"I will and thank you for all your trouble."

Mr Fairway climbs up to the front of the carriage and Joshua waves them off.

Three weeks have passed when a messenger boy comes to Alvington Manor asking for Lord Dryer. He is shown into his study by Gareth, who waits patiently by the door. The boy looks pale and shocked.

Joshua is immediately concerned. "What can I do for you, young man?"

"Please could you come to Abbey Farm, mister? Louisa Bonfield is asking for you; her sister Millie has been found drowned."

The news hits him like a punch in the stomach. "Oh my good Lord," he stammers, "poor Louisa, she must be devastated – Gareth, ask Billy to bring round the curricle immediately will you please."

"Of course, my Lord."

He turns to the lad. "What is your name, sonny?"

"Tommy, sir."

"Would you like a quick drink before we go?"

"Yes please, sir; I am thirsty, 'cause I ran all the way here."

Joshua rings for Rosa. "Rosa, would you take Tommy to the kitchen and give him a glass of ginger beer, please? Then bring him back here so that I can give him a ride back to Abbey Farm."

"Yes, my Lord. Come on, Tommy, it's this way."

Joshua gets his hat and riding coat and pulls on his long boots. However is he going to be able to console poor Louisa? Perhaps he should take Rosa with him, but no it is no place for a woman, that is for sure.

Billy has brought the carriage to the front of the house and he and Tommy climb in and are soon on their way. "Is there anything else you can tell me, Tommy?"

"No, sir. The constable is there, but I was not allowed to go near, sir."

"Well, thank you for running all the way to fetch me. Here is a little something for your trouble."

The boy's eyes light up at the sight of the coin and he holds out his grubby little hand. "Thank you, sir, I have to work all year rook-scarring to earn me a crown."

The carriage has to pass the pond on its way to the farm and Joshua can see the men gathered around the body of a young girl. They drive into the farmyard and he instructs the boy to go inside the house, before rushing off in the direction of the pond.

He can see Louisa down on her knees weeping over her sister while the doctor is examining the body. His heart goes out to her. He rushes towards her and gently he lifts her to her feet and enfolds her in his arms.

"There, there; hush, Louisa, don't cry, there is nothing you can do for her now."

"But they are saying she has killed herself. I didn't realise she was so unhappy... so unhappy that she could not face her life any longer," she sobs. "How can I tell Ma and Pa that our Millie has drowned herself?" She looks up at him. "How can I?"

"I don't know, Louisa, but she is out of her pain now." He looks down at the body laid in the grass, mud and pondweed in her hair. He recognises the young girl that he saw on the day he travelled to Alvington Manor with Mr Fairway, her beautiful, thick, wavy, red hair now lank and filthy, her face as white as porcelain. She had been a very lovely young girl, just like her sister Louisa and he is surprised that he did not make the connection before now. Had the horseman and the argument been something to do with this?

The constable approaches them. "I understand, my Lord, that you are the new owner of Alvington Manor?"

"I am, constable. My name is Joshua Dryer and I am Louisa's employer."

"Constable Gundry," he says holding out his hand. They both shake hands. "Well, it would all seem pretty cut and dried; I believe that the young lady has taken her own life. Neither the doctor nor I can see any foul play here; naturally it is very distressing for her sister."

Joshua gives Louisa a gentle squeeze. "Is it not possible that she was taking a shortcut and slipped in the mud, banging her head on one of the rocks surrounding the edge of the pond?"

"It is possible, my Lord, but there is no sign of any injury, so very unlikely." The constable continues, "Anyway, we will remove the body back to the morgue and send someone to the glove factory to inform her parents. Shall I tell them that her sister is with you, my Lord?

"Yes, if you could ask them to come to Alvington Manor to fetch Louisa, then I can help them with the funeral arrangements and deal with the undertakers if they wish me to."

"Thank you, my Lord, pleased to make your acquaintance; no doubt we will meet again."

"Come, Louisa, they are going to take your sister away with them for forensics and then we will be able to have her back for the funeral. You come with me for now to Alvington Manor." He walks her back to the curricle and helps her up. She sits beside him, weeping silently as he drives her back to his home.

Once back at Alvington Manor, Joshua sits Louisa down by the fireside and asks Rosa to get her some hot, sweet tea. Louisa is aware that her parents will have no idea why their daughter might want to take her own life and she does not know how she is going to be able to keep it from them and everyone else. *Poor little Aurora really has lost her mama now.* She weeps for the loss of her sister, the mother of her little niece and a close companion that she thought she would have for life, but for the devilry of Nathan Meakins.

When her parents arrive, Joshua shows them into the same room and leaves them alone together for a while, going off to ask cook to organise refreshments for them all.

On Joshua's return Mr Bonfield stands up and moves forward to shake his hand. "I am very grateful to you, my Lord, for taking such good care of Louisa. It is a great shock to us all, but they were both especially close and it will be some time before any of us can come to terms with it."

"Believe me; I am very sorry for your loss."

"We would have liked to have the service at our church in Preston Plucknett, but because they say she took her own life she cannot be buried in consecrated ground."

"She couldn't have taken her own life. She was a very happy child. How could she have taken her own life?" Mrs Bonfield protests weakly.

"Well, I will have a word with the Reverend David Phelps and persuade him that there is no proof that that was her intention. As far as I am concerned, you are welcome to have the service here at Alvington Manor if you wish and I am sure we can find a suitably secluded plot in the grounds behind the little estate chapel."

Mrs Bonfield bursts into tears then, the relief overwhelming her. "You are very kind, my Lord, that means so much to us."

"I will make the arrangements with the reverend and let Louisa know when he can do it, once we have the go ahead from the police. Which undertaker would you like me to contact?"

"I think that Montague's would be fine, don't you dear?"

Mrs Bonfield wipes her eyes with a handkerchief. "Yes I do. They have a beautiful glass hearse and a fine pair of black horses with plumes."

"That is decided then."

There is a quiet tap on the door and Rosa enters with a small trolley and the refreshments.

Joshua takes a while to persuade the vicar that no one can be sure that the young girl had intended to take her own life. "It is not as if she had hung herself, or cut her wrists, it could just as easily have been an accident and it is not fair to her, or her family, that she should be excommunicated on such flimsy proof."

Finally he agrees and a week later the funeral service takes place in Alvington Manor Chapel. The people are all dressed in their black and milling about outside when the hearse arrives. Joshua thinks Mrs Bonfield will be satisfied because, as she requested, the hearse is pulled by a fine pair of matching black horses and they look magnificent with their polished tack and feathered plumes. The coffin is covered with a large spray of white chrysanthemums and nerines with some feathery greenery. It is lifted onto the shoulders of the undertakers and the family and friends all file into the chapel behind them.

A lot of villagers from Preston Plucknett attend, including Mr and Mrs Poulton and Tommy from Abbey Farm. Both Louisa and Millie's school friends also attend and soon the small chapel is filled with their singing. Joshua sits with the rest of the Alvington Manor staff in the small south aisle of the chapel where he can look through into the knave and his sympathetic eyes are on Louisa throughout most of the service. She sings quietly, pausing intermittently as if her heart is breaking. His feelings of sorrow and tenderness are overwhelming and he longs to be by her side supporting her.

After the service Reverend Phelps announces that the committal will be attended by the family only and that Lord Dryer has arranged for tea and sandwiches in the Orangery and the remainder of the congregation make their way slowly there to wait for the principle mourners.

In a secluded spot behind the chapel, as Joshua promised, the committal takes place and Mr Bonfield has his arms around his wife and Louisa, as they sob quietly and remember Millie in their own personal ways.

Afterwards they wipe away their tears and join their friends for the funeral reception. Thankfully everyone avoids the rumour that Millie took her own life, because Louisa and her parents have no idea how they could answer such an accusation. They are all very relieved when finally the last of their friends give their condolences and leave for home.

After everyone has left Joshua takes Louisa to one side and suggests that she should take a few days off work to come to terms with what has happened, but she cannot bear the thought of being in her home alone with her memories. "I will not be able to put it out of my mind for a second, if I stay all day at home. At least at Alvington Manor things will be going on that will create a distraction to some extent."

"In that case why don't you move into the Dower House? There is a room spare upstairs next door to Rosa's, and it would save you the trek from Preston Plucknett morning and night?"

Louisa looks at him with eyes full of gratitude. "I would like that, my Lord, our home is so full of memories and I cannot get poor Millie out of my head for a moment."

"Then I shall ask Billy to bring round the landau and he can take you and your parents home. He will wait while you collect your things together and you can return with him and stay here with us in the Dower House."

"Thank you, my Lord. That is very kind of you."

"I am doing you no special favours, Louisa; it is commonsense to have all the staff within easy access to the manor. Although I am sure you will be even more pleased, as the weather deteriorates and you no longer have to put up with your twice daily walk."

"I am sure you are right. Thank you, my Lord."

"You are very welcome, my dear."

CHAPTER 3 *(September – October 1851)*

ALL HALLOWS EVE

Amy Proctor is the new girl employed to replace Millie Bonfield at the Meakins' residence, Summerville House. She approaches the property from the direction of Stoford, where until today she lived with her mother and four younger siblings. Her father, who was a bricklayer, has recently been killed in a tragic accident; he was buried alive when a building trench collapsed upon him and now Amy has to find work whilst the rest of her family are sent to the Coker Poor House.

The child is weeping as she goes, for the loss of her beloved father, the shame of her mother and brothers and sisters having to go into the poor house, for the loss of her happy family home and the premature end of her carefree childhood. As she approaches the house she can see that it is huge and she is frightened and intimidated, but her mother has arranged for her to go into service here as a kitchen maid, so that she can earn £15 a year and she has to be brave.

She puts down her bag on the wide steps and smears away the tears. Then she lifts the huge knocker on the large front door and hears the echo of the sound from inside. The door opens and a snooty man looks down his nose at her.

"You need the back entrance, stupid girl," he says and shuts the door in her face.

She is taken aback. She doesn't know where the

tradesman's entrance is and so she walks around the house to the left. Eventually she finds the kitchen lobby and knocks again. Jean Hawkins, one of the housemaids, answers her knock and takes her to the housekeeper.

"This is Amy Proctor, the new live-in kitchen maid from Stoford, Mrs Faversham," says Jean Hawkins.

"I see." She turns to Amy, "Well, you are late. You should have been here an hour ago. We expect you to start work here at six and not a moment later."

"I am sorry, ma'am, but I had to help my mother with my brothers and sisters packing up their belongings to go to the poor house. It will never happen again, not now I will be living in."

"It had better not. Show her up to her room, Hawkins, and be quick about it."

"Yes, Mrs Faversham."

Jean Hawkins leads her up the back stairs, up and up, eventually reaching the attic where she is shown into a tiny room with sloping ceilings and a slit window. The room contains a wooden bed, a wooden ladder-backed chair, a simple dresser and a washstand, with pitcher and bowl and cupboards underneath for storage. It is dark, hot and airless, lacking any colour or cheer. Her heart sinks – she feels as if it is a prison cell and she can see no way out.

"There is your uniform." Hawkins points to the bed. "Be quick and put it on and leave your bag, otherwise we will both be in trouble."

Downstairs the staff are rushing around like there has been a medical emergency and Amy is anxious to know her duties. Mrs Faversham calls her into her room. "Right, Proctor, your duties are to assist Mrs Chubb, the cook, in the kitchen in whatsoever she requires. Stand still and look at me when I am talking to you."

"Sorry, ma'am."

"I am to be addressed as Mrs Faversham."

"Sorry, ma'am… I mean Mrs Faversham." She tries to stand stock still before this unapproachable woman, but the embarrassing heat suffusing her cheeks she cannot hide.

"As far as Sir and Lady Meakins and their family and guests are concerned, you will be invisible to them at all times. If one of your betters should pass you in a corridor, or on the stairs, you must turn your face away and keep in tight to the wall, averting your eyes."

"Yes, Mrs Faversham."

"If a family member requests you to walk with them to carry packages, you will be expected to walk a few paces behind them. You must only speak when spoken to and otherwise you must never be heard by them. Always respond to an order and always use the proper address – sir, ma'am or miss. Except in return to a greeting offered, never even say 'good morning' or 'goodnight' to your employer, and never, ever, offer your opinion to any member of the family."

She looks sternly at her. "I warn you now that if you are responsible for any breakages or damages in the house, the value will be deducted from your wages."

Amy is horrified at this; there will be so many beautiful and costly items that the loss of any one of them would leave her with no money for the foreseeable future.

"You are expected to be punctual at all times, including mealtimes."

"Yes, Mrs Faversham."

"You shall not receive any visitors, family members, or friends into the house or servants' hall without the consent of Mr Morton the butler, or myself. 'Followers' are strictly forbidden, any fraternisation and you will be dismissed immediately."

"I understand, Mrs Faversham."

"You had better understand, Proctor, or you won't last five minutes here. Go and find Cook; she will give you your instructions."

"Yes, Mrs Faversham."

The cook asks her to make a start by feeding the chickens and collecting the eggs from the chicken run for breakfast. Once outside in the fresh air Amy becomes distracted, looking all about her and curiously trying to take in her strange new environment; soon Cook is at the back door, shouting for her to get a move on. As a punishment for being so slow she has to clean out the larder and she is soon up to her elbows in water and lye. She is busy all morning scrubbing the shelves and dusting the jars of preserves.

Later they all sit down for some bread and cheese. There is a household staff of around twenty and Amy is too overwhelmed to take in all the people around her. The man who answered the door to her and who was so unkind is Wadman, the first footman. He is very tall with good features, but is obviously mean spirited and Amy is very wary of him. She is questioned by Apsey, Olivia Meakins' ladies maid, about her background, but once she has told them of the loss of her father and the poor house she is left alone.

During the afternoon she is peeling vegetables and scurrying to and fro with pails of boiling water for the cook. She burns her wrist on a hot pan and rubs it with a slice of raw potato, as her mother had taught her. She is too afraid to mention it to the others, but it is still hot and sore, especially when she is washing all the pots and pans at the end of a sixteen hour day, after the family have finished their evening meal.

That night she tosses and turns in the little wooden bed. She must get to sleep, or she will not be awake by five thirty in the morning. She has asked Jean Hawkins to make sure that she is woken up; she is so terrified that she will oversleep and break her promise not to be late again.

Amy has been working in the kitchens for several months and she has become used to the hard work and drudgery, fetching coal and laying all the fires, lifting heavy pans, scrubbing everything in sight and the lack of an occasional kind word. She now knows the names of all the kitchen utensils and pieces of furniture that were unfamiliar to her when she first arrived and she knows all the members of staff, including who she trusts and who she does not trust. She is still quite reliant on Jean Hawkins who, although not exactly friendly, has always been dependable and not unkind to her. The one highlight of her week is when Bobby Tomkins, the butcher's boy, delivers the meat. He always gives her a friendly smile and a wink and she finds herself blushing at the thought of him.

However, it is at this time that one of the other housemaids is taken ill with scarlet fever and is immediately sent back to her home. This means that there are duties to be performed in the main house and she becomes a between maid for a while. She has not been allowed to venture there until this morning and she is apprehensive lest she encounter any family members whilst going about her duties, and especially nervous that she might break one of the articles of fine china. However, Hawkins is showing her the ropes and on her first day she is relatively safe cleaning the windows in the main hall.

Suddenly the front door opens and Nathan Meakins strides in, handing his hat, whip and gloves to Wadman with a curt command, "Get the stable boy to take care of Diablo."

"Yes, sir."

Amy looks out of the corner of her eye to see what the young master looks like and is surprised to see how handsome he is, with his light brown wavy hair and side whiskers touching his wing collar. He is, of course, beautifully and fashionably dressed. Suddenly he is looking in her direction and she quickly averts her gaze.

"Who do we have here, Wadman?"

"This is Proctor, sir, the new kitchen maid. She is standing in for the housemaid who has scarlet fever."

"Come here, girl; let me have a look at you."

Amy anxiously puts down her cloth and goes to stand before the young master. "How old are you, Proctor?"

She knows enough to look him in the eye when spoken to. "I am thirteen, sir."

He is looking her up and down and she feels uneasy, wondering what he is thinking. He licks his lips as if he is savouring her and with this dreadful thought she trembles uncomfortably.

"Is that you, Nathan?" It is his mother's voice, coming from the direction of the drawing room.

"Run along then, back to your work; we don't want Mama to find you slacking, do we?" It is an attempt to appear friendly, but Amy does not trust this man and she turns away from him quickly. He strides off into the drawing room and, relieved, she returns to continue her task.

Hawkins is up the wooden ladder and she watches

Amy returning to her work, observing the small, neat, youthful figure with the fine blonde hair, neatly coiled and pinned under her cap, and the huge innocent blue eyes. Sometimes she is glad that she does not have a pretty face like Amy and Millie before her. Unfortunately she has the same manly nose as her brother and frizzy, wiry hair, but at least it means that she is left alone by the young master.

Nathan Meakins' sister Olivia was born thirty-eight years ago on the Eve of All Hallows and is said to be blessed with the ability to converse with all things supernatural. She remains unmarried, having been jilted at the church ten years earlier by her fiancé who desperately wanted to travel to South Africa to prospect for gold. She refused to go with him and after much agonising he left her at the altar. Rumour has it that he is now a millionaire, but it is diamonds that have made his wealth and Olivia is bitter that she not only lost her lover, but also his fortune.

On Friday 31st October it is her birthday and she has made special plans for her personal celebrations this year. She is going to give herself to the warlock. His coven name is 'Jaldabaoth' after the Lord of the Underworld, who raped the first woman and seduced the first humans into sexual intercourse. Olivia has no wish to end up an old maid, but time is running out and she is determined to experience union with a man and does not care even if it results in conception. The ceremony will take place in an oak grove at Newton Hollow on All Hallows Eve. She is the witch maiden and the coven will witness her sacrificing her purity to their warlock.

The night is crisply cold and Olivia is glad of her red hooded cloak as she walks with her ladies maid, Apsey, up the hill to Newton Hollow. They are following the warlock, who carries a flaming torch, and Olivia is excited to be the focus of this important ceremony. She is known in the coven as 'Jahi' after the Demoness of Lasciviousness.

Apsey's name is 'Lilith' in the coven. She was a fertility goddess and the Greek Goddess of the Dark Moon.

As they approach the oak grove they hear chanting and see the shadows of the hooded witches circling around the flaming markers of a five-sided inverted star shape, etched out within a circle. The witches go around the pentacle with their besom brooms sweeping the area clear in readiness for the Samhain ceremony. In the centre is a large flat slab of rock that serves as their altar and the high priestess, cloaked in black, stands at the head of this altar. She lifts up from the centre of the stone slab and holds aloft a large, wooden-horned, head with evil, glowing, red glass eyes glittering in the light from the flaming torches around her.

Jaldabaoth places his torch in the last remaining point of the pentacle and is handed the ceremonial horn and gourd, which he passes to Lillith.

The priestess proceeds with the ceremony. "Come, Jahi; sit on the sacred stone and we will bless and cleanse you of your sins."

Jahi goes forward and sits on the stone slab.

"Come, Lilith, and purify your mistress." Lilith removes her mistress's hood and sprinkles spring water over her forehead from the gourd.

"Jaldabaoth, come forward and kneel before the sacrificial stone." The warlock kneels at Jahi's feet and Lilith pours spring water over his head.

The high priestess continues, "You have been cleansed of your sins. It is time to cast off your robes."

Jaldabaoth and Jahi both remove their cloaks to reveal their naked bodies beneath.

"Let Jahi offer her purity to Jaldabaoth."

The circle of witches then moves slowly in an anti-clockwise direction around the outside of the pentacle, chanting their ancient incantations. Jahi lays back on her red cloak, symbolic of the loss of her maidenhead, and Lilith is expected to stroke and touch her body intimately to ready her for Jaldabaoth.

When she is ready Jahi shivers as Jaldabaoth leans over her and kisses her on the mouth. Suddenly and unexpectedly she feels something cold and hard between her legs and she cries out in pain as he uses the ceremonial horn to break her virginity, before covering her writhing body with his own. She clings to him, absorbing the warmth of him as he enters her enthusiastically. They are to copulate until both are satisfied.

The witches dance increasingly faster as, excitedly, they watch the naked bodies fulfilling the pagan ritual.

Jahi experiences rippling waves of pleasure, like the symbolic witchcraft concentric circles. She feels her body responding, melting and moulding to him until she experiences her first orgasm. She feels the muscular tension building in him until he reaches his climax within her and her initiation is over. Lilith passes Jaldabaoth his brown cloak and then helps her mistress on with her red cloak. Jahi is glad to have experienced what she should have enjoyed ten years earlier with her jilting husband. Now at least one of the mysteries of humankind has been revealed for her. Words are chanted over the blood smeared horn and then all in turn drink from a bottle of mead, before dispersing back into the darkness once more.

Unbeknown to them, the scene is witnessed by Jean Hawkins who, filled with curiosity, had followed the trio from Summerville House. She is shocked, frightened and sickened by what she has seen. The knowledge of the existence of a coven meeting in Newton Hollow is disturbing enough, but the fact that Nathan Meakins has quite openly had sex with his own sister is even more appalling.

CHAPTER 4 *(October 1851)*

COUNTRY PURSUITS

Joshua keeps a wary eye on Louisa over the next few weeks. He misses the familiar sound of her humming as she goes about her domestic duties. She looks so downcast in her black bombazine, even though it is trimmed with crape and she still wears the crisp, white cap and apron. He also notices that she is avoiding the company of the other girls during her breaks and one day he finds her in the library, seated in a shaft of light from the window and reading one of his books. She jumps up guiltily as he walks in. "I am sorry, my Lord, I hope that you are not displeased."

His voice softens, "Not at all, Louisa, you are welcome to make use of the books here at any time you are at liberty. Would you like to keep that one with you to read?"

"Are you sure, my Lord?"

"Of course, as long as you return it to the shelves when you have finished with it, I have no objection whatsoever. What is it that you are reading?

"*Oliver Twist*, by Charles Dickens, my Lord."

"Ah, about the little orphaned boy. Yes, it is a good story with a rewarding conclusion, if I recall. Dickens is a great writer; he really brings his characters to life. You will enjoy it, Louisa."

"I am sure I will, my Lord, I enjoyed reading the serialised *David Copperfield* last year in *Household*

Words, my ma's magazine, so I am already a bit of a follower. Thank you, my Lord, 'tis the one thing that absorbs me and distracts me from my melancholy thoughts." She closes the book and goes to leave.

He feels disappointed. "Please don't disturb yourself on my account, I have just come in to study my law books and we can sit in here together and read in peace and quiet."

"That is very kind of you, my Lord, but I have to get back to work now. I am most grateful that you will allow me to use the library and I surely will again in the future, because I see there is also *Nicholas Nickleby* on the shelf."

Joshua looks along the rows of book spines. "There are many authors exhibited here that I have not even heard of. Perhaps we can compare notes as we go along?"

"I would like that, my Lord," she smiles shyly, dips a small curtsey and leaves the room.

He watches her go, admiring her grace and beauty. Her thirst for knowledge, for someone of such limited means, impresses him.

That night Joshua tosses and turns before dropping off into a fitful sleep. He dreams of discovering Louisa floating in the pond, her red hair fanning out and floating on the surface with her feet among the water lilies, like Ophelia from Shakespeare's play *Hamlet*. Then the body is on the shore of the pond, blanched and bloated and he is standing beside it and comforting Millie on the death of her sister. He wakes in a distressed state before the sad reality calms him again.

On Portland, Joshua's sister, Rebecca, is at the shop helping her mother when the postman puts his head around the door and the familiar bell jingles. She greets him cheerfully and he hands her the mail. She thumbs through the small pile before putting it on the counter for her mother and among the letters she recognises her brother's hand.

"Ma, there is a letter here from Josh," she cries! "May I open it?"

Her mother is pinning up the hem of a gown on a tailor's dummy and she is holding a selection of pins in her mouth. "Yes do and read it out to me," she manages, because of years of practice, to say this out of one side of her mouth.

"Dear Ma and Pa and Becky,

I hope this finds you all in good health. I am writing to invite you all to spend the Christmas vacation with me here at Alvington Manor, (at least Christmas Day and Boxing Day). I believe, Mama, that you will enjoy being waited on for a change and it will be a good opportunity for you to meet all my helpful staff and see this beautiful estate where I am now domiciled.

If you are in agreement I will send John Moore with the landau on Christmas Eve. I know that you will be in demand with the shop, right up until then. Maybe Ben would like to come along too? Perhaps you could ask him, Becky?

"Oh, Ma! That is wonderful; do you think Pa will agree?"

"I don't see why not, we hardly ever leave the island, we could all do with a break and it will be wonderful to see the house and grounds and to see Josh, we haven't seen him since June. What else does he say?"

"Umm," Rebecca scans the page to find her place.

"… Also I want to commission Pa to construct a small boat with a shallow draught for the pond at Alvington Manor that will take about four people, plus the row man. I don't know how long it will take for you to do this, but if it is completed in time for Christmas, I can send Billy Riddick with the farm wagon. Let me know what you think as soon as possible, so that I can make the necessary arrangements.

Your loving son and brother,
Joshua."

Having shut up the shop at the end of their working day, Violet and Rebecca return home and Violet prepares their supper. When Matthew comes in from the boatyard he kisses Violet on her cheek and she passes him the letter.

"Not a letter from our Josh! Well, that is unexpected." He removes his boots and goes into the scullery to wash his hands.

Rebecca is bursting to tell her father the news, but she manages to contain herself and watches his face as he slowly reads her brother's words. "So he wants us to go all the way to Somerset just to spend a couple of days?" He speaks thoughtfully, "'Tis hardly worth the effort is it?"

"Well, it will make a nice break for us all and it will be lovely to see him," Violet says persuasively.

"What about your ma and pa and brothers, and mine and Hannah and Johnny, what will they do without us at Christmas?"

"But we have seen them every year since time immemorial," protests Rebecca.

Matthew laughs, "That is a slight exaggeration isn't it, Becky?"

"No it isn't, Pa, we always do the same thing every year and I so want to go, please, Pa. He has even invited Ben."

"I am only joshing with you, Becky; of course we can go, I am curious to see this wonderful estate, just as much as you two are."

"Oh thank you, Pa," Rebecca hugs her father excitedly.

Her mother smiles happily. "Well, Becky, it looks like you and I will have to get busy making some new gowns and a riding habit for you. Not forgetting we still have to make the waistcoat and cravat for you to give to Ben for his Christmas present, in addition to all the other presents for the rest of the family."

"I promise I will help you, Ma." She goes to the dresser and takes out the cutlery to lay the supper table. "Have you read the rest of the letter, Pa?"

"I was just reading it; it looks as though your cousin Ben and I are also going to have our work cut out, designing and building this little rowing boat that Josh has requested."

"I expect Ben will enjoy helping you with that, but I am sure he will want to see it launched as well. Will you ask Ben tomorrow for me, if he will be able to come with us, Pa? Only I don't want to go out tonight, as it is already dark and it is pouring with rain."

"Of course I will, but don't be disappointed if he says no. Christmas is a family time and he may feel that his place is with his mother."

"Try to persuade him, Pa, I will really miss him if he doesn't come and I know he will want to see our Josh. He has told me often enough how he is lost without his best pal. Besides, his mother does have all those brothers and sisters of hers to spend her time with, after all."

The following morning Matthew tells Ben that he has been invited to Somerset for Christmas and Ben is flabbergasted.

"Do you think you will be able to come with us, Ben?"

"I would really love to, Matthew, but I will have to be careful how I handle me ma. You know what she is like and she only has me at home."

"Well, Becky asked me to remind you that you both usually go to see her brothers and sisters to celebrate and so your mother would not be completely on her own."

"Yes, I suppose it is true that all her younger brothers and sisters do get together with us on Christmas Day. You never know, she may let me go just this once, it is worth a try."

Ben manages to persuade his mother to let him go on this occasion and he and Matthew are soon working hard to finish off their outstanding commissions in order to start work on Joshua's boat, with the aim that it might be completed by the time of their visit.

Violet replies to Joshua, saying that they would all like to accept his kind invitation and that Matthew is trying to complete the building of the boat in time and they would keep him informed if there was any delay.

Back at Alvington the weather is getting colder and early one frosty morning in November, John Boucher and Isaac Warren are seen by the footman approaching the manor, pushing a younger man ahead of them. John is moving him forward by prodding him in the back with his gun. His spaniel, Honey, is snapping at the man's heels. The younger man has a heavy sack bag slung over his shoulder. On reaching the front door Isaac Warren knocks and they wait for the response. As the door opens John Boucher lowers the gun. Porter lets them in and John breaks the gun, leaving it in the porch with Honey on guard. He asks to see Joshua and the three men are shown into his study. Joshua is seated at a large, mahogany, pedestal desk. He looks up from his work.

"Good morning gentlemen, what can I do for you?" He smiles amiably and immediately notices that John is red in the face with indignation.

"I am sorry to disturb you, my Lord, but Isaac and I found this young villain on your land with this sack full of coneys and I wondered what you wanted me to do with him."

Joshua frowns. "I see." He pauses. "This is indeed a grave matter. What is your name?"

The blood has drained from the lad's face and John Boucher answers for him, "It is Raymond Hawkins, my Lord. He is related to the Hawkins family up on Camp Road. I believe he is Jack's nephew and he lives up Dray Road at Odcombe."

"Well, I don't suppose you are aware of this, young fellow, but I am studying the law books to become a Justice of the Peace and it just so happens that I have a couple of volumes which record the recommended sentences for crimes against society, such as this." He looks from the lad to John Boucher. "Was he carrying a weapon, John?"

"No, my Lord, he was using a wire."

Joshua takes down one of the heavy volumes and scans the index; he turns the pages and reads to himself, while the three men wait patiently. "Hmm, well if you had been carrying a weapon they would stretch your neck, but as it is, the worst that could happen would be that you are transported to a penal colony, such as New South Wales, for fourteen years. Having said that, once you are there you would have to fund your own way back and so for most folk it is a sentence for life."

The boy looks anxious and apologetic. "I am sorry, my Lord, but there are so many coneys up the sloping valley sides and we so rarely get to eat a bit of meat, I didn't think you would miss a few."

"Well, that is not really the point, is it, lad? You knew you were breaking the law of the land, and it is my duty to see that the law is obeyed." He speaks sternly, but cannot help feeling sorry for the young man.

"Please give me another chance, my Lord; my pa has been sick for weeks now with a bad chest and unable to work and my ma only takes in a bit of gloving, I won't go poaching on your land no more, you have my word upon it, my Lord."

Joshua cannot help think that there, but for the grace of God, it could be him in those shoes. "I will let you off in this instance, Master Hawkins, but if I come across you again in these circumstances, on my land, or anyone else's, it will be a different matter, I assure you. I don't expect any reprisals against my loyal gamekeeper here, either. Thank you, John, for your swift action; please, would you mind taking the game down to Flora?" He winks at him. "Tell her she can have one for her family, the rest for the kitchen, and leave one in the sack bag and return it to me."

John picks up the sack. "I will, my Lord, thank you." As he closes the door behind him Joshua turns back to the poacher. "How old are you, Master Hawkins?"

The lad clears his throat, "I am nineteen, my Lord."

"What is your occupation, apart from poaching?"

"I do a bit of beating for the local shoots hereabouts, but I don't have no training for nothing else." He hangs his head shamefully.

"Well, I think it is about time at your age that

you thought about taking on some kind of apprenticeship, don't you?"

"Yes, my Lord, I will give it some thought."

John returns with the poacher's bag. "Right then, John, you had better give him back his bag. There is enough for a coney stew in there, but now my gamekeeper is going to escort you off our land and I don't want to see you back here again."

"Thank you, my Lord. I won't be back, you have my word and I am grateful for you not reporting me to the constable, my Lord."

"As long as you remember that I am no soft touch; if there is a next time, it will be a different matter."

"I understand, my Lord." John Boucher and young Hawkins leave the room and Isaac Warren turns to follow. Joshua delays him. "Thank you for helping John to bring the lad to me, Isaac; I have been meaning to visit Home Farm and meet the rest of your family, but I have been very preoccupied with my studying and the construction of the jetty on the pond, plus we had poor Millie Bonfield's funeral. However, I would like to take this opportunity to invite you all to our Christmas party on Christmas Day. It will just be estate staff and my close family and yourselves."

"Why, thank you very much, my Lord. Shall I ask my Beth to come and see Flora to help with the preparation of the victuals, my Lord?"

"That would be much appreciated, thank you, and if you would like to go and see Flora now she can give you one of those coneys."

"Thank you, my Lord; I will and I look forward to seeing you on Christmas Day."

They shake hands and Isaac leaves.

During December the staff are all busy making

arrangements for the guests who are coming from Portland to stay for the Christmas festivities. There is a special Christmas market, held in Ivell in the market square, during the second week of the month and Joshua takes Louisa and Rosa into town to choose decorations for the eight foot pine tree that Robert and Harry Sandford have uprooted and placed in a large barrel for the hall.

As they enter the market square, the smell of spiced mulled wine is evocative of past years. They pass the food stalls selling candies, cheeses, wines and other Christmas fare and the different aromas waft around them. The stall holders are all wrapped up against the winter cold and are rubbing their hands, or stamping their feet, to keep warm. Some of the stallholders are selling leather gifts, others handmade clothes and basketwork. Louisa is attracted to a tiny white cotton broderie anglaise dress and is looking at it wistfully when Joshua comes up behind her.

"Are you thinking of Aurora?"

"Yes, I was. I think it would be just right for her by the summertime."

"Then I will purchase it for her." He takes out his purse. "How much for the child's cotton gown?"

"Two and four pence please, my Lord, there is a lot of work in the embroidery anglaise." He pays the woman and she wraps the gown in brown paper and hands it to him. He places it in Louisa's basket.

"Thank you, ma'am." He smiles at Louisa. "I think she will look adorable in that when the summer comes."

They wander on, meandering among the other shoppers until they come to the Christmas decorations, where Joshua purchases a box of forty small, white candles in silver clip-on holders, plus four boxes of ten Christmas crackers for the tables, while the girls continue to look around. Rosa finds some strings of pretty red and white beads, twists of candy and a number of wax figures, such as angels and gingerbread men.

Louisa chooses various silver wire ornaments in the shape of bells, snowflakes and stars, some silver tinsel and a variety of glass baubles. They also buy some multicoloured paper flowers and some beaded decorations that have come all the way from Germany.

When Joshua has paid for it all, and Rosa and Louisa's baskets are quite full, he says, "That should all look quite eye-catching together with the crocheted snowflakes, stars and little baskets that Mrs Abbott has made."

"I think so, my Lord," Louisa smiles up at him. "Oh, and we had better get some sugared almonds to go in the baskets while we are here."

"Well remembered, Louisa."

"Do you think a length of wide, red ribbon would look nice tied round the barrel under the tree? Shall I see if they have some?" asks Rosa.

"Yes, that is a good idea."

While Joshua and Louisa walk on back to the confectionery stall, Joshua sees a large, shining star to fix to the top of the tree and he goes to pay the lady for it. A little further on, while he is purchasing the sugared almonds, Louisa notices the stall selling holly wreaths and her thoughts immediately fly to the tragedy of her poor, lost Millie. Her eyes fill with tears and she decides to buy a wreath for her parent's front door. She chooses one with holly, mistletoe and some realistic wax Christmas roses set amongst the greenery. She wipes the tears from her eyes as Joshua rejoins her. "This is for my ma and pa, my Lord. Can I drop it off on the way back home?"

"Of course, Louisa, of course you can." He

sees her sad eyes and understands immediately what has distressed her.

"Thank you, my Lord."

"Maybe you or Rosa could make a larger one like it for our front door. After all, we have plenty of greenery and we have the real Christmas roses at home in the glasshouse."

"I am sure we can, my Lord."

Rosa joins them. "This has been such fun. It is all so merry and everyone seems to be so joyful. I am really looking forward to Christmas this year."

"Me too," Joshua smiles, but Louisa's eyes are still full of sadness. He tries to cheer her up a little. "Shall we have some mulled wine before we return home?"

"Yes please," both girls reply in unison and he is rewarded with a smile from both of them.

On their return the girls set to work with the decorations. Louisa adorns the Christmas tree while Rosa goes outside to collect greenery for the table decorations and the holly wreath. Joshua gets a step ladder and places the star on the top of the tree and Louisa hands him some tinsel and beads for higher up the tree. They work together in contented harmony and soon the tree is festooned from top to bottom.

They both stand back to admire their handiwork. Louisa gives a sigh of satisfaction, "It is so beautiful."

"It is, isn't it?" agrees Joshua. "I have never seen such a large tree, with the exception of the huge tree that they have in Easton Square on Portland. I cannot wait for my mother and Becky to see it; they will be so amazed and impressed."

Joshua receives a letter from his mother saying that the small craft is completed, as planned. The days fly by and soon Louisa has organised the bedrooms, allocating Joshua's parents a double room with a view over the gardens and the duck pond. Benjamin, she has put in a smaller single room and Rebecca is allotted a pretty little room near the nursery. She has beaten the feather mattresses and aired all the bedding, which is crisp and fresh, and made up the beds and laid the fires in readiness for their arrival.

At Home Farm Isaac has killed a pig and is providing Flora at the big house with the pork, plus two geese, two capons and two hare ready for boiling and roasting, and a large truckle of cheese straight from the vat. He leaves Beth demonstrating to his daughter, Lucy, how to make meat cake according to her grandmother's receipt.

"First you mix together the flour and the butter into a thick paste, and put some on the bottom of a baking tin." Lucy is speckled with flour as she struggles with the wooden spoon in the stiff flour and butter mixture.

"Then you cover that with the chopped beef, onion and herbs, then more paste, then more meat and flavouring until the baking tin is full and topped with the paste. Then when you have done all the layers it is baked in the oven and cuts up just like a cake when it is cold."

"It sounds real tasty, Mama."

"It will be, sweetheart, and made by your own fair hands." She kisses her affectionately on the top of her head. "While you are doing that I will make the coney pies, and together with the junkets, your apple pies, my cider cake and all the meat your papa has prepared, I think we will have contributed quite a lot to the festivities, don't you?"

"There will be a lot of folk there though, Mama, do you think that two meat cakes will be enough?"

"Well, Flora says that there will be two tables

and so one for each table should be sufficient. Besides, she is the one who will have to ensure the quantities are adequate, not us. We can just enjoy ourselves, once we are done here." She flours the scrubbed wooden kitchen table and rolls out the pastry and mother and daughter hum some Christmas hymns and tunes as they work.

When Isaac arrives at the manor kitchen he finds Elsie and Emily washing up baking tins and Flora busy preparing mince pies. He can see that preserves and plum puddings are already on the shelf for the feast. He greets them all as he brings in the jointed meat, game and poultry. Flora is grateful for his contribution and helps him stack it on the marble shelves of the cold cupboard. Then she takes him into the pantry and shows him the large, rich Christmas cake, some small cinnamon cakes, tarts and custards that she has also prepared.

"I see you have been very busy, Flora."

"That I 'ave and both Emily and Elsie 'ave been run off their feet clearing up after me."

Isaac laughs, "I bet they have. I have just left Beth and Lucy also fully occupied in the kitchen with preparations for the party, but I will let Beth tell you what they have prepared."

Flora wipes her hands in her apron, "Come and see what else I have 'idden away as a surprise."

He follows her into the dark corner of the pantry and she shows him the dusty bottles of primrose wine that she made the year before last. "This is a very strong tipple, Isaac, as it consists of primroses, lemons, ginger, cinnamon and sugar but," and she emphasises this, knowing Isaac's favourite tipple well, "mainly brandy."

He grins at her, "Mm I can't wait; Beth is

bringing a couple of bottles of each of her honey, elderberry and dandelion wine, so it should be a real party what with all the ale and spirits the master will provide."

They walk back out into the kitchen and Flora lowers her voice. "I know for a fact 'ee already 'as a barrel of beer, brandy and Madeira wine, so there will be fun to be 'ad. You and my John 'ad better watch it though, I know what you are like when you two get together and you must set a good example to the younger ones." She nods in the direction of Elsie and Emily. "We don't want any bad behaviour, or in future years we may go back to the old ways."

"That is true, Flora; this is so much jollier than those years of gloom, when his grandfather ruled the roost."

Flora looks him in the eye and emphasises, "We don't want to go back to that ever, do we, Isaac?"

He grins back at her and shakes his head like a naughty schoolboy. "No, Flora, we do not."

They both laugh good-naturedly and Flora returns to planning her cooking schedule. "I will cook up the 'ams this afternoon and I think I will put the 'ares in a milk and egg pie, which will be nice served cold. Then tomorrow I will concentrate on the geese and the rest of the pork."

"Mm, Flora, my mouth is watering. Lucy was making some meat cake as I left and I am really feeling hungry now. I had better be off home for my luncheon; I will just drop the truckle of cheese in before I forget."

"Thank you, Isaac, I am much obliged. That will go nicely with my pickled eggs and pickled onions."

CHAPTER 5 *(December 1851)*

CHRISTMAS AT ALVINGTON MANOR

The day before Christmas Eve, Billy is up with the lark and goes across to Home Farm to harness Hercules and Perseus, the shire horses, and hitch them between the shafts of the wagon. His journey has been brought forward a day in order that Joshua's step-father, Matthew, and his cousin Ben will be at the other end to help load up the boat and secure it for the homeward conveyance.

Thankfully the weather is exceptionally mild for December; nevertheless, Billy is wrapped up well with a heavy fustian coat and cap, muffler and gloves. The roman road traverses the high, rounded, undulating hills of Dorset throughout a considerable part of his journey and the wind is straight off the sea. Fluffy clouds scud the skies, their shadows chasing over the rolling hills, but the rain holds off and, thanks to the newly macadamised road, Hercules and Perseus are able to average about five miles an hour.

Eventually Billy crosses the ferry bridge and arrives at Portland at around noon. Having taken the wagon straight to the boatyard to meet Matthew and Ben, they help him to unhitch the shires and lead them to the stables alongside Caraway's, Violet's old faithful horse. Caraway neighs and stamps her feet in excitement at having visitors and Thomas the stable boy gives her an apple. Then he gives Hercules and Perseus a bag of oats each, rubs them down and covers them both with a rug. Matthew and Ben take Billy to the Cove House Inn for refreshments, before loading up the boat with the help of some of the fishermen there.

Because he cannot complete the journey there and back in daylight, his return to Alvington Manor is delayed until the following day. This gives him and the shires a well deserved rest and he will be able to sleep that night in Joshua's old bedroom. He is made very welcome by Joshua's family and after supper, while Joshua's mother Violet is clearing away, he joins Matthew, Ben and Rebecca in a game of cards.

Billy is up at dawn on Christmas Eve and, with the help of Thomas, he hitches the two shires between the wagon shafts and sets off home with his unusual load. The wind is far stronger on Portland than it was the previous day and he holds his cap in place by tying his muffler around it. He leaves the family busy packing up their garments and their gifts into a large leather trunk ready to be strapped to the pillion seat at the back of the landau when John Moore eventually arrives.

Some time after Billy has left, Ben turns up with his bulging duffel bag slung over his shoulder; he wears a smart, dark blue jacket and a blue and mustard shawl-collared waistcoat with a matching mustard coloured cravat and some cord trousers. Violet and Rebecca meet him at the door of Cove Cottage. "Wow!" says Rebecca. "You look very fetching, Ben."

He smiles back and raises his eyebrows at the sight of the two women: Violet with her hair pinned up prettily underneath a very dainty hat adorned with artificial flowers and feathers, and Rebecca in a neat little bonnet tied under her chin with a pretty bow matching her outfit. They both are wearing smart travel jackets nipped in at the waist over the top of their long skirts, buttoned boots and gloves. Violet's whole outfit is a dark leaf green and Rebecca's a deep blue jacket and blue and gold plaid skirt.

"You both look like city folk," he laughs, as Rebecca holds out her hand to be kissed, and drops a small curtsey. He takes her mother's hand and kisses her as well, not to leave her out. After all Violet is still a very attractive woman even though, according to Matthew, she was thirty-seven last birthday. "I will go and wait at the end of the lane for the arrival of the carriage," he says and wanders off down the path.

Matthew comes to the door to see what is happening and they explain that Ben is standing guard. "That is a good idea, as the groom will be unable to turn the landau along here outside the cottage, and Ben can come and give us a shout when he gets here." Matthew is dressed in his Sunday best and looks very smart in his moleskin trousers, matching waistcoat, brown frock coat, white stiff-collared shirt and green and brown cravat.

They all go back inside and Violet makes sure all is tidy within, then Matthew puts the trunk in the porch along with the ladies' reticules.

It is not long before Ben is running back along the narrow lane. "He is here, come along; he is waiting at the end of the path."

They step outside and Matthew locks up the door to the cottage and they all set off, Violet and Rebecca ahead and Ben helping Matthew with the trunk, bringing up the rear.

John Moore takes the trunk and straps it onto the pillion seat at the rear of the landau, whilst

Matthew hands Violet up into the carriage, followed by Rebecca and then he and Ben climb aboard. The groom takes his seat at the front and clicks his tongue and flicks the reins and they set off down the hill.

"Oh, Ma, this is so grand, isn't it?" whispers Rebecca.

"I never thought I would see the day that we would all be riding out in such splendid style," replies Violet.

"Look, there is Susan Atwool; give her a wave!" cries Rebecca.

They all wave out of the windows and laugh at the astonished look on their neighbour's face. "It won't be long before that is all around Chiswell, I'll be bound," chuckles Matthew.

"This is so exciting!" Rebecca can hardly contain herself, as she looks out through the windows of the carriage and enjoys the changing vistas passing before her. They are soon across the causeway and leaving Portland behind them. Weymouth is very quiet at this time of the year and the sea and sky are a cold murky grey, nevertheless folk are still promenading along the esplanade, well wrapped up against the cold; last minute shoppers are rushing along laden with parcels and they even pass one poor man struggling against the wind, dragging a Christmas tree behind him.

"He is a bit late with that; they are going to have their work cut out to decorate it, as well as everything else by tomorrow, aren't they?" says Violet.

"I wonder if Josh has put up a tree?" muses Rebecca.

"I don't know, Becky. We have so much to look forward to seeing; it is going to be such an amazing change for us all, isn't it?" says her mother.

"I cannot wait to see the boat launched on the lake," says Ben enthusiastically.

"I am looking forward to that too, Ben," agrees Matthew.

Thus the journey is spent surmising on their destination and commenting on the passing landscape. The time seems to pass very slowly and at each toll house they step down and stretch their legs, partaking of some refreshments at a post-house in Dorchester.

Eventually, John Moore slows the horses. He calls out to them, "You can see the manor house if you look down into the valley on your right." They all lean forward to look across the fields and beneath them they can just make out the roofs and chimneys of Alvington Manor, nestled among the trees in the valley below.

"We will soon be there." Rebecca smiles with relief, "My backside is feeling a touch flattened, bouncing up and down for so long."

"That won't do it any harm," quips Ben.

"Hey, don't be so cheeky, Ben," she responds indignantly, but they all laugh.

"I think we all are in the same boat, Becky," says her father.

"It is obviously a 'flat-bottomed' boat then," laughs Ben.

They are still laughing and giggling when the landau swings through the gate of the manor and across the gravel to the front entrance.

Gareth opens the front door, now decorated with the Christmas wreath that Rosa has made, and Michael Porter walks elegantly down the steps to open the carriage doors and hand the ladies down. He removes their trunk and, before Gareth can take them through into the hall, Joshua is there to greet them.

"Wow! Don't you all look stylish!" he exclaims. There are hugs and kisses for the women and handshakes and back slapping for the men. "I am really pleased you could all come, I have been so looking forward to showing you all around."

"We too have been eagerly looking forward to our visit, ever since you invited us, Josh," says his mother.

He introduces them, "This is my butler, Gareth Williams, and my footman, Michael Porter. Come through to the drawing room and I will ring for some refreshments."

They follow him, wide-eyed and looking all around them. As they pass through the oak panelled hallway, they all comment on the height of the ceilings. When they enter the drawing room Violet's eyes are immediately drawn to the tall mullioned windows and the view of the terrace, gardens and down to the pond with the green fields beyond. She walks across the thick, Persian carpet and looks out at the scene from there, then turns back to her son. "What an attractive room this is, darling."

"It is even more beautiful in the summer sun, Ma, when the gardens are a riot of colour."

"I am sure," she smiles.

Both Matthew and Ben are standing with their backs to the roaring fire and Rebecca is studying the paintings, obviously old masters; the one on the wall opposite the fireplace is a portrait of the 10th Earl of Westmorland by Thomas Lawrence and two of the paintings are by Van Dyke.

Violet is impressed at how elegantly the room is furnished, admiring the beautiful Louis XV chairs with twin matching sofas in gold upholstery. The wallpaper is pale blue and gold and on the walls are some sparkling Queen Anne and Chippendale mirrors. On the side opposite the windows there is a large Sheraton buffet table, covered in highly polished silverware and above this hangs some Jacobean needlework.

Joshua pulls the cord to ring for some refreshments and moments later Rosa answers. He introduces her to his family and asks for the tea and sandwiches prepared earlier by Flora and she goes off to fetch them.

"I expect you are all rather travel-weary; when we have eaten I will get Louisa to show you up to your rooms, so that you can rest and wash and change before dinner. There is plenty of time for me to show you the grounds on Boxing Day."

"Did the boat arrive in good shape, Josh?" asks Ben.

"Yes it did and it is down by the edge of the pond ready for its maiden voyage."

Matthew and Ben walk over to the windows. "I see what you mean about it being more like a lake; it is definitely big enough to have a bit of fun on."

"Yes, it will be rather special to be able to use it on hot summer afternoons." He went to a bureau and took out a cash box. "Here is what I owe you, Pa. I have put in a bit extra as I felt that what you asked for was not enough."

"There is no need for that, Josh. It was a fair price."

"Well, I think you both deserve a Christmas bonus as well."

"Thank you lad, that is very generous of you. I will, of course, split it with Ben."

Rosa then returns with the food and they all enjoy the smoked salmon and ham sandwiches, some slices of cherry cake and cups of China tea.

Afterwards, Louisa shows them upstairs to their bedrooms. In Violet and Matthew's room she explains, "There is hot water in the ewers and fresh soap and towels laid out for you and I have hung up your gowns in the closets."

"Thank you, Louisa, I am sure we will be very comfortable," says Violet.

"Dinner is served at seven of the clock, ma'am, but the master will be in the drawing room from six of the clock onwards to serve you with aperitifs."

Matthew smiles at her. "We will look forward to that with eager anticipation."

"I will see you tomorrow morning, and wish you a goodnight." Louisa smiles and then she turns to Ben and Rebecca, "Please come this way."

They follow her along the passageway to the rooms that she has allocated for them and she leaves them to their ablutions.

Later, they are sitting dressed for dinner and relaxing with Joshua in the drawing room. He is serving them with ladles of hot rum punch and telling them what has happened on the estate since June, when he first arrived. He explains how he has been studying to become a Justice of the Peace and his mother is pleased that he is looking so settled and seems to be so eager to become a respected member of society.

Ben, however, looks uncomfortable and Joshua notices him whispering something to Rebecca. "Is something wrong, Ben?"

"No, Josh, it's just that I just don't want to be reminded of the great British justice system that is all."

"I am sorry, Ben, I didn't think. But you have no reason to feel uneasy, we all know that it was not your actions that led you to Dorchester gaol, but those of your devious uncle."

"I know, but it doesn't stop the memories from haunting me to this day."

"No, I suppose not, but as you know, my own father was brutally killed by a treacherous smuggling gang and so I do believe that there has to be a deterrent. I was very lucky to have Matthew step in and take care of my mother and me. However, I give you my word that I shall always endeavour to be fair and just." He helps himself to some more punch, "In fact, only last month we caught a fellow poaching on the estate and by rights he should have been transported, but I have warned him of this and let him off this once, but next time he will go before the justices."

"It seems to me that the law is harsher with the poachers than it is with the smugglers," comments Ben.

"Well, I think that is because it is mostly the landowners who make up the rules and unfortunately a lot of them actually benefit themselves from the smuggling, but lose out with regard to poaching. I have to say I would be even more severe with the so-called gentlemen who fund these smuggling runs, who profit from the misery and cruelty of the gangs that terrorise innocent folk, while maintaining an air of respectability."

Rebecca joins in, "But, Josh, Ben was just trying to be kind to his uncle and take him out fishing and he deceived him," she protests. "How many other folk, accused of dishonesty, have been unable to prove that they are guiltless? You can be hanged for stealing a sheep can't you?"

"Yes, you can, in addition to manslaughter and murder, also for burglary, forgery, and sexual assault, but the judge does have it in his power to commute the sentence to life imprisonment."

"Well that is not much consolation if you are

actually innocent, is it?" says Rebecca earnestly. "If a felon has been hanged and then found in due course to be blameless, it is too late to save him then."

"Well, Becky, I don't think we have to worry, none of us are likely to be convicted of any of those crimes, are we?" laughs her father in an attempt to lighten the mood.

Joshua realises that it is time to change the subject. "Anyway, Becky, I am sure this will interest you far more; something else happened here that was very sad and mysterious in the autumn."

Rebecca is immediately intrigued. "What was that?"

"Rosa found a little foundling, abandoned here, hidden under the clock tower early one morning. She brought her into the kitchen to warm and we decided to keep her. She is being cared for by Susan Moore, who has a small son of her own. She has been her wet nurse and we have named her 'Aurora'."

"Will we be able to see her, Josh?" asks Rebecca eagerly.

"Of course, she will be coming to the Christmas party tomorrow and eventually, when she has been weaned, she will live down here with us."

"Why did you call her Aurora? I have never heard of that name." Violet asks.

"Well, it means 'new dawn' and apparently it was the name of the princess in *Sleeping Beauty* and the staff all decided that it was the most appropriate of all their suggestions."

"Well, it is very pretty."

There is then a tap at the door and Michael Porter enters. "Dinner is served, my Lord."

"Thank you, Michael." Joshua stands up and puts his empty punch glass upon the silver tray, on the buffet table. "Your dinner awaits, ladies and gentlemen," he says, as they too put down their glasses and he ushers them from the room.

They all enjoy a tasty meal of beef stew and dumplings served by Elsie, while Michael Porter serves more wine. This is followed by apple cake and custard. During the meal Matthew and Ben tell Joshua about the boatyard; Violet tells him all about her shop and how busy they are and Rebecca joins in when it comes to all the gossip about their family, friends and neighbours. "Guess who we saw as we were leaving in the landau?"

Josh, knowing that it could be anyone, hazards a guess. "Aunty Sarah?"

"No, Susan Atwool. So, like Pa says, that will be all around Chiswell by now." Rebecca looks and sounds like an old fishwife nodding away and her older brother laughs at her feeble attempt to sound worldly wise.

After dinner they return to the comfort of the drawing room for coffee and nightcaps by the fireside. Once this is served the remaining staff retire for the night and in the gentle flickering of the firelight Joshua decides to quietly tell his family about the death of Louisa's poor sister, Millie. He explains the circumstances in which she was found and he finds their concern for Louisa touching.

"There is something else that I witnessed back in the summer and I am now sure that it is connected. On the day that I first came to Alvington Manor I passed an attractive red head, I did not know at the time, of course, that it was Millie. She was running through the fields in great distress down towards the road on which Mr Fairway and I were travelling, but up on the hill astride a horse was a gentleman watching her and I concluded that they had had a lover's tiff, but in retrospect it must have been far more serious than that, for her to take her own life."

"So you don't think it was an accident then?"

"No, Pa, I don't. We persuaded the parson that it may well have been an accident so that the poor lass should not be ex-communicated and we could have the service here in the chapel, but I believe that she was so unhappy that she killed herself. Louisa has been much troubled by her sister's death and so please be diplomatic in your dealings with her."

"Which one is Louisa again?" asks Ben.

"She showed you all up to your rooms earlier, she is the chambermaid."

Violet looks assiduously at Joshua. "The rather attractive one dressed in black with the copper coloured hair?"

"Yes," says Joshua, feeling his cheeks growing hot at the thought of her.

His mother comments, "I thought it strange that a young girl like that should choose to wear black under her pinny and I did notice that all the other girls were wearing that pretty shade of dove grey."

Rebecca is looking thoughtful and then, as if inspired, she says, "You don't think that the little abandoned baby might be Millie's child, do you?"

Everyone is silent contemplating this suggestion.

"It is possible, Becky, I hadn't thought of that, but it would explain a lot," says Joshua thoughtfully. "I don't know why I hadn't thought of that probability before." He would give anything to know the identity of that arrogant man. *Poor Louisa! That would make the baby Aurora her little niece. Maybe it was her who had left the baby for us to find.* "Well, you will all see Aurora tomorrow and you can make up your minds then."

The fire collapses a little in the middle and Joshua gets up from his seat to riddle it with the poker. It is too late to put another log on and so he damps it down. "I suppose that, as we will be up early in the morning to exchange our gifts and to receive our Christmas party guests, we should think about retiring for the night."

"Yes, darling, it has been quite an eventful day for us all and it is already past our bedtime." She kisses her son on his cheek. "Goodnight, my dear. It is so nice to see you looking so well and happy."

"I am very happy here, Ma, I feel as if I belong. All the staff have made me feel so welcome."

"That is wonderful, Josh, it is a great relief to your pa and me to know that you are content."

Rebecca says, "I think you look like a proper country squire, Josh, don't you, Ben?"

"Yes, my friend, you really look the part," agrees Ben.

Joshua laughs, "'Tis not a drama I am in, you know, this is my life now."

"And a very good one too, as far as I can see." Matthew pats him on the back, as they all move to retire for the night. "We'll see you at breakfast, Josh."

"Yes, goodnight everyone, I hope you will all be comfortable." Joshua turns to extinguish the lamps and candles and then follows his family up to bed.

On Christmas morning Violet awakes and immediately goes barefoot to the windows. She draws back the curtains and looks out onto the gardens, to check the weather. The lawns are crisp with frost and the sky a clear blue; she stretches and gives a contented sigh. Matthew smiles to see her silhouetted in the early sunlight. It is chilly and she puts on her robe and moments later there is a gentle tap at their bedroom door.

"Come in," she responds and Louisa pops her head around the door.

"I have some hot water here for you, ma'am, and would you like me to light the fire?"

"Thank you, that is very kind." Violet steps back and lets Louisa into the room. As she goes about her tasks Violet watches her covertly. She moves with grace and poise but there is an imperceptible aura of sadness around her.

As she goes to leave the room Louisa turns and smiles. "Cook says that breakfast will be ready at eight of the clock. Is there anything else I can do for you, ma'am?"

"No thank you, Louisa, we will both be down to breakfast shortly."

Violet and Matthew meet Rebecca on the landing. "Merry Christmas, Becky."

"Merry Christmas," she says gaily and kisses her parents. They go downstairs together.

"Did you sleep well?" her mother asks her.

"I did and I was lovely and warm. Louisa had left a hot charcoal warmer in the bed for me."

"I know, we had one too, we were really snug as bugs last night."

Moments later Ben and Joshua join them in the dining room and they sit down to a hearty breakfast of hen's eggs, bacon, bread and butter and a cup of cider, served again by Elsie the kitchen maid. With breakfast finished they all go and fetch their gifts and meet back downstairs in the drawing room.

They sit in a semicircle in front of the fire and while they take it in turns to hand out their parcels, Joshua is toasting chestnuts in a long handled roasting pan. Being the youngest and most eager, Rebecca goes first. She has a silk folding fan, hand painted with tiny violets, for her mother, who unties the parcel and exclaims happily at the charming present, taking it out and fanning herself coyly. "This is lovely, darling, and so clever to find one with violets."

Ben has unwrapped the cravat that she had made for him and he knots it in a careless bow, flowing away from his neck in fine romantic style. "What do you think?" he asks Rebecca, who smiles lovingly.

"It looks charming," she replies.

She passes her gift for her father and watches as he unties the wrapping. It is a pair of Berlin work slippers and he removes his shoes and tries them on. "Look at that; a perfect fit," he says.

"They are embroidered by my own fair hands, Pa. Do you like the rich colours of burgundy, green and gold?"

"I do, sweetheart. They are lovely and comfortable too."

For her brother she has a quill pen and inkwell set. "Just the thing for my studying Becky, thank you very much."

Violet then hands out her presents from herself and Matthew. She gives the smart hand-crafted waistcoats, one each to Ben and Joshua. Both Molly and Rebecca had helped her with the finishing touches but she was very pleased with them and so are the boys. Although she has already given Rebecca the outfits made for their visit, she has also purchased a pair of kid gloves to give to her daughter as a surprise. Rebecca is thrilled, trying them on immediately. "They fit like a glove, Ma." Everyone laughs.

Violet then passes the largest box to her husband

and inside is a new beaver top hat that she purchased in Weymouth on her last visit. He tries it on, then gets up to look in the mirror and walks round the room like a toff until they are all laughing again. Then he returns to his seat and gives Violet his gift of a fur wrap and matching muff. Violet has no idea what is inside the parcel and opens it carefully. As her hands touch the soft fur she smiles at her husband and removes the items from the box. "That is a wonderful present darling and just what I need for our journey home," and she gives him a kiss.

Joshua passes around the chestnuts and mulled ale that Flora prepared earlier and left by the fire. "Mm, I love roasted chestnuts," says Rebecca taking a couple, "and this hot toddy is delicious." Everyone enjoys a little drink and a few chestnuts.

Violet has one more parcel tucked behind her. "This one is for you, Josh, from your grandparents. They asked me to bring it for them. We will be exchanging the rest of our gifts with them when we invite them to dinner on our return." She passes the gift to her son.

"Thank you, Ma." Joshua opens the wrapping to reveal a nightshirt in soft, white, peached cotton twill. "Your grandma did the smocking herself," says Violet.

"It is very fine, tell them thank you from me and I will send a hamper of Christmas fare back with you for them all."

Joshua then goes to his pile and passes his presents around. He has a beautiful cashmere shawl for his mother and she wraps it around herself. "This is gorgeous darling and so soft."

"I thought you would like it, Ma."

Rebecca's gift is a silk parasol, hand-painted with bluebirds. "Look, Ma, I won't have to borrow yours anymore. It is lovely, Josh, thank you so much."

For Ben and for his father he has a smart cigar box, each containing the best Brazilian cigars. The men smell the aroma of the cigars. "Mm, I love that rich Brazilian tang," says Matthew.

"Thank you, Josh, we can enjoy them this evening after the party," added Ben. "Right, now it is my turn. I am afraid my gifts are more modest, but I hope that you will like them nevertheless. This one is for you, Becky."

Rebecca takes the gift and opens it inquisitively. Inside is a dainty marcasite brooch in the shape of a slender ribbon tied in a bow, and a pair of silk stockings. Rebecca is thrilled and jumps up and kisses her precious cousin on his cheek. "Thank you, Ben, it is a lovely gift. These are my first silk stockings and I will treasure this lovely brooch always. Will you pin it on for me?"

"Of course, let me see." Rebecca holds up her chin as Ben carefully pins the brooch in the centre of her satin blouse. She stands up and looks in the mirror.

"It looks very pretty, darling," says her mother.

Ben then passes Violet her gift from him, which is a mother of pearl hat pin and some lace-edged handkerchiefs, made for him by Matthew's sister, Hannah. She is very moved by his thoughtfulness. "Thank you, Ben, that is very kind of you and I love both items."

"You are most welcome." He then picks up his last two parcels, "I have spent many a night by candlelight labouring over these, so I hope that you like them." He hands his boss Matthew and his cousin Josh a parcel each, which they open together to reveal two quite different ships in bottles.

"Why, these are exquisite; what a lot of work there is in them," says Matthew.

"Thanks, mate," says Josh touching his shoulder

warmly. "This will always remind me of my trip to New Guinea in the Methodist missionary brig."

Ben is pleased and relieved that they all appreciate his choices and they spend the rest of the morning together in relaxed harmony enjoying the mulled ale, until the guests start to arrive.

The banqueting hall is laid out with two long tables. Both the tables and the silver cutlery have been polished until they gleam and sparkle and all the best crockery is filled with the most delectable fare. Joshua is amused to see the shock on Ambrose Fairway's face when he realises that the guests upstairs and the staff downstairs are all celebrating at this Christmas banquet together.

Joshua's family, the Warrens, the Moores, the Fairways and those in the Dower House are to sit at one table and the other table headed by Gareth and Mrs Abbott is to seat the remainder of the staff. Rosa has done the table decorations with Christmas roses from the glasshouse, dried flowers, holly, ivy and old man's beard. Louisa has made the place name cards and decorated each of them with tiny sprigs of holly and everyone is wandering around the tables to see who they are sitting with. There is a hum of happy voices as people admire the Christmas tree decorations and all the tiny, twinkling candles. Mrs Abbott lights the table candelabras and Gareth asks everyone to take their seats.

Joshua sits at the head of his table and after saying Grace he carves the hams and the baked fowl, while Isaac and Beth are seated at the other end and Isaac cuts up the beef and the bacon chine, and Beth passes around the platters of meat. For a while Louisa and Rosa stand and rearrange the dishes, in order that both ends of the table can choose from all that is laid out, then they sit down as well and join in the feast.

Gareth and Mrs Abbott are at the head of the other table and John and Flora Boucher at the opposite end and. While the men are busy carving, Flora is helping Elsie and Emily on her table to pass around the platters of meat and to respond to any requests from those seated. There is a buzz of elated chatter as Michael Porter fills the glasses with Madeira wine and little Luke squeals excitedly in his highchair, squeezed in between his mother and Bunny, the youngest of the Warrens. Aurora is sleeping peacefully in a Moses basket in the corner of the room, having just been fed by Susan Moore.

Rosa, Louisa, Lucy Warren and Clara Fairway are all seated in the centre of Joshua's table opposite each other, with only Lucy's brother Jacob caught in the middle between Clara and Rosa, periodically blushing and laughing out loud at their conversations. Whilst they talk Rosa keeps catching the eye of Malachi Warren and her pretty face flushes when she smiles at him and he gives her the slightest wink.

This doesn't go unnoticed by Louisa, who is thrilled to have witnessed this secret attraction between them. She thinks that they will make a good match; the Warrens are a quality family, hard-working and good-looking and Malachi especially has a sort of animal magnetism that is very appealing. She glances to the top of the table where Joshua is talking animatedly to his parents, with Ben and Rebecca listening intently. His handsome face is illuminated by the soft candlelight and, as he laughs, his eyes sparkle. When he looks at his mother, Louisa can see the affection between them. She wishes that he would look at her with such warmth and she realises then that she is falling for him. She finds him absolutely fascinating, but she has to tear her eyes away, because it would not do for anyone else to know how she feels, least of all Joshua himself. She is reminded of how this situation was the ruination of poor Millie and that dark cloud of unhappiness descends upon her once more. Clara and Lucy are talking about playing the piano and so she turns to Mr Fairway on her left and asks him if he would mind passing her the meat cake that Lucy made. She helps herself to a portion and hands it back to him. She serves herself a small amount of red cabbage to go with it and takes a mouthful of the mixture. "Mm, Lucy, this is delicious."

Lucy beams with pleasure at the compliment. "Thank you, Louisa, 'tis my great grand mama's receipt."

"You will have to give the receipt to Flora so that we can have some more of this."

"I will do." She nods and smiles.

Jacob helps himself to a little of his sister's meat cake and some of Flora's hare pie, then passes the dish along the table for John and Isaac. The Madeira wine is going down well and soon Michael is going around and topping up some of the glasses.

When everyone has had their fill of all the savoury food, Flora and Beth ask Emily and Elsie to clear away the dishes whilst they go to the sideboards and replenish the tables with the puddings, desserts and sweetmeats.

"Flora, that hare pie was scrumptious, how did you make it?" asks Beth. "Everyone has been commenting."

"Well, first I skin the 'ares and remove their insides, cut the meat up into small pieces and soak the pieces in milk for an hour. Then I place the 'are pieces in layers, with layers of a mixture of apples, onions, 'ard boiled eggs, seasoning and so on. Then I add some brown sugar and two glasses of port wine and I put it into the oven to bake. While it is baking, I mix four eggs with fresh cream and, when the dish has been cooking for about an hour and an 'alf, I pour in the egg mixture and put it back into the oven until the eggs are set."

"I would be really grateful if you would write the quantities down for me, because Isaac was really impressed and it is always good to give the family something different for a change."

"Of course, perhaps we could do a swap – my 'are pie for your meat cake."

"Yes, that is a bargain; I will send Lucy round with it after Christmas."

They serve the junket, plum pudding, fruit tarts, mince pies and the apple pie with custard or fresh cream to whoever wants it. When everyone has been served with something of their choice, Flora and Beth sit down to enjoy their own puddings.

Susan Moore manages to help herself and Luke to a dish of junket before Aurora wakes up and starts to grizzle for attention. Susan leaves unobtrusively with the baby to go upstairs to the nursery and feed her.

Finally, Beth and Flora cut up the Christmas cake into small squares and serve each person with a slice. They lay a platter of cinnamon cakes and a platter displaying slices of cider cake on each table, together with the bottles of homemade wine.

It is early evening by the time everyone has eaten their fill of desserts and the ladies retire to the drawing room; Flora, Beth, Elsie and Emily all help to clear the tables. Rosa and Louisa serve the men with the cheese and pâté and a variety of pickles, fruits and toasted bread; and while Gareth and Michael serve the port, Joshua, Matthew and Ben hand around the cigars.

Rebecca goes off to the drawing room with Clara, Lucy and Lettie Boucher. Rebecca and Lettie chatter away happily while Lucy and Clara play the spinet.

"Can you ride, Becky?" asks Lettie.

"Yes, I often ride my ma's horse, on Portland."

"I sometimes exercise the horses here with Billy for the master. Would you like to see around the estate and hereabouts with me tomorrow?"

"If it is clement weather I would. I have brought my riding costume with me and after all this food some fresh air and exercise would be beneficial for both of us."

"Yes, I must say my corset is feeling a little snug," laughs Lettie. "Perhaps you could suggest it to your brother, Becky?"

"I will, when they join us."

Lucy is playing 'It Came upon a Midnight Clear' and soon everyone is joining in with the singing. When the men and the remaining women join them, Elsie uses the bellows to heat up the samovar to make some tea. Joshua and Michael serve wine to those who are not yet ready for tea, and then they all join in the singsong. Clara plays 'Green sleeves' and 'Oh Suzanna', John Boucher sings a hunting song and Isaac an old poaching song, with everyone singing the choruses. Sarah Moore brings Aurora down after her nap and the girls take it in turns to nurse her. Rebecca has never cuddled a babe-in-arms before and she is besotted. Aurora is a contented little soul, full of smiles and enjoying the attention. This is a particular treat for Louisa; Joshua and Rebecca watch with interest at the way she interacts with the little one. Joshua suspects that Rebecca is right.

Rosa, on the other hand, is looking very content sitting between Malachi and Jacob; a rose between two thorns, as Beth Warren points out approvingly to her husband. Granny Warren and the Smiths are seated together in the most comfortable chairs nearest to the fire, in respect of their great age. Matthew and Violet share one of the sofas and Bunny Warren and Toby Boucher are sitting on the carpet making a house of cards. Rebecca makes special friends with Lettie and they are busy chatting with Lucy and Emily, being younger and nearest in age to them. Clara, Louisa, Lottie and Elsie are also nattering to each other and altogether they make a happy group. Rebecca takes this opportunity to ask Joshua if he minds if she goes out for a ride with Lettie the following day.

"Not at all. She will be able to show you all around and you will get a better idea of the extent of the grounds, but I think it might be a good idea for Billy to ride with you."

Rebecca turns to Lettie. "Lettie do you mind if Billy comes too?"

"No, of course not. It is only right and proper that we should be chaperoned," she says, fanning herself, cheekily.

Joshua laughs and, catching Billy's attention, he asks, "Billy, would you please prepare Cassiopeia, and the bay – what is she called? – Capella, for the girls to ride tomorrow morning? You can exercise Andromeda if you would like to join them."

"Of course, my Lord, I will look forward to that."

Rebecca smiles, "Thank you Billy, I will be ready at about half past ten I should think, only I would like to look around the garden with Joshua and the family first. Is that fitting for you, Lettie?"

"Yes, I will meet you both at the stables at half past ten."

Billy nods to himself. "That will give me plenty of time to get the horses tacked. I think it is going to be cold but dry and sunny tomorrow, so wrap up warm."

Finally they play charades and, as they all watch Maud Porter doing her mime, Billy, Jacob, Robert and Harry Sandford are in a separate group, desirously watching the young ladies all dressed in their best finery.

Everyone is a little inebriated and all are stuffed full of the Christmas fare. Soon Granny Warren is snoring quietly and Beth and Isaac decide it is time to take her and Bunny home. Lucy is to stay on a bit longer with Malachi and Jacob, but the Smiths and the Hodinotts decide that they are ready to take the long walk up the hill back to Camp Road, and the Moores also need to put the babies to bed. In the end the Camp Road families all leave together for company on the way and they go off in small groups, with their Christmas boxes ready for Boxing Day tucked under their arms and singing Christmas carols.

Mr Fairway and Clara are also ready to leave and they offer Louisa conveyance in their carriage, as she has a day off with her family on Boxing Day. She asks Joshua for permission to leave. "Do you mind, my Lord? Only Clara and her father have offered to give me a ride."

"Of course not, Louisa, but first come with me to the kitchen because Flora has prepared a box of goodies for you to take home to your family for Boxing Day, to go with your meal tomorrow."

She follows him down to the kitchen and he hands her the parcel.

"Thank you, my Lord. It has been a lovely party and it was very nice to meet your family." She is feeling very self-conscious, alone with him in the silent kitchen. "Merry Christmas, my Lord; I had better get along because they will be waiting upon me."

"Merry Christmas, Louisa." He is looking into her eyes and she is afraid he is going to kiss her on the mouth, but then he takes up her hand and kisses it tenderly.

She curtseys and blushes. "Goodnight, my Lord." She turns then, her heart thumping, and rushes back along the servants' passageway into the hall, where thankfully Clara and her father are waiting for her.

The remaining staff are busy tidying up as Joshua returns and he and his family relax together, enjoying a nightcap with the younger Warrens and Billy Riddick. Ben sits next to Rebecca and Billy sits himself down next to Lucy. Rosa is soon back and makes a beeline for the chair next to Malachi. Rebecca has drunk more than she has ever drunk in her life and is very giggly. Lettie too is a little tipsy, but the atmosphere in the room is relaxed and homely and all enjoy winding down from all the noise and gaiety of the party.

Gareth and Mrs Abbott pop their heads around the door and say goodnight and eventually the Bouchers, the Warrens and Billy also depart for their beds.

Rosa leaves on Malachi's arm and he walks her to the door of the Dower House kissing her goodnight in the frosty moonlight. Billy is not brave enough to kiss Lucy goodnight; the fear of rejection is too great, but he kicks himself for the lost opportunity, as he watches her walking away on the arm of her brother, Jacob.

Joshua dowses the fire and the lights and he and his family all retire.

CHAPTER 6 *(December 1851)*

BOXING DAY

The following day, with the exception of Billy, Mrs Abbot and Gareth, all the staff go home to their families for Boxing Day. A cold buffet has been left for those remaining.

As Billy predicted the weather is dry and sunny, but the ground is hard and twinkling with frost in the early sunlight. After breakfast Rebecca dresses in her riding habit and joins the rest of her family for a tour around the grounds. She has never seen Joshua looking so proud, as they all admire the immaculate gardens, although obviously not at their best midwinter. The snowdrops are a picture, spread in a white speckled swathe down the lawns, as far as the pond. They visit the glasshouse to see the camellias, already their fat buds are beginning to open in the warmth.

"It is much warmer inside here in the sun," says Violet.

"Well, the glasshouse is warmed by long pipes that run water heated from a wood burning stove and chimney stack at the other end of the building."

"No wonder you have such lovely plants, Josh. Are these orchids?"

"Yes, Ma, they are beautiful aren't they? And these are hibiscus… and look, Ma," Josh points, "this is a grapevine all along the wall so we will have plenty of grapes in the summer. There are figs, too."

"You are so lucky, darling."

"I know I am, and I intend to make the most of it."

Rebecca and her mother follow the men through to the end of the path, enjoying the perfume of a multicoloured display of hyacinths, before they exit the glasshouse.

"Shall we launch the boat, Josh?" asks Ben enthusiastically.

"Why not? Come on, Pa, let's get her onto the water."

Violet and Rebecca skirt the mass of snowdrops and wander down, following the men.

It does not take the three of them long to push and slide the small craft into the water and they hold it against the jetty for the ladies to climb onboard. Soon Matthew and Ben are seated opposite them and Joshua is rowing. They go around the small island and can see the ducks sunning themselves on their ramps in the shelter of the willow fronds, evergreen ferns and among the yellow flowers of winter aconite. It is very peaceful; all they can hear is the flip flop of the oars on the water.

"Oh! Look at that funny little duck with the lovely markings," says Rebecca with delight.

"It is a Mandarin drake, Becky. The lake is fully stocked with ornamental birds, such as the Carolina and the Mandarin ducks, Gorgany and falcated teal, and Argentine shovellers. They all enjoy the luxury of an island duck house where they are safe from predators."

"This is very pretty, Josh," says his mother.

"I know, Ma, I never tire of it. There is a huge clump of arum lilies on the edge of the island that look wonderful in the summer and are especially beautiful in the moonlight."

"You are very well informed about all the different plants, Josh."

"Well, I have been talking to the gardeners, but I saw the arum lilies growing wild all around Cape Town when we docked there en route to New Guinea."

Suddenly a fish jumps out of the water and plops back down again, sending circles of rippling water towards them. "You have some fish in here, too, then, Josh," comments Matthew.

"Yes, but I am not sure what." They all stare into the water in the hope of catching sight of some and identifying them, but that must have been an exception because the rest are obviously staying deep because of the cold. They go all the way around the island and Joshua manoeuvres the boat back to the jetty and they all disembark.

"Right, shall we go and see the chapel now?"

"Yes, I think we had better, because I have to go and meet Lettie and Billy presently," Rebecca reminds them. They all follow Joshua around to the western side of the house and down a neat, fine-gravel path to the heavy oak door of the small, traditional chapel.

"Oh isn't it charming, Josh? What a pretty setting for a wedding." Violet smiles at Rebecca, who flushes crimson at the thought of it, because Ben is standing right beside her. It is Joshua who replies, "I think that will be some time off in the future, Ma, but yes, one day I am sure I will take my vows here."

The sun is streaming through the stained glass window above the altar and dust particles glitter in the shafts of light. They move around the nave, admiring the craftsmanship in the vaulted roof and the colourful painted murals on the walls.

"I have been to all the Sunday services here, although we share the Reverend Phelps with Odcombe and Montacute and the service is at Montacute today. He is a very pleasant man and he is going to nominate me for the position of Justice of the Peace as soon as I attain my majority."

"That will be good for you, darling; it will give you something useful to occupy yourself with."

They all wander around looking at different aspects of interest. Violet is reading the epitaphs and memorials of Joshua's ancestors; Matthew and Ben are admiring the woodwork and carvings in the pews and choir stalls and the magnificent roof structure, whilst Rebecca loves the religious paintings and stained glass windows.

After a while Rebecca decides it is time she left. "I am going to go and meet Lettie and Billy now, Josh. I don't expect we will be back until after luncheon, but we can help ourselves to something on our return. Please don't wait for us before you dine."

"All right, Becky, we will see you later. Don't be too reckless; give the horses a chance to get used to you first."

"Don't fret, I will be careful, Josh."

"Enjoy your ride, darling," says her mother.

"I will, Ma. See you all anon."

They all say their farewells and she takes her leave of them.

Billy is ready with the three mares, all saddled and waiting in their stalls. As Rebecca arrives he brings out the beautiful grey. "This is Cassiopeia," he says, as he leads her to the mounting block. "She is gentle, responsive and amenable. I am sure you will like her."

Rebecca strokes her neck and then stands on the block and mounts her side-saddle, then walks the mare around the stable yard.

Lettie arrives moments later and Billy leads out the bay for her. Lettie is used to riding Capella and she is soon mounted and ready to go, as Billy goes to fetch Andromeda for himself. Lettie holds her steady in position for him to climb astride and then they are off trotting through the gate and into the pastures of Home Farm.

They have a canter through the fields with Billy opening the gates for them to pass through. Rebecca is not confident enough to jump side-saddle. She is used to riding Caraway bareback on Portland during the summer months, but it would not be the thing to do here.

They ride alongside the stream for a while and then turn northwards up the hill towards Camp Road, their own and the horses' breath misty in the cold air. As they go Rebecca hears an unfamiliar sound. "What is that noise?" she asks, listening carefully.

In the distance is the sound of a hunting horn and hounds baying. "It is the hunt and I think they are getting closer," calls Billy.

"I have never seen a hunt before," replies Rebecca excitedly.

"It is quite a spectacle when they are in full cry, with the horses and huntsmen in their bright red coats and the pack of hounds with the fox in sight."

"It is so cruel though," comments Rebecca.

"Well, you may get to see it close up," warns Lettie.

At the top of the hill they turn west towards the entrance to the lane, leading down to Lettie's home, known as Keeper's Cottage. Suddenly they spot the red fox, running for its life. The animal bursts through a hole in the undergrowth at the top of the hill and then tears down the field along the line of the hedge. The hounds are soon on its heels. The noise of them must be terrifying for the poor, fleeing creature.

As they go along Camp Road, Rebecca spots the huntsmen bringing up the rear, the horn sounding triumphantly, the hunt master shouting, "Tally ho." The hunt splits as the bold and the brave fearlessly jump the dry stone wall bordering the road and land heavily in the field beyond, while the more cautious take their horses down Pound Lane.

Rebecca and her friends can see the excitement in their own horses, their ears pointing forwards, their sideways stepping and frisky behaviour. Billy comes to a halt on the top of the hill and they watch the scene from this vantage point. The fox has found cover in a copse at the bottom of the lane, behind Alvington Manor Chapel, and they watch as the hounds with their tails erect and wagging excitedly weave in and out of the undergrowth.

They decide to make their way down the lane and as they go they hear the baying of the hounds rising to frenzy and in amongst this a terrified squealing and yelping. The hunt master blows the mort, a mournful call on the hunting horn to signify the demise of their prey.

As they reach the bottom of the lane the huntsmen are all making their way towards the hunt master, who is dismembering what is left of the fox and dividing the prized parts among the riders.

Rebecca is horrified. "Oh the poor animal, what a dreadful way to die."

Billy recognises the hunt master as Nathan

Meakins and they watch as a small lad on an equally small stocky pony is led forward. He must be the youngest member of the hunt, at around ten years, and his lack of enthusiasm is evident.

Nathan Meakins looks impatient. "Come here, lad, what are you dithering about? This is your first hunt, is it not?"

"Yes, my Lord."

"Well then, you are a novice and the youngest, and have earned the honour of being blooded."

"Thank you for the honour, my Lord, but I do not relish it."

"Come, don't dilly dally; I haven't got all day."

The lad reluctantly dismounts and his portly father encourages him to go forward. Nathan Meakins picks up a piece of the dead animal and daubs the child's face with the still warm blood. The child visibly cringes. Meakins then removes the brush and tosses the remains of the carcass to the hounds.

Rebecca is horrified. "This is quite barbaric, Lettie, I have never seen anything quite so shocking; that poor, young boy."

"I know it is disgusting, but it is the tradition of the countryside."

Suddenly they are spotted by Meakins and he rides over to them.

"What are you all staring at?"

Rebecca sticks out her chin. "We were watching you cruelly butcher that innocent animal," she says boldly.

"Well be on your way, this is nothing to do with you. It is hunt business and not for the eyes of wenches." He turns his mount in front of Cassiopeia and flicks his whip. He is so close that his horse kicks out, catching Rebecca on her shin and causing Cassiopeia to shy.

"Ouch!" Rebecca cries out in pain and just manages to keep her seat, but Meakins does not even look back. Tears prick her eyes. "What an arrogant man!" She tries to hold Cassiopeia steady, as she takes the reins in her left hand and rubs her leg vigorously with the right to alleviate the smarting.

Billy moves Andromeda forward and catches hold of Cassiopeia's head, calming her. "Don't get on the wrong side of him, Becky. He is Nathan Meakins and he would make a bad enemy."

As they turn the horses and move away, Rebecca says angrily, "Wait till I tell Josh what has just happened on his land, I bet he won't want the hunt riding rough shod across the Alvington estate again."

"Is your leg alright?" asks Lettie, concerned.

"It will be, nothing is broken, just badly bruised. I have some arnica ointment, but it is back at home on Portland."

"Well, we could pop in to see if Ma has a remedy. She likes to make herbs and potions and I am in no doubt she will have something that will help."

"Are you sure she won't mind, Lettie?"

"No, of course not, but let us get out of the way before more of these arrogant toffs decide to push past us in the lane," suggests Lettie.

"Good idea," says Billy, "and I will stay with the horses while you go in with Lettie."

They trot back up the hill to Keeper's Cottage and the girls dismount and hand the reins to Billy, who leads them to a wide part of the grassy verge and into a gateway where they graze contentedly.

As they approach the cottage Rebecca can see beyond it into their back garden, where there are dead rooks strung up in the trees. It looks macabre and Rebecca wonders uneasily what she will encounter inside.

Keeper's Cottage is built of the local ham stone from Hamdon Hill, with a thatched roof and, like most workers' cottages, it has two rooms up and down. The front garden is small and protected by a white picket fence and gate and Rebecca can see from the rambling stems and thorns that there are roses climbing over the porch, which must look a picture in the summer. There is a holly bush in one corner and the bare branches of a deciduous bush on the opposite side. In the centre is a short flagstone path to the front door.

Lettie opens the door and Rebecca follows her inside. She is relieved to find herself in a well lit, neat and tidy parlour, with homemade curtains at the windows, rag rugs on the floor, a corner cabinet displaying the family's treasures and a small sofa with two armchairs. Along one wall there is an oak side cabinet, upon which there sits a glass dome, housing a stuffed pheasant. Through the glass doors of the cupboards below Rebecca can see a blue and white Spode china dinner and tea service on display.

There is a fireplace with a mantelpiece, on which stands a brass candlestick at each end and a black marble mantel clock in the centre. Between the ticking clock and the candlesticks are two white Staffordshire porcelain dogs at either side. Under the mantel the open fire is lit and crackling and the room is snug and warm. Rebecca warms her hands by the fire. On one side of the hearth there is a polished brass shell case holding tapers. In the corner, between the fireplace and the window, is another tall, glass-fronted case that holds two shotguns, one double barrel and one single bore.

Rebecca can hear voices from the other room and she follows Lettie through into the kitchen. Toby is playing with a spinning top on the kitchen floor and chatting to his mother as she prepares the table for their Boxing Day meal. Mrs Boucher is pleased when Lettie walks into the kitchen. "Ah! just in time to 'elp me, Lettie."

"Oh, Ma, I still have Becky here with me. She has been kicked by Nathan Meakins' horse and has a nasty bruise on her shin. I wondered if you had a remedy we could apply for her?"

"I'm sure I do 'ave somewhere. I expect I still 'ave some infusion of comfrey and we can soak a compress in it and 'old it against the painful area. Let me just look through the cupboard 'ere. Ah! 'ere we are." She shakes the bottle. "There should be enough 'ere. Get me some muslin, Lettie, and Toby could you go and tell your pa that dinner will be about 'alf 'n hour." Toby wanders off into the garden and Lettie runs upstairs and is soon back down with the cloth. "Come 'n sit 'ere, Becky," says Flora. "Lift up your skirt a little so that I can see the bruise."

Rebecca rolls down her woollen stocking.

"Dear me, it does look red and swollen, but this should cool it down for you." She soaks the muslin in the infusion of comfrey and administers it to the bump on Rebecca's shin.

"Oh, that has really taken the sting out of it already. Thank you so much, Mrs Boucher."

"My pleasure, ducky. I should leave the muslin 'eld in place by your stocking. That's right. You can take the rest of the bottle with you, because I 'ave plenty of comfreys in the back garden and I can easily replace it in the summer. But, before you go, you must 'ave a drink of wine with us and I will add in a few drops of catnip juice, which should also 'elp."

"That is very kind, Mrs Boucher, but Billy is waiting for me with the horses, so I had better not tarry."

"Here then, take this little bottle and add it to your wine when you 'ave your dinner this evening." She pours off a small amount into a tiny bottle and Rebecca puts it into the pocket of her skirt with the comfrey.

"Thank you very much, Mrs Boucher. That is very thoughtful. I too am interested in herbs and potions, but I have never heard of these before. I suppose because Aunty Sarah only ever used arnica, but I can already feel the benefit."

"They're both very effective and are useful to keep in the cupboard. Tell your family I enjoyed meeting 'em all yesterday and look forward to seeing you again soon."

"We enjoyed meeting you all too. It was a lovely party and I feel quite sad to be saying goodbye." She kisses Mrs Boucher on the cheek. "You stay here and help your ma, Lettie. I am sure Billy and I can manage with the three horses." She turns to leave and then turns back. "Is there a place where I can mount Cassiopeia?"

"Yes, I will show you, follow me."

Outside, Billy is waiting in the gateway and Lettie points out the stone pillars either side. "If you climb the gate and step onto the pillar, you will be able to mount easily."

Lettie holds Cassiopeia in place; Rebecca follows her instructions and is soon seated comfortably.

"Thank you Lettie. It has been an eventful morning, but I did enjoy our ride and seeing the fox and the hunt riding out across the valley – apart from the kill and that horrid man."

"I did too. Maybe we will be able to go out again next time you come to stay."

"I would like that, Lettie. In the meantime I will write to you. Enjoy the rest of your Boxing Day, farewell."

"Bye, Lettie," adds Billy as Lettie waves them both off, and with Billy leading Capella they both ride back down the lane towards the stables. Fortunately there is no sign of the huntsmen. Rebecca holds onto Capella's reins while Billy dismounts and stables Andromeda. Next, he deals with the bay and finally he helps Rebecca down from Cassiopeia and leads her into the last stall. He fills their mangers with oats and soon they are all chomping happily.

"All that fresh air and exercise has given them an appetite," he comments.

"Me too and no wonder, it has already gone two of the clock," says Rebecca, as she looks at the clock tower.

"Let's go and see what we can find in the kitchen."

After they have both eaten, Rebecca goes upstairs to freshen up and change into her day gown. She leaves the comfrey in place under her stocking and goes downstairs to find Ben and the rest of her family. She bumps into Joshua in the hall and he tells her they are all in the 'Oak', or the smaller drawing room, and he gives her directions.

Rebecca discovers this to be an oak panelled room with comfy armchairs, a thick Wilton patterned carpet and a glowing fire. Ben and Joshua have been playing chess and the board is set with an unfinished game, whilst Matthew and Violet are sharing pages of the *Western Flying Post*. They all look up as she enters.

"Hello there, we thought you must have got lost!" says her pa, smiling with relief to see her back again.

"Sorry I was so long, but there was a bit of an

incident with another horse and I got kicked in the shin."

"Are you all right, Becky?" asks her mother with concern.

"Yes, Ma, I am fine. I went to see Lettie's mother and she has given me two remedies and I am already feeling the benefit of the comfrey."

"What happened?"

Rebecca is about to explain when Joshua returns. "Did you have a nice ride, Becky?"

"Yes, Josh, it was very enjoyable, but did you not hear the hunt?"

"We heard them in the distance and I caught sight of some stray horses riding down the valley, but that was all. Why? Did you get to see them?"

"Yes we did, a bit too close for comfort. They were all on your land, right behind the chapel. I was surprised you didn't come out to see what the commotion was about."

"I didn't realise they were that close."

"It was rather horrid actually. They caught the poor little fox; the pack of hounds ripped into it and then the hunt master finished it off. It was very cruel. Then he smeared the face of one of the small lads with part of its bloody carcass. It was awful; it was obvious that the boy did not expect that to happen to him and he looked horrified."

"I had no idea, Becky. It is not as if I have given permission for the hunt to ride across the estate lands."

"Then to cap it all the hunt master came up close to us and told us to leave. That it was none of our business and he called me and Lettie 'wenches'. Then he turned his horse so close to mine that it kicked back and caught me on the shin."

"The nerve of the man, telling *my* sister what to do on *my* land, when he is the one trespassing! I wish I knew who he was, I'd give him a piece of my mind!" says Joshua indignantly.

"Billy recognised him. He said his name, but I cannot remember. I think it may have been Nathan something."

"Was it Nathan Meakins?"

"Yes, that was it, Nathan Meakins. Do you know him then?"

"I know him by reputation only, but he is purported to be arrogant and heartless and, from what you say, these rumours are not wrong. I am, nevertheless, looking forward to meeting him in the flesh, so that I can make up my own mind. However, when I do, I plan to make him aware in no uncertain terms who he is now dealing with at Alvington Manor."

Joshua uses the bellows on the samovar, partly to relieve his anger, but also to heat it up ready to make tea for everyone. Rebecca goes to help him pass around the cups of tea and the cinnamon cakes. Whilst they are eating and drinking, his good nature returns and he goes back to his game of chess with Ben. Rebecca looks at the fashion pages and advertisements in the *Western Flying Post* and shows her mother anything that interests her. They while away the remainder of the afternoon in relaxed harmony.

At around six of the clock Mrs Abbott taps on the door and informs them that she has laid up the dining table with a cold collation, a variety of desserts and a selection of wine. Joshua asks that she, Gareth and Billy join them and so extra places are laid and they all sit down to enjoy their Boxing Day supper.

Rebecca adds a few drops of catnip to her

cowslip wine and they all take pleasure in their last evening together. For the moment she is determined to enjoy the surroundings and Joshua's company as much as she possibly can. Tomorrow will be a long day with the journey back to Portland, but she knows that she must return with her parents and Ben to go back to school.

She is very impressed with Alvington Manor and although she has only been here two days she already feels at home. She will miss the new girlfriends that she has made because, apart from Ben, she has few friends on Portland. She is also sad to be leaving little Aurora, but most of all she will miss her big brother Joshua.

CHAPTER 7 *(Easter – June 1852)*

OSTARA TO SAMHAIN

As the New Year moves into spring Amy has settled into a familiar routine at Summerville House and although the work is little more than drudgery, day in day out, she is young and strong and is coping well. It gladdens her heart to hear the dawn chorus in the mornings now and to see the tall stems and bowing buds of the Lent lilies swaying in the breeze. Purple, white and yellow crocuses are already flowering under the trees and along the driveway leading to the manor. She is a lucky girl to be working in this beautiful place, compared to the rest of her family. Even though a mean spirit seems to envelop the house, her surroundings are quite charming.

It is such a pity that everyone inside always seem to be in such ill humour. The young mistress particularly never ever smiles and always snaps her commands at the staff. She does not even go out riding, as she did when Amy first came to work here. The only one who smiles at her is the young master, but she knows in her heart it is insincere and it makes her feel uneasy.

At Easter time Bobby Tompkins delivers the meat order and as luck would have it she is standing nearest to the back door. "Morning Bobby, how are you today?" she asks gaily.

"I am very well thank you, Amy," he replies as she takes the basket from him and removes all the meat, placing it in the meat safe in the larder and returning the basket to him. She is absolutely thrilled when she secretively slips a painted egg into her hand. "For you," he whispers with a wink.

She blushes, mouthing back, "Thank you," then pops the small gift into her pocket before anyone notices.

"It is cooked, so you can eat it if you want to," he smiles down at her lovingly and she has to stop herself from going up on tiptoe and kissing him, he is so good and sweet and kind.

"I will treasure it," she whispers back.

"Amy, what are you two whispering about?"

"Nothing, Mrs Chubb, I was just giving Bobby next week's order." She raises her eyes; *why couldn't she just let her have a few precious moments with her friend?*

"Well, hurry up about it, the range needs black leading," says Mrs Chubb impatiently.

Amy passes him the list with an expression on her face that hopefully conveys 'sorry Bobby I would love to chat, but fraternisation leads to instant dismissal' and she says, "Thank you, Bobby, see you next week."

At the end of her busy working day Amy drags her weary body up the stairs to her room. She places the candle on her dresser and sits down on her bed. She cannot wait to have a proper look at Bobby's gift. She puts her hand in her pocket and draws out the egg. It has been dyed red and then hand painted with a ring of green alternate circles and crosses around its middle. *They are supposed to mean hugs and kisses; perhaps he loves me?* Then she sees the heart shapes painted in gold around the bottom of the egg and the silver stars decorating the top. It is absolutely delightful. *I wonder if he did this himself.* It doesn't matter, the meaning is clear: he wants her for his sweetheart and she is happier than she has ever been in her whole life. She puts the egg under her pillow to keep it close and safely hidden from view, but it will be back in her pocket tomorrow.

On Easter Monday morning Apsey announces that her mistress is feeling unwell and she will take breakfast in her room. The young master has gone to a cockfight and Sir Oliver and Lady Annabel are visiting their friends, the Dampiers, at Montacute House, so the house is particularly quiet.

Amy is helping Hawkins clean the chandeliers and renew the candles and, because no one is around, they are able to talk. "Where has the young master gone to see the cock fighting?" She asks Hawkins.

"Catkin Mill," says Hawkins.

"It is a cruel sport, I think," says Amy.

"It is what he enjoys – cruelty. He will be in his element, with the benefit of a bit of gambling on the side," replies Hawkins sagely. "You need to be wary of him, Amy; try never to be alone with him, he cannot be trusted."

Amy is surprised that Hawkins is showing concern for her and that she called her 'Amy' and not 'Proctor'. "He does scare me, it is true. He always seems to single me out for his attention and I would far rather be invisible to him, as we are supposed to be."

"I fear it is too late for that, now he has spotted you, but he is a dangerous man so try to be cool with him. Don't give him the slightest encouragement."

"I won't, but I am afraid I will annoy him and I fear his bad temper."

"You should, Amy. Stick close to me while you are on housemaid duties, there is safety in numbers."

"I will. Thank you, Jean." She calls her by her first name, grateful for her friendship and Hawkins does not correct her. She is tempted to confide in her about Bobby Tompkins, but decides better of it. You never know if in the future someone might find it to their advantage to betray a confidence, so instead she changes the subject.

"Do you know what ails the young mistress?"

"I have no idea," Hawkins replies, but despite her answer, there is a tiny seed of suspicion already germinating in her subconscious mind.

Hawkins has regularly noted her master and mistress leaving the house after nightfall during periods of full moon and at times of equinox and solstice and presumes they are going, as before, up to Newton Hollow. She is too anxious to follow them again for fear of discovery, but as the summer solstice approaches her curiosity gets the better of her. She has grown suspicious as to the health of the young mistress, who has been indisposed for at least the last six weeks and keeping to her rooms with only Apsey in attendance.

Hawkins is not to know that Apsey has been giving her mistress tincture of vervain, the enchanter's plant, to stimulate contractions and that three days ago she prematurely gave birth to a son. Apsey was her midwife and somehow they managed to keep the child's birth a secret from the rest of the household.

Hawkins is quite sure that they will not miss out on the summer solstice and she has decided to keep a lookout for anyone leaving the house on the night of the 20th June. Sure enough at about half past four in the morning she is awoken by the sound of footsteps on the gravel down below her window.

She jumps up off her bed, fully dressed and, looking out of the tiny window, she can just make out the three cloaked figures setting off up the hill to Newton Hollow. She can only assume that her mistress, regardless of having been indisposed, must have a very good reason for making the effort to join the coven. This time she is going to follow them again.

Her heart is thumping with anxiety lest she be discovered, but she quickly creeps down the stairs and out through the kitchen lobby. With shaking hands she carefully unbolts the back door. She will have to be back just before six, or her absence will be discovered.

She soon catches sight of them up ahead, as the mistress seems to be making hard work of ascending the hill. On reaching the oak grove Hawkins observes them, as they place their flaming torch within the pentacle as before. She creeps stealthily behind some bushes to observe their ritual.

The other ten coveners are standing around with their offerings for the Sun God, as the high priestess lights a candle and places it on the right hand side of the altar. "I, Ishtar, light this candle in the name of the Sun God. I call our spiritual father forth to bind and protect our coven, I call you forth to hear our pleas and in return we offer our gifts to you."

The coveners take it in turns to make their offerings of bread and fruit and wine, breaking off some bread and fruit and placing it in the ceremonial gourd and then pouring the red wine over it. Then they toast the Sun God by saying in unison, "As we eat of this bread and fruit, and drink of this wine, we give blessings and thanks to the Sun God, on whom all living things depend."

They then mill around eating the bread and

fruit and drinking the red wine, talking and dancing, until a blushing pink glow is seen in the eastern sky. Hawkins sees Ishtar call Olivia to her.

"I understand, Jahi, that you are offering to sacrifice Helios to the Sun God." As the high priestess talks to Olivia, Hawkins recognises her as the woman who lives in the round house at the very top of the hill. Her words are chilling, but Hawkins does not fully understand their meaning and she crouches lower in the bushes, unable to tear herself away.

"I am," says Olivia, but tears are brimming in her eyes.

"Are you sure this is your irrevocable decision?" asks the high priestess.

Meakins steps forward. "She is sure Ishtar, we are both sure," he intercedes firmly.

"Then make ready," instructs Ishtar.

The sacrificial stone slab has been scrubbed clean and a bed of moss is arranged upon it. Hawkins watches as Olivia, or 'Jahi' as they call her, steps forward; but she gasps in horror as her mistress draws from the shelter of her robe a tiny, sleeping baby, swathed in muslin. She unravels the swaddling and he awakes with a start, his tiny limbs spreading wide as he cries out in fright. Olivia hesitates and then bends over the child and kisses him on his forehead, before laying him on the bed of moss and covering his body in the loose strips of muslin.

Hawkins is appalled; surely they are not going to slay that poor, innocent baby? She feels physically sick with fear and can hardly bear to watch, but however horrific she has to keep silent witness.

Ishtar sprinkles spring water over the child's forehead and he cries even louder. "We pass into your hands this progeny of mankind. If it be your will, we ask you to bestow upon him immortal birth, so that he may be born again and allow us the gift of your sacred spirit to continue to warm and nourish our world and light the fire in our hearts."

Jean Hawkins watches from her hiding place in terror as Ishtar passes Jaldabaoth the ceremonial sword. Using the sword Jaldabaoth scratches the shape of the pentacle around the child. Ishtar and the other coveners begin to mumble what sounds to Jean Hawkins like a load of gibberish, but as the rising sunlight pierces through the trees, it reaches the stone altar and falls on the child. Jaldabaoth raises the sword and the chanting grows to a crescendo. Jean Hawkins puts her hand tightly over her mouth as the sword slices across the child's throat, silencing his cries instantly. Bright red blood pumps out, seeping through the white muslin and through the moss, onto the sacrificial altar. Jean Hawkins loses consciousness.

When Jean comes round the sun has risen and the pagans are gone. It was no nightmare; it was real. She is covered with scratches from the hawthorn bush, behind which she had been hiding. Her cloak is snagged by the blackthorn and as she struggles to her feet, she puts her hand through the tangle of briar rose, hawthorn and deadly nightshade, to make sure there are no fragments of her clothing left behind. The only evidence of what has occurred are the ashes that remain on the sacrificial altar.

She weeps for the poor, little, hapless mite being born to those devils. She crosses herself and gives thanks to God that she was not discovered having passed out in the bushes on the edge of the oak grove. The blood drains from her face; at least she hopes she was not discovered. She feels shaky and nauseous. *What if the noise of her falling had drawn their attention, but they decided to let her believe that she was safe, when in reality they had plans to deal with her in their own nasty, satanic ways?* She cannot bear to think of that. *No, surely they would have dealt with her then and there and she would also be among the ashes of the sacrificial fire by now.*

Her mouth is dry and her body feels taut with fear. To be on the safe side, she must arrange some amulets in order to protect herself against the evil that prevails here, and in that house. At the very least she can hang a horseshoe on the inside of the door to her room.

She can see the round house through the trees and is afraid the high priestess might see her as she hurries away, but she forces her shaking legs into action and hastens back to Summerville House for fear of being missed. Still trembling, she takes the back lane that leads straight to the kitchen lobby, but she has the presence of mind to collect some eggs before entering by the back door. She looks at the kitchen clock: five past six. She must pretend that she was up and out before the door was due to be unbolted by Mrs Chubb at six o'clock.

CHAPTER 8 *(August 1852)*

OVERLOOKING AT HOME FARM

On Portland, Rebecca cannot wait until her school year is over. She has been a pupil teacher for the past year and before that she was a monitor. On her last day she is given her school certificate and her tutor tells her that she would make a good schoolteacher if she wished to follow this career, but Rebecca is happy to leave her school days behind her. She will not miss the scrape of chalk on slates, the musty smell of the teacher's well worn books, the coughs and sneezes of the small children and the feeling of being trapped on glorious summer days, when she so often longed to be free.

The windows of the schoolroom were too high to see anything but the sky; when they showed only blue and the sunlight poured in on them Rebecca yearned to be out in the fresh sea air, clambering over the rocks and listening to the skylark high above Royal Common. She would prefer to be searching for blackberries, picking her herbs, finding the bee orchids – anything rather than being shut in without any view of the outside world.

She is longing for another adventure and Joshua has invited her to spend the summer at Alvington Manor. Billy Riddick is to collect her the following day. She will miss Ben and her family and she will miss the island, but there is always a lot going on at Alvington Manor and she is looking forward to riding and having fun with Lettie, developing her friendship with Lucy, Clara and the maids: Rosa, Louisa, Elsie and Emily.

The journey there, however, is best forgotten, as it rains constantly and Rebecca is very weary by the time they arrive. Poor Billy must be soaked to the skin, as on the top road the heavy rain is wind driven, but at last they pull in through the gates of the manor and Rebecca is able to stretch her stiff limbs and disembark.

Michael Porter holds an umbrella over her as he hands her down from the carriage, taking her box for her. Once inside Joshua rushes forward to greet her. "Oh dear, Becky, you must have had a dreadful journey with such poor visibility." He kisses her on her forehead. "Come and rest yourself in the drawing room and I will ring for afternoon tea." He calls out to Billy. "Thank you, Billy, Flora has victuals prepared for you in the kitchen." Billy touches his cap and manoeuvres the carriage forward and off around into the stable yard.

"Thank you, Josh. It was rather a shame, because it poured down all the way here and I was so looking forward to seeing the sun on the fields, on the yellow gorse and purple heather, and the farm workers haymaking as we went by." Rebecca follows him up the wide steps and in through the heavy oak door. "As it was, the fields were deserted and the sheets of rain all but obliterated any view at all."

"Well, with any luck it will have cleared the heavens ready for your stay here with us."

"I hope so, Josh. I have been so longing to get out and enjoy some fresh air."

Joshua puts his arm around his sister and they go through the hall and into the Oak. Elsie answers Joshua's ring and is soon back with the prepared tray of sandwiches and cake, followed by Emily with the tea tray. Joshua asks Emily to pour the tea and serve them, as he can see that Rebecca is quite exhausted from her long journey. Then he turns to Elsie. "Elsie, would you mind asking Susan to bring Luke and Aurora along later to see Becky before they go back home to Camp Road?"

"Of course, my Lord. Shall I suggest in about half an hour, my Lord?"

"Yes, Elsie, thank you. That will give Becky time to recover from the journey and to enjoy the refreshments you have made for us."

The two girls leave the room and Joshua passes Rebecca the plate of sandwiches and she helps herself. "So, Becky, what is all the news of Portland?"

"Well, Ma is still very busy at Fortune's Corner and Pa and Ben also have a lot of commissions in the boat yard, so they are both very content. Molly is still helping Ma full time and I help out on Saturdays." She takes a bite of her sandwich. "I enjoy it, we hear all the gossip through the shop and the latest talk is all about Queen Victoria's visit with Prince Albert, who came to inspect the progress of the breakwater in July. The paddle steamers were packed with onlookers trying to catch a glimpse of the royal party."

"I can imagine. Did you go to see them yourself?"

"No, I didn't, Josh; we have to live with the commotion all the time and I would rather avoid it, given the choice. The breakwater and the prison work parties are such tourist attractions that the steamboats come from Weymouth to Castletown twice daily with day trippers. We are inundated with Kimberlins at the moment."

Joshua nods. "Well that is progress and the harbour is going to be something very special when it is completed. We Portlanders should be very proud of it."

"Oh, I am sure we will be when it is all completed, but in the meantime it is quite disordered. They have even replaced the horse-drawn wagons with a brand new steam railway engine, for drawing the trucks loaded with stone from the base of the incline out to the end of the staging. Portland has changed beyond all recognition, Josh. It is not peaceful any more but a hive of trade and engineering."

"Well, although it is peaceful here it is also rather hectic during the summer. At Home Farm they have been very busy with the haymaking and now they are reaping and binding, and harvesting the mangelwurzels."

"Mangelwurzels? What are they?"

"They are like turnips or fodder beat, good food for the cattle." Joshua pours himself some more tea. "But it is still peaceful and on hot sunny days you can sit in the garden sometimes and all you can hear is the eerie cry of the buzzards echoing soulfully across the valley, as they soar overhead on the thermals."

"How lovely." Rebecca sips her tea. "Do you have skylarks here, too?"

"Yes, I often hear them hovering above the ridge during the summer. That is my favourite recollection of Portland."

"Mine too." She agrees wistfully. "Do you spend much time in the garden, Josh?"

"Yes I do, when the weather is clement. Sometimes we picnic on the lawn to allow Luke and Aurora the benefit of the fresh air. Luke is walking now and is quite active, whereas little Rora sits quite happily with her dolly."

"It will not be long now before she is also running around, then you will have your work cut out."

"Yes, she will be a year old next month. She has

grown a lot since you last saw her and she is really very bonny. Susan Moore feels that she is nearly weaned and she has started introducing some cow's milk diluted half and half with some boiled water and a little sugar. She will soon be able to live down here with us all the time, if the Moores can bear to be parted from her."

"I cannot wait to see her." Rebecca lowers her voice. "Have you found out any more about her parents?"

"No, nothing significant," Joshua replies quietly. "But I think you hit on something when you suggested that she might be Millie's baby, because as her hair is beginning to grow thicker, there is definitely quite a red tinge to it."

Rebecca whispers, "Does she resemble Louisa?"

"It is too early to tell yet, Becky, but if they are related I am sure it will come out eventually. Millie was the image of her sister."

There is then a gentle tap at the door and the sound of childish voices beyond.

"Come in," calls Joshua. The door opens and in steps Luke with his mother behind him carrying Aurora.

Rebecca holds out her arms to the little lad. "Hello, Luke, come and give me a big hug." The child steps forward, but then turns to hide his face in his mother's petticoats.

"Come on, sweetheart, don't be shy," encourages Rebecca.

"He will be fine in a moment, ma'am, he just needs to get used to you that is all," says his mother. "Would you like to nurse Rora?"

"Yes please!" Rebecca holds out her arms as Susan Moore puts the baby on her lap. "Hello my precious, how you have grown." She kisses the child on her cheek and is rewarded with a smile. Rebecca sees immediately what Joshua meant about the colour of her fine, wispy hair. As Rebecca nurses Aurora, Luke loses his shyness and is soon chatting away to Joshua and his mother. He is not quite talking in sentences yet, but it will not be long.

Susan Moore asks, "Do you mind if I sit down, my Lord?"

"Of course not, Susan, is something wrong?"

"No, nothing is wrong, my Lord, but I have something to tell you." She sits down. "I am expecting another child in the spring and I wanted to warn you that it might be better for Rora if she was to be settled back down here before then, as I will not be able to cope with all three of them."

"Well congratulations! That is good news, you and John must be very pleased."

"Yes, we are, my Lord, although I am sad to be losing the little one here. Luke will miss her terrible, I know."

"Well, he will be welcome to visit whenever he likes as they grow up, after all they are like brother and sister, aren't they? It will perhaps be a little easier for Luke with another little playmate soon to arrive, but Aurora may feel it more to be robbed of her playfellow."

"I will bring him with me every time I come to help Lottie with the laundry and they can play together then."

"Thank you Susan, I really appreciate all you have done for Aurora. She may not have survived without your kind help and nurture."

"It has been my pleasure, my Lord; she is a dear little thing and much loved by all of us. Shall we keep her with us until her first birthday in September to give us a bit of time to get used to the idea? Then I'll bring her and her few things back down here."

"Yes, that is a good idea and we can give her a little birthday party to welcome her home."

Rebecca slept well that night. The following morning the rain has cleared and she is looking forward to visiting Lettie. As Joshua has an appointment in town she sets off early to stroll up the lane to Keeper's Cottage. Her skirts are hitched up to avoid the mud and she feels like a proper country maid as she skips along, avoiding the puddles. She can see the men in the fields harvesting the root crop and as she approaches the cottage she sees Toby outside feeding their pigs. She waves to him and calls out, "Morning, Toby."

"Morning, ma'am. If you have come to see Lettie she is inside doing some baking for Ma. I will tell her you are here." He runs inside and moments later Lettie has opened their front door and is welcoming her in.

Rebecca beams at her. "Hello, I couldn't wait to come up and see you to tell you that I am going to be here for a few weeks, staying with Josh."

"Oh! That is good news, we shall be able to go out horseback riding again. Come inside, Becky. Would you like a glass of ginger beer?"

"Yes please, I would love one."

Lettie pours them both a beaker each and they sit down in the kitchen. "I was just preparing a rook pie, ready for Ma to put in the oven when she comes home from work. I only have to roll out the top and I am done. Would you like to go down to Home Farm to see Lucy this afternoon? We can take Toby with us and he can play with Bunny."

"Why not? It promises to be warm and sunny all day and we ought to make the most of it."

"Well, we can have some bread and cheese for

our lunch here if you like, before we go. There are chives in the garden and some pickle in the larder."

"If you are sure you can spare it."

"Of course, I'll just give Toby a shout and he can bring in the chives when he has finished with the pigs." She calls to Toby from the back door and then returns to rolling out the pastry.

"Shall I prepare the sandwiches, while you are doing that?"

"No, you just sit tight, there is plenty of time and it will be better if I clear this away first."

"So, Lettie, what is all the news since I was last here?"

"Well, Rosa has been walking out with Malachi Warren since the Christmas party and they both seem to be very happy together. There is talk of wedding bells among the maids and Rosa is definitely besotted."

"I am not surprised at that, something was definitely brewing between them at Christmas. I am really pleased for them, they make an attractive couple and I should think that he will make a good, hardworking husband. He is very handsome in a wild untamed sort of way. He reminds me of Heathcliff from *Wuthering Heights*."

"Does he? I have not read it."

"Oh Lettie, it is very passionate and romantic. I will see if we have it at Alvington Manor."

"I am not very good at reading, Becky; don't have much call for it."

"Then I will read it to you and you will see that it is really worth the effort. We can sit out on the lawn at Alvington Manor on sunny afternoons, once you have done all your chores."

Lettie laughs. "That sounds very leisurely and ladylike; my Ma can serve us afternoon tea. His old lordship would turn in his grave."

"Ah, but young Lord Dryer is in charge now and I am sure he will approve."

Toby comes in with the washed chives, just as Lettie finishes crimping the pastry on the pie. They all sit around the kitchen table and help themselves to the bread and cheese with chopped chives and pickle and beakers of cider.

"Would you like to come with us to Home Farm after our victuals, Toby?"

"Yes, I would, because I have some more pheasant feathers for Bunny."

"What is her proper name?" Rebecca asks Toby.

"I don't remember, do you, Lettie?"

"I think it might be Beatrice, but I am not certain. Why?"

"Well, on Portland, where I was born, those creatures are thought to be a bad omen and we never say their name for fear of bad luck."

"Oh dear, well I don't know if she will answer to Beatrice, but we had better explain it to her."

"I don't want to upset her by putting her off the name she has always been known by."

"Well, maybe you can just avoid calling her anything," suggests Lettie.

"I will give it a try."

They wash up their crockery, pack it away in the kitchen china cupboard and are soon off to see their friends. The girls hitch up their skirts as Toby hops from one rut to another. Rebecca feels the hot sun beating down on them and she soon hears the eerie cry of the buzzards overhead. Looking up she spots three of them soaring high on the thermals, just as Joshua had described.

"Look at those beautiful birds; they make it look so easy to fly."

"I dreamt that I was flying once," says Toby. "I ran along the top of the hill and then I took off and glided down over the valley just like those buzzards. I could see my own shadow chasing over the grass and it was wonderful, I really believed that I was flying, but when I woke up, however hard I jumped up and down, I couldn't get off the ground!"

Toby looks very comical jumping up and down to illustrate his story and they all laugh. "I don't think it is possible for us to fly. If God had wanted us to fly he would have given us wings like angels," says Lettie.

"But angels and fairies can fly, so why not us?" asks Toby.

They didn't want to destroy his innocent faith by disillusioning him.

"That is true," says Rebecca. "Maybe we need the magic fairy dust. Perhaps the tooth fairy sprinkled you with some dust before your dream and that is why you were able to do it."

"I hadn't thought of that; I will look out for that next time I leave a tooth under my pillow," says Toby earnestly.

As they walk along butterflies flit among the wild flowers and a wren sings its shrill melody from the top of the hedgerow. Bees busy themselves in a hum of activity and all the natural sounds are those of contentment. They skirt Alvington Manor House and go through the stable yard towards Home Farm. Capella whinnies at the sight of them, but they pass on, this time eager to see their friends.

On reaching the farm Rebecca follows Lettie through a covered lean-to outhouse area where there is a well set in the middle of a flag stone floor, a sink and storage shelves for farm and gardening implements and, in the corner, piles of boots, gaiters and clogs. Lettie knocks on the back door of the farmhouse.

Beth Warren answers their knock. "Why, Becky,

'tis you, what are you doing back here?"

"I have come to stay for a while with Joshua, Mrs Warren, and we thought we would call and pay our respects."

"Well, go on through. Lucy is practising the piano and Bunny is drawing."

They all go through into the parlour where they find old Granny Warren asleep in an armchair by the fireplace, Lucy at the piano and Bunny sitting in the light from the window drawing a specimen of rosebay willow herb. Toby goes immediately to Bunny and gives her the pheasant feathers.

"Thank you, Toby, would you like some paper and a pencil to draw?"

"Yes please." He sits down at the table and they chat quietly together.

Lucy stands up to greet them. "This is an unexpected pleasure; I didn't expect to see you, Becky. Of course you have finished school now and I suppose you will be looking for something to entertain and occupy you. Are you thinking of staying here with your brother?"

"Not permanently, no. I plan to return to Portland shortly, because I hope to be betrothed to Ben when I am sixteen. He is my childhood sweetheart and I don't want him to forget about me and fall for someone else while I am away. He is very dear to me, but he is also very busy working with my pa." She smiles self-consciously. "I so enjoyed meeting all the girls here at Christmas time; my ma thought that a little summer holiday and a bit of fun before I return and settle down to family life would be good for me. I don't have many girl friends on Portland and Ma is very happy that I have come to be with Josh, to see how the estate is run and to learn a little bit about society and social etiquette."

Lucy is intrigued. "Are you and your brother going to visit the other big houses hereabouts and leave your cards, so that you will be launched into calling card society?"

"I really don't know. Josh is very busy with his studies at the moment, but when he is a Justice of the Peace it will probably be expected of him. However, I doubt he is in any hurry to behave as the idle rich and, as I am only here for a short holiday, I doubt we will get involved with that. Besides, I think that it would be rather boring."

"I would love to visit the big houses, to see the beautiful gardens and look around inside at the expensive furniture and paintings and experience how the other half live," says Lettie with a sigh.

"Oh, I agree that would be interesting," admits Rebecca, "it is just that once you have seen all the impressive properties, you would still be obliged to entertain people that you probably have nothing in common with and to return their visits on a regular basis, for if you did not you would cause offence."

"You would also have to dress appropriately and not wear the same costume twice, which would be extremely expensive and you would be forever at the dressmakers," adds Lucy.

"Yes, well at the moment Joshua is not, as far as I know, involved in that social circle; probably because it is usually the women who start it."

"The thing is," adds Lucy, "he is an eligible bachelor and as soon as folk hear that he has a sister staying with him, then the calling cards might come, as eager mothers try to get an introduction for their unmarried daughters."

"Oh, I hope not, Lucy, because I don't think that will suit him at all. He will not want to be tied by convention; he may well ignore these people and unintentionally cause offence."

"Well, perhaps we had better keep your presence here quiet," laughs Lucy.

"I am happy with that," says Rebecca smiling. "Anyway, changing the topic, what is this I hear about Malachi and Rosa?"

"They are walking out, it is true and they are very happy together. I have never seen Malachi so smitten. He has started saving hard and is seriously looking to settle down."

"Where will they live?" asks Rebecca.

"I don't know, but there is a small hamlet just off to one side of the estate and a cottage there would suit them very well. Rosa could continue to work at the big house and Malachi will always be needed on the farm. As the eldest brother he is destined to take over when Pa retires."

"Well, that is a social event to look forward to. What else is happening this year?" asks Lettie.

Lucy looks thoughtful. "I suppose harvest supper is next, early in October, and then the Saint Leonard's Day fair in November."

"Well, before that, in September, Aurora is a year old and we are going to have a small birthday party for her. I plan to stay here at least until then," says Rebecca.

Lucy's mother puts her head around the door. "Would you all like a cup of tea and some cake?"

"Yes please," they all chorus and soon they are all sitting around the large scrubbed kitchen table eating slices of cherry cake and supping their tea with Lucy's mother.

Before long they hear Malachi grumbling to his father in the outhouse and the sound of water being pumped from the well.

The door opens and Isaac enters, looking annoyed and perplexed. Granny Warren stirs from her doze and Beth looks up, concerned. "Whatever is wrong Isaac?"

"Two of my best dairy cows have got the milk fever," he answers irritably.

"Oh no!" Beth says dejectedly, a worried look on her face.

Malachi enters, wiping his hands on a cloth and the room suddenly seems crowded. He hangs the cloth on the fireguard and leans against the chimney breast with a look of concern on his handsome, rugged face. His mother pours him a mug of tea and he takes it from her, his large fingers too big for the handle. He wraps them around the mug and takes a mouthful.

Rebecca is aware of the odour of the working men permeating the room. The smell of good honest toil, not unpleasant but unmistakably masculine and she suddenly feels timid.

"Do ee think you've been overlooked then Zak?" asks Granny Warren, fearfully.

"I cannot think of anyone who would do that to us, Ma, can you?"

Malachi looks up and speaks thoughtfully, "But after losing the little piglets last month it makes you wonder, don't it?"

"Shall I ask me Ma to come with a charm for it?" asks Lettie with concern.

"I don't know, child, I cannot afford to lose them like last time."

The room falls quiet. Lettie finally breaks the silence, "It cannot do any harm to ask my ma to call around with a remedy, in case you have been ill wished."

"Thank you, Lettie."

"What is ill wished?" whispers Rebecca looking puzzled.

"It means that someone has ill will towards you and they may have put a hex on you or your livestock," explains Lettie.

129

"Surely no one would do that to Isaac?" she replies, her voice low.

"It does happen round here, we do have a lot of cunning folk." Lettie turns to the farmer. "Do you suspect anyone, Malachi?"

"No I don't, but you cannot be too careful, so I think we would appreciate your ma doing what she can, don't you, Pa?"

"Yes, Lettie, please ask her to come over as soon as she can, lass."

"I will, Mr Warren, as soon as I see her tonight."

Rebecca then plucks up courage to speak to everyone, despite feeling reticent in front of the men, especially Malachi. "We have a place called Conjuror's Lodge on Portland and 'tis said they are involved with the crafty sciences. 'Tis just round the corner from where we live and Ma is always anxious that we should stay away from them."

"Don't worry, Becky, my ma has a lot of remedies, charms and incantations against the evil eye. I am sure she will be able to help."

Rebecca turns to Bunny, her nerve returning gradually. "We have a lot of superstitions on Portland, too. For instance I cannot say your name; no one will say it on Portland for fear of an ill omen. There have been so many problems in the quarries due to those creatures undermining the ground. They all come out of their burrows on Hamm Beach, running into Chiswell whenever the sea floods us and so whenever anyone sees one, we are fearful of what is to come. In all my life I have never uttered their name, which unfortunately happens to be your name. I wonder if you would mind me calling you instead by your Christened name?"

"But I don't like Beatrice!" wails Bunny. "It sounds like beetroot."

Malachi and her father suppress their laughter at this.

"It is a lovely name and it means 'bringer of happiness and joy'," says her mother, "which is why we chose it for you, darling."

Rebecca is thoughtful, "How about I call you 'Bonny' instead?"

"Yes, I prefer that," says Bunny, nodding in agreement.

"That is settled then, Bonny it is."

After they have finished their tea, Lucy gives Rebecca an impromptu piano lesson and she enjoys it so much that they arrange to meet regularly, in order that she can teach her to play properly.

Preparations for Aurora's birthday surprise are in full swing. Joshua has bought her some pretty clothes from the town, John Moore has made her a jointed peg doll and Susan has dressed it as a gift from their family. Mrs Abbott saw an advertisement in the *Household Words* magazine for the Dean Book Company, illustrating their selection of 'rag books for little children' and she sent away for three of these. Flora has made a birthday cake decorated with some sugar icing and all the maids have helped with the preparations.

Louisa has for some time been working on a rag dolly. She found some wool that she dyed with madder and then added some weld to make an auburn shade and she plaited the wool for her hair. She has gone through her mother's sewing box and made a long, blue frock for it, with a little white pinny. For her face she has glued green and black felt eyes and a little red felt mouth.

When Susan Moore arrives with the children, Joshua takes them into the drawing room where he has placed some cushions on the floor for them to play. John Moore had, earlier in the day, brought down most of Aurora's belongings on his way to the stables and Louisa has already taken them up to the nursery. During the afternoon members of staff pop in at various times to give the child their gifts. She is quite bewildered, but Luke is happy to help her unwrap the presents and they play well together. He proudly shows her the peg doll that his father has made, saying 'Papa', and then he watches as she chews happily on its head.

Ben had made a Noah's ark for Rebecca to give to Aurora from both of them and he had been busy carving small animals to go inside. Joshua had been impressed when she showed it to him earlier. "Give her your present, Becky; they will be able to play together with that one," he says. Rebecca hands the parcel to them and watches happily as they tear off the wrapping.

Luke is very excited and pulls out the animals one by one, whilst Aurora is fascinated by the double doors at the front of the ark. They play together contentedly whilst the adults watch over them and chat.

"That was a clever idea to make a stand for it, Becky, and I like the bright colours. Please thank Ben for us, won't you?" says Joshua.

"Of course I will. He will want to hear all about it when I get back."

"Luke really loves that, Becky." Then in a lower voice, "Do you think Ben might make one for us to give to Luke for Christmas?" asks Susan. "I will gladly pay him for his time."

"I am sure he would love to. He is never happier than when he is working with is hands."

There is a tap at the door and Louisa pops her head round. "May I come in to see the birthday girl?"

"Of course, everyone is welcome, come and sit

down." Joshua indicates a seat beside him and Louisa diffidently sits there, still clutching her gift. She reaches down and passes her present to Aurora. The child looks up at her with big, pale, aquamarine coloured eyes and holds out her hands to take it.

"She seems to be getting the idea now," says Josh, laughing.

Luke comes to help, instantly curious, and together they strip off the paper. Aurora immediately clutches the doll to her and will not let Luke take it. Louisa can see that she loves it and tears come into her eyes. She whispers to her, "She is called Millie, darling, and she loves you very much."

Joshua hears her and his heart aches for her. It is as they had suspected all along; how can she bear it?

Mrs Abbott then comes in, followed by Flora with the birthday cake, and Elsie and Emily with the other party fare. They place the food on the buffet table and Susan gets up to select some food for the children's picnic. Joshua suggests that Susan has Luke on her knee and that Louisa looks after Aurora. Louisa is secretly thrilled and picks up the little girl, who straight away reaches for her new rag dolly. Louisa sits Aurora comfortably upon her lap and tucks the rag doll, Millie, under the child's arm, cuddling them both tightly to her. Rebecca passes her a plate of food for them to share.

After they have all eaten the sandwiches and sweet meats, Flora lights the candle for the children to blow out (with a little help from Susan) and they cut the cake. Mrs Abbott then gives Aurora her gift and watches expectantly as the child rips off the wrapping. Louisa helps her turn the pages of the rag books and the child basks in all the attention.

Joshua is moved by the scene of the two little red heads together and is convinced now that Millie was the child's mother.

Mrs Abbott interrupts his thoughts. "Do you know, that is the first time I have ever purchased a gift for a child. I would have loved to have had children of my own. This is the nearest I have come to it and I feel like her grandmama."

"Then that is who you shall be," says Josh. "There is an opening for a grandmama and I cannot think of anyone else who would make a better job of it."

Mrs Abbott beams from ear to ear. This is the happiest Joshua has ever seen her.

Soon the leaves are falling and a misty, mellow autumn is upon them. The harvest service in the estate chapel is arranged early in October. Alvington Manor is radiant in its autumn colours this year. Louisa is looking forward anxiously to the service on Sunday, as her parents are to accompany her and it is the first time they have all been together there since Millie's funeral. Her mother has made her a new costume for her birthday on 3rd October and she plans to leave off her mourning costume and wear it to the harvest service at the end of the week.

As they enter the chapel Louisa feels all eyes are on her and her parents, and she self-consciously takes her seat and bows her head in silent prayer. She is aware, however, of Joshua seated several rows in front of her and facing the altar. They all stand and join in singing the first hymn: "For the beauty of the earth, For the glory of the skies, For the love which from our birth, Over and around us lies, Lord of all to thee we raise, This our grateful hymn of praise…"

Joshua can recognise Louisa's melodic contralto voice over and above the rest of the congregation.

After this hymn he is to take a reading and he climbs up into the small pulpit. As he turns to face the congregation, he looks towards the sound of that sweet voice and he spots Louisa in her new costume. It has a beautifully fitted dark green jacket, with russet coloured cuffs and lapels. This really complements the rich colour of her hair, which is pinned up artistically with a tortoiseshell comb. She has never looked so lovely. He is aware of his heart racing and his hands shaking as he clears his throat to read from Psalm sixty-five, 'Praise to God for his Salvation and Providence,' verses eight to thirteen.

After the reading Joshua steps back down to rejoin the congregation. He catches Louisa's eye and smiles appreciatively at her, she smiles back as they all join in singing the hymn, 'We plough the fields and scatter the good seeds on the land, and it is fed and watered by God's almighty hand...'

During this hymn Emily, Elsie, Toby, Bunny and other estate children all take their families gifts of fruit and vegetables and place them at the altar, ready for Billie Riddick to take them to the Coker Poor House after the service.

Reverend Phelps then takes the blessing and finally the dismissal. After the service they all file into the Orangery for their harvest supper.

Louisa and her parents follow Mrs Abbott and Gareth down the path. A jay and a magpie are squabbling noisily in the copse to their right and orange and yellow leaves flutter to the ground around them. The autumn sunshine is glinting on the glass of the Orangery as they approach. There is a background hum of animated chatter as they step through the glass doors.

Rebecca immediately catches Louisa by the

hand, holding her back, as her parents make their way towards the buffet table. "Wow, Louisa, look at you! You look marvellous, that bottle green colour really suits your eyes and your lovely auburn hair. That nipped in jacket shows off your trim figure beautifully, where did you get it?"

"Thank you, Becky, my ma made it for me, for my nineteenth birthday."

Rebecca is impressed; this being her own mother's line of work she can appreciate the skills involved. "My goodness, Louisa, what a good job your mother has done; but when was your birthday?"

"Last week, the 3rd October."

"Oh I didn't realise! Happy birthday for last week." She kisses her on her cheek. "Well, you look marvellous." She turns and spots her brother. "Doesn't she, Josh?"

Louisa looks uncomfortable as Joshua, looking so smart in his expensive tailor-made clothes, turns towards them. "Doesn't she what?"

"Doesn't Louisa look wonderful in her new costume?"

"Yes, she certainly does." Joshua smiles at Louisa, takes her hand and kisses it. "She is a very beautiful young woman." He winks at her surreptitiously, turning away suddenly to circulate among his guests.

Louisa knows she has gone bright red and she feels hot and flustered. Why did Becky have to make a public show of her! Rosa and Elsie both saw and now she will be mercilessly teased. She joins her parents as they eat from the buffet and they all wander over to Gareth for a cup of cider each. The food is wholesome and tasty and the atmosphere is jolly. After they have eaten, her parents want to slip away to pay their respects to Millie and so she quietly leaves with them. They walk together back through the fallen leaves and around to the rear of the chapel.

They stand together at the graveside, her mother weeping and her father with his arm around her. Louisa is too angry at what happened to her sister to weep, but she is trying to concentrate on her thoughts for Millie, trying to convey to her that Aurora is safe and well and happy. But she cannot dispel the thought of the intimacy of that wink, and the tingling sensations that run through her every time she sets eyes on her master. She cannot end up as Millie has done. She must avoid him as much as possible; she must hide her true feelings for the sake of her future happiness.

Back in the Orangery, Rebecca is looking after Aurora. "You know, you could stay here and become Rora's nanny, Becky, if you wanted to. She has really taken to you and everyone else is very busy with their regular occupations. If Ma and Pa and Ben can do without you, why don't you stay on for a few months while Rora settles in? It will be a real help for us."

"Are you sure, Josh? Only I think I might quite like looking after her. I could stay on for a while at least and see how we all get on together."

"Well, if you are in no doubt, I will write to Ma and Pa and see if they agree."

Rebecca smiles up at him. "Yes, I think I would like that."

It is decided that Rebecca shall stay on until the following summer and she soon falls into a routine that suits both her and the baby. She enjoys the life at Alvington Manor there is always something of interest going on and always someone to talk to among the staff. Emily is the same age as Rebecca and she is the one who keeps her up to date with all the gossip, the next event of note being the Saint Leonard's Day fair.

CHAPTER 9 *(November 1852)*

THE SAINT LEONARD'S DAY FAIR

On the third Friday in November, Joshua has given leave for everyone to go to the Saint Leonard's Day fair. The schools are closed, because this year the circus is coming to town and everyone can watch the procession for free, even if they cannot afford the tickets for the performances. Mrs Abbott is happy to stay behind and look after Aurora, and Joshua has a lot of paperwork to catch up on.

The day turns out to be unseasonably mild, with a light breeze and scattered clouds. All the young ones meet up at Home Farm and then set off in a hum of enthusiastic chatter towards Huish Field. Beth Warren has told them what was advertised on the poster that she saw at the corn exchange. Malachi and Jacob are both looking forward to the animal market, but Lucy wants to see the production of *Robin Hood* in the theatre tent. Bunny and Toby are both excited at seeing the waxworks. "And I want to see *Snow White and the Seven Dwarfs* too," adds Bunny excitedly.

"Well, I can't wait to see the Circus Menagerie, they say it will be the greatest pageant ever witnessed and I have never seen all those wild and exotic creatures before."

"Neither have I, Becky. And I want to see all the different horses and ponies as well," says Billy. "They said in the *Western Flying Post* that there will be 200 of every kind and description."

"Flora read that out to us and she also said there would be lions and tigers, llamas, emus, ostriches, buffaloes and baboons, to name but a few," says Rosa.

"Yes, and um, kangaroos, camels, yaks and dromedorararies, whatever they are," replies Elsie.

"Dromedaries! They are like camels, but with two humps," says Louisa.

"How do you know that?" asks Elsie.

"Oh I saw a picture in a book, in the library I think," says Louisa dismissively, brushing it aside, "I would really like to hear the African Shaman's show. He is supposed to be able to cure ailments and he sells charms as well."

"I don't know, Lou, that is a bit risky; they are also called witch doctors and can do bad things as well as good," says Rebecca.

"Well, I think it would be very interesting and I would have thought you would too, Becky," says Lettie. "Especially as we need to find something to help Isaac's cows."

Malachi overhears their conversation and joins in. "I agree with Lettie, it is worth listening to him at least."

"Well, we must find out what time his show is when we get there. I think Flora said that it was going to be in the cattle market. He is coming every day for two weeks to address the crowd, pull teeth, sell his charms and potions and cure ailments," says Louisa.

As they enter Huish Field they can see the advance party of the travelling circus have already arrived and have erected the huge tent. In the top corner of the field are all the various circus wagons and corrals, and a variety of circus folk going about their business and setting up among the stalls. Then they hear the town crier ringing his bell and proclaiming the times of all the events taking place that day. The procession of animals goes from below the cattle market up to Huish Field at eleven o'clock and the Shaman Nsukwini's show is at quarter past ten.

"If we go now to the cattle market, we can join the procession of animals back up here, after we have seen the Shaman," suggests Louisa.

"As long as we get back up here in time for *Robin Hood* and *Snow White*, that will be fine, because everything else is going on all the time," says Lucy.

"I am not sure I want to walk all the way down to the cattle market just to listen to some old witch doctor," says Elsie in an aside to Emily.

"I don't want to, Elsie; I don't think you should mess with all that black magic stuff," says Emily. "I would rather stay up here."

As they all walk through the crowds of people now milling among the stalls, Bunny spots the marionettes. "Oh please let us watch the puppet show – look, they are so funny."

"It looks like it is *A Midsummer Night's Dream*," says Louisa.

"How do you know that?" asks Rebecca.

"Well, there are fairies and a king and queen and a person dressed as a donkey, so it must be."

"You are very clever, Louisa," says Lettie.

They watch with Bunny and Toby for a while, who want to stay to the end, then agree to leave them in the charge of Elsie and Emily. They are to meet later at two of the clock, either in the tableau tent, where they are showing *Snow White*, or the theatre tent. They carry on past the fire eater and the strong man, stopping to watch the contortionist for a while.

"I bet you couldn't get into that position," Malachi whispers to Rosa saucily.

"I hope I should never need to," she whispers back, laughing and slapping him playfully.

Finally they reach the Shaman, who is attended by three black women in native costume and a small black boy playing cowhide drums, whilst the women dance and swirl to the rhythm and wiggle their behinds, so that their feathered costumes shimmer and shake.

"I'd like to see you in those costumes," whispers Malachi. "Would you dance for me like that?"

"Wait and see when we are married," Rosa whispers back seductively.

Despite their low voices, Louisa can sense the strength of the love growing between Rosa and Malachi and she is aware of a sense of longing in herself. The two girls have become good friends since Christmas, on their outing into town with Joshua and decorating the tree together. She looks up at Malachi's brother Jacob, standing alongside her. He is a nice, kind, attentive young man and it would be very convenient if she could love him. They would make a happy four indeed, but there is no frisson of excitement and pleasure when he glances in her direction, as there is from her master. Louisa sighs and turns towards the witch doctor; maybe he has some magic potion that will help her.

The Shaman is sitting cross-legged on a brightly coloured blanket. He is wearing a vibrant red costume, decorated with tiny multicoloured beads; a wide beaded belt, with a leopard-skin draped over him and a leopard-skin hat. Slung over his shoulder is a leather-bound stick, sprouting long strands of animal hair at its end. Before him is a large cooking pot placed on a tripod over a small fire. Boiling water bubbles away and the Shaman is dropping strange objects into the water, as he hums and wails in time to the drums. Rebecca draws closer for a better look and she can see small animal skeletons, odd bones and shells, animal hair and a cow-horn. The Shaman is adding some liquid from different bottles, then he waves his leather wand over the strange smelling pot and mumbles and chants in his native language.

"Zis is potion for muscle and joint pain," he says once he has finished his concoction. "Who among you would like to wake up without pain in muscles or bones?" There is muttering among the crowd. He stands up and waves his wand over the crowd. "Come, do have taste from ladle."

An old hunch-backed man steps forward. "Anything is worth a try when your body is twisted and misshapen like mine." He screws up his face as he takes a sip. "Why, 'tis not bad at all, it tastes like it has alcohol in it." Suddenly more folk are showing an interest.

"Only two pence for bottle and will last you all winter my friend."

The Shaman ladles the potion into a bottle for the man and more people come forward to try. All purchase a bottle and soon the cauldron is empty.

The Shaman then goes to the back of his covered wagon, where he has shelves packed tightly with many bottles of potions and different jars of cream. The black women help him to sell them to the crowds. There are also scary instruments for pulling teeth and displayed on a large wooden tray is a selection of shining, beautifully coloured, semi-precious stones. "These are my healing stones." He picks them up one at a time, calling them by name. "I have purple amethyst, tiger eye, cornelian palm, red jasper, hematite, rose quartz, green aventurine, blue lace agate, lilac fluorite, serpentine, malachite and white howlite. You can choose any three for a penny and I will tell you their properties."

"I would like some of those pretty stones, Mal, and did you hear him? One is called malachite!"

"Come and choose what colours you like and I will buy you some." Rosa and Malachi step nearer to the back of the wagon and listen; while the Shaman tells each person the best use for the stones they are choosing.

"I would like the malachite, to remind me of you, and the rose quartz and amethyst," whispers Rosa. "He says the rose quartz is the stone of love."

"We will ask him what the others are for." Malachi gets the man's attention and asks him, "Which is the malachite?" The man selects the green, marble-like malachite stone and passes it to Malachi. It feels beautifully smooth in his large hands.

"It bring calm and peace for you, help with sleeping, very good protection from sorcery and black magic."

"Really? Did you hear that, Rosa?"

"Yes, I did."

"Do you have any other stones that have that quality?"

"I do, good sir. Tiger eye also protect from ill will and bring good luck, prosperity, wealth and success. This one help make you powerful."

"What about that one?" Malachi points to the silvery black hematite that he is attracted to.

"That one like protective fire, make you alert, good for hearing and awareness."

"And that one?" Malachi points to the rusty-red coloured stone.

"That red jasper, good for energy and vitality."

"Can I have the red jasper, the tiger eye and the silvery black one, please?" He turns to Rosa. "These are for me." Then he turns back to the Shaman. "And I would like the rose quartz, the malachite and the amethyst for Rosa, please."

"Thank you, sir, two pence please." He wraps up the stones and passes them to Malachi.

Malachi and Rosa work their way around the people huddled behind the wagon to the back of the queue where the rest of them are waiting. Malachi unwraps and separates the stones to give Rosa hers.

"Look, we have bought some stones and these are going to be very useful." He shows them the tiger eye and the malachite.

"Why do you say that, Mal?" asks Lettie.

"Well, we have been hoping to get some kind of amulet to protect our animals from the evil eye and both the malachite and the tiger eye will help. I think that is good value for tuppence." He slips his own into the pocket of his breeches and hands the remainder in their wrapping to Rosa.

"That is lucky, Malachi. Ma and Pa will be pleased, but it seems to me that you should be our protection, for you are similarly named," says his sister smiling.

"This one is for love," says Rosa, showing the girls the rose quartz.

"That is funny, you have chosen malachite and rose quartz, which is like Malachi and Rosa. It must be a good omen."

"Do you know, I hadn't realised that," says Rosa laughing.

"You will have to have a child called Amethyst," laughs Rebecca. "Shall we choose some, Lettie?"

"Yes, let's. I quite like the idea of the rose quartz," says Lettie.

"I would also like to choose some," says Louisa.

The girls all choose the same: rose quartz, blue lace agate and the tiger eye.

"That way we get the protection of the tiger eye, the love from the rose quartz and the healing and calming effects of the blue agate," says Louisa.

"… And the blue lace agate gives kindness, patience, wisdom and peace. I think that one is a good one, don't you?" says Rebecca.

"I think they are all very beautiful, even if they don't work. They feel nice to hold, too," says Louisa.

"Oh I am sure they will work," says Lettie confidently.

Billy plucks up the courage to ask Lucy if she would like some, but the others are all turning away and the queue is so large now that she declines. "I would buy them for you, Lucy. Wouldn't you like some rose quartz?" he asks hopefully, but Lucy just smiles sweetly.

"It is too late now, Billy, we want to keep up with the rest and we don't want to miss the menagerie parade." She takes his hand and drags him after the others. Billy is thrilled at this development and savours the feel of her hand in his for those few moments.

They follow Malachi and Jacob around the cattle market, as they view the animals for sale. The brothers are critical of the livestock available and shortly turn their attention to the coming parade. The townsfolk are lining the street to see the free show and before long they hear the music of the band. Then along comes a fabulous gilded carriage, pulled by four cream horses in polished leather harnesses and decorated with shining horse brasses. A lady dressed as Britannia is riding on top holding a golden shield and trident, and wearing a Greek helmet. A lion is lying at her feet. The crowd gives a cheer as the procession reaches them.

"Is that a real lion?" asks Lettie. "Yes, look it is moving!"

"Mercy me! She must be the lion tamer," says Billy.

"I hope it cannot get down from there," says Lettie, concerned.

"No, can't you see? It has a chain around its neck," says Malachi as the carriage passes by.

"My goodness, look, there is an elephant!" cries Rebecca. The Indian elephant is magnificent, dressed in its ceremonial red silk blanket with tassels all around it; a silk forehead square, with a large Indian silver jewellery tassel hanging down his trunk; a silver necklace from which is attached tiny bells and silver tail and head ornamentation. Riding the elephant, seated on red velvet cushions in a silver gilded box seat is the circus owner, with the portreeve seated behind him. The elephant plods on, waving his trunk from side to side.

Malachi leads the group of friends slowly up the hill as the animals pass alongside them. "Those camels are a bit smelly," complains Louisa.

"Watch out for that ostrich!" shouts Billy, as the ostrich takes a peck at Lucy's hat.

Lucy screams and grabs her hat. "Shoo!" She waves her hand at the big bird and he wanders off, unconcerned, following the llamas.

"It must have been the feather that attracted him," laughs Louisa.

Some of the animals are linked together in their species groups with their trainers leading them and controlling them, but the lions, tigers, kangaroos, emus, chimpanzees, baboons and buffaloes are all conveyed in horse or camel-drawn cages, the horses sporting fabulous plumes. There is also a foal wagon and everyone is especially taken with the foals and the baby apes and their antics.

Finally they are back at Huish Field and the animals are being corralled ready for their performances later. The friends can hear loud cheering and shouting coming from the lower corner of the field and they curiously make their way towards the sound. People are crowded around a roped off area.

"It is the boxing ring and the prize-fighter has just knocked out the landlord of the George Inn," says Malachi, looking over the heads of the crowd. "I think it was an unfair fight; the 'Wessex Wonder' is a fit young man with bulging muscles, whereas the landlord is past his prime and slightly overweight." The landlord soon comes round after a sniff of sal volatile. He stumbles to his feet and takes his purse for taking part in the competition. They edge forward to the front of the crowd.

Malachi reads the sign. "They are paying a florin to anyone who has a go and ten golden guineas to the victor, or one guinea to anyone left standing after six rounds."

"Crikey! Do you think we should have a go?" asks Jacob.

"Well, if I go first and come back in one piece then maybe you could, but I am definitely going first." Malachi steps forward with his hand in the air as the showman calls out for contestants.

He spots Malachi. "Step forward, young man. Who is your second?"

Malachi looks back at Jacob. "Jacob, will you be my second?"

"Of course I will."

"Malachi, are you sure this is a good idea?" calls Rosa anxiously.

"Malachi, don't be stupid, Ma will kill you!" cries Lucy.

"Then I have nothing to lose," he says, laughing.

"What is your name, lad?" asks the manager.

He thinks for a moment. "Malachi the Magnificent," he says with a grin, stripping off his jacket, waistcoat and shirt. Rosa looks up at him proudly. He has a fine, tanned, muscular body and she is aware of the murmur of appreciation from the women in the gathering.

The Wessex Wonder looks him up and down and flexes his muscles like a strutting cockerel, then returns to his corner where he has words with the bruisers who are backing him.

The showman rings his bell, introduces his new combatant to the crowd and runs though the rules for them. "There will be no biting, no kicking and no clawing of the eyes." Then he asks them to return to their seconds to wait for the bell. As it rings out the two men spring forward, their arms held high and bobbing and weaving around each other. Malachi gets in the first punch and the crowd scream out, "Mal-a-chi, Mal-a-chi", eagerly supporting their local man.

Among the crowd Lettie recognises Raymond Hawkins of Odcombe, who is among those who are shouting their support. Until recently he was the bane of her father's life with his poaching and then he sees her looking in his direction and grins at her knowingly. He is with Thomas, his cousin, and Robert and Harry Sandford. Despite her father's frustration Lettie is attracted to him and, blushing, she smiles back at him. He takes this as an invitation and encourages the lads to join the girls at the ringside.

"My goodness, that rose quartz is working already," she whispers, as she smiles at Rebecca.

Rebecca looks at the lads, as they move in. "Which one?" whispers back Rebecca.

"The tallest one, wearing the red neckerchief, with the big brown eyes."

"He is quite handsome, in a roguish sort of way. Are the two blond lads twins?"

"No, they are brothers – three years between them."

"They are nice looking too, but nothing compared to my Ben. I am really missing him; he would have loved all this."

Billy is too busy watching the fight to notice at first, but when he sees the four lads he sidles up to stand beside Lucy protectively.

Then the Wessex Wonder hits home and knocks Malachi off balance. Rosa grips Lucy's arm and cries out in concern, as again the crowd roar out their support for him. He soon regains his defensive stance. As the minutes tick on slowly there is a lot of body holding and punching, then Malachi pulls back and directs a left hook at the fellow's jaw. He staggers backwards unsteadily into the ropes, just as the bell rings.

Malachi returns to his corner and feels in the pocket of his breeches for his handkerchief. Instead he finds the stones and he strokes and fondles them optimistically. "I believe these stones are working, Jake, I have never felt so invincible."

Jacob wipes the sweat from his brother's face with a damp cloth. "Don't be too cocky, Mal, you'll get yourself hurt." Malachi takes a swig of water, then he is up on his feet again for round two.

This time the Wessex Wonder really means business. He did not appreciate that last left hook and he catches Malachi with a hefty clout to his cheekbone, ripping the skin open in a red gash of blood. Malachi's head jerks back with the impact and blood and sweat rains down on the crowd.

"Oh no! I knew he would be harmed, we should have stopped him, Rosa," says Lucy, really worried now. Malachi hardly notices, as his adrenaline is pumping and he skips and dances around his opponent who keeps missing his aim.

"Don't worry, Lucy, he is definitely faster on his feet than the Wessex Wonder," says Billy reassuringly.

The crowd are getting excited, sensing the man has met his match. Malachi does not notice the blood streaming down his face and neck as he slams home another weighty blow, making good contact with the chap's chin. The man drops to the floor.

"He has gone down like a sack of spuds!" yells Harry Sandford, triumphantly.

The crowd erupts as the showman holds up Malachi's hand and proclaims him the winner. As the showman hands over the ten guineas Malachi wipes his hand across his cheek and notices the blood. Malachi asks him, "Where is my florin? Surely I am entitled to that for taking part, as well as the prize money."

"Ah yes, sir, you are of course correct," and he hands over the florin.

"Thank you. Please give my apologies to the Wessex Wonder when he eventually comes round."

Jacob slaps him on the back. "Well done, Mal. I cannot believe you have won and in only two rounds!" He passes him his clothes and Malachi puts them on.

Rosa rushes forward to the ropes. "Mal, you are bleeding, are you all right?"

"All right? I feel incredible, it was great, Rosa, and look – we have ten guineas towards our wedding. I will keep the florin, you can have the guineas when we get home, but make sure you put them somewhere safe." He hugs her as the showman approaches him. "Are you up for another opponent?"

"Of course he isn't. Can't you see he is bleeding badly?" says Rosa spiritedly.

Malachi is aware that if he fought again it would really upset Rosa and his sister. "I would be, sir, I really enjoyed that and I will be here again next time you are here, rest assured, but I have my family and friends here and I ought to see them home safely." He climbs over the ropes and turns away to join his friends.

The showman shouts out, "Let's have a big hand for Malachi the Magnificent!" The crowd applaud enthusiastically, and Malachi waves both arms in the air as he walks away.

"I know you did not enjoy that spectacle, but I loved it, Rosa. The only thing is I should have pickled my hands in astringent first. I will be better prepared next time, as they are quite swollen."

Rosa tucks her hand in the crook of his elbow and looks up at him with loving concern. "What do you mean, you will be better prepared next time?"

"Rosa, I loved it; it is the easiest money I have ever earned, that is for sure, and I didn't even realise I was cut, I was so keyed up."

"I don't think you should do it again, Mal, 'tis a dangerous sport. I believe you will need some stitches in that cut and it will probably leave a scar."

"Don't you worry, love, it is just a graze. Besides, a scar will look good for next time."

All the lads, including the Sandfords and the Hawkin boys, cluster round him, offering their congratulations and shaking his bruised hand carefully.

"I think we should go home and see to that cut, Mal," says Lucy, concerned for him.

"But I thought you wanted to see *Robin Hood* in the theatre tent, Lucy?"

"Well, let's just wander back in that direction and see what we can see on the way."

The boys follow them as they pass the tableau tent and peep inside to see *Snow White and the Seven Dwarfs*. "The little dwarf people are fascinating, aren't they? They are so cute," says Lettie.

"Can you see Toby and Bunny in there?" asks Louisa.

"No I can't," says Malachi. "We will have to try the theatre tent."

As they go various local people come up to offer their congratulations to Malachi, and he tells Rosa that it makes him feel 'on top of the world'. They reach the theatre tent at ten past two and as they stand in the entrance they can see their friends with Bunny and Toby on the raised wooden stands. "It is a penny to go in," says Jacob, "and the next showing is at two thirty."

"I feel fine, honestly," insists Malachi. "Let's all go and get some pies and then go in to watch the show. We will have a bit of a rest then, before walking back home."

"That is a good idea," says Rebecca, looking at Lucy for confirmation.

"All right," agrees Lucy. "But do say if you change your mind."

"Are you boys coming to see the show too?" asks Lettie, looking at Raymond Hawkins hopefully.

"I don't have any more money I am afraid," he says.

"I have only a penny left I am afraid," says his cousin.

"I can lend you some, Ray," says Harry Sandford. "You can pay me back when you next get paid."

"Thanks mate," says Ray, who doesn't want to be the odd one out. Besides, he wants to sit near to Lettie.

They all go and choose their pies and Malachi buys four extra for Bunny, Toby and the girls. Then they return to the marquee, hand over their pennies at the entrance and take their seats in a large group, as near to Bunny and Toby as they can get. Lucy takes the extra pies and passes them to Elsie to share them out. Bunny looks horrified to see that her big brother has been injured. "Whatever has happened to Malachi, Lucy?"

"Don't worry, he is fine and he won a prize in the boxing match."

"Gosh!" She waves over to her brother and mouths, "Well done, Malachi."

Toby calls out, "Thank you for the pies."

They all sit in their rows munching on their pies as the showman cracks his whip and announces the beginning of the performance. The show is amazing, with Robin Hood and his merry men, some of whom are clowns and midgets, getting up to all sorts of revelry. The archery is fantastic and Maid Marion is a wonderful, bareback horse-rider. They all thoroughly enjoy the spectacle.

After the event they re-group outside the theatre tent. Lettie tells the boys that she is taking her brother home with the Warrens, Rebecca, Elsie and Emily. It has been a long day; they are all tired and she has seen enough. The boys decide to walk with them and as they leave Huish Field behind them they are telling everyone about the freak show. "There was lots of little folk, midgets and dwarfs doing conjuring and acrobatics and Siamese twins, a giant strongman and an armless woman who could play the piano."

"No, we didn't see that," says Rebecca.

"We did, didn't we Elsie? And we saw the mermaid, and the strange creatures in jars," says Emily.

"Yes, they were weird and you must have seen the tiny twin horses, they were only about so high." Robert Sandford is demonstrating by holding his hand about two feet from the ground.

"Oh! I would have liked to have seen those, they sound so delightful," says Louisa.

Robert and Harry then focus their attention on

Louisa as they go along, describing all they had seen in detail and behaving like gentlemen in their concern for her.

"Mind that puddle, Louisa," says Harry.

"Look out for that bramble," says Robert.

"Here, let me help you over that stile," says Harry.

"I am fine, Harry, but perhaps you could lift Bunny over? She is only small."

Raymond Hawkins is walking alongside Lettie and Rebecca. "We were planning to watch the striptease and knife throwing show, but we missed it because we left early," says Raymond Hawkins. Then he drops his voice to a whisper, "No matter, it is worth it to be walking home with you, Lettie."

Lettie blushes with pleasure.

Quietly he says, "Can I hold your hand?" Raymond looks at her pleadingly and Lettie smiles. She takes his hand, hoping that Toby is too busy chattering to notice.

Rebecca tactfully drops back to walk alongside Lucy, Elsie and Emily. Jacob joins them and soon he and Elsie are chatting away together.

It is not long before they reach Home Farm and the friends all say farewell to the Warrens. Lucy invites them all in for a drink and they eagerly accept, but do not stay long.

"It is getting dumpsy, we'd best be making tracks," says Lettie, anxious to be home before dark.

They say their farewells and set off again, the Sandfords still pouring their attention over Louisa, and Malachi walking Rosa back to the Dower House. Elsie, Emily, Rebecca, Billy and Thomas Hawkins are in another group, whilst Toby is holding Lettie's hand as she walks alongside Raymond Hawkins.

At Alvington Manor they all say goodnight and

Lettie continues on up the lane with the boys, hoping that her father especially will not notice their companions. As they reach Keeper's Cottage Toby runs on in excitedly to tell his parents all he has seen.

Raymond grabs Lettie by the hand before she goes through the gate. He pulls her into his arms, his hand reaches up behind her hair and quickly he says, "I want to kiss you." Before she has a chance to stop him his mouth is down on hers tenderly, more tenderly than she would have imagined and she is unwilling to push him away.

Then she hears her mother's voice and comes to her senses. Gently she extricates herself from his arms and she says, "I must go, Ray, goodnight. I have had a lovely time." She squeezes his hand to let him know that his advances are not being rebuffed and turns to go inside. "Goodnight everyone!" she calls happily and runs in after Toby.

Unbeknown to Lettie, her father is not far away and is watching the scene through an eye glass. Raymond Hawkins is the last person he wants to be courting his little lassie and he is determined to put a stop to it at all costs.

CHAPTER 10 *(December 1852)*

THE TRUTH WILL OUT

Early in December Raymond Hawkins turns up at Summerville House with a group of beaters in readiness for a shooting party.

He manages to have a quiet word with his sister. "I thought you ought to know, Jean, that our pa is going downhill fast. The surgeon says it is not bronchitis, but consumption and I am sorry, Jean, but his days are numbered." Jean looks so shocked that he puts his arm around his sister to comfort her. "I think you ought to come home and see him before it is too late."

"Oh, Ray, I didn't realise he was that ill; poor Pa, I will talk to Mrs Faversham, I have not had any time off for such a long while, I cannot see why they would not allow me to have Christmas at home this year. I will speak to her now and let you know when you come back later with the hunting party for the shoot breakfast."

She then goes immediately to knock on Mrs Faversham's door. She hears the call, "Come in," and enters.

"Excuse me, Mrs Faversham, but my brother has just informed me that our pa is very poorly with consumption and I would be grateful if I could have some time off over Christmas to go home to see him."

"You are not on the rota, Hawkins."

"Please, Mrs Faversham, Raymond thinks that

he is going downhill fast and it may be my last chance to see him." She is looking over the desk at the upside down rota as she speaks, to see who is due for time off and recognises the two 'R's' for Ruby Reynolds written there. "Mrs Faversham, Ruby is no longer working here, Amy took her place and she will not be due time off yet. Please, can I not go in Ruby's place?"

"Amy did not take her place, she replaced Millie Bonfield, but you are right that Ruby is no longer here and so, under the circumstances, I think that would be acceptable. I will cross off Ruby and put your name in her place. But do not discuss this with the other girls. I do not want them thinking there has been any favouritism."

"I won't," she promises with relief. "Thank you, Mrs Faversham."

She returns to her work, saddened by the thought of her father being so unwell, but glad of the opportunity to spend some time away from the oppressive atmosphere of Summerville House. Later in the day, on the return of the shooting party, she is pleased to be able to tell her brother that her leave has been agreed.

The long walk home on Christmas Eve is going to be a pleasure for her. It is wonderful to be free of the chores, the anxiety and fear of the coven and out in the fresh open air where she can think straight. She hooks her basket in the crook of her elbow and goes up the hill towards Stoford, passing the copse where the coven meets. Should she tell her family what she has witnessed, or would it be safer to keep her own counsel? The question troubles her and the answer eludes her. Her family would want her to leave Summerville House, if they were aware of what was going on, but how could they manage without her contributions?

She turns right along Two Tower Lane and as she goes she can see the folly 'Jack the Treacle Eater' in the east of Barwick Park and then 'The Fish Tower' near to the roadside, and finally the 'Messiter's Cone' and she marvels at the workmanship and design of these obelisks. The Messiter family must have been very wealthy people to assign the building of these follies in order to be able to give employment to local labourers during the depression. They obviously wanted the best for their employees, unlike the Meakins. She wonders if their outgoing generosity had been a shield behind which to hide evil secrets after all. She would forevermore be suspicious of everyone.

She crosses the Dorchester Road and takes the lower East Coker Road, having to stand in tight to the hedge as a horse-drawn dog cart passes by. As she turns briefly onto the Ivell to East Coker Road it begins to rain and she pulls up her hood and wraps her cloak more tightly around her. Shortly she steps into the narrow bridleway that leads to Placket Lane. This footpath is damp and muddy underfoot, but a more direct route to Camp Road and she trudges along with the wet undergrowth brushing against her skirts, the rain blowing into her face and drips running down the bridge of her nose.

Once she is on Camp Road the wind whips across her from the left and if it was not for her warm, thick hood she would be suffering from earache by the time she reached Odcombe. Her buttoned boots are muddy and her feet are sore and damp, her arm is aching from carrying her basket, but she is nearly home. At last she reaches the finger post at the junction of Cherry and Donne Lane and crosses into Dray Road. She is wet and cold and aching all over and she is looking forward to a hot drink and something to eat.

Finally she enters Cobb Cottage, but she is shocked to see her emaciated father lying on the sofa by the fire, a spittoon on the rug beside him. He goes to sit up, but she stops him, seeing the effort in his face. "Hello my maid, what a lovely surprise," he says, holding out his hand to her. But as soon as he speaks he is racked with coughing.

She puts down her basket, passes him the spittoon and kneels down on the rug beside him. When he finally stops coughing she says, "I am sorry to hear that you have been so poorly, Pa. Ray told me, and that is why I was able to get a few days off, but I have to go back on Tuesday to start work again first thing Wednesday."

"It is so good to see you, lass, pull up a chair by the fire and take off that damp cloak, you must be chilled to the bone."

"I am feeling cold and weary, Pa, 'tis a long walk from Newton Hollow to here. Where's Ma and Ray?"

"Ray is out back, chopping wood for the fire and your ma is upstairs making up a bed for you. She has been busy all morning preparing the Christmas meal. She only finished her gloving yesterday. Poor woman, it makes me feel so guilty lying here like a helpless old man."

"It's not your fault, Pa; you are ill and I know Ma understands." She hears footsteps descending the stairs and the door beside the chimney breast opens.

She jumps up and hugs her mother. "Hello, Ma. It's so good to be home."

"Oh, Jean, you don't know what this means to us to have the whole family here together this year."

She kisses her daughter's cold cheek and then wipes away a tear, continuing cheerfully, "Ray got us a wood pigeon and a partridge for our dinner tomorrow and I have made some plum puddings and mince pies. We've got sprouts, parsnips, potatoes and some kale from the vegetable patch."

"My goodness, Ma, that all sounds like a feast," she smiles comfortingly. "Well, I managed to get some gifts off the pedlar who came calling at the manor and I have the rest of my savings for you and Pa." She hands her mother a chamois stocking purse, heavy with coins.

"Oh! Bless you child. This is a godsend."

"You are welcome, Ma, I only wish I could do more."

"Come, I must get you something to eat; you must be hungry after that long walk."

"I am, Ma. Could I have a nice mug of hot chocolate?"

"Of course, you sit down and chat to your pa and I will go and get it. Would you like some chocolate, Gabriel?"

"I would, Esther, thank you."

Raymond then comes in with an armful of wood for the fire and dumps it unceremoniously into the log basket. "You made it in time for luncheon then, Jean."

"Yes, I didn't tarry in this weather, besides I am looking forward to sampling some of Ma's home cooking."

"Well, I think we are being treated to her egg and bacon pie today."

"Mm, my favourite."

Christmas morning dawns cold but sunny. Jean looks through her closet and finds her old red Sunday best frock and puts it on with a green woollen shawl, matching woollen stockings and slippers. Then she goes downstairs to help her mother.

She had bought some lavender water and soap for her mother, some slippers for her father and a new catapult for her brother, plus some wrapping paper from the pedlar and she had wrapped and wax sealed the gifts in her room before going to bed last night.

They did not have a Christmas tree, but Raymond had brought home a branch from a fir tree and had stuck it in a bucket of soil and decorated it with painted fir cones. It is placed on a table in the chimney corner opposite the stairway door and they have arranged their presents underneath it.

After they have eaten their sumptuous Christmas dinner they sit around the hearth and exchange their gifts. Her family are all pleased with her presents and in return she receives a beautiful new pair of dove grey kid gloves from her mother and father.

"Oh, Ma, they are beautiful and made by your own fair hands."

"Well, your pa paid Mr Giles for the materials from his savings and I made them up at home."

"Thank you, Pa. They feel so soft and fit wonderfully well and I love the colour."

Raymond then gets up to pass her his gift. "I hope you like this. It is my new hobby, but I am just a novice really." He hands her a small parcel.

"Thank you, Ray." Thinking to herself, *this is the first time I have ever had a gift from my brother*, she removes the wrapping paper carefully to reveal a wooden hand-carved sculpture of a tiny robin.

"My word, Ray, this is truly magnificent. I did not realise you were so talented!"

162

"I thought you would like it, Jean. He has been busy working on it for ages," says her mother.

"I love it! It is really charming and I will treasure it. Thank you very much, Ray." She gives him a kiss on his cheek, which he immediately rubs away with the back of his sleeve.

"I am glad you like it, Jean, I thought a robin appropriate for Christmas. I used some of Ma's cardinal red to colour his breast."

"I think he has a genuine talent for wood carving, don't you, Esther?" says his father.

"I think he can do anything he sets his mind to, if only he had a bit more faith in himself."

"Well, maybe my little brother is growing up at last," says Jean grinning at him with sisterly warmth.

Later, when they are washing up the dinner things and their parents are relaxing together, Jean whispers to Raymond, "When we have the opportunity I need to speak to you alone."

"Why, whatever is wrong?"

"I cannot talk here. Perhaps we can take a walk tomorrow if the weather is good."

"Yes, of course, but you have me worried now."

"'Tis nothing for you to worry about, I just need to confide in someone. I need to share a burden, that is all."

On Boxing Day the weather has improved slightly, the rain has stopped and the wind dropped, but it is still dull and grey. After breakfast their parents are happy for them to go out for some fresh air and once they leave the bounds of Odcombe behind them, stepping out along Camp Road towards Alvington Manor, Raymond is eager to hear what has been troubling his sister. "Right, Jean, what is this burden you need to share?"

"I don't know how to tell you it all, Ray. I have had a frightful time, but I have to talk to someone, though you cannot tell anyone, not even Ma and Pa, for fear of both of us losing our jobs."

"This sounds serious."

"It is, Ray. It is fearful serious. Master Nathan and Miss Olivia are members of a coven."

"How do you know that?"

"Because I have followed them in their hooded cloaks and witnessed their pagan satanic rituals. 'Tis not a coven of white witches, Ray, they tend towards the dark side."

"What did you see?"

"I watched as Miss Olivia sacrificed her purity to the devil at Hallow tide. To symbolise this she had sex on their stone altar with the warlock."

"She did what?"

"She had sexual intercourse in front of all the witches, but the worst of it is that the warlock was Master Nathan."

"What! He had a shag with his sister! That is disgusting! It's unlawful isn't it? Isn't that called incest?"

"But it is even worse than that, because they begat a child."

"Crikey! How did they explain that?"

"They didn't, they kept the baby hidden."

"They must have had a job. You cannot keep a child quiet very easily."

"Well, they didn't have to for long. Olivia took to her room for a while to hide her condition and then to keep the baby out of sight. But the evil devils conspired to slaughter the poor little mite in a pagan offering to the Sun God. I was there when they did it, Ray, and I could do nothing. They lay him down on the stone slab and cut his poor little throat."

"My God, Jean! That must have been horrific!"

"It was, and you remember when Ma used to call you 'her little Ray of sunshine' when you were tiny? Well, they called him Helios after the Sun God and then sacrificed him. I just cannot imagine how they could do that to their own child."

"Well, it was evidence you see, Jean, of what they had done together, of their incest."

She nods her head sadly. "I don't know how much longer I can stand working there. The house seems shrouded in evil, now that I know what has been going on. I have hung a horseshoe on my door, but I feel I need some stronger medicine to protect me from being possessed by Satan myself."

"Well, perhaps we should go and see Lettie's mother."

"Who is Lettie?"

"Well, she is kind of my girlfriend."

"Your girlfriend?" Jean raises her eyebrows in surprise. "What do you mean 'kind of'?"

"Her father is the gamekeeper at Alvington Manor and he don't want me seeing his daughter, because he caught me poaching on their land, back in November last year. But we have been meeting up secretly sometimes, in an old hay barn, when the weather is good. She is really nice, Jean, you will love her and I am so lucky that she is sweet on me. I just wish I had a good job and then her family might accept me one day."

"I am happy for you, Ray, but we both need good jobs. I would do anything to change mine at the moment." She links her arm in his. "So you say her mother knows about the crafty sciences?"

"Yes, she is a hedge witch and healer and I am sure she would help you."

"But we cannot tell her what the problem is, for fear of it getting back to the Meakins."

"No, but there is no need for that, we can ask Lettie to craftily question her, without revealing why, and then maybe we can make up the amulet ourselves."

"It is worth a try, as it would ease my mind greatly. The thing is, Ray, there is another young girl started work there in the summer and she is only thirteen. She is innocent and pretty and I know the master has his eyes on her. I am anxious for her safety. Why, even now that I am away over Christmas I am worried that he might get his claws into her. Usually we stick quite close together, but left on her own I fear she will be in danger."

"What kind of danger?"

"Well, maybe they will be wanting another child to sacrifice. It certainly suits his nature to be the supplier of these illegitimate babies. He is having the time of his life, with no repercussions. He can charm the bloomers off the young girls and then terrify them into giving up their babies, for fear of losing their jobs and their reputations. I should hate to think that poor Amy would be put through the horror of all that. Olivia brought it on herself, but Amy is a different matter all together."

"Hmm, I can see why you are worried and want the protection of some sort of talisman," says her brother.

"Well, I don't know how we can devise a covert meeting with your Lettie."

"They will probably be going to church this morning; I heard Ma say there is no Holy Communion service at Odcombe because the vicar is going to Alvington Manor this Sunday."

"Well, we could go to church there; we share the vicar after all."

"That is true, Jean; we have as much right to go there as they do. We are already halfway there.

Come on then, we had better get a move on, it must already be half past ten."

Keeper's Cottage looks deserted as they pass by on their way down the hill. They can see folk arriving for the service all dressed up in their Sunday best and Jean is suddenly self-conscious lest she look out of place in her shabby clothes.

"Do you think we look proper enough to go to church, Ray?"

"Of course we do. You're wearing your Christmas gown, I've not seen you in anything nicer. I have left off my tatty old cap and have on my new wide-awake hat that Ma and Pa gave me. I think we are fine and dandy."

"Look, there is Uncle Jack and Auntie Molly with Frank and Thomas. Let us sit with them."

Jean is pleased to see family there and they both join them, exchanging greetings as they enter the small chapel.

"Well, I didn't expect to see you two here," says their uncle. "How did you manage to get Christmas off, Jean?"

"Well, it was really because Pa is so poorly with the consumption."

"I am sorry to hear that, I haven't set eyes on him myself for a while now. I will make sure that Molly and I visit him after Christmas."

"I am sure he would be thankful for that, Uncle Jack."

As they find a pew large enough for them all to sit in a row, she notes Raymond looking around for Lettie and spots him smiling at a pretty young lassie with a mass of brown curly hair. She smiles back warmly, revealing pearly white teeth and two deep and appealing dimples. *So this is Lettie*, she thinks. Her brother could do no better and she is pleased for them.

She kneels down and prays to God for help and protection against all the evils of this world, for help in improving the health of her father and for her brother to eventually be accepted by Lettie's parents. Her mind wanders a little throughout the service, but she is glad that they decided to join the congregation here, for she is very aware now of the existence of pure evil and for the need for folk to unite against it. She finds the presence of all these good and honest people comforting and decides that she will attend church more often in the future. For some reason, her mind turns to Amy and a shiver runs down her spine. She also silently prays for the protection of her new friend.

After the service the congregation file past the Reverend Phelps and he shakes their hands and has a few words with each of them. He is surprised to see that Jean and Raymond have gone out of their way to attend, even though they had to walk all the way from Odcombe.

"My sister was keen to attend, Reverend, she is home only for the Christmas break but she is usually away in service the other side of Ivell."

"Well, I am very pleased to see you both. How is your father keeping these days?"

"He is not doing so well, I am afraid, but he has really enjoyed having us all together this Christmas."

"I am sure, my boy; please pass on my regards to him and your mother."

"We will, thank you, Reverend."

Outside the chapel they wait to one side as the people slowly pass by. Lettie emerges before her parents and Raymond takes this opportunity to have a quick word with her.

"Lettie; this is my sister, Jean."

They both say Hello.

"She has a problem and she needs some way of

protecting herself from the evil eye. I will tell you more when we meet, but can you get something for her from your ma? She needs protection from a satanic coven, but I don't want your family to know the details for fear of it getting back to her employers and her losing her job. Can you try to get something and meet us in the hay barn tomorrow some time?"

"I will do my best, Ray. I will try and get there for about three of the clock. I cannot wait to see you, but I had better go before Pa catches us chatting. It is nice to meet you, Jean."

"Yes, I am pleased to meet you too, Lettie, and thank you, I am very grateful for your help."

"Well, I cannot make any promises, but I will do my best."

"Bye, Lettie, see you tomorrow," whispers Raymond, just as her parents and Toby emerge from the chapel porch.

They turn away to rejoin Jack, Molly and the boys, in the hope that they were not noticed by the Boucher family. They go along Pound Lane, up the hill towards Camp Road, chatting about their respective Christmases.

"I am glad it is all over, I always prefer Boxing Day myself, when you can all just relax and enjoy the time off," says their Auntie Molly.

"I can understand that, Auntie Molly. Our ma looked very tired last night, but we are just having a cold collation for our lunch today, so she has been able to relax with our pa."

"Would you like to come and have a drink with us before you return home?"

"Thank you that is very kind, but we had better go straight back, otherwise we won't be back in time for our lunch and I know Ma and Pa are looking forward to the company."

They say their farewells and turn towards

Odcombe. "We will have been gone nearly three hours by the time we get back," says Jean.

"Well, we didn't take into account going to the church service, did we?" replies Raymond.

"They will be worried, come on we had better hurry home," says Jean, quickening her pace.

The following day Jean and Raymond set off to meet Lettie in the hay barn. Raymond has his Christmas present for Lettie tucked in his pocket and Jean is looking forward to getting to know her brother's sweetheart and to being able to talk to her freely about her fears.

They reach the barn at ten to three, but Lettie is already there waiting for them. As soon as they enter the barn door Raymond takes Lettie in his arms and kisses her on the mouth. "I have missed you so much, Lettie, it is so good to hold you in my arms."

"I have missed you too, Ray."

"Did your pa spot us yesterday?"

"No, but Toby did and he wanted to follow you to say hello, but I put my finger to my lips and thankfully he kept quiet."

"Thank goodness. Were you able to get anything for Jean?"

"Yes, I have this tiger eye. It is a semi precious stone that I bought at the Saint Leonard's Day fair and, as you have more need of it than I do, you can borrow it, Jean, for as long as you need it."

"That is very kind of you, Lettie, thank you so much." She takes the small oval stone and rolls it around in her palm, before slipping it into her pocket.

"I also have this bottle with a charm in that you must bury in a churchyard."

"What is the charm in the bottle?" asks Jean.

"It is a piece of paper with something written on it," says Lettie.

"Can we take it out and see what it says?" asks Jean.

"I shouldn't if I were you, we don't want to interfere with its powers, do we?" says Raymond.

"I think it is better if you don't disturb the cork," says Lettie. "Anyway, what is all this in aid of?"

"Lettie, 'tis quite serious; our Jean has witnessed some dreadful satanic deeds in the name of witchcraft at a coven at Newton Hollow near where she works as a housemaid. The young master and mistress are both involved."

"Do you mean Nathan and Olivia Meakins?"

"Yes, and Olivia's ladies maid, Apsey," says Jean.

"What have they done?" asks Lettie wide-eyed.

"Well, firstly the mistress sacrificed her purity to the devil on All Hallows Eve, by having carnal relations with her brother at a witchcraft ceremony, while they all danced around them ecstatically and…" She looks at Raymond and he nods in agreement that she should continue. "Well, she conceived a child and the evil devils sacrificed the baby to the Sun God at the summer solstice ceremony. I was there, Lettie, when they slit the poor little child's throat and it haunts me that I could do nothing but watch from the safety of the bushes. Well, that is until I fainted."

"My God, Jean, no wonder you want protection from those devils!"

Raymond takes his sweetheart by the shoulders earnestly. "But you cannot tell anyone, Lettie. I know I can trust you, but neither Jean nor I can afford to lose our jobs there. I know I merely go beating, but it is the only money I earn and with Pa so ill we need every penny."

"Don't worry I will not tell anyone. I doubt they would believe me, anyway." She takes hold of both their hands in hers. "There is something else you can do. My ma always says that if you know who the witch is you should make a plan to draw her blood, by pricking her with a pin or something similar."

"Right, I will bear that in mind, but it is not easy to get close to the master and mistress. Maybe I could prick Apsey."

"I am sure it all helps. My friends and I purchased some stones from the Shaman at the Saint Leonard's Day fair because of all their magic properties. If I learn of any other forms of protection I will tell Ray and he can let you know when he next sees you. My ma is very good with this sort of problem; why, only last summer Isaac Warren had some trouble with his milking herd and after Ma helped him, with a charm and an oily clay dressing, they were all fine again."

"Thank you for your help, Lettie, I am very grateful. It has also been a comfort telling you both, for if anything dreadful should happen to me, you two will know where to lay the blame."

"Don't talk like that, Jean, I am sure they are unaware that you know of their secret lives, for surely they would have acted by now if they did."

"I think so too, Ray, but I won't be following them any more, I can assure you."

"I am glad to hear it."

"Anyway, enough of that nasty talk," he turns to Lettie. "I have a little Christmas present for you, Lettie." He draws his gift from his pocket and hands it to her. "It is only something home-made, but I hope you will like it."

"Oh thank you, Ray, I also have something hand-made for you," and she takes from her cloak a larger package and passes it to him.

"You go first, Lettie," he says.

Carefully she unwraps her present and is thrilled to find a small, wooden, carved kingfisher, painted with aquamarine and dark sienna, with flashes of a pale stone colour each side of its neck.

"Oh, Ray, did you really make this for me?"

"I really did. Do you like it?"

"Of course I do, dearest Ray. I love it, it is exquisite, but you must open yours now."

He carefully unwraps his gift with the two girls watching. It is a woollen scarf, knitted in greens and blues. "It is very nice, Lettie, lovely and soft and warm and ideal for today. He wraps it around his neck, covering his old red neckerchief. "Thank you, Lettie, it is lovely and it matches my breeches."

"I like your new hat, Ray. I noticed it after church yesterday. Is that a Christmas gift too?"

"It is yes, my present from Ma and Pa."

"Well, I like it very much, don't you Jean? It makes him look like even more of a dandy, don't you think?" she says laughing.

Jean laughs too. "Yes, you are right, it really suits him."

"Come here, you," cries Raymond, taking Lettie in a tight hold and kissing her on the mouth to silence her mirth.

They make a lovely happy couple and Jean is pleased for them, despite experiencing a twinge of sadness that she has no one special with whom to share her own happiness or her fears, apart from her family. She notices the pile of haystacks in the corner of the barn and the loose hay that carpets the floor of the barn and wonders how far her brother has gone with Lettie. She looks to be only just old enough, but even so it wouldn't do his case any good with her family if he was to get Lettie into trouble.

"Well, I had better be getting back, Ray, before I am missed. When shall we meet again?

"How about next Tuesday? I am sure that will be fine, but I will drop by and leave a note if I am unable to come that day to let you know another time."

"All right, Ray, I will see you in my dreams until then. Thank you for my lovely present. I think I might show Toby, he will be so impressed."

"Make sure he doesn't tell your pa though."

"I will." She turns to Jean. "Goodbye, Jean. It has been nice to meet you and I hope the charms will work. I will let your brother know if I think of anything else to help."

"I am very grateful and I hope that your ma and pa soon realise that Raymond is not all bad. He has a very kind heart."

"I know and I am sure Pa will come round in time, it is just that we do not want to be kept apart in the meantime." She turns and kisses Raymond on the lips and he wraps his arms around her in a warm embrace.

"See you on Tuesday next week, sweetheart. Fare thee well." Lettie then quietly leaves the barn and they follow a short while later.

As they take the route back home, Jean is pondering how she should broach the subject that is on her mind, but eventually she just blurts it out. "That barn is an ideal meeting place for a couple of lovers, with all that comfy hay all over the place and I am concerned. Have you done anything that might risk Lettie being with child?"

"What do you take me for, Jean? I am trying to impress her father with how responsible I can be. I am not going to completely ruin my chances, am I? If only I had a proper trade I might stand a chance."

"They will come round I am sure, but it certainly

would help your case if you found yourself a decent position with good prospects. I really like her, Ray. She is good for you."

"I know she is and I adore her."

On their way back, they pass Odcombe Church. "If we had a trowel we could bury the witch bottle here in this churchyard."

"Let us just have a quick look. There may be a piece of slate fallen from the roof that we could use," suggests her brother.

They have a quick look around, but are unable to find anything suitable. "Don't worry Ray," she says in a low voice, "I can borrow one of Pa's trowels and do it on my way back to Summerville tomorrow morning. I will leave the trowel here behind the wall for you to find and return."

"No need for that, I will come with you and I can dig the hole for you then," he whispers back.

She shakes her head, "No, Ray, for the spell to work I think I have to do it myself."

"Well, I can be your lookout then."

"Thank you, that is a good plan and you will be a great help."

The following day is thankfully dry and sunny, if a little cold. Jean is upset at having to say goodbye to her father, for fear it may be the last time she sees him alive, but she has no choice and tries bravely to hide her fears. "Bye, Pa, I have had a lovely time with you all. Please take care of yourself and keep your strength up by eating all Ma's delicious meals. I will be thinking of you over at Newton Hollow and praying that you soon feel yourself again."

"Don't you fret, Jean, I am in good hands here with your mother."

"I know you are, Pa, and thank you, Ma, for

looking after me so well. The Christmas meal was absolutely delicious and I love my gloves – thank you, both of you. Ray is going to walk with me for company for part of the way, but I had better go; it is a long way and I will need to rest this afternoon, before being up at dawn tomorrow."

"Well, it has been a pleasure having you here with us this yuletide, sweetheart, and please remember that if you ever decide you want to come home, there is always a room here for you. You could take on a bit of gloving like I do; it won't pay so well, but at least you would be with the family."

"I may take you at your word one day, Ma. I will see how I get on, only at the moment I have a new young friend working there and I think she needs my support."

"Well, think on it, Jean, is all I am saying."

"I will, Ma." She kisses her mother and her father struggles to his feet to say goodbye. She kisses him on his cheek and they both wave from the parlour window as she sets off with Raymond at her side.

She smiles merrily and waves back to them until she reaches the junction. "Have you got the trowel?" she asks her brother.

"Inside my jacket," he reassures her.

"Good, then let's get the deed done."

As Jean buries the witch bottle she says a few words in the form of a prayer, because she needs all the help she can get. "Please, dear Lord, protect me and my family from all evil persons, all witch charms and all ill wished things." Then, as an afterthought, she adds, "And please protect my friend Amy from all persons with evil intent too, particularly at Summerville House."

She breathes a sigh of relief as she finishes covering the bottle with the soil and some loose leaves to avoid discovery. Ray then gives a cough to warn her that someone is walking by and so she stays concealed until he whispers, "All clear."

She then leaves the churchyard and rejoins him outside the perimeter wall. "I feel much better now that has been done. At my first opportunity I am going to prick Apsey with a pin to draw blood and block her supernatural powers. I will make it look like an accident, but I cannot risk that with the master and mistress for fear of being dismissed."

"Well, if Lettie comes up with any more ideas I will come and let you know. We are here supporting you, Jean; you are not alone and if you need help, or if you are at all frightened, you must come home. Bring Amy with you if you have to. You cannot live your life in fear."

"No, you are right, of course, Ray. There are other places we can work and if it gets unbearable that is what we will do. Thank you for listening and for helping me. You go on back now and take good care of Ma and Pa."

"I will, I promise. Good luck, Jean."

"Bye, Ray, thank you."

They both wave as Jean sets off alone. She fondles the tiger eye in her pocket for reassurance and mentally prepares herself for the long walk back to Summerville House.

CHAPTER 11 *(Spring 1853)*

GOWNS AND GARTERS

For Rebecca the winter passes with lots of crisp, frosty walks and fireside playtimes with Aurora. Soon the weather improves and all the spring flowers are basking in the gentle sunlight.

Susan Moore has a little girl in April and they call her Lilly. Rebecca takes Aurora up to Camp Road in her perambulator to see Luke and his new baby sister. Aurora and Luke play together as always and Rebecca chats to Susan about the birth of her daughter. It appears that Susan has no problems with childbirth or with caring for the babies and she is blissfully happy.

"Will you have any more children, do you think?" asks Rebecca.

"It is in the hands of the Lord, Becky, but I do hope so. I am never happier than when I am suckling my wee babies."

"I cannot wait to have a family of my own, either. You are very lucky, Susan, because both of your children are healthy and beautiful."

"I know, we are truly blessed. John and I are very thankful for it."

As Rebecca walks slowly back down Pound Lane she muses over where she and Ben will eventually live in Chiswell and whether or not they will be blessed with children. She decides that ideally she would like two girls and two boys, and she dreams of her future happiness with her beloved Ben.

Joshua has had invitations and calling cards left over the Christmas period to visit local landowners and he feels the time has come to pay back their hospitality with a select summer ball. Mr Fairway and Clara are invited to the ball and Mr Fairway asks Joshua if Louisa might be allowed to accompany Clara. Joshua agrees and all those in the Dower House are invited to attend, so that Louisa will not be singled out for special attention. Because of this Lettie is among the extra help he has brought in for the event. Joshua wants his sister also to enjoy the party but she declines the invitation, preferring to remain anonymously in the background looking after Aurora and enjoying the spectacle from the gallery. Mrs Abbott has written all the invitations and Joshua has arranged for a pianist and the string section of Ivell Town Band to come to play for them.

A fortnight before the occasion Clara brings a selection of gowns for Louisa to try on.

"Oh, Clara, they are beautiful! Thank you so much for bringing them. What colour are you wearing?"

"This peach-coloured one; I thought I would bring it to show you, what do you think?" She holds out the dress with its white floral underskirt and plain peach-coloured silk overskirt, revealing the patterned material in a wide front central panel.

"I particularly like the off the shoulder, tiered and frilled white lace collar that hides the capped sleeves underneath. I am going to wear it with these white lace gloves."

"It is lovely; won't you put it on and show me, while I try on the others?"

They are in Louisa's bedroom in the Dower House and, in addition to her own gown, Clara has brought three others for Louisa to try on; a lemon one, a rose-coloured one and a deep blue one. Louisa is drawn to the beautiful tiered midnight blue taffeta and she tries that one on first. It has a pretty, plunging, frilled, cream lace décolletage and a nipped in waistline.

"Oh, Clara, it feels wonderful; can you do up the buttons for me please?"

"That looks marvellous on you and it is a perfect fit."

"I don't think the lemon shot silk is really my colour, but I think I will try on the rose one just in case I like it better." The rose embroidered muslin dress has burgundy-coloured scalloped lace, drooping in folds from the waistband, and a dark burgundy-coloured velvet bodice, decorated with some more of the burgundy lace. Clara has brought with her the matching burgundy lace gloves. The whole effect reminds Louisa of pink rose petals with their darker underside, but it does not go with the rich auburn hue of Louisa's hair.

"This is a beautiful dress, Clara, but I think I prefer the blue one for me."

"I agree, Louisa. That is the one for you. It is glorious, put it on again."

"I can see why you chose the peach, Clara. It really suits your colouring and is so pretty."

Once Louisa has put the blue gown back on, the two girls experiment with their hair pinned up in different styles to go with their costumes. Suddenly Louisa has a horrid thought. "Oh dear! Oh Clara, I have no dancing slippers to wear."

"Try on my shoes; see if we are the same size."

Louisa unlaces one of her ankle boots and tries on Clara's left shoe. "It is too small, Clara. Oh dear, I cannot wear my old boots." She removes the shoe despondently. "My only hope is perhaps Rosa has some she can lend me, I will ask her later."

"Does Rosa have a gown? Because she could borrow one of these if she wants to."

"That is very kind of you, Clara, shall we try her room and see if she is there?"

They go along the landing to Rosa's bedroom and tap on her door. She answers their knock quite quickly and stands back in surprise to see them all dressed up in their finery.

"My goodness, don't you both look splendid!"

"Clara wondered if you had a gown for the ball, Rosa, only she has two spare if you would like to try them?"

"That is very kind of you, Clara, I was planning to titivate my Mayday frock, but I will look like the country cousin compared to you two."

"Please do try one on, I think the rose-coloured one will look fabulous on you," says Clara enthusiastically.

Louisa watches as Rosa removes her clothes and dresses in Clara's gown and then she broaches the subject of the shoes. "Rosa, I have a bit of a problem, you don't happen to have a pair of dainty shoes I could borrow by any chance?"

"I am sorry, Lou. I only have the one pair and I will be wearing those myself."

"It is so disappointing, but I will have to tell the master that I will not be able to attend the ball, because I will look ridiculous in Clara's dress with my buttoned boots," says Louisa sadly.

"Oh, Louisa, that is such a pity. I was looking forward to having some fun with you and Clara, and you look so lovely in that gown," says Rosa dejectedly.

"There is still two weeks to go before the big day, maybe we could make some," suggests Clara.

"I would not know where to start; besides, we don't have the materials and I don't really have the time, as we are working later each day to help with the preparations and I am on duty next Sunday."

"Oh dear, Louisa. Don't look so sad, I am sure we will think of something."

On Monday morning Louisa approaches Joshua's study nervously. What will he think of her having no suitable shoes? She taps lightly on the study door and hears his response, "Come in." Gingerly she opens the door and enters, standing before him at his desk.

He looks up and smiles. "How can I help you, Louisa?"

"I am sorry, my Lord, but I am unable to attend the summer ball."

"But I thought you were looking forward to it?"

"I was, my Lord, but I have no suitable dancing shoes."

"Oh, forgive me; I did not think of that, Louisa, I am sorry. Please don't look so crest-fallen, I am sure we will be able to get you a pair in Ivell. You can accompany me to the cordwainer in the borough and we shall have some made for you."

"Are you sure, my Lord?" Louisa's eyes fill with hope.

"Of course, we cannot let Clara down after all her help with your gown."

"I am most truly grateful, my Lord," she says, smiling shyly.

"Is that the only problem? Do you have everything else you need?"

"I do, my Lord, thank you."

"Perhaps we should go on your half day."

"That is Wednesday, my Lord."

"Well, if you could wait for me in the vestibule after you finish your duties then we can go in the curricle."

"Thank you, my Lord. May I return to my duties?"

"Of course, Louisa. I will look forward to our jaunt on Wednesday." He says this with a glint in his eye and she knows he is teasing her, but does not dare to comment.

Louisa is waiting in the front entrance at noon when Rebecca joins her. "Are you coming to town too, Becky?" she asks.

"Yes, Joshua has to purchase some more maids outfits from the drapery and I thought I would like to try one on for Lettie. She is about the same size as me and Mrs Abbott has given him the details of the other three girls from Coker."

Louisa smiles with relief, she will not be so nervous with Rebecca there.

"Isn't this exciting, it promises to be such a spectacle." Rebecca adjusts her sun bonnet impatiently. "I have never been to a ball before; I shall so enjoy watching all the dancing and seeing all the wonderful gowns."

"Why didn't you accept your brother's invitation to join us, Becky?"

"Because I would rather watch it all from the gallery; I don't know the dance steps, I am not good at making the small talk and I would be nervous without Ben. Joshua was quite upset when I said I did not want to join in. He said it was partly for me that he had decided to have the ball, but I explained that I would prefer to enjoy myself watching the spectacle without getting all het up and I think he understands. Besides, Lettie is joining the maids and will need some help."

"I am nervous too, you know, and I am sure Rosa is as well, but it is a wonderful opportunity for us and very kind of your brother to allow us to join in."

With that, Joshua arrives. "Are you ready, ladies?" They both reply in the affirmative. "Billy is bringing round the landau as there are three of us."

First stop is the cordwainer's in the borough, where the man takes Louisa's measurements and she chooses a stylish design in the finest, softest kid. The slippers will be ready the following Wednesday and she is very happy with her choice and the man's attention to detail.

The next stop is the drapers in Silver Street, where Rebecca tries on the dove grey dress for Lettie and Joshua purchases four sets of white caps and aprons for the extra girls and the correct sizes of grey frocks, plus a new footman's livery for John Moore. Louisa is looking at a pair of very fine, cream lace, elbow-length gloves. Suddenly she feels someone standing close behind her and spins round. Joshua says, "Try them on, Louisa, and see if they fit you."

Her face burns as she tries on the gloves shakily. They are too loose for her.

"Do you have any more gloves like this in a smaller size, Mrs Burton?"

"I will just look for you, my Lord." The proprietor opens a drawer behind her deep wooden counter and searches among its contents, bringing up a smaller pair triumphantly. "Here we are, madam, would you care to try them on?"

"Yes, Mrs Burton, she would, thank you very much." Joshua takes the gloves and passes them to Louisa, who trembles self-consciously as she tries them on. Joshua can see immediately that they are a perfect fit. "They will do fine, Mrs Burton, what is the total please?"

Rebecca comes up to see what is going on. "The

master has bought me some cream lace gloves to go with my outfit; they will match beautifully with the neckline of Clara's gown." She lowers her voice, "He is too generous though, it makes me feel beholden."

"Don't be silly, Lou, we have to keep up appearances; we don't want all the local upper-crust landed gentry looking down on us, do we?"

"No, I suppose not."

"Well, there you are then, just enjoy it. You have a nice pair of evening gloves and some lovely dancing shoes; all you need now is a gown of your own." She laughs and Louisa laughs with her.

They walk with Joshua back to the landau. "Thank you, my Lord, for the gloves and dance shoes, I am most truly grateful."

"You are very welcome, Louisa, but in return I would like the first dance."

"Of course, my Lord," she says uneasily. She feels the blood drain from her face. *How will she be able to stop her heart racing wildly once held in his arms? How will she be able to dance with him and hide from him her true feelings?*

When Louisa returns from town Joshua drops her off at her home for the rest of her half day. On her parents return from the glove factory that night, she shows them the lace evening gloves that Joshua has bought for her and tells them about the dancing shoes that he has ordered to be made especially for her to go with Clara's gown.

Mrs Bonfield is thrilled for her daughter. "Oh how I would love to be there, you are so lucky, Lou."

"You just watch out for those toffs, Lou Lou, don't let them take advantage," warns her father.

"I won't, Pa. Rosa and Clara will be there with me all the time."

"That is all right then, but stay among your friends, there is safety in numbers."

"What colour is your gown, Lou?" asks her mother.

"It is a deep midnight blue."

"Ah! That will look lovely with your red hair. Would you like me to cover your hair comb with some blue cloth and decorate it with some cream lace flowers?"

"Oh, Ma! That would be lovely if you could."

"I will see what I can do between now and next Wednesday."

The following Wednesday Joshua sends Louisa with Billy into Ivell to pick up her dancing shoes. She tries them on in the shop and, when the cordwainer has his back to her, she does a few dance steps to test them out. It is like walking on air they are so comfortable. Joshua has paid for them in advance and, as long as she is happy, she can walk out of the workshop with them. She thanks the cordwainer for his wonderful workmanship and goes out to the waiting gig.

Billy drops her off at her home and she rushes indoors so that she can try them on again. On the mantelpiece she spots her comb, transformed into a pretty blue and white lace floral fascinator. "Ma, you are so clever, it is beautiful," she says to herself.

When her parents arrive home, tired from a hard day's work at the factory, Louisa has made a savoury cobbler for their supper.

"What is that tasty, mouth watering smell coming from the kitchen?" says her father. "I am starving."

"I have made us some supper, Pa. Thank you so much for titivating my hair comb, it looks wonderful, Ma." She pins it in among her thick curls high on the back of her head, with the white lacy bits hanging down.

"It looks even better than I imagined, love," says her mother.

"And look at my lovely new dancing shoes," she says, popping on the shoes quickly to show them off.

"You will look a picture, Lou Lou, I am sure," says her father.

"They look lovely, darling; I only wish I could see you in the gown as well."

"Nevermind, Ma; one day I will have one of my own, even if we have to make it ourselves from old curtains." They both laugh.

"Do you have a necklace?"

"Not a suitable one, no."

"Well, I have a pearl drop on a choker that I wore on our wedding day. Do you think that will go with your gown?"

"Let's see." They go upstairs to her parent's room and her mother goes to her bottom drawer, where she still has her wedding costume. From a velvet covered box she takes the pearl drop necklace.

Louisa has never seen it before. She tries it on her slender neck and with the comb the effect is delightful. Louisa can imagine herself in the whole costume and she kisses her mother warmly. "This would be perfect, Ma. Are you sure you don't mind me borrowing it?"

"Of course not darling, when else is it going to see the light of day!"

"Thank you, Ma, what good fortune that it all matches so well."

From downstairs they can hear her father.

"Come on, you two, hurry up, my stomach thinks my throat has been cut."

Later that evening Elsie has lit the gas lamps in the ballroom and Louisa joins Rosa, Clara and Mrs Abbott there to rehearse some of the dances that the town band players are likely to select. But they soon realise that they need four more people, preferably men, to rehearse properly. Mrs Abbott sends Louisa to ask Joshua if he and Gareth would care to join them and Rosa runs off to find Billy Riddick and Malachi. Because Lucy and Isaac are with Malachi at the time, they decide to come along to help and Isaac brings his concertina, Lucy plays the grand piano and Mrs Abbott calls out the moves as they dance. Of course Rosa is paired with Malachi, Mrs Abbott with Gareth, Clara with Billy and Louisa with Joshua.

"I think we should commence with the easier dances to warm up and so we shall start with the military two step," says Mrs Abbott. "Each couple stands in a circle, the gentleman with his partner on his right, arms around each other's waist, and all facing anti-clockwise. Start with your outside feet. Right: Isaac, Lucy, off you go."

The music starts up and Mrs Abbott calls, "Heel, toe, heel, toe; step forward for the count of three: one, two, three. Turn towards each other, arms round the waist. Heel, toe, heel, toe; step forward to the count of three: one, two, three…"

Louisa cannot believe Joshua is so close, she can feel his muscles through his shirt when he has his arms around her, she can feel his warmth and she is loving it.

"Turn to face each other, jump and kick right leg to the left, jump and kick left to the right.

Gentlemen raise your right hand above your head and ladies a complete turn underneath and then polka to the count of eight. One, two…"

Despite her anxieties Louisa cannot help but enjoy dancing with her master. He is so handsome and he looks so gently and kindly towards her, it is easy to imagine there is love between them. Their dancing is in perfect time with the music and it is natural and instinctive.

"Once more from the beginning, heel, toe, heel toe…"

"Well done everyone, that was excellent," says Mrs Abbott. "Now let's go through the Gay Gordon's before we try the quadrilles."

"I like the Gay Gordon's but it does make me feel rather dizzy," says Rosa.

"Well, just spin a little slower, Rosa, and see how you get on," says Mrs Abbott. "Now gentlemen, the shadow hold please, ladies on the right, your right arm over their shoulders holding their right hand, and your left hand across your chest holding their left hand. No, Billy, all facing anti-clockwise please and starting with the left foot. Right, we are ready, music please. Walk forward for three and on four about turn to the right and walk backwards for four: one, two, three, four and repeat…"

"Next, drop the shadow hold but remain side by side, gentlemen take your partner's left hand in your right hand and raise your arm for the lady to spin underneath: one, two, three, four, five, six, seven, eight. Not too fast, Malachi, poor Rosa doesn't like it."

"Sorry, Rosa."

"Well done, now into a waltz hold and polka round the room for a count of eight and back to the shadow hold to start again. Excellent, I think you are all familiar with that one now. How do you feel, Rosa?"

"The room is still spinning; I think I might have to leave that one out on the night."

"Well, I am afraid the quadrilles are more complicated. Has anyone danced these before?"

"I have danced the mazourka, the caledonian and the lancers before," says Clara timidly.

"Well, I think I will need your help with this then, Clara. If you could help Billy, Rosa and Malachi and I will concentrate on Mr Williams, Lord Dryer and Louisa. Now, before commencing each quadrille the music plays eight bars, during which time the gentlemen salute their partners, after which they salute the other couples. Alright, let's form the square, ladies on the gentleman's right and we will start with the mazourka." She goes to the piano to help Lucy find the correct music.

"Mrs Abbott could take this up as a side line; she is so good she terrifies me," Joshua whispers to Louisa, who giggles covertly, aware of a certain intimacy between them.

"Well I am very glad of the lessons, because I am sure I would make a fool of myself and any partner without them."

Mrs Abbott returns taking her place next to Joshua with Gareth next to her, forming the right hand corner of the square. Lucy and Isaac play the first eight bars and after the salutes they all join hands and form a circle.

"Now then, four bars to the left and four bars to the right. Advance with joined hands to the centre, through four bars and then retire back to reopen the circle, through four bars and then back to: four bars to the left and four bars to the right. Top couple, Clara and Billy, and bottom couple, Mr Williams and myself, make a *chaine Anglaise*, that is, we advance and Clara and myself cross over, Billy and Mr Williams link their left arms at the elbow and turn rapidly, which makes a change of ladies. Then Billy moves forward and dances with Louisa and Gareth goes forward and dances with Rosa, we all repeat the figure and then return to our original partners."

"That is good; now Rosa and Malachi, Louisa and Joshua perform the same figure."

There is then a lot of hesitation and giggling as they don't quite get it right and thus the evening progresses, until finally they have also practiced the lancers, the Caledonian quadrille and lastly the minuet, which is somewhat more sedate even though the movements are quite complex.

Finally Joshua suggests they all go and have a nightcap before retiring, everyone by this time being quite weary. Clara declines, as it will be quite late by the time she gets home and Billy goes off to the stable to get the gig.

"I did enjoy that and I am so glad we had lessons tonight. I would have been at a loss without them," says Rosa to Mrs Abbott.

"Do you think that maybe we need some more practice and should have another go tomorrow?" asks Louisa eagerly.

"Well, it really depends on Isaac and Lucy, you had better ask them," says Mrs Abbott.

They are both happy to play for them and when Billy brings the gig round they ascertain that everyone without exception all enjoyed it so much that they agree to meet the following evening. "Don't worry, Clara, I will come and fetch you and take you home like today."

They all wish Clara and Billy goodnight and follow Joshua through into the Oak. There he hands round Madeira wine, port and brandy according to taste. Louisa has a glass of Madeira; she has not tasted it since Christmas and has forgotten how sweet and potent it is, but she thoroughly enjoys it, possibly consuming it rather too quickly. She decides to broach the subject that has been worrying her recently. "Have you had many acceptances to your invitations, Mrs Abbott?"

"Yes, nearly all have responded. Unfortunately the Dampiers of Montacute House are going to be away in London and Mrs Moreton of West Coker Manor is in a delicate condition and thus confined, so they have declined. But Samuel and Edith Bridewell, plus Alicia, Keziah and Serena of Clifton Maybank have accepted. The Helyars of Coker Court, um… the Seymours from Sutton Bingham Manor, plus Rupert and Ashleigh; the Stourtons of Preston Plucknett and there was someone else… ah yes, Sir Oliver and Lady Annabel Meakins of Summerville House, plus Nathan and Olivia have all accepted also."

Louisa turns pale, despite the Madeira wine. She knew in her heart that he would be there, but she dreads it.

Joshua is listening to the conversation knowing that, although he is aware it is going to be difficult for Louisa, he put the Meakins' family on the guest list in order to meet this man for himself. He watches her reaction now and realises that he will have to be vigilant on the night and ensure that she is not too upset by this encounter.

CHAPTER 12 *(June 21st 1853)*

THE SUMMER BALL

The day of the ball turns out to be fine and sunny and Alvington Manor is a hive of industry, with everyone – including the extra maids, Lettie and Rebecca – caught up in the preparations. Soon the house and all the china, glasses and cutlery are sparkling brightly. Louisa and Rosa have been busy decorating the ballroom; the bandstand, the side tables and the gallery balustrading are all festooned with garlands of leaves and flowers. John Moore has placed flax torches all along the carriageway and around the front gravel courtyard, ready for lighting as darkness falls.

Joshua is himself up a step-ladder replacing the candles in the chandeliers as Rebecca passes them up to him. For Mrs Abbott it is very strange to have Joshua and his sister getting so involved with the organisation of this party. She is used to being instructed by her employers and a strict social code, where the domestic staff never fraternises with the upper echelons. For her this is a refreshing change, if a little disconcerting, but she is quite certain that their guests will frown on this liberal arrangement.

Finally their work is done and Mrs Abbott and the girls leave to prepare themselves. Louisa washes her hair with a henna shampoo, rubbing it dry with a towel, then winding it up in rags. She strips and washes herself at her washstand. She dresses in her chemise, drawers and hooped petticoat and then her corset. She runs along the landing and taps at Rosa's bedroom door. "Rosa, can you please lace me up?"

Rosa emerges dressed in her robe, her hair also in rags. She has just put some rouge on her cheeks and has not smoothed it, making her look like an Aunt Sally doll. "Come on in; just let me finish doing my face, Lou."

Moments later Rosa is pulling the laces tight, while Louisa holds tightly to the bed post and then Louisa does the same for Rosa. They both look at each other and burst out laughing. "My! We look well endowed," says Rosa, "and these gowns are not going to cover much either. Will you help me with my gown Louisa and then I will come and help you with yours?"

Louisa lifts the gown over Rosa's head; she slips her arms through the sleeves as it drops down into place and Louisa buttons the back. Rosa adjusts the folds to sit nicely over her petticoats and turns to look in the mirror.

"Oh, Rosa, you look beautiful."

"Do you think Malachi will think so?"

"Of course he will, he would have to be blind not to. Come on, let's go and do mine."

Soon both girls have dressed themselves and their hair and are ready for the ball. They go downstairs to their small drawing room to wait for Mrs Abbott. Gareth is going to pop over to accompany Louisa and Mrs Abbott, and Malachi is calling for Rosa.

There is a tap at the door and Gareth enters. "Are you ready?" he asks.

Louisa calls to Mrs Abbott, whose room is on the ground floor, and she emerges all dressed up in her finery.

Gareth looks impressed. "Why, Mrs Abbott, you

look very handsome this evening, and you too my dears, most attractive. Please take my arm, ladies."

"I am going to wait for Malachi," says Rosa, smiling, "I am sure he won't be long."

Louisa and Mrs Abbott take his proffered arms and they set off to the ballroom, where they join those of the staff attending who are milling around chatting. Louisa spots Joshua instructing Gareth and Michael; she is observing him when he glances in her direction and notices her dressed in all her finery. His look of warm appreciation is gratifying and she smiles back happily.

In next to no time the guests are arriving, carriage after carriage turning into the driveway and guests alighting, one after the other. Elsie takes their hats, canes and jackets, and Emily escorts them through to the ballroom, where the band is playing Chopin's prelude in E minor and two maids are stood with trays of champagne.

Michael Porter, dressed in his gold braided footman livery and wearing his powdered wig, announces each party as they enter the ballroom. "Samuel and Edith Bridewell, with their daughters Serena, Keziah and Alicia."

Joshua greets them, introducing them to Louisa and Mrs Abbott. Louisa thinks that Alicia must be the youngest, but they are all very pretty and beautifully dressed. Mrs Abbott engages their parents in conversation and the girls turn to Louisa. "Would you care for some champagne?" She asks them.

"Oh yes please, I love bubbly," says Alicia.

Louisa passes them all a glass.

"What a glorious evening and still so warm outside," says Serena.

"Yes indeed, we still have the windows open in here for the fresh air," agrees Louisa, trying her best to keep up appearances.

"Have you come from afar?" asks Keziah.

"Not at all, I live in the Dower House."

"Oh, I am not familiar with it," says Alicia.

Then, thankfully, Clara and her father arrive. "Please excuse me," says Louisa and she joins Clara just as the Seymour's are announced and Rupert and Ashleigh join the Bridewell girls.

Then the Reverend Phelps arrives with the curate from the Coker parish.

Louisa whispers to Clara, "Keziah Bridewell has just asked if I have travelled far and I said from the Dower House!"

Clara giggles, "Well you spoke the truth."

"Yes, but the funny thing is, she replies, 'Oh I don't know it', as though it is a fancy manor house somewhere!"

Clara chuckles again, "Well, it is not her fault she doesn't know who we are, is it?"

Malachi is escorting Rosa across the drive when the Meakins' carriage rolls up. John Moore, dressed in his new footman's livery, opens the carriage door and hands down the ladies.

Malachi had mentioned to Rosa as soon as he saw her that he felt a little uncomfortable in his unfashionable burgundy jacket, but she had reassured him that it was perfect, because it matched her gown so well. However, as Nathan Meakins steps down from the carriage he throws Malachi such a demeaning look that he wants to challenge him over it.

Rosa feels his muscles stiffen in the crook of her elbow. "What is it, Malachi?" she asks.

"It is that arrogant snob, looking down his toffee-nose at me."

"Just ignore him, Mal, you cannot make a fuss and let Joshua down. We are honoured to be invited."

"Well, don't let me catch him alone, is all I can say."

They follow the Meakins family into the house and, whilst they are handing over their outer garments to Elsie, Rosa and Malachi go on ahead and are announced first. They go immediately to join Louisa and Clara.

Michael Porter then announces, "Mr and Mrs Oliver Meakins, their daughter Olivia and their son Nathan."

Louisa turns around surreptitiously. She does not want him to recognise the family resemblance, but she has to see this despicable man who had, in effect, murdered her little sister. How she despises him; she feels her skin prickle with goose-bumps all over and she shivers in distaste. He looks so cavalier, so relaxed. He should pay for what he has done, but what influence has she to achieve this?

She watches as he makes a beeline for Alicia Bridewell who, with her sisters, is chatting happily with the Seymour brothers and filling up their dance cards. She sees how Alicia is taken in by him and she feels sorry for her.

Then she notices Joshua watching her. She smiles and turns away to her friends. "Shall we reserve ourselves a table?"

"Yes, let us go towards the back so the music is not too loud and we can talk," suggests Rosa. Malachi leads the way and the girls select a table in the corner, put their reticules and fans down on the white tablecloth and take their seats. One of the new maids is circulating with a tray of champagne and they each take a glass.

Clara giggles, "Look at that Serena, she is using

her fan to speak silently to Joshua."

"What do you mean, Clara?" asks Louisa in concern.

"Well, you see, she is looking at Joshua whilst carrying her fan in her left hand and holding it in front of her face."

"And what is that supposed to mean?" prompts Louisa.

"It means that she desires his acquaintance." The girls all surreptitiously watch them. "You see, and now she has closed the fan," says Clara excitedly.

"So has she changed her mind then?" asks Rosa.

Clara shakes her head. "No, not at all, she is saying that she wishes to speak to him."

Rosa is fascinated. "What, by simply closing her fan?"

"Yes."

"Well, what if Joshua does not know about this coded message?" asks Louisa, with concern.

"Then she will be disappointed, won't she." They all laugh.

"Can you see Mrs Abbott? She is talking to Oliver Meakins and is drawing her fan through her hands, what does that mean?" asks Rosa.

"I hate you," giggles Clara.

"I don't suppose she realises what she is doing," says Rosa, "but I would have thought she would have learnt the language of the fan when she was young."

"Well, Alicia Bridewell is being very forward. Do you see her with Nathan Meakins? She is holding the handle of the fan to her lips. That means kiss me," says Clara knowingly.

"I notice she has made sure that her parents are stood behind her and are unable to see what she is up to," says Rosa.

"Well, she is welcome to that one, I cannot stand him," says Louisa.

"She has spotted us," whispers Clara, looking away.

"How do you know?" asks Rosa.

"Because she is twirling her fan in her left hand and that means 'we are watched'. If it was her right hand it would mean 'I love another'."

"Well, I see I have a lot to learn," says Malachi wryly.

Rosa laughs, "You have no need to worry; I don't know the messages myself yet."

"Well, you will be safe from unwanted admirers if you fan yourself very quickly," Clara reassures her. "That means 'I am betrothed'."

"You had better remember that one, Rosa," says Louisa smiling.

"Don't you worry, Malachi, no one here measures up to you."

Malachi beams at Rosa and kisses her affectionately on her forehead. As he looks back up he notices Nathan Meakins watching them.

The bandmaster then announces the first dance, which is a military two step. Louisa sees out of the corner of her eye Joshua putting on his white gloves and making towards her. He bows and says, "I believe you promised me the first dance, Louisa."

She takes his proffered hand and he leads her to the dance floor. Malachi is partnering Rosa, and Clara is spotted by Ashleigh Seymour, who smiles and bows and she accepts his hand. The couples arrange themselves in a circle and the band starts off… heel toe, heel, toe, Louisa remembers it well from their rehearsals and enjoys dancing with Joshua.

"I would like to book the last dance with you, Louisa, and a couple in the middle, if I may."

"Of course, my Lord, it will be my pleasure,"

she says between moves. "At least we are used to each other, I am quite anxious about dancing with another partner."

"You will be fine, Louisa, you are a natural."

"Thank you, my Lord."

"I must say, you are looking quite beautiful tonight."

"Thank you, my Lord."

"That gown really is a gorgeous colour and suits your rich, auburn hair wonderfully."

"Thank you, my Lord."

"Are the slippers comfortable?"

"Yes they are, my Lord, thank you."

"I am glad." She is aware of him looking at her as they dance. "I like the pretty comb in your hair."

"Thank you, my Lord; my mother decorated it for me."

"Well, I think you are the prettiest maiden here this evening."

She feels hotter by the second as he is looking down intently at her. "Thank you, my Lord," she says self-consciously. She feels embarrassed and foolish. All she can say is 'Thank you, my Lord'. *He must find me very boring, but what else should I do? I am beholden to him for everything!* When the dance ends they return to their table and Louisa writes on her card the dances that Joshua selects.

Joshua leans in close to her and says in a low voice, "Mrs Abbott tells me it is not good form, apparently, to monopolise a lady, otherwise I would pick you for every dance. But I am forced to dance with others and so I must go and reserve some more partners. I will join you in the mazourka later." He turns to Malachi. "Come on, Malachi, you need to book a few more dances; let's go and book up the Bridewell sisters."

Louisa fans herself very quickly to cool her burning

cheeks. *Why does he always say such flattering things to me?*
He must be aware of the social barriers between us.

Clara notices. "If you keep doing that, Lou Lou, everyone will think that you are engaged."

"Whatever do you mean?"

"The rapid fanning, that is what it means."

Louisa's face goes even redder. "That I am engaged to Joshua?"

"No!" Clara laughs, "Just that you are engaged."

With that Louisa notices Nathan Meakins making a beeline for their corner.

"I need some air, excuse me." She takes the back door from the ballroom before he notices her, but she remains there in the shadows listening and peeping occasionally until he has gone.

Nathan Meakins books Clara for the mazourka quadrille and asks Rosa to dance the Gay Gordon's.

"I am sorry, but I am afraid I must decline…"

Before she can finish what she is going to say he stalks off muttering under his breath, "I was only being charitable, offering you my hand in the first place."

Rosa is offended. She looks at Clara. "I was only going to ask if he might select another dance, as I am unable to do that one, I get so dizzy. There was no need for him to be so insulting."

They watch as he goes off in a huff towards the stairs to the gallery, where Rebecca and Lettie have a bird's eye view of the gathering.

The Seymour brothers then turn up and ask the girls to reserve the lancers for them and when Louisa returns they each book her for the Gay Gordon's and the minuet.

Rebecca and Lettie have been having a break from their duties and are leaning over the gallery balustrade watching all the goings on. Lettie has been telling Rebecca who is who among the guests.

"Don't I recognise that man down there?" She nods in the direction of Nathan Meakins.

"Yes, don't you remember the hunt on Boxing Day? He was the man whose horse kicked you."

"Of course, that's right. He seems to look younger in his frock coat, but yes, I remember it well. I had the bruises as a reminder for some time."

"Do you see Mary Sandford dancing with Jack Hawkins, and their partners Molly and Percy sitting it out?"

"Yes."

Lettie drops her voice, "Well, Mary and Jack are having an affair."

"How do you know that?"

"Harry Sandford told me that Jack was always popping in to help his mother and then one day he caught them kissing. He hates Jack now."

"Oh, that is sad for Percy and Molly."

"Oh, they don't have a clue."

Rebecca then notices Nathan Meakins making for Louisa and Rosa's table, but her thoughts are interrupted by Elsie's voice. "Lettie, can you please help me with the buffet?" Lettie turns to go.

Rebecca says, "I'll be along in a minute, I am just observing something."

Rebecca watches as Louisa leaves the ballroom; she sees Meakins booking Clara for a dance and she notes him walking off in a huff after speaking to Rosa. It is a good job Malachi wasn't there. Then she realises that he is making towards the gallery. She hesitates as he strides up the stairs and, as he reaches the gallery landing, she turns and walks off slowly down the corridor towards the bedrooms, in the hope that he hasn't noticed her. He is fast on her heels: suddenly, alarmingly, she is grabbed from behind and pushed through the nearest door. It is the room opposite the nursery. *What is he going to do to her? Should she scream?* Her blood runs cold. She is afraid of frightening Aurora; afraid of Meakins discovering the child, but she also realises no one would hear her downstairs over the noise of the band.

She tries to dodge him and escape, but he shoves her roughly onto the bed. He is strong and angry. She is terrified and mute with fear. She fights him, kicking and scratching, but he quickly drops his trousers and is upon her, using his body to pin her down. He smells of the Makassar oil in his hair. The more she kicks and struggles the more excited he gets and he laughs at her feebleness. He puts his hand over her mouth, pulls up her skirts and pulls her drawers down to her ankles. The pain as he enters her, tearing her pure and chaste body, is sharp and quick, but as he moves powerfully and agonisingly inside her she wants to vomit.

"You know you like it, so why fight me?"

His knees are digging into and bruising her legs, his free hand is squeezing her breast tightly and painfully… and then it is tangled in her hair, pinning her head to the bed… then his mouth replaces the hand over her mouth, and he bites her lip and she tastes blood and he is squeezing her other breast firmly and aggressively… and his tongue is penetrating in and out… and touching her tongue. It is unbearable. Whenever will it end? Then she can feel him twitching and ejaculating inside her.

She gasps for air, as he collapses on top of her and then removes himself from her person, wiping his shameful organ against her drawers. He stands up and pathetically she pushes her skirts down to hide her disgrace.

"You've never had the honour of a gentleman

like me before, have you?" She can hear him pulling on his trousers and buttoning his flies. "You're a buxom wench and I like my tarts virginal," he says harshly, as he moves towards the bedroom door, and then he sniggers. "Don't you want to say thank you for my favours?" He opens the door and Rebecca cringes as the lamplight from the corridor falls on her, and she turns away from him. "Please yourself," he says, as he closes the door and goes off back to the dancing.

Rebecca lays there in the darkness, her tears soaking the pillow. *How can she bear this? The anger and humiliation will live with her forever. This moment was supposed to be warm and loving and reserved especially for her Ben. However can she hide this from them all?*

Joshua and Louisa are taking the floor for the mazourka with Rosa and Malachi when Nathan Meakins returns to the ballroom and, as promised, requests the pleasure of Clara's hand for this dance. To Louisa's vexation they join their quadrille, along with Keziah Bridewell and Rupert Seymour. Louisa spends all her time avoiding his glances, her eyes only for Joshua and her friends, while Malachi cannot take his eyes off Meakins, just waiting for another slight to either him or to Rosa. Joshua seems to be observing the man surreptitiously.

They are glad when the dance is over. As Louisa, Rosa and Malachi return to their table, Meakins escorts Clara back with them and then excuses himself, and Joshua goes off to announce a short interval and that buffet refreshments are being served in the dining room.

While Lettie is serving Louisa and her friends, she mentions that she hasn't seen Rebecca for some time. "I've not seen her for a while, not since we were chatting together up on the gallery."

Louisa recollects Meakins striding off angrily towards the gallery stairs and alarm bells ring. Not yet having selected her food, she decides to go and find Rebecca. From the gallery she looks down at the dwindling numbers of folk left in the ballroom. There is no sign of Rebecca. She decides to peep in on Aurora while she is upstairs and check the bedrooms before going down to the kitchen.

Aurora is sleeping soundly, but as Louisa creeps back out onto the landing she can hear the sound of someone weeping. She listens at the opposite door and there it is, the sorrowful sound of someone crying. She opens the door quietly and sees Rebecca lying on the bed, weeping her heart out. She enters the room and closes the door silently behind her and then opens the curtains to let the moonlight in. Rebecca opens her eyes warily.

"It is only me, Becky," she whispers. "Whatever is wrong?"

"Oh, Louisa, it is too horrible. I cannot tell you." She turns her tear-stained face away from her.

"Of course you can, Becky. We are friends, we can tell each other anything."

"I cannot, it is unspeakable and I am ruined."

"Becky, whatever is troubling you will be improved by sharing it with a friend."

Rebecca fumbles in her pocket for her handkerchief and then wipes away her tears and blows her nose. She looks up at Louisa revealing the pain in her eyes. "I am so ashamed, I was so stupid, but... I cannot bear the truth of it alone, do you swear... it will be just between the two of us?"

"Of course, Becky, whatever has happened?"

"It was that revolting Nathan Meakins. I was watching him from the balcony as he went over to your table and I saw you leave." She sniffs. "He seemed annoyed with Rosa and stalked off in a huff. Before I could think straight, he was striding up the stairs to the gallery. I did not want to meet him going down... because he was horrid to me the last time when his horse kicked me... and so I was trying to avoid him by going into the corridor to the bedrooms, but he followed me. I was scared he would discover Aurora... but I had nowhere to turn. He came up behind me and pushed me in here..." She bursts into tears again. "And he raped me Louisa... he raped me."

Louisa feels outraged, but she pushes her anger aside and puts her arms around Rebecca. "There, there, don't cry, Becky. He is not worth it and I am sure he will get his comeuppance. Come on darling; let me help you to your own bedroom." She settles Rebecca in her own room and goes down to the kitchen to tell Lettie that Rebecca is unwell with a headache and that she has retired early. Then she goes back up with a ewer of hot water for her to wash and a mug of hot chocolate.

"Thank you so much, Louisa. You had better go back, or you will be missed."

"Don't worry, they are all eating at the moment, so I have not missed any dances, but I will go back now and leave you to sleep. I am truly sorry this has happened, but please try not to worry and we will talk confidentially tomorrow."

As Louisa descends the stairs she can hardly contain her fury with Meakins. He is nowhere to be seen in the ballroom and so she goes to the dining room. The room is almost empty and the food somewhat disseminated, but Meakins is at the far end of the buffet table talking to Mr Bridewell. Louisa picks up a plate and makes her selection, working her way towards the two men. As she reaches them she hears Mr Bridewell saying to Meakins, "I will go and tell her the good news," and he goes off in the direction of the ballroom.

Louisa is steeling herself for a confrontation when Meakins suddenly notices her standing nearby. "Do I know you?" he asks her, looking puzzled.

"No, Mr Meakins, we have never been introduced."

"I am sure we have met before, I never forget a pretty face."

This comment alone is enough to incense her, and she says in a firm but low voice, "Don't you try your smarmy ways with me, sir. We may not have been introduced, but I know what you are capable of." Then she adds bitterly, "I suspect you are confusing me with the memory of my dead sister."

She can see the light dawn in his face. "You were responsible for her suicide and now I know you are guilty of raping a friend of mine, so keep away from me, or you will rue the day."

Meakins grabs her arm. "How dare you speak to me like that! That little maid was begging for it, and as for your sister she couldn't keep her hands off me. You make sure you keep your mouth shut! You are no match for me, missy. You're just a cheap trollop like your sister before you."

Louisa shrugs off his hold on her arm and, her promise to Rebecca forgotten, she says defiantly, "I wouldn't want to be in your shoes if Lord Dryer ever discovers that you have raped his sister." The look of dismay on his face is reward enough for now and Louisa turns from him to return to the ballroom.

As she settles down next to her friends, she watches Meakins as he rejoins the Bridewell family. His countenance is completely transformed into a charming personality again. She sees Mr Meakins senior and Mr Bridewell going towards the bandstand. "Before the dancing begins again, with your permission Mr Dryer, my son would like to make an announcement."

Nathan Meakins then takes the hand of Alicia Bridewell and leads her to join their fathers. "I have known this charming lady for some time now and, since all her family and close friends have already been informed of our relationship, I have been granted permission by her father to make this declaration. I take great pleasure in proclaiming the betrothal between myself and this lovely lady, Miss Alicia Rose Bridewell."

He lifts her hand to his lips and kisses her as everyone applauds. Joshua looks for Louisa's reaction, noting her black expression. Louisa wants to murder him.

The band strikes up for the Gay Gordon's and Louisa and Clara are partnering the Seymour brothers. Joshua is dancing with Serena Bridewell, Keziah is partnered with Gareth and Mrs Abbott is dancing with Malachi, but Louisa notices curiously that Meakins is not dancing.

Whilst politely talking with Alicia and her family, Meakins is using this opportunity to observe everyone while they are unaware. He understands the language of the fan from years of social intercourse with women. He notices a table of two people, where their respective partners are dancing together, and he picks up the message 'follow me', where the lady is holding her fan in her right hand in front of her face.

The lady gets up to leave and the man follows her. Intrigued, Meakins follows them furtively. They go outside into the garden and Meakins observes them from the cover of the front porch. He observes them kissing in the moonlight. He has seen enough. On his return to the ballroom the Gay Gordon's is ending and the lancers is next on the cards. He is partnering Serena and as Joshua returns her to their table he engages him in conversation.

"Wonderful party, dear boy, but there are quite a few people here who I am not familiar with."

"That is probably because a number of them are the estate staff."

"That is very charitable of you, dear boy. I wouldn't recommend it myself; I think the hoi polloi need to be kept in their places."

"Well, they work very hard for me all year; the least I can do is allow them to let their hair down once in a while."

Joshua turns away from him just as Jack Hawkins and Mary Sandford return to their seats and he feels a tap on his shoulder.

"Who, for example, is that gentleman?"

"That is my ploughman, Jack Hawkins."

"Any relation to Raymond Hawkins of Odcombe?"

"Yes, I believe he is his uncle."

"That is interesting. You see, his nephew works for me occasionally."

"Indeed." Joshua is not enjoying this man's company and is glad when the music strikes up for the lancers. "Please excuse me; I am booked for this dance." He goes to find Louisa.

Joshua is aware of Louisa's increased animosity towards Meakins, but nevertheless he is disappointed that she should be so subdued in his company. "Louisa, has something happened to make you so despondent?"

She sighs deeply and then smiles, "I am sorry, my Lord, I don't mean to be rude. It is that arrogant man Meakins, he is so two-faced. I feel sorry for that Alicia; she does not know what she is taking on."

"I am sure you are right, Louisa, but please don't let it spoil this lovely evening. I am so enjoying dancing with you."

"I am enjoying the dancing too, my Lord."

"It is such a pity Becky did not want to join us. Come to that, I haven't seen her for ages; I hope they are not working her too hard in the kitchen."

"No, my Lord, I saw her earlier and she has had to go and lie down with a headache."

"Oh that is a shame, she looked so happy when I saw her before with Lettie."

As the evening progresses the dance floor is taken over by the younger ones; their elders, energy abating, taking to the sidelines and drinking their nightcaps. The last dance is a waltz and Louisa is taken on a dreamy romantic journey in the arms of her master. She will remember the pleasure of that romantic music and being held gently in those strong muscular arms forever. The only thing to mar her pleasure is the thought of poor Rebecca, lying traumatised upstairs, and the supercilious grin of that conceited rogue Meakins.

The following morning the sun is shining and Joshua is doing his morning exercise rowing around the lake. Louisa watches him for a moment as he moves quickly with powerful strokes, his white, loose-sleeved shirt catching the sunlight. He looks magnificent, so fit and handsome that she cannot stop the yearning in her heart. She turns away, lest he might see her watching him and goes into the house and upstairs to see Rebecca. Something is bothering her about Rebecca's story last night.

She taps gently on Rebecca's bedroom door and enters to find her still in bed.

"How are you feeling, Becky?"

"Sore and bruised and miserable," she replies not lifting her head from the pillow.

"Shall I fetch you some breakfast, sweetheart?"

"No thank you, Louisa, I really don't feel like eating."

"Becky, can I ask you something?"

Becky turns towards her slowly, as if her head is hurting her. "Of course, what is it?"

"You said last night that you were watching Meakins from the balcony, and you saw me leave the room.

"Yes, I did."

"Why were you watching him?"

Rebecca struggles to sit up and puts her hands through her hair distractedly. Louisa plumps up her pillows, and then finally Rebecca seems to come to a decision. She replies, "It was because he was walking in your direction and I wanted to see your reaction."

"But why?"

Rebecca hesitates, for she is sure now that their assumption about Meakins was correct and she does not want to upset Louisa, who has been so good to her, but she cannot lie to her friend. "Because, Lou Lou, Joshua and I believed that Aurora could be your poor sister's child and that Meakins was the loathsome man responsible for her pregnancy. After last night I am certain it is true."

"And that was why you did not want Aurora to wake up?"

"Yes, I did not want him to discover her and possibly put two and two together, like we did."

Louisa sits down beside her, on the edge of the bed. "I see. Well, Becky, if you want me to keep quiet about the awful events of last night then I hope I can count on you to keep quiet about Aurora's father. Please don't confirm your brother's suspicions, as he may feel obliged to inform him."

Rebecca takes Louisa's hand in hers. "It is true then, Louisa?"

"Yes, it is true and I hate that man more than anyone has ever hated anyone in the history of mankind."

Emotional tears fill Rebecca's eyes at their shared wretchedness. "Me too."

"Becky, you are so like my little sister was, so gentle and trusting and naïve."

"To our cost," she replies bitterly.

"Yes, but from now on, I will be like your big sister and look out for you and Aurora. It will be our secret." She wraps her arms around Rebecca and gives her the longest, warmest hug.

CHAPTER 13 *(July 1853)*

CRAFTY SCHEMING

Since Christmas, Hawkins has been racking her brains for a clever way of drawing blood from Apsey. She has thought of using sewing pins, hat pins, even kitchen utensils, but none of her ideas are easy to execute and time has gone on without her accomplishing this task. However, in June the Bridewell ladies are invited to attend for afternoon tea on the lawn at Summerville House. The staff are under pressure to perform their duties meticulously and Mrs Chubb is barking out her orders anxiously from early morning.

Apsey is in the kitchen preparing a breakfast tray for Mistress Olivia and Hawkins suddenly has a plausible plan. Uncharacteristically, she offers to take a damask rose from the arrangement in the drawing room for the mistress's tray. Apsey, always eager to please her mistress, accepts her offer. Hawkins is back in the bustling kitchen in a jiffy, but as she is passing the single bloom to Apsey she suddenly turns, pulling it away just as her hands close over the flower stem and the thorns rip across the palm of her hand. "Ouch!" she cries, looking angrily at Hawkins.

Hawkins looks at the beads of blood with concealed satisfaction. "I am sorry, Apsey, I thought I heard Mrs Faversham calling for me."

"You did that deliberately," says Apsey suspiciously. "I've a good mind to report you to my mistress."

"Of course I didn't, Apsey. You should have been looking what you were doing anyway."

"Come on, you two, stop your bickering and get out of my way," says Mrs Chubb impatiently.

"You had better watch your step, Hawkins. I only have to have a word with my mistress and you will be ancient history," says Apsey haughtily.

"I said I was sorry; it was an accident, there is no need to get nasty," says Hawkins, more confident now that Apsey will have lost her powers of witchcraft.

Apsey picks up the breakfast tray and, tossing her head self-importantly, she marches off to attend her mistress. There is no time to waste arguing, for she has promised to prepare some belladonna drops for her mistress's eyes, as she will be competing with the lovely Bridewell sisters later that day.

No one notices as Hawkins smiles with satisfaction at a task perfectly executed.

The food has been prepared, bees are buzzing in the beautifully manicured borders, two squirrels are playing tag around the newly mown lawns and buzzards are soaring overhead as the sun beams down from a clear blue sky. Wooden folding tables and chairs, with fringed green and cream striped parasols, are set out on the terrace. Lady Annabel has ordered jugs of Pimms Number One Cup and sherry cobbler to be available to the ladies. Nathan and his sister both appear to be agitated as they await the arrival of their honoured guests, but soon they hear the sound of their carriage approaching on the gravelled driveway.

Morton is about to greet the party, with Wadman and the second footman there to hand the ladies down, when Nathan Meakins brushes them aside, and with Olivia also in attendance they personally welcome them into their home. He takes the girls' mother by the arm. "Come on through, ladies, we have everything ready for you out on the terrace, so that we can all enjoy this beautiful sunshine."

As they walk through the French doors out into the garden, Mrs Bridewell says, "How charming!"

Nathan Meakins says to the company in general, but is looking straight at Alicia, "Mama has organised some refreshments for later on, but first I thought you may like to have a game of Pall Mall."

"Oh yes, that is a splendid idea," she looks at her sisters. "We love playing Pall Mall don't we? Come on Keziah." She goes to pass around the mallets. "Are you going to play too Serena?"

"Of course," says Serena, not wanting to be left with the mothers. "I was just going to say hello to Lady Annabel first."

"Oh dear, of course, where are my manners?"

Lady Annabel gets up to greet their guests and the ladies all curtsey, making their personal greetings in turn. Lady Annabel indicates the seating and Mrs Bridewell accepts immediately. "Would you like to take tea, Mrs Bridewell, or would you prefer something a little more summery?" she asks, indicating the jugs of sherry and Pimms Number One standing in buckets of ice.

"I think I ought to take the tea please, Lady Annabel, if it is not too much trouble."

"Not at all; are you young ladies going to play first, or are you also ready for some refreshments?"

Alicia claps her hands gleefully "Oh! Pimms is my absolute favourite, but may I please have some after our game?"

"I think we would all like to play first and then take our refreshments afterwards. Thank you, Lady Annabel," says Serena.

"Of course." She turns to Amy, who stands on duty discreetly beside them. "Proctor, could you please take the cold drinks back into the kitchen for now and ask Hawkins to bring out the tea?"

"Yes, ma'am." Amy picks up the Pimms and goes into the house to give the message to Jean, returning to remove the second jug moments later. On her return she stands in attendance for the duration of the afternoon.

She is impressed by the beauty of the scene before her; the ladies in their colourful gowns and parasols make such a pretty picture against the smooth green lawns and the herbaceous borders. The three Bridewell girls, although they may have different characters, are all full of fun and happiness. There is not a cross word between them and overall Amy thinks they are perfectly lovely girls. She enjoys listening to their happy chatter, the occasional click, as the mallet makes contact with the wooden balls, the birdsong and the buzz of insects, busy in the gentle warmth of the sun.

She can see why the young master has suggested the game of Pall Mall, for it gives him the opportunity to have the occasional intimate conversation with Alicia, who giggles coquettishly at his suggestive comments. She is one of those girls who have a twinkle in their eyes that instantly attracts the men and Amy can see that Nathan Meakins already believes her to be a juicy peach, ripe for plucking.

They are playing the singles version, and Nathan has decided to tutor his fiancée. Olivia and Serena have the black and blue balls and Alicia and Keziah the red and yellow. Amy observes that, although Alicia has a good eye for the ball, Olivia keeps hitting her red balls out of the way, preventing her from running the hoop. She also notes Nathan frowning at his sister, aware that her competitive nature is trying to undo any unfair advantage that he may be giving to his fiancée.

Nevertheless it is Keziah who is the first player to score seven hoops and she is therefore the winner of the game. By the time it has finished all the young ladies are ready to sit down and relax over their refreshments. They all, including Nathan and Olivia, partake of the Pimms, finishing with a glass of the fruity sherry cobbler.

There is a variety of finger sandwiches, freshly baked scones with local clotted cream and a selection of preserves and French pastries, all laid out on silver platters and tiered cake stands. Amy serves the food and pours the drinks; with each glass she fills, her thirst becomes stronger. Whilst the ladies are seated under the parasols she is standing in the full sun. She is grateful for the slight protection of her white cap, but she would give anything for a sip of the sherry cobbler, with its fruity bouquet tempting and tantalising her the whole afternoon.

She listens to the ladies idle chatter until Keziah makes a newsworthy comment. "Papa tells me that according to *The Times* the Russians are occupying territories in the Crimea and our government are concerned about it. Do you think this might mean war with Russia, Nathan?" Amy assumes she directs her comment to Nathan because he is the only male present.

"I have no idea, Keziah, and I could not care less. I believe in making love not war."

Olivia looks contemptuously at her brother. "Let us hope not, Keziah, I understand that France is joining Britain in trying to negotiate their withdrawal, so let us pin our hopes on that."

Nathan Meakins is too busy dancing attention on Alicia to want to get into political conversation with mere women, but even so at one point during their respite he passes behind Amy and has the audacity to pinch her behind. She nearly cries out indignantly, she is so taken by surprise, but she manages to keep her composure. He gives her a sly grin and returns his attention to his fiancée. How dare he do that with Alicia and everyone else sitting right there! She feels suppressed annoyance at his presumptuousness and sympathy for the poor, unsuspecting girl who is beguiled by his two-faced charm.

She is holding up the heavy silver teapot and pouring fresh tea through the silver strainer into Lady Annabel's delicate china teacup when the afternoon is suddenly marred by the arrival of some wasps, attracted by the smell of the preserves and the fruity drinks. Nathan Meakins comes into his own, thwacking away these irritating insects with a fly swatter. However, his erratic waving and flapping only seems to annoy the wasps until one manages to sting Olivia near her eye.

"Ouch! Get it off me, Get it off me!" she screams, as her brother attempts to knock the insect away. "That is your fault, Nathan, agitating them like that. How would you like to be stung?"

"I am sorry, Olivia, I was just trying to protect our guests."

"Yes, well you managed to scare them towards me, thank you very much." She gets up in anger and marches off into the kitchen for some vinegar.

"Oh dear, I was only trying to help!" Nathan sounds contrite, but he is grinning.

"Poor Olivia, it must be horrid. I have never been stung by a wasp before," says Alicia, "but Keziah was stung by a bee, weren't you, Keziah?"

"Yes, I was; it was very painful and we had to get the sting out, then Nanny rubbed it with blue bag to take the pain away."

In the kitchen there is an argument going on about whether it should be vinegar or Reckitt's blue for wasps.

Mrs Chubb intervenes, "It is definitely acid for wasps and alkali for bees," and she passes the vinegar to Olivia, who administers it underneath her eye.

Hawkins cannot help but wonder if this stab by the wasp will affect her powers of witchcraft. If so, it has been quite a successful day.

Later on, after their guests have left for home Jean Hawkins recognises her brother and her Uncle Jack coming up the driveway to the house. They go towards the tradesman's entrance and she rushes down to the kitchen in a panic to see them, fearing the worst.

"What are you doing here? Is Pa all right?" She asks them anxiously.

"Don't worry, Jean, we are not here because of Pa, he is much the same as he was at Christmas. No, Nathan Meakins has asked to see us here. He apparently has work for us."

"What, both of you? I thought you were happy at Alvington Manor, Uncle Jack?"

"I am, Jean, I'll not be leaving there; no, it is what they call moonlighting, I think, but we cannot turn down the opportunity for a bit of extra cash, can we?"

Jean lowers her voice and whispers to her brother, "You know that sharp little job I had to do Ray?"

"Yes, how did you get on?"

"I have done it, today actually, craftily with a rose."

"Well done you."

Then Mrs Chubb comes out of the larder and

Jean says, "Follow me, I will show you to Mr Morton's room and he will know where to take you to find Mr Nathan."

Morton shows them into a small study where Nathan Meakins is seated behind his desk. He looks up, "Ah thank you Morton." He waits until Morton has left the room. "Good to see you gentlemen, I have a little proposition to put to you. Please take a seat."

The two men remove their hats and sit down on the opposite side of the desk.

"Some gentlemen from the coast are doing a regular run inland with some free trade goods and their route passes via Corscombe and Halstock along secluded footpaths, one of which is Gulliver's Lane, which comes out just alongside your cottage at Camp Road," he says, looking at Jack. "What I would like is for you two to intercept the landsmen, telling them that you are acting on behalf of a 'Squire Brandon' and that you are there on his behalf to collect his share of the crop."

Jack Hawkins shakes his head in disappointment. "I am sorry, Mr Meakins, but I wouldn't have come if I had known it was to do with shady dealings with smugglers. You should be doing your own venturing, without endangering innocent folk in your schemes."

Meakins laughs snidely. "Hardly innocent, Mr Hawkins; I know all about you and the delectable Mary Sandford. I have seen you with my own eyes, kissing and canoodling outside in the moonlight at the Alvington Manor summer ball. Surely you don't want to risk a Skimmington if news of that gets out? I can assure you it will, if you refuse to co-operate with me."

Raymond looks shocked at this information and

Jack is speechless. He can easily imagine the pain it would cause everyone, including his wife Molly, Mary and her husband Percy and their families, if their effigy's were paraded on donkey-back through Odcombe and along Camp Road, so that all their neighbours would know of their shame.

He looks despondently at Ray, and then turns back to Meakins. "You give me no choice," he says bitterly. "But it is against my nature to be involved with those ruthless, wretched villains. If any harm should come to either of us, I assure you now that you will pay the price, one way or another, sir. I will take precautions so that folk will know where to lay the blame."

"Look, Hawkins, all I want you to do, once in a while, is meet the mule train at the end of Gulliver's Lane. State your business with their leader and then lead off my mule over Alvington Manor land, downhill towards the new railway route and I will meet you along the way, somewhere near the border with Broad Leaze Farm. The contraband has been paid for in advance. I am one of the venturers who have employed the freighter to charter the vessel, but I have given a false name to protect my family's reputation. All you have to do is remember the name 'Squire Brandon' and they will happily give up the cargo.

"You will need to carry some form of protection the first time, as the batmen can be a little rough if they feel at all threatened. I will give you a letter of authority for you to show the freighter, but once they know you, it will be a piece of cake."

"What will you pay us Mr Meakins, sir?" asks Raymond, turning his wide-awake hat round and round in his hands awkwardly.

"You can share a 'dollup' of tea."

"We would prefer hard cash, if you please, sir.

Young Raymond wouldn't have much use for a load of tea and he isn't likely to be telling his family where it came from neither, nor me mine."

"In that case you can have six shillings a head."

Jack hides the fact that he thinks this a lot of money and asks immediately, "How will we know when there is a run and what time they are due?"

"It will more than likely be a moonlit night, because they keep to the same routes and do not carry torches to draw attention. They stop during the daylight hours en route at pre-arranged farms and then traverse on through the night to Odcombe and across Hamdon Hill, then onward straight up to Bristol where they dispose of their wares and return with more contraband to sell along the way. The next run is due Tuesday week, because it is a full moon. It will be about four in the morning, because of the longer hours of daylight, but later on in the year it will be earlier, so you will just have to keep your eyes peeled for an hour or two either way."

"How often are you expecting these runs?"

"No more than four times a year, probably less. Raymond will pass on my instructions and we shall see how it goes. Are you going to accept the work or not?"

Jack looks at Raymond and raises his eyebrows questioningly. Ray nods his head in agreement. "We are, sir, even though it is against my better judgement," says Jack.

"Fine, well I cannot think of anything else we need to discuss. I will meet you, as I said, sometime after four in the morning, which should give me time to get the mule back here before too many folk are abroad. Thank you gentlemen and good day."

CHAPTER 14 *(July 1853)*

REBECCA'S SHAME

As the summer months wear on Rebecca becomes aware of feeling sick in the mornings and she fears the worse. She is out of her mind with worry; *surely that one moment of terror could not have resulted in her being pregnant?* As the days go by her breasts grow tender, the sickness continues and she is certain. *She cannot keep the offspring of that vile man!* If it was not for Ben she might have considered it, as Aurora is such a beautiful child, but she does not want Ben to know of her shame. She has agonised over her decision, but she is desperate. *She has to find a way to abort it before her condition is noticed.* As the distressing weeks go by she somehow devises a plan.

She asks Lettie to join her for a morning ride and they set off together happily. She always rides the gentle Cassiopeia and Lettie is on Capella; they trot through the meadow and jump the stream at the bottom of the valley. The September mists are lifting and the gentle sunlight has a calming effect on Rebecca. *She can do this, she must just keep calm.*

"Let us have a gallop across towards Broad Leaze Dairy up past the rookery, along Camp Road and back down Pound Lane. First to go past your cottage is the winner."

"All right," says Lettie. "Ready, steady, go!" They both spur the horses on and set off at a gallop. Rebecca takes the lead and jumps the first hedge safely with Lettie flying over it moments later. They gallop across the next field and Rebecca lets Lettie take the lead as they approach the next hedge. Lettie jumps it with ease, but as Rebecca follows she slips her feet from the stirrups and unhooks her left leg from under the lower pommel and as Cassiopeia's rump is high in the air, Rebecca is thrown off, landing heavily onto her stomach on the hard ground of the bank. She cries out in pain and Lettie turns to see what has happened. She pulls up sharp bringing Capella around to go back and see what damage has been done.

She dismounts and runs to her friend. "Are you hurt, Becky, what happened?"

"My stomach, I have hurt my stomach!" she cries breathlessly.

"Can you stand up?"

"Please give me a minute, Lettie; I need to get my breath back."

"Does it hurt anywhere else?"

"It hurts all over, Lettie. It even hurts to breathe."

"Just stay there and rest and I will go and get help." Lettie can see John Hawkins ploughing the field adjacent to Broad Leaze Farm and she clambers back up onto Capella and rides like the wind to try to attract his attention.

Rebecca lies on the damp grass. She can see blood pooling around her and knows that she is miscarrying. *Thank the Lord for that!* It has worked, and she loses consciousness.

When Rebecca comes around the doctor is holding some sal volatile under her nose. Joshua, Louisa and Lettie are standing around her bed, all looking very concerned.

"How do you feel, young lady?" asks the doctor.

Rebecca groans with a wave of pain. "I have stomach cramps and I feel sick and weak and I ache all over."

"It is not surprising, you took a nasty tumble and you are lucky that you did not break your back, my dear."

Joshua is looking concerned. "Whatever happened, Becky? You are such a good rider."

"I don't know, Josh. Somehow my feet came out of the stirrups and as Cassiopeia jumped I was thrown off. I fell onto my stomach and was winded, and I banged my head." She groans again as another wave of pain causes her to draw up her legs.

"Well, Mr Dryer, I think I ought to examine your sister thoroughly. Could we have some privacy, if you please?"

Rebecca manages to speak, despite the pain. "I should like Louisa to stay as my chaperone, please doctor."

"As you wish, my dear."

The doctor sees Joshua and Lettie from the room and then proceeds to examine Rebecca. As he presses down gently on her stomach Rebecca cries out in agony. She can feel herself losing more blood and then something more solid comes away. The doctor wraps it in the towelling used to stem her bleeding and a shocked Louisa replaces it with clean material. "I am very sorry, my dear, but you have lost your baby." Louisa comforts Rebecca, as she weeps in a confusion of sadness, bitterness and relief.

"I am truly sorry, but I am sure there will be more babies. You are still very young. He goes to his medical bag. "I can give you a bottle of Agnus Castus, a tincture made from the chaste tree berry, which should help to balance your hormones and restore you to good health. You need to have complete bed rest for at least ten days and I will call daily to monitor your progress."

He turns to Louisa, "You will need to give her forty drops daily in a glass of her favourite liquid and keep an eye on the bleeding. I need to be informed if she becomes at all feverish. You must understand it is important that all the foetal material is expelled."

"I understand doctor; I will attend to her while she is confined."

Rebecca reaches out to him, "Please doctor. I beg you for discretion, my brother does not know about my pregnancy."

"I understand and I can assure you that anything that you have told me, or wish to tell me in the future, will be treated as confidential. I will see you tomorrow morning, my dear." He picks up his medical bag and Louisa accompanies him downstairs.

Every day the doctor calls on Rebecca, but despite the chaste berry tincture she seems to become progressively worse. Louisa is worried, not only by the fever, but by Rebecca's constant weeping. She confides in Lettie, "She is not getting any better and she seems to have lost the will to live."

Lettie's feelings were hurt when Rebecca chose Louisa over her to stay with her when the doctor called. She has avoided visiting her friend, but when Louisa tells her that Rebecca is not getting any better, she feels guilty for deserting her and she decides to visit. She takes some calf's foot jelly and some honey with her. Whilst sitting by her bedside and holding her hand she plucks up the courage to speak.

"Becky, why did you choose Louisa to stay with

you and the doctor? Have I done something to offend you?"

Rebecca is feverish and exhausted and guilelessly replies, "No... course not... it was because she knew about Meakins' assault."

Lettie is stunned and asks her, "What assault?"

She answers her breathlessly, "I am sorry Lettie... didn't want anyone to know... but I think I'm going to die. Meakins raped me... wanted to lose his baby."

"Oh, Becky, how dreadful!" Lettie is shocked and confused. "How did Louisa find out?"

"She found me... night of the ball." She reaches out and takes Lettie's hand, "Please, Lettie, I want to see Ben... before I die... will you run and tell Joshua for me?"

"Of course I will. I will go and tell him now. May I speak to my ma to see if she can give me something to help break your fever?"

"Yes, Lettie... I am frightened... don't want to die," she whispers, tears brimming her eyes.

Lettie brushes the damp hair off her forehead and gently wipes away the perspiration from her face. "You are not going to die, Becky. You are too young and I won't let you." She kisses her friend gently on her fevered cheek. "I won't be long."

She goes immediately to tell Joshua that Rebecca is asking for Ben and he instructs Billy Riddick to go to Portland and bring him back with him. Lettie then goes to the kitchen to ask Flora what she would recommend to help break Rebecca's fever and help with her stomach cramps. She gives her some chamomile tea. "I will ask Emily to take her up some more later, she will need to drink a cupful five times a day," says her mother.

She takes the drink upstairs to Rebecca, feeling much better being able to help. Rebecca takes a sip and then lies back down; Lettie has to keep encouraging her to get her to drink the whole cupful.

"If you have a little sleep now, either myself or Emily will come back later with some more for you. Joshua has sent Billy off to bring back Ben."

"Thank you, Lettie," she says breathlessly. Then she asks her, "Where is Louisa?"

"She is looking after Aurora at the moment."

"Thank you for coming to see me, Lettie, I feel a bit better already."

Lettie strokes her friend's forehead gently; her hands feel cool against Rebecca's burning skin. "You go to sleep now and let the medicine do its work. I will pop in later."

The following day Ben arrives just as the doctor is leaving and he overhears him talking gravely to Joshua. "She is a bit better this morning, but she is still not out of the woods yet."

Joshua turns and sees Ben. "Ah, Ben, I am so glad you are here. She has been asking for you." Ben feels Joshua's left arm around his shoulder as he shakes him by the other hand. "Doctor, this is my cousin Ben who is Rebecca's sweetheart."

The doctor turns to look in his direction as he holds out his hand. "This may be just what she needs to take her mind off her troubles. I am glad you could make it, my boy."

Ben smiles amiably as he shakes the doctor's hand, "Me too." He turns to Joshua. "Matthew said I could leave immediately, he also is very concerned. May I go up and see her now?"

"Of course, go on up, Louisa is still with her. I will just see Dr Gillingham out and I will follow you."

He rushes anxiously up the wide stairway, hearing Joshua saying goodbye to the doctor and then making arrangements for some refreshments to be sent up to Rebecca's room.

As soon as Rebecca sees him she breaks down in tears. "Oh, Becky, I didn't expect that reaction," he says kissing her gently. He is shocked at how pale and wan she looks. "This fall has really shaken you up, hasn't it?"

Through her tears she tells him, "I am afraid, Ben... afraid that I am going to die. And I didn't want to die... without seeing you again and saying I'm sorry... so very sorry."

He sits down on the edge of her bed, feeling very concerned. Whatever can she mean? "Why are you sorry, sweetheart? It was an accident. Please don't blame yourself, and why should you die?" He takes her hand in his. He can see that she is struggling with some kind of dilemma and then her words take his breath away.

"No, Ben, it was no accident. I threw myself from the horse deliberately."

He is stunned and confused. "But why, Becky? I thought you were happy here with Joshua?"

Becky's face is blotchy with her tears. "Oh, Ben, 'tis not Josh troubling me... 'tis that devil, Meakins. Please don't tell Josh about this, but... he raped me at the summer ball."

Ben is pale and silent with suppressed rage and Louisa approaches him cautiously. "It is true, Ben, Becky swore me to secrecy, but I have been looking after her. I found her the night it happened, but she begged me to keep it secret. She was so terrified; I felt I had to abide by her wishes."

Ben is no longer able to contain himself and he jumps up, pacing the room, filled with impotent anger. "Well, I am glad she had someone to confide in. I am so sorry I was not here to protect you, Becky. If I can just get my hands on his puny, upper-crust neck, I will strangle the bastard!"

"But that is not everything, Ben," says Rebecca, the pain evident in her face. "That was vile enough, but then I discovered that I was carrying his child… and all I could think of was you, my love… and how this would come between us. I knew I had to get rid of the baby somehow."

Realisation dawning on him, he looks even paler as he struggles to suppress his fury; "Hence the fall not being accidental," he says bitterly.

"No, Ben, it was an act of desperation," replies Rebecca, the tears streaming down her face.

Louisa puts her arm around Rebecca to comfort her, as Ben sits back down on the edge of the bed, taking her hand in his and trying to take it all in.

Louisa explains to Ben, "Of course the doctor realised that she was miscarrying and he has been treating her confidentially, but Becky has been so unhappy, her progress has been faltering and she has become afraid."

Joshua then enters the room with a tray of refreshments; he passes Louisa the chamomile tea and she lifts Rebecca's head from the pillow for her to drink. There is an uneasy quiet in the room and then Ben angrily breaks the silence.

"I am sorry, Becky, but Joshua needs to know what you have been going through."

Rebecca looks horrified and cries out breathlessly, "Don't, Ben, there is no need to worry Joshua further… I feel so much better now that you are here."

"That is not my only concern." He turns to Joshua and emotionally blurts out the whole story before Rebecca can stop him. "Joshua, that bastard Meakins raped your sister at your summer ball and as a result she conceived a child. She has been so desperate that she deliberately fell from the horse, in order to lose the baby."

Joshua is stunned; his expression passes from sorrow, guilt and through to anger. Although he does not doubt his cousin, he is compelled to ask, "Is this really the truth, Becky?"

Ben watches her, as she gives a deep sigh and then answers reluctantly, "Yes, it is true. I didn't want anyone to know… I was so ashamed… and so worried, but I was in terrible pain afterwards… because in addition to my injuries… I was also miscarrying."

"I am so sorry, Becky. I cannot believe he could be so evil, but you should have told me, we could have dealt with him there and then. I think it is too late now to get him to pay for what he has done through the law."

"I could never have faced him in a court of law, Josh… so what was the point in disclosing what had happened and sullying my reputation? I never thought I would have conceived a baby first time. That was the tragedy of it… I was so worried, I did not know where to turn."

"Bugger a court of law, I would take pleasure in killing him myself at the moment," says Ben vehemently.

"I agree he needs to be taught a lesson, but his is an influential family. We need to plan, rather than act instinctively, as we would both like to do. I think we must be more devious than that," says Joshua thoughtfully. "I am really sorry, Ben, I know you feel that I should have taken better care of Becky, but she hid the truth from me. I had no notion of the wickedness this man is capable of, or any inkling of what went on that night."

Ben observes his friend, as he paces the room

distractedly. He knows Joshua is hurting as much as he is and yet he is still trying to work out how to make amends and cook Meakins goose, once and for all.

Louisa then finds her tongue and speaks bitterly, "He thinks he is so superior that he is untouchable. I feel angry for the sake of Becky, but I also feel sorrow for poor Alicia. She has no idea of the type of man she has agreed to marry."

Joshua is listening carefully. "Maybe a word in a certain person's ear might settle a few scores," he says thoughtfully. "I think I might pay a visit to the Bridewells this afternoon."

"Please don't do anything that might sully Becky's reputation," says Ben. "She has suffered enough at the hands of that scoundrel."

"Never fear, I will swear whosoever I confide in to absolute secrecy. That is why I want to go in person and not put pen to paper." Joshua goes to his sister and kisses her gently on her forehead. "Don't you worry about a thing, Becky, for I am going to make sure that he pays one way or another. Nathan Meakins will not get away unscathed after his despicable treatment of you." They all watch as he strides out with purpose.

Despite being consumed with vengeful thoughts, Ben spends the rest of the day reassuring Rebecca and watching over her while she sleeps. Her breathing seems more regular now that the combination of her confession and her beloved Ben's presence has lifted her spirits.

When Joshua arrives at Clifton Maybank Manor he is shown into a very pleasant drawing room where he finds Serena playing the spinet. She stops immediately to welcome him and suggests they take a walk in the orchard. Her two sisters follow at a discreet distance. Serena, being the eldest, is expected to find herself a husband before her younger siblings are married and this is why they are affording her the opportunity to talk with him privately. Joshua realises that he may be giving the wrong impression by his visit, but he is determined to carry out his plan.

"Serena, I have something to tell you which may adversely affect your sister Alicia's future. I don't find it easy to put this into words, and I need to keep this information strictly between ourselves and your sister, Alicia."

"This sounds very serious, Joshua; whatever is it that could possibly threaten my sister's future?"

"It is her fiancé. He is not all he makes out to be."

Serena looks shocked, "Is there some scandal attached to his name?"

"I am afraid it cannot be a public scandal, because innocent people will be hurt, but I can assure you he is a very evil man."

"Please do not hold back, Joshua, your information will be safe in my hands."

"On the evening of the summer ball at Alvington Manor he raped my sixteen year old sister. She was terrified; she had never been with a man before. She then discovered that she was pregnant. She was so distressed that she threw herself from her horse, in order to miscarry, and she has been very ill with pain and fever ever since."

"Oh, Joshua, how dreadful! Your poor little sister; and my sister Alicia will be devastated."

"I realise that you are in a difficult position being the bearer of such bad tidings, but I cannot bear the thought of there being any more victims of this aggressive sexual deviant. You see, I don't believe she is the first." He decides to confide all. "I am almost certain that he seduced and abandoned Millie Bonfield, the poor young lass who committed suicide last year. The previous week we found a baby abandoned in the clock tower and we have been looking after her ever since. I believe her also to be his child, but I have no proof and this definitely must go no further than between the two of us. I do not want him to get his unworthy hands on our little foundling."

"I appreciate your coming to tell me this. It must be hard disclosing the desperate position your sister is in, but I will do my utmost to persuade my sister to break off her engagement. She will, however, have to give her reasons for her actions and this may mean more trouble for you and your family."

"I welcome the challenge of any trouble from that quarter. Don't you worry, Serena, just do your best to make Alicia see him for what he is. For I cannot wait to see the look on his face when he is turned down by your beautiful sister, even if he does come running to lay the blame at my door."

A few days later Joshua is at the front of the house. He is overseeing the planting of two stone urns each side of the porch, when a furious Meakins rides up the driveway on a frisky dappled grey horse. In that moment Joshua recognises the horse and remembers again the man on the hill, watching as a distressed young red head ran away from him, and he knows for certain that he is the father of Aurora.

"Good day, Mr Meakins, what can I do for you?" he asks, in a restrained manner.

"Don't you 'good day' me, Dryer!" he yells angrily. "You who dare to slander me! I have come to tell you to keep your big nose out of my business, or you will rue the day. Because of you, Alicia Bridewell has seen fit to call off our engagement."

"Well, as far as I am concerned she has had a lucky escape."

"What business is it of yours?"

At this moment Ben comes out to see what the shouting is about.

"You can accuse me of slander if you wish, Meakins, but I have two witnesses who will support my version of the story if you wish to persist in your innocence. You know as well as I do that you are guilty as sin."

Ben grabs the reins of his horse and lowers his voice menacingly, "You abused my Becky and I challenge you to a fight. Get down off this filly and fight like a man, you coward. Come on; pick on someone your own size."

The horse bucks and shies away from Ben, but he hangs on doggedly. "You think you can do what you like, you arrogant bastard. Get down and defend yourself." Meakins uses his whip on Ben, but he treats it like a fly swat, "You're just a pathetic bully and abuser of women. Come on, fight like a man, you great pansy."

Finally Meakins breaks free of Ben's hold and he turns the horse away in anger and embarrassment, the gardeners having witnessed his humiliation. He cracks his whip against the horse's rump and gallops off down the drive.

They all stare after the man in disgust. "I think we have made an enemy there, my friend. I doubt he has ever been spoken to like that in his whole life."

Joshua also really wanted to accuse him of

mistreating Millie, being responsible for her ruin and ultimate suicide, but he cannot put this into words for fear of losing the little lass who has become so dear to them all. However, he knows now that he needs to speak to Louisa. He finds her upstairs, dusting in Rebecca's room and keeping her company.

"How are you this morning, Becky?"

"I actually feel a little better, Josh; I think my temperature is going down at last."

"She has had some porridge as well this morning," says Louisa encouragingly.

"That is good, I am sure you will soon be right as rain. Louisa, may I speak to you in my study when you have finished here?"

"Yes, of course, my Lord."

Later on Joshua hears a tentative knock on his study door and Louisa enters.

"Louisa, come and sit down, I need to talk to you." Louisa seats herself the other side of his desk and he comes around to sit on the desk beside her.

"Louisa, I have not said anything to you, but I have for some time suspected that Meakins was the devil who seduced your sister and is therefore also the father of Aurora. This was confirmed this morning when he turned up outside and I recognised his dappled grey horse."

Louisa hangs her head in shame and sadness; her subterfuge is over.

"You see, when I first came here to Alvington Manor, I witnessed him on his horse up on a hill watching as your poor sister ran down towards our carriage in a distressed state. I thought at the time it was a lovers tiff, but following events have proved it was far more serious. It was you who abandoned the child under the clock tower, wasn't it?"

"Oh, my Lord, I am so sorry, but I had no choice… Millie begged me to take her and I didn't know what else to do." She is weeping now and the sight of her is heart wrenching.

"I didn't want Nathan Meakins to have any claim on her. I doubted he would want her, I was sure he would deny his paternity, but there was just a chance he could get his clutches on her. My ma and pa don't have any idea, and my pa would kill him if he knew." The tears are running down her face.

Joshua puts his arms around her and gives her his handkerchief. "Louisa, don't distress yourself, there is no way that we are going to betray that little mite. Her home is here with us and I will never turn her away, you have my word on that." She looks up into his face with relief and he is filled with desire, but he simply strokes her hair and kisses her cheek. Then he drags himself away. "You may also be interested to know that Alicia Bridewell has broken off her engagement to with."

"I am glad; she doesn't deserve to be sentenced to a life with him."

"No woman deserves the likes of him, but I don't think he will take this lying down either."

Rebecca is not sure whether to go back to Portland with Ben or to stay at Alvington Manor, but Joshua persuades her to stay, at least until her strength is restored. Later, downstairs in his study, he persuades Ben to go back home to reassure their parents and to preserve his sister's reputation.

Joshua is anxious to get Ben away from this emotive situation, fearful that he might take the law into his own hands and do something they would all regret. He puts his arm around Ben's shoulders in a brotherly fashion. "Be assured that I will deal with Meakins. Let Becky stay here with us to recover, where she will be well looked after. Our folk at home will be none the wiser, preserving her reputation on Portland and preventing our parents' anxiety."

"I can see you have a point, Josh, but please take good care of our Becky when I am gone. I know I must return to help her pa and to earn a crust, but I find it hard to turn my back on that evil man."

"Please, be not concerned about that scoundrel. I will deal with him in my own way. Rest assured he will not get away unscathed after his dealings with our Becky, I promise you."

Ben goes upstairs to say his farewell to Rebecca. "Your brother has persuaded me to go back to Portland, even though all I want to do is rip that bastard's heart out. But I suppose that will only make matters worse and your parents will be worried until I return. You must stay here until you are fully recovered, Becky, and I must return to my work. I will miss you but you are in safe hands here." He leans over her and kisses the top of her head gently.

"Good bye, Ben. Thank you for coming to see me. I was truly afraid that I was going to die and never see you again. I am so glad you came and I am not scared now, I am determined to get strong again and not let that devil beat me."

"You are making good progress, Becky. You have colour in your cheeks and you are eating again. Before long you will be fully restored and Billy will bring you back home to Portland and your family. Take good care of her, Louisa." Then suddenly he has to leave the room for fear of tears.

With Ben leaving her so suddenly, Rebecca is

again filled with doubt and anxiety lest he might feel differently about her, now that another man has sullied her. He was so full of anger towards Meakins, that for most of the time he was with her he seemed to show her only compassion and she is fearful she may have lost her dearest, truest love. She resolves to recover her strength and return to Portland to find out the depth of his feelings for her and, if he still loves her, to never leave his side again.

On his return home Ben reassures Rebecca's parents, telling them only that she has fallen from her horse and suffered considerable bruising, but is mending quickly now and not to worry. Putting on an animated face he tells his mother, despite the accident, what a wonderful time Rebecca is having, about the grand ball, the manor and the huge estate.

Unfortunately, Annie is afraid Ben will become discontented with his simple life on Portland, when if she had only played her cards right with Richard Dryer it could have been her and Ben living the high life. She has been lonely while he has been gone, missing her son dreadfully and she has become bitter again, as she was back in her teens. "I don't want to hear about that Joshua and his wonderful good fortune all over again, Ben. You need to get back to working for Matthew and stop gallivanting all over the countryside."

Ben does not understand why his mother is so resentful. "Ma, Becky was badly hurt. She fell from a horse. Of course I would go to her if she is asking for me and Matthew didn't mind, he was as worried about his only daughter as I was."

However, his false gaiety is hard to keep up, as the longer he is away from Becky the more he worries about her health and her safety, and the fact that he didn't really reassure her of his continued loyalty and love. He worries about her state of mind; *if she is capable of throwing herself off a horse, what else might she consider doing?*

Unless Josh sends another carriage for him, he can ill afford to visit them again so soon. Maybe it is better for Becky to let her memory of the incident fade before they meet again.

CHAPTER 15 *(October 1853)*

THE AMBUSH

On the 1st October 1853 there is much excitement in the town, with the opening of Ivell's first rail branch line link at Hendford, from Durston near Taunton, on the main Exeter to Bristol line. The first passengers to arrive are to be met by the portreeve and other town officials. Joshua has decided to accept an invitation from David Phelps to go along and join the crowds of well wishers and witness the historic moment. Aware that the huge steam-train passes quite close to the edge of the estate, Joshua wants to be among the first to see the mechanical monster bringing passengers to their town.

It is not long before they hear the shrill whistle announcing the arrival of the train and soon they spot the steam bellowing from the chimney as it approaches the station. Among the passengers to descend from the locomotive are directors of the Bristol and Exeter Railways and the crowds watch as the portreeve steps forward to welcome them.

"This is a momentous occasion, David. It should help hugely to bring prosperity to our town."

"Let's hope so, Joshua. We don't want Ivell to get left behind all the other towns that are more progressive, do we?"

As the crowds disperse after the speeches Joshua notices Sir Maurice Moreton, another Justice of the Peace, present among the dignitaries. He lifts his hat in greeting, but there is no opportunity to talk and Sir Maurice responds in kind.

Jacob Warren, whilst tending his sheep, observes Nathan Meakins on horseback, lurking under an old oak tree in the shadows of a moonlit November night. He immediately goes to inform Joshua.

Joshua sends Billy Riddick to fetch Malachi. "Ask him to join us in the copse near Broad Leaze Farm, by the withy pool, but to avoid the location of the ancient oak where Meakins is lurking." Then he sets off with Jacob to find out what Meakins is up to. It is not long before Malachi stealthily joins them in the copse, where they remain concealed together and watch and wait.

Joshua is disappointed when he recognises the familiar features of his ploughman Jack Hawkins in the company of his nephew Raymond approaching and leading a heavily burdened pack mule. They pass over the reins to Meakins, who hands them their reward and leads the animal away. Raymond and Jack Hawkins then return back up the hill towards Camp Road.

Joshua signals to Malachi and Jacob to follow him, taking a short cut through the woods in order to ambush Meakins before he reaches the edge of the estate.

They manage to take him by surprise and Malachi pulls him from his horse. He is determined to teach this arrogant prick a lesson and when he tries to struggle free Malachi and Jacob both enjoy knocking him about and roughing him up a bit, while Joshua holds the reins of the animals. Indignantly he speaks out. "Get your mongrels off me, Dryer!"

Joshua pretends to suddenly recognise him.

"Bring the villain here where I can see him properly, I am sure I recognise that voice."

Malachi drags him to his feet and out from the shadows, so that Joshua can see his somewhat battered face in the moonlight. He cannot help smiling in satisfaction at the state of him.

"Nathan Meakins, I thought I recognised you. I think you owe me an explanation. What the devil do you think you are doing trespassing on my land at this time of night, with what looks like a consignment of contraband? Is there no end to your villainy?"

Meakins sullenly brushes off his clothes with his free arm and then wipes it across his face, before condescending to answer. "I could have your yokels here charged with assault, for Christ's sake. I am just doing a bit of free-trade business. There has never been a problem before."

"No, I am sure my old grandfather was totally ignorant of what was going on, right under his nose," says Joshua angrily. "It was damned smugglers who murdered my father and I will not sanction smuggling across my land. I am seizing this animal in the name of Her Majesty's customs. Jacob, take the beast back to the farm where we can unload him and see what we have here and you, Meakins, can get off my land, but I assure you, you haven't heard the last of this." He passes the reins of the grey to Meakins. "I don't want to see you on this estate ever again for any reason, and that includes your fox hunting cronies. Do you understand me?"

Meakins snatches the reins from Joshua and inelegantly swings himself into the saddle. "Who made you judge and jury, Dryer? You jumped up sailor boy. Don't go thinking you have seen the last of me, for you will be very much mistaken."

"This may come as a surprise to you, Meakins,

but I swore an oath of allegiance to the crown before the Lord Chancellor Cranworth last month and, as a Justice of the Peace, I will be presiding over the next quarter session. I am quite sure that I haven't seen the last of *you* just yet." With that he slaps his horse's rump and the grey sets off at a gallop.

The following day Joshua sends Billy to summon Jack Hawkins to the house. On his arrival he is shown into the study. Joshua is aware that Jack has no idea why he has been summoned and he stands before him waiting patiently for him to speak. He remains seated at his desk, surrounded by his law books and a large stack of Justice of the Peace magazines. He is staring blankly at the ship in the bottle that Ben gave to him, which is placed on the front of his desk, wondering how best to deal with the situation.

Finally, he speaks. "Jack, I and two witnesses saw you last night with your nephew Raymond leading a mule across the Alvington estate, heavily loaded with contraband goods." He notes with some satisfaction the look of guilt on his ploughman's face. "I am very disappointed in you, Jack. I took you for an honest man. What do you have to say for yourself?"

Jack hangs his head in shame. "I am sorry, my Lord, it were that Meakins fellow. I should never have got involved with 'im, but for Mary.

"Whatever has Mary got to do with it?"

"Well you see sir; he did spy on us at the summer ball and was threatening to tell folk of our tryst, if we did not comply with his wishes."

"You are having a relationship with Percy's wife, Mary?" Joshua is astonished.

"Yes, my Lord... we have been especially close friends for years... and it has recently become more serious... I love her as much as I love my own wife... but I don't want to hurt either of them, my Lord." Jack's voice wavers, falteringly.

Joshua deliberately sounds stern as he issues an ultimatum. "Well, I have called you in today to say that unless you stop your dealings with Meakins and with the smugglers, I am afraid you and all your family will have to leave the tied cottage on Camp Road and thus you, Frank and Thomas will lose your jobs on the estate."

Jack looks very shocked at this. "I don't want me and my family to leave the estate, my Lord... I don't want to be involved with the smugglers... but I don't want a Skimmington, neither."

He remains firm. "In that case you have no choice but to break off your relationship with Mary Sandford and you must tell Meakins he no longer has any hold over you. He knows that I am aware of his illegal activities and I am not going to turn a blind eye to it, so I believe that once you have done the right thing, by Percy and your wife Molly, you will have a clear conscience and that is worth its weight in gold, I can assure you."

Jack lowers his head shamefacedly. "I will do as you say, my Lord, and stop the affair." His eyes fill with tears and his bottom lip quivers, trying to gain control. "I promise to talk to Mary and tell her how it will become public knowledge if we risk continuing and how me and my boys could lose our jobs and our cottage." He roughly wipes the back of his hand across his eyes, "And I give you my word I will have no dealings with Meakins ever again. I do not like or trust the man and I believe he is a bad influence on our Raymond."

"How come he got Raymond involved?"

"Well, the poor lad was unemployed and his family are desperate for money, my Lord. He was already caught up with Meakins, his sister being a maid at Summerville House, and she was getting him a bit of work here and there, beating."

"But why do you think he required your assistance?" He is puzzled. "Why could he not take delivery of the mule himself?"

"I believe Meakins did not want to be recognised by some of the landsmen who come via Gulliver's Lane. They are a ruthless bunch of reprobates who come up from the coast and travel on over Hamdon Hill to the fosse way, thence onward inland up to Bristol and then they return with further contraband brought into the docks up there. His involvement was secret, my Lord, for we were told not to name him, but to say that we were there on behalf of a Squire Brandon, my Lord."

"Well, Jack; as long as you give me your assurance that you will keep away from the smugglers and cease all dealings with Nathan Meakins I will allow you to continue to work as my ploughman and to live in the tied cottage with your family."

Joshua can see the relief run through him. "Thank you, my Lord. You won't regret it. I truly appreciate your clemency; it means the world to me and my family. I promise I will tell Raymond to inform Meakins that because we have been discovered we can no longer do his bidding."

Joshua then says casually, "You can also tell your nephew that if it is an honest day's work he is after, to come and see me and I will see what I can arrange."

Jack Hawkins looks like a weight has been taken from his shoulders. "Oh that is very good of you, my Lord. You see his father, my brother, has consumption and times are hard for their family. I am sure he will come and see you shortly, my Lord."

The following day Raymond approaches Summerville House. He knows he has to inform Meakins that their cover has been blown and that he and his uncle are no longer in a position to help him, but he is anxious as to the man's reaction. Meakins will just have to make alternative plans to get a return on his investment.

As expected the man is angry and informs Raymond that if he cannot be relied upon, he no longer wants him helping with the beating. "Get out of my sight before I sack your sister into the bargain."

Raymond leaves hastily; their family would never survive without the little help that Jean provides, especially if, in addition, there was another mouth to feed.

Meakins is in a foul mood and after Raymond has gone he paces the room angrily. Joshua Dryer is getting the better of him and he does not like it. As he turns back and forth across his study he catches sight, through the corner of the window, the little kitchen maid being kissed by the butcher's boy outside in the driveway, partly hidden by the magnolia tree.

Aha! That little madam knows fraternisation is forbidden; perhaps he can cheer himself up with a bit of sport in that direction. He watches surreptitiously until he sees her waving him goodbye. *Oh, how sweet*! He cannot wait to see her expression when she realises that she has been discovered disobeying the household rules.

He goes out through the French doors and around the back of the house to the tradesmen's entrance, where he waits beside the porch to catch Amy on her way back to the kitchen. As she approaches he steps forward and is gratified to see that his sudden appearance frightens the child, who blushes crimson, guiltily.

"Good Morning, Proctor, and what have you been up to, missy?"

Amy hesitates and then stutters, "I… I was just feeding the hens, sir."

"Were you indeed? I have never heard it called that before."

"I beg your pardon, sir?"

"Feeding the hens, Proctor; with your tongue halfway down the butcher boy's throat."

Amy looks down at the ground and shuffles her feet nervously. "I am sorry, sir. It was just a little kiss, sir, it don't mean nothing."

"You know very well that all the staff here are forbidden any form of fraternising with the opposite gender on pain of instant dismissal."

"Please, Sir. It was just Bobby being cheeky, Sir, we haven't done nothing."

"Except the kiss, which any man would take for an invitation."

"I am truly sorry, sir. Please give me a second chance."

Meakins moves towards her and takes her chin gently in his right hand raising her face to look him in the eye. His voice is seductive as he says, "You are such a sweet, innocent child, Proctor. I am sure I could forgive you if you were particularly nice to me."

"What do you need me to do for you, sir? I am a hard worker, ask Cook. I can clean shoes and sew and mend and darn too, sir."

"Oh I am sure I will come up with something, Proctor, when the time is right. Just you remember that you are indebted to me and I expect to be repaid."

She lowers her eyes shamefully. "Yes, sir. Thank you, sir."

That afternoon Raymond turns up at Alvington Manor and asks to see Lord Dryer. He is shown into his study and Joshua looks up from his desk.

"Good day, Master Hawkins, I understand you have graduated from poaching on my land to smuggling." He sounds very severe.

"Yes, my Lord. I am very sorry, my Lord."

"Is that all you have to say for yourself?"

"I was desperate, my Lord, and that Nathan Meakins thinks he owns you if you work for him. I was afeared I would lose the little I do get from the beating, if I did not go along with his plans. He is a nasty piece of work... and he was blackmailing my uncle into the bargain."

"I am aware of that, Master Hawkins, but how can I have peace of mind enough to employ you on the estate, if you have leanings toward law breaking? I warn you that I now hold the office of Justice of the Peace and will no longer tolerate any wrong doing."

Raymond is suddenly afraid that he was asked to see Lord Dryer simply to be humiliated and that he had no intention of employing him at all. "My Lord, if you could see your way to giving me reliable employment, I will willingly serve you honestly and diligently. I want to turn over a new leaf; I just need the opportunity to do so, my Lord."

"In that case I am prepared to give you the benefit of the doubt, but bear in mind you are bound over to be of good behaviour. I trust you understand that you are on trial here?"

"Yes, my Lord."

"I am going to put my best and most honest employee in charge of you and you will be under his supervision at all times." As Joshua pulls the bell for Gareth, he observes the tension in Raymond's shoulders relax with relief.

"What is it that you are offering me, my Lord?"

"I want you to be apprenticed to the gamekeeper, John Boucher, and I assure you he will have no truck with idleness, tardiness, or dishonesty. Do we have a bargain?"

Raymond smiles at the irony. "We do, my Lord, I am truly grateful to you for the opportunity to prove myself. You will not regret it, my Lord, I give you my word." *What will Lettie's father think of this! No matter, he will show him just how hard working and reliable he really is.*

Gareth enters the study.

"Right, be off with you, then, to commence working with John Boucher." He turns to Gareth, "Gareth, would you please take Master Hawkins here with you to find John and tell him that he is to be his new apprentice?"

"Yes, my Lord."

Joshua stands up to indicate that his interview is over, but as Raymond turns to leave he adds, "Do not forget, however, that we are all like one big family here and you must bear in mind that I employ your uncle and your two cousins. I don't expect you to let them, or me down."

"I won't, my Lord, you have my word, and thank you, my Lord."

After the two men have left, Joshua picks up his hat and sets off to the stable to find Billy Riddick.

"Please set up the gig, Billy, I want to go into town on court business."

He has decided to visit the police station in order to put a covert plan into operation. However, after speaking with the police constable, Joshua realises that he needs to discuss his problems with the other local Justices of the Peace and with this in mind he invites them all to dine with him at Alvington Manor.

The Reverend David Phelps, Mr Samuel Bridewell Esq of Clifton Maybank, Sir Maurice Moreton of West Coker Manor, Viscount Seymour from Sutton Bingham Manor and Lord William Helyar of Coker Court all attend. They have been shown into the oak and are all sitting around a lively log fire in comfortable armchairs, supping a variety of alcoholic beverages served by Joshua himself.

Joshua believes he can count on David's and Sam Bridewell's support, after Alicia breaking off her engagement, but he is not sure of Lord Helyar or Sir Maurice Moreton because of their close friendship with Oliver Meakins. Neither, for that matter, does he know how close the Seymour brothers are to his son.

He decides to tread very carefully without mentioning any names. "Right gentlemen, I have invited you all here for several reasons; firstly to meet together on an informal basis, as I am new and have a lot to learn about the extent of our jurisdiction, plus I wish to make better acquaintance of you all. Secondly, because I have a dilemma which requires very careful handling, but before I elaborate I would like us all to sit back and relax and enjoy the light supper that my wonderful cook has prepared for us, so please do help yourself from the chiffonier, before the victuals spoil in the warmth from the fire."

The men all rather self-consciously help themselves from the platters displayed on the large, four-door, rosewood chiffonier. Joshua cannot help but smile. These men are always waited on hand and foot, but he deliberately wants to keep the company exclusively private and therefore the servants have all been dismissed for the evening.

Lord Helyar is swirling around his brandy bowl and talking loudly to Sir Maurice Moreton about the Russians destroying the Turkish fleet at Sinope and his fear that British and French troops would go to war against Russia. Samuel Bridewell is leaning back in his seat, stroking his greying beard and talking at the same time to Maurice Seymour about the cotton weavers strike in Lancashire and the Preston lock out, as reported in the *Illustrated London News.*

David Phelps sidles up to him. "What is this really all in aid of, my friend?"

"I want to call out the militia to take on a smuggling gang that passes by the edge of the estate on a regular basis, but I am reluctant to blurt out my intentions before ascertaining whether or not I can trust all the parties present."

"Oh my dear chap, these are all fellow members of the courts of justice. I am sure you can rely on them all."

"Even if this may involve a well-known family with whom some of the people present are friends?"

"Ah, my boy, I see your predicament. Tell me who it is you believe to be involved and maybe I can help."

"It is Nathan Meakins."

"Hmm, I understand you have a bit of a quandary. That man is certainly a loose canon. He is a member of the Black Panther Club and I believe that the Seymour boys have also recently joined. It might be a good idea to sound them all out, by asking their opinion of this club for a start."

"That is a good idea. Why don't you bring it up, David, as you seem to know more about it than I do?"

"I can certainly do that; I will wait until they are all sitting down again."

After the men have partaken of their victuals and are all seated once more, Joshua passes around some cigars and David Phelps brings up the subject of the Black Panther Club. "I have heard rumours that Catkin Mill is the meeting place of a so called 'gentleman's' club called the Black Panther Club and, according to some of my parishioners, all kinds of debauchery is taking place there: gambling and prostitution, even black magic has been whispered about. What do you all feel about it, as a possible enticement to young people hereabouts?"

"I am sure I have no idea what you are referring to, but I certainly would not condone any such association if it really did exist, especially going on within my own parish!" says Lord Helyar, haughtily.

"I have to admit, William, that I have had my suspicions for some time that some place existed locally for lewd goings on. My fear is that my two boys will be led astray, so I would be very much against such a club," says Sir Jeremy Seymour. "They are already far too friendly with that rogue Nathan Meakins, but you know the attraction of a bad boy among their peers. I feel sorry for Sir Oliver, fathering such a nasty piece of work."

"Well, I am glad that you both feel this way, because I have had several clashes with Meakins junior and one involves a lucrative smuggling gang," says Joshua. "I feel that if only I could get hold of the members of this gang, I would have a way of exposing Nathan Meakins for the rogue he really is."

"I see, and is this why you brought us here?" asks Lord Helyar.

"It is, my Lord. I am relatively new hereabouts and I needed to get to know you all better and then sound you out with regard to dealing with this gang. I wish to be in a position to call out the militia the next time the smugglers are due to pass my estate."

"Well, you have my agreement. What do the rest of you say?" says Lord Helyar.

They all immediately agree that it is their duty to prevent smuggling and if Meakins' boy is involved, then so be it.

"I appreciate your solidarity gentlemen, but I must ask you for complete secrecy or my plan will not work."

"That is taken as read, my boy."

"What is your cunning plan, Joshua?" asks David, smiling.

"Let me explain," says Joshua.

CHAPTER 16 *(December 1853)*

SEDUCTION AND DISCLOSURE

Ben's mother Annie is sitting with her sister May beside the fire at the Cove House Inn, on Portland enjoying a rare evening out, while Ben and his uncles are involved in a game of darts. It is their brother Eddie's twenty-eighth birthday and so a celebration is underway. Their large family have taken over most of the bar area with their cries of encouragement and frustration coming loud and clear from the men. No one pays any attention to the noise until a tall Kimberlin enters the inn through the main door, a blast of cold wind accompanying him and Annie is suddenly conscious of her family's rowdiness.

"Ben, get them to keep the noise down can't you?" she says to her son, as he passes his mother drinks for herself and her sister.

"Oh, Ma, don't fret. They are doing no harm, just enjoying themselves. No one is paying no mind."

May is staring at the stranger. "Who is that, I wonder?" says her sister.

"I have no idea, but I would like to find out," she says with a grin.

Annie Stone is still a comely woman at forty-three and she has not yet given up hope of finding herself another husband. She watches with growing interest as the tall, handsome man takes a seat at the bar and orders a double scotch. He has a lyrical Scottish lilt to his voice and Annie is overcome with curiosity. She wonders how old he is. He has crinkly salt and pepper coloured hair with wide sideburns and she guesses he is about fifty, by the white flecks in his eyebrows, but nevertheless he looks elegant and distinguished compared to the local fishermen that usually congregate in the Cove House Inn.

He is observing all around him, particularly the darts match, but she is extremely surprised when he catches her eye and moves towards the fireplace to take a seat beside her. "I trust you will forgive my intrusion, but it is a cold night and I would appreciate the opportunity to warm myself by the fireside and take advantage of some charming company into the bargain." His voice is fluid and musical and puts her in mind of spring water trickling over pebbles into a Scottish loch. Annie has almost forgotten that May is sitting there beside them.

"Of course, sir, you are very welcome." Annie leans back and pulls a stool towards the fire. "You are a stranger here on the island; we have a special name for foreigners here don't we, May? A Kimberlin is what you are, sir. Have you travelled far?" she asks, wasting no time at all.

"I come originally from Aberdeen up in Scotland, but I love this part of the world especially the coastline."

"We have lived here all our lives; our families before us were Portlanders through and through. I've no wish to go anywhere else, have you, May?"

As the Kimberlin looks towards Annie's sister, Annie looks pointedly at her and jerks her head towards the men, trying to get her to leave her alone with the Kimberlin.

"No, all our kin live here near about and it is good to have that support when you have a big family. Anyway, I am going to take a turn with the birthday boy, so I will see you later." She gets up and tactfully goes to join her brothers.

"Can I get you another drink? I am sorry, what is your name, my dear?"

"Annie, Annie Stone, and yes, I would like a little nip of gin, if you don't mind."

He goes to the bar and shortly returns with the drinks, having asked the barmaid to keep a watchful eye and to top up their drinks when needed. He passes Annie what looks to her to be a rather large gin and she is impressed with his generosity.

"I would like to thank you, but you didn't give me your name?"

"It is Alistair McNab," he says with a seductive smile.

"Well, thank you very much, Alistair, this is very kind of you."

"You are very welcome, my dear." Annie cannot believe how well this is going. She has not had any attention from a man, in whom she might have any possible interest, since her William died eighteen years ago and she cannot believe her good fortune.

Whilst they chat amiably he continues to ply her with drink. He tells her tales of the beauty of Scotland and the highlands and she thinks he is the most romantic of men. He avoids all talk of his recent history and current position.

She tells him tales of smuggling and wrecking and of the superstitions of the island, whilst he listens avidly and she believes him to be fascinated by her charm. On one occasion he accidently touches her knee and when she looks up at him he winks at her suggestively. She points out the members of her family, including her son, Ben, and he encourages her to talk about him. "I cannot believe you have such a strapping son; you don't look old enough, you must have been a child bride when you entered the kirk."

She laughs at this and goes on to tell him how it is just the two of them now, as they lost his father eighteen years ago in a fishing accident. "Our Ben was no more than a nipper."

"And now as a full grown man he is following in his father's footsteps. That is as it should be."

"Well, no sir, not really." Annie is tempted to tell this handsome fellow the truth; after all he does not know anyone hereabouts and so is not likely to want to get involved with local gossips. She hesitates.

"No?" McNab prompts her gently.

"No, sir, but you see," her voice is barely above a whisper, "'tis a secret never to be repeated. No one around here knows and it would cause much trouble if the truth were told."

"Well, you are the only one who has given me the time of day and so I am not likely to tell a soul, am I?"

"Just between you and me then, sir, I will tell you only this. My dear husband was not his true father; my son is related to another who was murdered."

Here his interest is aroused; she has had enough drink to loosen her tongue and he decides the time is right to suggest he sees her to her home. "I think that now might be a good time to walk you home. I will just settle my account, my dear."

"That is very kind of you; I do think I have partaken of rather too much gin than is good for me." Annie says her goodbyes to her family members and, with her eyebrows raised in anticipation, she gives a wink to her sister.

On his return McNab holds out his arm and offers, "Here, take my arm and I will see you safely to your door."

Once outside they can hear the waves thundering below them and the suck of the undertow. The cold

December air hits Annie hard. McNab has to physically support her as they walk across the pebbles and into Big Ope, the rough track that leads from the Chesil beach back down into Chiswell.

He decides to probe gently to find out more, before it is too late and she loses consciousness. "You have got me curious now, Annie, so tell me who is the man who was your son Ben's real father, and how come he was murdered?" He talks to her gently, as if genuinely concerned and she is beguiled by him.

"He wuz my Richard." She stumbles along hanging onto his arm. Her words are slurred as she confides in her new friend. "He wuz Dryer, the new preventive man, and no one liked him round here because they wuz all smuggling. He wuz mine ffirst and then he ffell for that ffancy piece, Violet Allen, and they married."

She twists her ankle on a loose pebble, but the pain is dulled by the amount of alcohol she has consumed and she is eager now to tell her new friend how hard done by she had been. "By the time I ffound out that I wuz carrying his child, Violet also became pregnant, but her child was born early and Ben wuz not born until few days later."

She is slurring so much now, that McNab is finding it hard to understand her. "That was not sooo bad because I love my ssson more than life itself, but the worse thing was his father was murrrderred by a ruthless sssmuggling gang. His father was of the gentry and it broke my heart when Joshua, who is accshally Ben's half brother, hinherited a huge estate in Somerset. My Ben thinks he's his cousin, but he's really his half-brrother and I cannot tell him ffor ffear of what he will think of me."

"I am sure he will always admire and love the

259

person who has nurtured and protected him into adulthood, you must have no fear, my dear. You will always be his mother."

"That's true enuff, sir."

On reaching her front door McNab has to help her turn the key in the lock, but as he is about to turn away to his lodgings, feeling satisfied knowing that he has a bonus coming for this information just in time for Christmas, she is up on her tiptoes flinging her arms round his neck. She tastes of gin, but gives him a surprisingly passionate kiss and he cannot help but think it is a shame to lose this opportunity and he follows her inside.

When Annie awakes the following morning she is disappointed to find herself alone in the bed and unhappily nursing a dreadful hangover from the night before. She is somewhat bemused having thought she was onto a good thing with Alistair McNab. However, she has no recollection of disclosing her long held secret.

She can hear Ben moving around downstairs and she decides to put on her dressing gown and go and see him before he sets off to work. She gasps in pain as she puts her feet to the ground and discovers her ankle to be painful and swollen from where she twisted it the night before. She struggles downstairs.

"Good morning, Ben," she says as she enters from the stairway.

"Good morning, Ma, you look a bit worse for wear this morning!"

"Yes, I have a swollen ankle and a dreadful headache; well, I did have a bit of a skin-full last night."

"So I saw, Ma. Who was your companion in crime?"

"Oh, he was just some Kimberlin hailed from Scotland and enjoying these parts. He was very interested in our coastline and hereabouts."

"Was he? Well I heard he seemed to be very interested in you, Ma."

"Don't be daft, lad, he was just being friendly."

"Hmm! Anyway, changing the topic, how are you getting along with that shawl for our Becky, Ma? 'Tis not long to Christmas now and I am sure she will soon be home. You did promise me you would get it finished in time."

"Don't you fret, lad." She limps across to the sideboard and takes out her knitting bag holding up the soft woollen shawl. "Look, I have only the fringing left to do now. It is almost completed."

"That is coming along nicely, Ma, thank you."

"Well, it is made from wool from our own Portland sheep and I spun and dyed the wool myself, it being the softest, non-scratchy wool and beautiful to work."

"I am sure she will love it and it will go very well with her plaid skirt."

"That was what I thought; so you think she will like it?"

"Yes Ma, as I said, I am sure she will love it."

On McNab's return to Summerville House he goes straight away to find the young master and pass on the interesting details. Nathan Meakins is delighted when he realises he has information that will take the smile off the pompous Lord Dryer's face and he immediately saddles his horse to go and spread his malicious news.

This Christmas Joshua has decided that it will be a

quiet affair and he is simply organising a Christmas meal for the household staff. He will give all the outlying staff a Boxing Day gift of a pheasant for each family and for the Bouchers' a hamper of sweetmeats and puddings, Madeira wine and brandy.

Out of all his staff Louisa is looking forward to the celebrations with the most eager anticipation. She has helped Rosa decorate the Christmas tree and the drawing room and has constructed the wreath for the front door. Becky is restored to good physical health but she is still very melancholy. She has missed Ben so much and has decided she would like to return to Portland for a traditional Christmas with her family. Their mother Violet is unable to travel to Somerset, having an inner ear infection that is rendering her dizzy, therefore she and Matthew have decided to stay on Portland for the festivities this year. This suits Becky admirably, because she would prefer to see Ben without all the people around and so Joshua arranges for her to be conveyed home with Billy Riddick.

There is an emotional farewell from Lettie and all the staff and Louisa holds up Aurora for a kiss from Becky. Becky cannot look at the child now without thinking of the one she has lost, but she still loves her with all her heart and tears fall at their parting. She promises to return with Ben from time to time to see them all and they wave as the landau sets off up Pound Lane towards Camp Road. Once it has passed out of sight Louisa carries Aurora back into the house along with the other staff and takes her upstairs to the nursery, to put her down for her morning nap.

Just moments after Becky's carriage leaves, Nathan Meakins turns into the tree lined driveway from the easterly direction of Preston Plucknett. He has the audacity to ride right up to the manor house, despite being ordered never to trespass on the Alvington Estate property again. He dismounts and bangs the knocker loudly, until Gareth opens the door to him, whereupon Meakins pushes past him and strides through the hall and into Joshua's study, with Gareth trotting behind him and protesting wildly.

"Tell your butler to piss off, Dryer, I have something to say and I will be heard. It can just be between the two of us, or for the ears of the whole household, it is your choice."

"Leave us, Gareth, I will call if you are needed."

Gareth leaves the room, closing the study door behind him, but Meakins wants the whole household to hear what he has to say and deliberately re-opens the study door before he tells Joshua what he has learned in a loud voice.

"My steward has just returned from a trip to that heathen island known as Portland where your family hail from and it was there in a pleasant little tavern that he encountered a very obliging woman. They spent a congenial evening together and during an intimate moment she revealed that you and her son Ben are not, as you might believe, cousins, but you are actually blood brothers."

Joshua is shocked at his words and takes a moment to take in what he has just heard. Then, aware that both Gareth and Rosa can probably hear what has been said, he finds his tongue and retaliates.

"You are a nasty, evil, trouble maker, Meakins, who is unable to control his sexual desires and to whom the law means nothing. You have been banned from my land in the past because of your depraved conduct and for smuggling, and your only possible reprisal is to come up with a bunch of vindictive lies designed to cause me and my family embarrassment."

Meakins places his hands on Joshua's desk and leans forward threateningly. "You are not going to brow beat me that easily, Dryer," he says, laughing smugly. "You see, my steward got this information direct from the whore who slept with your father — the mother of your bastard brother!"

This is too much for Joshua, who jumps up from his seat and is around to the front of the desk in a moment. Angrily he grabs hold of Meakins by one arm and the back of his riding jacket and flings him toward the open door. "I will not have you making up a load of malicious lies to insult me and my family, simply to divert attention from your own culpability. You can get off my land, never to step foot on it again. I give you my word, I will see you next in court."

He calls out for Gareth and Michael and they come immediately to assist him. "Come and see this villain off my property," he says furiously, shoving him toward them. They take him and throw him down the outer steps and almost under the hooves of his horse, who shies away. He stands up and brushes himself down indignantly, then, swinging himself back up into his saddle, he cries out angrily: "You think you can treat me like this, the son of Sir Oliver Meakins, when you are nothing more than a jumped up sailor boy. Think again, Jack Tar!" He then spurs his horse and gallops off.

Joshua returns to his study and pours himself a large brandy, then he asks Michael, Gareth and Rosa to follow him into the library.

"I am sure you overheard much of what that arrogant fop had to say and I am sure that I don't need to tell you it is all a load of nonsense. However, I expect you to treat what you overheard with the utmost confidentiality. I do not want to hear his lies repeated among the staff and I am confident that I can rely on your absolute discretion."

"Of course, my Lord."

"Thank you." He turns to his butler. "Now, Gareth, I would like you to act as head of the household over the Christmas meal on my behalf, as I have decided to accompany my sister on her journey back to Portland. I would be grateful if you could make haste to pack a travel bag for me, with clothes adequate for the Christmas break." He then addresses Michael. "Michael, could you please go and ask John Moore to saddle Capricorn for me?"

"Yes, my Lord."

"Thank you."

Finally he looks towards Rosa. "Rosa, please could you pass on my apologies to all the staff for missing their Christmas meal. All the preparations are in hand and I am sure Flora will manage superbly as usual with help from the rest of the staff. I will be back in the New Year."

"Yes, of course, my Lord."

Moments later Gareth is back with a duffel bag and soon Joshua is mounting his horse to set off after Becky. He is shocked and confused by that man's evil insinuations and he intends to confront Annie first with Meakins' allegations. If, heaven forbid, she says there is any fact in the tale, then he will check with his mother and Matthew to see what they know. Finally, if the tale turns out to be true after all, he feels duty bound to inform Ben and his sister. However, he is convinced that if there was any legitimacy in the story at all, his mother and Matthew would also know of this and they would not have kept it from him for all these years.

He catches up with the carriage and hails Billy, who brings the vehicle to a halt. Becky looks out of the carriage and is surprised and pleased to see him as he ties his horse to the back of it and joins her for the journey, simply adding that he too would like to spend Christmas with the family this year.

Rosa waits until suppertime to tell the staff of Joshua's plans. As they all congregate in the kitchen for their late meal, she makes her announcement.

"I am afraid Lord Dryer has decided to join his family on Portland for the Christmas celebrations and so Gareth is going to be in charge in his absence. He asked me to pass on his apologies to you all for missing our Christmas meal, but he said that all the preparations are in hand and he was sure Flora would manage superbly as usual, with help from the rest of us. He will be back in the New Year."

"But it is all a bit sudden isn't it? I thought he was looking forward to our party," says Louisa sadly.

"Don't worry, Lou Lou, while the cat is away the mice can play!" whispers Elsie cheekily.

"I heard that, Elsie Hall, and you can be assured that there will be no monkey business while I am around," says Mrs Abbott sharply.

"I was only jesting, Mrs Abbott, trying to cheer Louisa."

"It won't be half as good without him, Elsie, and you know it," says Louisa quietly.

Emily whispers to Elsie, "Do you think Louisa is sweet on Lord Dryer, Else?"

The two girls study Louisa furtively and Elsie looks back, smiling and nodding her head in agreement.

Louisa is devastated that she will not have the pleasure of seeing Joshua over the Christmas period and cannot hide her disappointment, but she does not want anyone to suspect that she has fallen in love with her employer. However, Rosa too notices her unhappiness and is tempted to tell her the truth about what has happened, but she has given her word.

At Summerville House the following morning the day dawns crisp and clear. Amy is wrapped up well against the cold, as she enters the kitchen after feeding the hens. She removes her cloak and clogs and warms her hands by the fire. She has been avoiding the master, but she is anxious that he will come in search of her, in order for her to pay her debt. Jean is busy in the main house and cook is following a recipe from the *English Woman's Domestic Magazine*.

Mrs Faversham enters the kitchen, her chatelaine's chain jingling and announcing her presence. "Proctor, Hawkins needs help with the Christmas decorations in the drawing room. Make haste, I want it finished by morning break."

"Yes, Mrs Faversham."

Amy straightens her cap and tidies her apron as she makes her way to the drawing room. She is just about to leave the service passageway when she spots Nathan Meakins passing by in the hallway. She makes herself invisible against the passageway wall, but not quickly enough. He turns into the passageway furtively and, taking her arm, pulls her back out of sight.

"Good morning, Proctor. Now is the moment when you can be nice to me." His voice is oily and seductive.

"How do you mean, sir?"

"Why, a little kiss on the cheek would not go amiss." He turns his cheek towards her to be kissed.

"I don't like to, sir, it is not proper."

He looks taken aback. "You don't like to? Do you not find me at all kissable?" He sounds playful, but there is an undertone of menace.

"It is not that, sir, but it is not my place to kiss my master."

"But, as you say, Proctor, I am your master and therefore it is your place to do as I request. Come now, just a little peck will do no harm, or I will be offended. After all, it was not a problem with the butcher boy." He points his finger to the spot on his cheek where he expects her to kiss him.

Amy is trembling, as she reluctantly moves to kiss him on the cheek, but as she does so he turns quickly to catch her full on the mouth. He pushes her back against the wall and his mouth is hard on hers, his tongue probing and intruding. She can feel his hand fumbling among her petticoats. She is mortified, even more so when she hears footsteps and Apsey turns into the passageway and witnesses her humiliation.

Meakins releases her from his grip and she turns hastily from him. Brushing away her tears, she rushes off towards the drawing room, her face crimson with shame.

Jean looks down from a stepladder as she enters the room. "Mrs Faversham said she would find someone to help me; I am glad it is you, Amy."

Amy takes a deep breath and, hiding her feelings behind a smile, she says, "Me too. What would you like me to do to help?" Now was not the time to tell her friend what had just happened.

"Well, if you could pass me some of the baubles for the top of the tree it will save a lot of time."

Amy hopes Jean will not notice how much she is still trembling.

CHAPTER 17
(December 1853)

MASKING AND UNMASKING SECRETS

Rebecca is standing in the window and looking out over the rooftops to the sea, feeling relieved and thrilled to be back at home on Portland where she belongs. She can see miles along the coast towards Sidmouth and Seaton. She gives a gentle sigh; she has missed this wonderful island with its wild beauty, almost as much as she has missed her family and Ben.

She hears someone enter the room and turns away from the window. Joshua is dressed for outdoors. "Where are you going, Josh?"

"Whilst Mama is still indisposed, I thought I would like an early morning stroll to blow the cobwebs away."

"Well, I am going to go and see Ben. Would you care to walk with me?"

"Yes, of course. I will go with you as far as Big Ope and then I'll go on alone, so that you can meet up with Ben privately." He did not want to tell Rebecca that he was going to seek out Ben's mother.

As they step outside a cold wind blows off the sea and they both wrap their cloaks more tightly around them. "I didn't realise it was this cold, but I really cannot wait any longer to see Ben."

"He will be pleased to see you again after all this time and to see how well you are looking, Becky."

"Do you think so, Josh?"

"Of course."

"I hope so, Josh, I have missed him so much."

"Well, pass on to him my good wishes and I will see him on Christmas morning."

They part company at the bottom of Big Ope.

Rebecca finds Ben, as expected, in the boatyard with Matthew and after the usual greetings she asks her father quietly if he could spare Ben for a short while so that they could have a stroll together. He agrees amiably, happy to see his Rebecca back home again where she belongs.

Rebecca takes Ben's hand shyly and they walk off along the beach together to talk.

"I have missed you so much," he says, gently looking down at her.

"Me too."

"I have been worried about you. How are you feeling? Are you quite recovered?"

"Yes, I am quite back to normal again now." She smiles.

"I am sorry that I was such little help or consolation to you, but I was so angry with that bastard. When I got back all I wanted was to hold you in my arms and console you, but I felt so out of water back there in that huge house, with all those people around. I just couldn't think sensibly, but as soon as I got back here, all I longed to do was go back to Somerset and make you realise how wretched I felt for you."

"Don't worry, I do understand Ben, but I was afraid that you would think less of me because of what that Meakins did to me."

"No, not you, Beck. It wasn't your fault, but I could have killed him, which is why Josh made me leave. Plus we didn't want to alert your parents to what had happened either. I love you, Becky, you know that don't you? Are you going to stay back here with us now?"

"Do you want me to?"

"Yes, of course I do, I have been lost without you."

"Then we must tell Josh together. I don't think he will mind too much."

Annie is surprised to find Joshua on her doorstep when she answers his knock.

"Good morning, Joshua, I am afraid Ben is already at work with your stepfather."

"It is not Ben I came to see, Mrs Stone. I wanted to have a chat with you, actually."

For some reason a sudden chill runs down her spine. "Well, you had better come in then." She stands aside and Joshua enters the small cottage.

"I have had a visit from a very unpleasant man, who tells me that his steward gleaned some information from you regarding my father and his relationship to Ben. Unfortunately, it has put me in a position where I am forced to ask you directly: is it true that my dear friend and cousin is in truth my half brother?"

Annie is stunned. She feels sick as realisation dawns on what must have happened. She had never wanted anyone to know that Richard Dryer, and not her husband William, was Ben's real father and is mortified that Alistair McNab must have been able to glean this information from her by getting her drunk. She sinks back into an armchair behind her. "I am so sorry, Joshua, I would never have let on, but he got me drunk."

Joshua can tell from her expression that the

story is true and he is devastated. "But why did you never tell us?

"It was my secret. I never wanted your mother to know. She was already married to your father by this time and shortly afterwards I heard that she was also pregnant with you. Please, Joshua, I beg you to keep it between us. It is better that Ben does not know the truth. You must agree that he and Becky are made for each other and it will be such a shock to realise that they are, in effect, stepbrother and sister. What will he think of me for hiding it from him for all these years?"

"But if what you say is true, they are not blood relations; Ben's parents would be you and my father Richard Dryer, but Becky's parents are my mother Violet and my adoptive father, Matthew."

"I know, that is why I never said anything," agrees Annie, "but it is true, Joshua, that you and Ben are half brothers and share the same father."

Joshua looks very despondent. He had always thought of his father as a hero, battling against the smugglers and losing his life into the bargain. "He really must have been a very shallow fellow. He could not have loved either of you, to treat you in this way."

It is difficult for Annie to admit to this, for she had always been so jealous of Violet, but she has to tell Joshua the truth. "No, Joshua, your father was very much in love with your mother. It was partly my own fault that he used me, for he was so handsome and charming, I would have done anything for him." She gives a deep sigh. "But it was not me he loved and I was soon to learn a very hard lesson."

"My problem is that now Meakins knows, he is shouting it to all and sundry, implying that Ben has a claim on the estate. Some of the staff overheard what he was saying and it could be all around the estate by now, so what am I to do?"

"I don't know. I am very sorry that I was so stupid. I cannot believe that canny Scot was so conniving to get the information out of me."

"Did my father know?"

"Yes he did and he offered financial help in caring for Ben, but I did not want his help. I was angry with him and I turned him down and insisted that it was kept a secret for all our sakes."

"What about my mother? Does she know?"

"I am quite sure your father would not have upset your mother by telling her what went on between us before they married, so I don't think so. But even if she does know, she has kept it a secret all these years and will be very upset to hear that you have found out the truth and will not want it public knowledge here, either."

"That is all well and good, but I feel that I have to tell Ben and maybe even offer him a share in the estate."

"Please, Josh, I don't want Ben to think that I have lied to him all these years. Please go back to Somerset and find out if he would be entitled to anything, before you make any hasty decisions."

"But whether he is or not, does not stop me acting however I feel is right and just, does it?"

"Well, I think that you should first talk to your solicitor before you do anything rash. Besides, I am sure that Ben could never get used to such a lifestyle, he is more than happy working with Matthew and fishing, as long as Becky feels the same."

"But I don't see how we can keep it a secret any longer. The truth always has a habit of coming out, eventually."

On Christmas morning Joshua gives his parents the hamper that he had prepared for Rebecca to take for them and is now helping Matthew stack some driftwood for the fire and rearranging the furniture. While Rebecca is busy helping her mother by preparing the Christmas meal, to which their grandparents and Ben are invited, along with their Uncle Robert and Aunty Hannah. When all the dinner guests have arrived, the family sit down together and open their presents, before it is time for Hannah and Rebecca to serve their meal.

Violet is feeling a little better and is very happy to be able to come downstairs at last and watch everyone exchanging their gifts. She and Matthew were going to give their present for Joshua to Billy to take back with him, but they were delighted to find instead that, as well as their Becky, he had decided to spend Christmas with them. They had bought him a beautifully tooled leather satchel and, as he draws it carefully from its wrapping, Violet explains, "It is for you to use for your documents when you are working as a Justice of the Peace."

"Oh my goodness! Thank you so much, it is absolutely perfect. What a good choice." He kisses his mother and shakes Matthew by the hand.

Rebecca's paternal grandmother has made her some lace-edged handkerchiefs, from herself and Matthew's father, and her maternal grandmother has made her a silk reticule as a gift from herself and Violet's father.

For Joshua, Matthew's parents purchased twelve plain handkerchiefs and his grandmother has embroidered his initials in one corner, each in a different colour. Violet's parents give him two pairs of braces for his trousers.

Hannah and Robert have brought some wine and a Christmas pudding for everyone and Ben has contributed some porter. For Rebecca, who he has been missing so sorely of late, and who, in his estimation, deserves special attention this Christmas after what she has been going through, he has bought a double-ended scent bottle; one end is for her perfume and the other end for her smelling salts. It is in a beautiful, ruby-coloured glass and has silver tops at each end. He observes her anxiously lest she does not like it.

"Oh, Ben! It is beautiful, I love it. Thank you so much, you are so thoughtful."

He is relieved; it is obvious that she is thrilled. "Well you will need something to go in it now," he says.

"Don't worry, I have some rose water."

"Here, open this one." He hands her another small parcel. Inside she discovers a bottle of French Lily of the Valley perfume. "My favourite!"

He grins at her pleasure. "I bought it from the emporium in Wyke Regis."

She takes off the stopper and inhales the subtle flowery perfume. "Oh lovely, look, Ma," she thrusts the bottle under her mother's nose.

"Very nice, Becky," she smiles at her daughter. "You had better take that with you when you go back to Somerset, otherwise there may be none left when you return."

"I am not going back to stay with Josh, Ma. I have decided to stay here. I really have been rather homesick in Somerset and I am looking forward to helping you in the shop and to seeing more of Ben."

"Oh, I am pleased, Becky. I have missed you too." She holds out her arms to give her daughter a big hug and Becky smiles to be back safely in the arms of her mother. Then she looks up guiltily at her brother.

"I am sorry, Josh, I meant to tell you first. I have loved being there with you, everyone is so friendly and kind, but I do miss Ma and Pa and Ben so much."

"Well, I can certainly understand why you are homesick, but we will all miss you, Becky, especially Aurora," says Joshua kindly. He knows only too well the true reason why Rebecca has decided to return to Portland and he understands that she wants to turn her back on her past traumas, but he is anxious not to raise suspicions in their parents. "Well, you are all welcome to visit whenever you like, you know that."

"I am sure we will take you up on that sometime soon, Joshua," says Matthew.

There are lots of expressions of appreciation as the others all exchange their gifts, until finally Rebecca opens her last gift. Violet has been busy making clothes for her daughter's Christmas present and Rebecca is thrilled with the lovely, rich-coloured gowns and matching jackets.

"Oh, Ma, these are beautiful! Do you mind if I pop upstairs and try them on?"

"Of course not, darling, I will just go and put the finishing touches to our dinner."

"No Ma, you stay there, you are still unwell. I will try them on later."

After their meal Rebecca helps her mother with the washing up, whilst her mother sits on a stool and dries the dishes.

"You never told me how the summer ball went, Becky?"

"Oh, it was marvellous, Ma. I decided not to attend the ball, but to help behind the scenes. It was great fun and such a spectacle."

She cannot let her mother suspect the trauma of what had really happened that night and so she regales her with the truth of how she had felt, prior to the moment of her attack. "We were so busy, Lettie and I, serving the refreshments, but we did have a break and we went up onto the gallery to look down on the ballroom. The music was so wonderful and all the dancers looked so glamorous, the men in their dinner jackets and the ladies festooned in their colourful gowns and glittering jewellery. It was magical, Ma."

As the tone in her voice alters, her mother glances up at her, "It must have been magical, Becky, for the memory has brought tears to your eyes, darling."

Rebecca blushes guiltily and brushes away her tears with the back of her hand; she must not let her mother suspect anything, "Well, I suppose I should have dressed up and joined in the dancing, but I didn't want to let Joshua down, not being used to the social etiquette and having to learn all the dances beforehand. I thought it better to enjoy it all as an observer instead. Besides, Joshua needed the extra help and Lettie and I were quite a team."

"Did your brother dance with anyone in particular?"

"Well, there were the Bridewell sisters, I think he rather took a shine to Keziah and he was very chatty with Serena, but he also had several dances with Louisa, according to Elsie."

"Hmm, that is interesting," says Violet thoughtfully.

"He also danced with Mrs Abbott and Mrs Seymour, do you find that so interesting Ma?" laughs Rebecca.

In the afternoon Aunty Molly and Uncle John join them with their two little children, Matilda and

Reuben. There is plenty to eat and drink and Rebecca is very relaxed back in her parent's homely cottage.

Violet had asked Ben to make another Noah's Ark for her, as her Christmas gift for her godchildren, and they watch as the children tear the gift from its wrapping. Matilda and Reuben are immediately enamoured with the tiny animals and soon they are playing with it together on the rug beside the fire.

Joshua watches his mother and Matthew chatting with their friends and family. They are both happy and relaxed and he is reluctant to tell his mother what he has recently learned. She will not want to hear that her husband fathered a child with Annie Shaddick. He finds it hard to imagine the difficulty Violet would have gone through, harbouring the secret of his true relationship to Ben all these years, if she did know the facts. *Surely she cannot even suspect the truth? Thank God Becky is Matthew's daughter; otherwise she and Ben would be committing incest. Should he confront her, or is it best to let sleeping dogs lie?*

Apart from this dilemma Christmas is a relatively happy time for Joshua, visiting his grandparents and uncles and telling them all about the estate, about the staff and the baby Aurora and what he is going to be doing from now on as a Justice of the Peace. While he is visiting his grandparents to say goodbye, however, he notices a lantern hanging on a hook in their scullery.

"Grandma Mary, do you mind if I borrow that lamp? Only I have a little job to do and that will be perfect for my needs."

"Well, I don't know what you would want with that, 'tis an old smuggler's spout lantern."

"I realise that, but it will be very handy for my gamekeeper."

"Well, we have no use for it any more, so I am sure you can have it, my dear, if it will be useful."

"Thank you, Grandma; it really will make a big difference."

"You are welcome, Josh, of course you are." She plants a kiss on his cheek, and they share a pot of tea with his grandfather before he takes his leave.

CHAPTER 18 *(January 1854)*

WASSAILING IN THE NEW YEAR

On New Years Day Joshua leaves Rebecca behind and returns to Alvington Manor without divulging their secret, or broaching the subject of Ben with his mother. The first thing he does is go and see Mr Fairway at Battens for his advice, who suggests that he keeps things between them, rather than arrange to see anyone else and he would go over the will again.

The following morning Mr Fairway visits Alvington Manor with what he believes is good news. "I have discovered that, as he had no knowledge of the whereabouts of your father at the time he made his will, Christian Dryer simply left everything to 'the oldest surviving male blood relation'. I believe that you are the firstborn, are you not?"

"Well, there are only a few days between us, but yes I am."

"Well, there you are then, despite you being related, you are still the firstborn and you are also legitimate, which your half brother is not, so as far as the law is concerned you are the rightful heir."

"But I still feel that Ben has a right to know that we are brothers and not cousins, as he believes."

"Well, that is up to you, my boy, but it may be like opening up Pandora's Box!"

"But if I don't tell him then someone else might."

"That is true, but if you do tell him then you will damage the relationships he has with his mother, Becky and yourself. Plus your mother and Matthew will learn of your father and Annie's long held secret. Is that not too big a price to pay for your peace of mind?"

"You have a talent for putting your finger right on the problem, Ambrose. I can see that you are right; disclosing the secret would be too distressing for all concerned. I will keep my own counsel and hope to God that no one else discloses the truth to them."

The following day is 5th January and many of the estate workers are going wassailing, the first fertility festival of the traditional calendar, a ceremony intended to begin the process of waking the fruit trees from their winter slumber and praising them for their previous fruitfulness. Lettie has arranged to join the maids for the occasion.

The ritual begins just before dark when the wassailing cup is prepared. Lettie's mother, with the help of Emily Potts, uses an old recipe called Lamb's Wool, made of hot ale, eggs, spices, sugar, cream and roasted apples and pours this into the huge ornate silver wassail bowl.

Later that night in the bitter frosty cold with stars sparkling overhead, small groups of estate staff and their families, muffled against the chill, proceed down the path into the orchard. Lettie has met up with Lucy and Bunny and the maids. They all proceed with as much noise as they can muster. Some carry flaming torches, others have long sticks and some have created utilised drums. Her father has his shotgun, and the kitchen staff have shared out their pots and pans.

Joshua and Malachi lead the way to the oldest tree in the orchard, each carefully holding a handle of the wassail bowl filled with the steaming brew, carefully trying not to spill it. The steam from the bowl mingles with the cloudy breath of all the people. At the largest tree, each participant takes a cupful of the brew with which to toast the most venerable tree and Joshua starts the chant, which he has only learnt since he came to Somerset.

"Health to thee, good apple tree, stand fast root, bear well top, pray God send us a good howling crop. Every bough, apples endow, every twig, apples big, health to thee, good apple tree."

Everyone drinks the health of the tree and then they join in with the chorus. *"Hats full, caps full, full quarter sacks full. Holler boys holler!"* Then everyone begins beating the trees about the trunks and branches to begin the process of awakening the orchard and starting the sap flowing up the trunks. It is accompanied by shouting and as much noise as possible, and John fires his shotgun up into the branches, to frighten away any evil spirits that might be lurking up there.

When all the noise and commotion is over, everyone bows to the tree and then young Toby is lifted up into the branches, where he is passed offerings of bread, cheese and cider to represent the spirit of the tree receiving the gifts.

Finally pieces of toasted bread soaked in cider are thrust up into forks in the branches or hollows in the other trees and left there as offerings, whilst the remainder of the wassail cup is sloshed over and around the trunk of the oldest tree.

The mouth watering aroma of the hot ale lingers in the air, as people turn to home. Lettie hears a cry from up above them. Poor Toby thought he was going to be left behind and all laugh at his indignant little face, as Malachi lifts him down safe and sound and then bounces him up again onto his father's shoulders to convey him home to his bed.

The girls linger, chatting and finishing up the contents of their wassailing cups, reluctant to leave behind the social event.

Lettie manages to get Louisa on her own for a moment. "How is Becky, Louisa, have you heard?"

"Yes, Lettie, she sent a note back for all of us saying that she was feeling much better and that she was glad to be back on Portland with her family and especially Ben. Joshua read it out to us when he got back. I believe Mrs Abbott has stuck it on the mantelpiece in the kitchen for anyone to read."

"Oh, I am so glad. I have been worrying about her."

"I am sure there is no need, Lettie, I do believe she is fully recovered." Louisa drops her voice. "I just hope that she will still be able to have more babies after going through all that."

"Oh, Louisa, I never thought of that."

"Well, Dr Gillingham gave her a clear bill of health, so hopefully there won't be a problem."

Lettie blurts out angrily, "That Nathan Meakins has a lot to answer for."

"I know, but…"

Lettie can see that Louisa is troubled by something. "What is it, Louisa? What were you going to say?"

Louisa moves closer to Lettie and whispers, "There is so much more sadness and pain he is responsible for, but it is too dreadful a secret."

"What, Lou, what is it?"

Louisa seems to be struggling with her conscience but finally she makes a decision. "I really feel now that because you know about Becky you should also know the rest. It is about Aurora. I am very sorry to have to admit it, but that devil Meakins is Aurora's father as well."

"My God, Louisa, he seduced your sister too!"

"Shush! Yes, Lettie, and I had to keep it all to myself, until Becky and Joshua discovered the truth. You must also keep it to yourself, Lettie, for I never want him to get his filthy hands on her."

"Of course I will, I love that little girl and we don't want her to end up dead too." Lettie blurts this out before she has thought of the consequences, but Louisa is thinking of her sister and does not pick up on her comment.

"I would rather die myself than have anyone touch a hair on her head," says Louisa fiercely.

Lettie has been sworn to secrecy by her sweetheart with regard to the coven and their evil activities, but maybe her friends and family should know about the dangers of tangling with this man. She decides to keep her own counsel until she has first spoken again to Raymond. "Don't you fret, Louisa; I know how to keep my mouth shut tight when necessary."

All the activity with his estate staff and their families distracts Joshua from his main worry, but the following morning he is again musing over the problem of Nathan Meakins and he decides to go out for a walk in the crisp winter air to clear his head. He follows the same route of the previous night and finds himself in the orchard again.

Unbeknown to him Mrs Abbott has asked Louisa to do a display of greenery for the hall table and she is also in the orchard selecting some winter twigs. In her trug she has a selection of evergreens, berries and pine cones and she thought a few small bare branches that had been knocked down the previous night would add a light touch to her arrangement. She gathers them up and then works her way along the hedgerow to search for some old man's beard. Unfortunately it is too early for pussy willow, which would have been perfect.

A robin perched at the highest point of the old apple tree serenades its mate, who is a few trees away and pecking eagerly at the tasty bread. Louisa searches through the branches to spot him, then she hears a man's voice. She winds her way through the apple trees until she finds him and is shocked to see that it is Joshua all alone and looking very tormented.

"Somehow I have to ensure that he doesn't get away with it all simply by paying a fine," he says to himself. As he does so he turns on his heel abruptly and sees her.

She clears her throat. "Pardon me, my Lord, I was just collecting some specimens for the hall." She feels guilty for sneaking up on him, but she had not expected it to be the master.

His manner changes immediately. "Ah, Louisa, what a gloriously fresh, bright morning. I just thought I would take a moment to clear my head. Would you care to take a stroll with me?"

"If you would explain to Mrs Abbott for me, my Lord, I would be delighted."

"Of course," Joshua holds out his arm for her. She takes it happily and they walk arm in arm through the frosty grass.

"I have missed our little chats, my Lord." She smiles shyly at him.

"Me too, Louisa." He gently pats her hand.

"Christmas was very dull without you. Gareth did his best, but he was no substitute."

"I know, I am sorry, but I had no choice but to go." He quickly changes the subject. "How is little

Aurora getting along? Do you spend much time with her?"

"Not really, my Lord, I pop up to the nursery occasionally and sometimes I see her down in the kitchen, but she is a bonny little lass and so happy, her mama would be so proud of her."

"I am sure. It is very sad that your poor sister was unable to cope with her horrible situation. You and your parents must have been so shocked. You have been very brave keeping this all to yourself, but we must keep up the pretence, for it would never do for that bastard Meakins to discover the truth."

Louisa is taken aback at her master using such language, but she could not agree with him more. "Well, he told poor Millie to get rid of it, but he never knew that the baby had been born. He probably believes that the baby died with its mother in the womb."

"That is just as well, for we really do not want him to get his hands on her."

"He will never hear it from me, my Lord; I would rather die than set eyes on him ever again."

Joshua relives the moment when he first saw Millie lying in the grass, her skin pale and translucent like alabaster, mud and pondweed in her hair and he cannot bear the thought of finding dear Louisa so tragically. "Don't talk like that, Louisa. I don't like to hear it; you are worth so much more than that. I would be lost now without you." He looks down gently at her and she blushes.

"Thank you, my Lord."

"I mean it, Louisa; I believe we are so much more than master and maidservant, I believe we have become friends and I would like it very much if you would call me Joshua at times when we are alone."

Louisa feels the heat flushing her cheeks with pleasure. "I would like that, my Lord, it means a lot to me… I mean… I would like that, Joshua, thank you." And she squeezes his arm affectionately.

"We have gone through a lot together, since my arrival here. Without your help and support I cannot imagine what would have happened to Becky."

"We have both gone through a lot with our sisters and all because of that fiend Nathan Meakins. God forgive me but I wish he was dead."

"Don't worry, Louisa, I have a plan that I hope will cook his goose once and for all."

"But how? With his family connections he thinks he is above the law."

"And that will be his downfall, Louisa. Believe me, no one is above the law and I intend to prove it." Joshua sees that Louisa is looking cold. "We had better get you back inside; I think the wind must be getting up."

CHAPTER 19 *(January 1854)*

THE BATTLE OF HAMDON HILL

Joshua checks *Jenks' Old Farmer's Almanac* to ascertain the following monthly full moons and he instructs John Hawkins to keep a look out, during the weeks that the moon is waxing to full moon and then waning, in the hope of catching the smugglers.

It is the end of January and for several nights now John Hawkins has kept watch over Gulliver's Lane. He is tired and cold and fears that he will fall asleep on duty, so he has enlisted Thomas to stand in for him, with instructions to wake him should he see the convoy of pack animals. He is soon snuggled up with his wife and snoring gently.

He has been asleep for about two hours when he feels his shoulder being shaken and he looks up to see Thomas standing there, silhouetted against the window in the moonlight.

"They are passing by now, Pa," he whispers.

John eases himself out of bed so as not to wake Molly and goes into Thomas's room, which overlooks the Alvington estate. He watches covertly until the last of the procession passes by and then he lights the spout lantern. The sulphurous smell wafts around the room as he signals the warning light to Joshua.

Joshua and Gareth have been keeping watch in turn from Alvington Manor and it is Gareth who is on duty and spots the flink. He rushes along to the master bedroom to alert Joshua. "Lord Dryer, sir, the moment has come. They have just passed Camp Road."

Joshua quickly pulls on his riding boots and his outer garments and is swiftly down to the stable where he finds Gareth has already woken Billy, who was sleeping in the straw beside Capricorn. Billy has hurriedly and efficiently saddled the black stallion. He is a little indignant at being aroused, but he is soon cajoled and ready to fly. As Joshua mounts the animal, Billy suddenly grabs his master's arm. "Let me go in your place, my Lord, I am a good rider and I won't let you down."

"No, Billy, this is something I need to see through from start to finish. Besides, I would never be able to forgive myself if anything should happen to you, whilst doing my bidding."

"Be careful, my Lord, don't take any unnecessary risks," advises Gareth.

"Do not concern yourself on my account, I am like a cat and have only used up a few of my lives."

"Good luck, my Lord," says Billy with concern.

"Thank you, Billy," says Joshua, as he urges Capricorn on with a flick of the reins. He is shortly racing down the drive in the direction of Montacute.

He rides as if the devil is on his heels; his blood is up, his heart pumping with excitement on this important mission. Although the moon is on the wane his route is well lit, as he passes through Montacute and on towards Stoke under Hamdon. A horse whinnies from a stable yard as he enters the village, and a dog barks from a small cottage as he turns left to go up the escarpment towards the summit of Hamdon Hill.

Capricorn is lathering and the frothy white sweat catches in the moonlight as a flock of sheep scatter.

He finally turns left again towards the Prince of Wales Inn, where a small detachment of militia is quartered. As he pulls the horse to a halt he is met by the captain and a militiaman on guard outside the inn.

"Halt! What is your hurry stranger?"

"I am Joshua Dryer of Alvington Manor, you are expecting me."

"We are, my Lord, what is your news?"

"The smugglers were last seen at Camp Road about an hour past and are due at any moment."

"Right, Perkins, let's raise the men." He sends his comrade off into the pub and Joshua watches as the men spill out onto the flagstones outside the inn, some yawning, some coughing and spitting, others straightening their uniforms and checking their muskets.

The captain says, "Right men, you have been briefed, but to re-cap: Sergeant Blake, I want B section to blockade the road down into Stoke under Hamdon to prevent them reaching the Fosse Way; Sergeant Flanagan, I want D section to disperse among the quarries, also making sure that escape down the westerly road into Chiselborough is thwarted. When they have passed that turning, on my command, we will make our move. Finally, Sergeant Cutter, I want A section to split and wait each side of the road at the southern edge of the quarry area and stay hidden as the smugglers approach. You are to wait until they have all passed by and then in a pincer movement bring up the rear to prevent them back tracking. I will be with A section and everyone waits until they hear my command. Is that clear?"

Each of the section leaders reply: "Yes, sir."

"Are there any questions?"

The men respond in unison: "No, sir."

"Right, off you go and take your places." He turns back to Joshua. "Thank you, Lord Dryer, your duty is done. If you wouldn't mind taking yourself and your horse off to the left over there to attend him and we will take over from now. It is likely the smugglers will be turning in this direction, as I believe, owing to the shiftiness of the landlord who is being closely watched, they may have been intending to break their journey here at the inn."

"I will certainly keep out of the way, for I have the greatest respect for your training and professionalism, but I am armed and rather than come to any harm myself, I will shoot if necessary."

"I understand, my Lord, but I would be happier if you could take yourself off into the stables, where you can watch the fun from there in relative safety."

With that the officer joins his comrades as they spread out among the quarries, their smart red tunics not easy to camouflage among the grassy banks and rocky dips of the rough terrain.

Joshua can see that the men are edgy, excited and looking forward to a bit of action. At last they have the opportunity to put to use all their arduous training. He waits anxiously, knowing that a lot depends on the outcome of this battle. He takes his pistol from his saddle bag and handles it appreciatively; it was his father's, one of a pair of Henry Nock, flintlock twenty-five bore duelling pistols and he is ready to avenge his father's death at the hands of the smugglers should any of them come his way. He is positioned behind the stable door, over which he has a good view of the approach to the inn, but he is unable to see the men who are now concealed among the humps and valleys of the open quarries. He waits anxiously listening for the slightest warning sound, but the only thing to break the silence is the eerie howl of a dog fox from the valley below.

Time seems to stand still and the cold is seeping into his bones. Joshua is beginning to think that the smugglers may have stopped off already at another gentlemen's house to overnight, which would ruin his plan completely, when he hears something and he stiffens in anticipation. The hairs rise on the back of his neck. Could this be the gang? What if it is a blood bath and it is his fault? He feels sick with anxiety.

Then he hears a command to the militia and the noise they make is blood curdling as they ambush the convoy. Some have no choice but to surrender immediately. Others abandon their pack animals and try to make a run for it, but the militia warn them to stand still or they will be shot. Only one rogue keeps running and is shot in the leg.

The captive convoy is strung out between the turning down the steep hill into Chiselborough and the Prince of Wales Inn; the leaders were nearly at the inn when the militia made themselves known. Joshua witnesses with pleasure their surprise, annoyance and frustration.

The militia are working along the line of the smugglers, tying the men's hands together and linking them to their animals, when Capricorn whinnies at the sound of the mules and Joshua observes that the smuggler who was leading the men has recognised the sound of a horse with which he could make a quick getaway. Joshua watches as the man makes a decision to move before he too is tied and it is too late. Calmly but gingerly the smuggler slinks into the shadows of the inn and works his way towards the stable. Joshua can see that he plans to make a run for the door behind which he is concealed. He primes his pistol. The man is waiting for a cloud to obliterate the moon, before he risks moving between the two buildings.

The more time passes, the more Joshua's tension increases. *Could he bring himself to shoot this man?*

Then a shadow passes across the moon and the man furtively makes a dash towards him. As he pushes open the stable door and silently slides inside, Joshua places his pistol against the man's temple. "I hope you weren't planning to steal my horse and add horse theft to your list of misdemeanours?"

The smuggler freezes. "Relax, soldier boy, hold your fire. I was only hoping to hide; I have a wife and family back home. I cannot face a prison sentence, let alone transportation. Can't you make out you've not seen me? 'Tis no skin off your nose, you have my word that I mean you no harm."

Joshua believes the man is terrified, but he showed pluck making a run for it and he is not prepared to give him another opportunity. "What is your name?"

"Why would I tell you that?"

"You are obviously planning to make another run for it, otherwise you would be resigned to telling me your name."

"It is Albert Johnson, if you must know."

"Well, Albert, I think we should go outside and join the rest of your cronies."

"Please, fellow, don't make me beg. Just wait a moment and hear me out, I can make it worth your while."

"I think you will find that it is worth my while to see all you villains safely behind bars. You see I am not one of the soldiers, I am actually the Justice of the Peace who organised this ambush and I am looking forward to meeting you all in my court in March at the Easter quarter sessions. But consider this; any information you or your friends are able to give me, with regard to the venturers who back you all financially, will be taken into consideration when deciding on your sentences, so think on that. Now, get back out there where the militia can see you." He points his pistol into the man's back and pushes him out through the stable door.

"Captain, I have another scoundrel over here."

The captain turns. "Well done, my Lord, I think we have a full house."

As an aside Joshua requests that Mr Johnson should initially be held with the ringleaders at the Ivell House of Correction and the captain is happy to comply.

Amy is sound asleep in her tiny attic room at the top of Summerville House. The moonlight is slanting across her peaceful face and she is dreaming of her father, as he was before his accident, when she is aroused by a creak and the sound of movement close by her. She opens her eyes cautiously and immediately is filled with alarm, as she sees the door to her room close behind a tall male figure and the smell of Makassar oil permeates the air. If it was not for the oil she might have thought she had seen the ghost of her father, but that hair oil is unmistakable. She is sure that Nathan Meakins was in her room.

Her heart is thumping so loudly that she fears he will hear it from outside the door. She is afraid to close her eyes lest he should return. What does he want from her? He is twice her age. The thought makes her blood run cold. After waiting and listening for a good half an hour, her heart rate returns to normal and Amy plucks up the courage to sneak into Jean's room.

She shakes her friend. "Jean, wake up, I need to talk to you. It is important."

"What is it? It is not daylight yet," she mutters hazily.

"I am sorry, Jean, but I need to talk to you. It is about Nathan Meakins."

"What about him?" Jean is suddenly alert and she raises herself up, to lean against the pillow on her elbow.

"I am sure he was in my room earlier." Amy sinks down onto the edge of Jean's bed

"What do you mean, earlier in the day?"

"No, while I was sleeping, just about half an hour ago. Jean, I am really frightened."

"Why, what are you not telling me? What else has happened?"

"Well, he caught me kissing Bobby Tompkins the other day and he said that he wouldn't say a word as long as I remember that I am indebted to him. I thought he just meant there was some domestic job that he would give me, but he has already forced me to kiss him and I am afraid of what he demands next."

"And so you should be. Why did you not tell me before now? There is only one thing he is after and only one person who will get pleasure from it. Listen to me Amy, you have to leave and right now, or you will be ruined. You must go straight away to Bobby and his family. They will care for you, Amy, they are kind people and you will be safe. Quickly, go and get your things together and we must sneak out before dawn."

Amy stands up as Jean pulls back her covers and lights her candle, quickly putting on her clothes.

"What do you mean 'we'?"

"I am coming with you, Amy, to make sure you are safe. I have had enough of this family and I don't want to work here a moment longer."

"But what about Cook and Mrs Faversham? We are letting them down."

"Don't give it a second thought, Amy, they have

not been friends to us. We are just servants and they don't care a fig about either of us, so why should we care about them? Hurry now, Amy, go and get ready and come back as fast as you can before folk are up and about."

Amy rushes off back to her room and is soon dressed, with all her worldly possessions bundled into her bag. She nearly forgets her Easter egg hidden under her pillow, but remembers just in time. She joins Jean, who is waiting for her on the narrow stairway, and together with hearts thumping they creep down the three floors to the kitchen. Jean reaches up and finds the key to the back door and in minutes they are out in the open air and running swiftly and silently across the damp grass, rather than the noisy gravel.

They are both breathless by the time they are out of sight of the house. Although grateful for the moonlight to light their way, it could also reveal their escape to any restless sleeper looking out of the front windows, but so far so good, there is no sound of anyone following. However, they need to get to Bobby's house before Meakins has the chance to sneak up on them.

As they follow the footpath that runs around the base of Summer Hill the scent of wood smoke becomes apparent and Amy notices Jean looking over her shoulder towards the top of the hill. She follows her gaze and can see a tiny glimmer of firelight through the bare trees and shadows passing across it at regular intervals. "Whatever is that, Jean?"

Jean whispers back, her voice full of fear. "I think we should make haste Amy, for it seems that there are witches abroad."

The faint sound of chanting wafts on the chill air and a shiver runs down Amy's spine. "Witches? Here in our copse?"

"Yes Amy, there is a coven who meets up there."

"Oh Jean, how dreadful! How long have you known about it?"

"I have suspected for months now, but we don't have time to talk about it, we must be very quiet and hurry away."

They hear a rustle through the undergrowth, a twig snaps and both girls freeze.

"What was that?" whispers Amy, gripping her arm in panic. They stay stock still for several moments, but no-one appears.

"Don't worry, it was probably just a badger," Jean reassures her quietly and they hurry on cautiously.

They can hear the running water below them as they cross the river, a ribbon of silver grey in the moonlight, and they can see the lights of the community ahead. The witches will not show themselves here and they relax a little. Amy's heartbeat slows to normal and her thoughts turn again to her future safety. "I am worried, Jean, about what Bobby's parents will say," she whispers breathlessly, as they both trudge along the road into the town.

"Don't worry about them, just ask to speak to Bobby first and we can both tell him what has happened. I am sure he will be able to talk them round."

"What are you going to do, Jean?"

"I am going to go home to my parents after I am sure that you are safe."

"Thank you, Jean; you have been such a good friend to me. I don't know what I would have done without you here. I would never have found the courage to leave like this."

"There is a lot you don't know about Nathan Meakins. He is the devil himself and you were next on his list of victims. I've seen the way he looks at you, Amy. He is like a spider with a fly and if, as you say, he was in your room then you have had a lucky escape."

"Why do you say that?"

"Because I know Nathan Meakins."

"But I don't understand," whispers Amy. "What do you mean, Jean, I was next on his list of victims?"

Jean hesitates. "The less you know the better, Amy, but you have seen for yourself how manipulative he can be."

"Yes, I have seen how smarmy he is and how he can change to being very mean in seconds."

"Oh, he can be charming when he wants something right enough. It is when he comes up against objection there is trouble, when he won't take 'no' for an answer. He might have had his evil way with you and ruined your reputation forever."

"My God, Jean, there will be pandemonium when they realise that both of us have left. He will be very angry."

"I don't care how he feels; we just have to make sure that we are both safely hidden from him forever."

"How will we manage that?"

"I have some friends who may be able to help us. But first you want to find your sweetheart, Bobby."

Amy notes with relief that they are approaching the shambles and signs of life are evident above the shops where people are preparing for another day. Cold and breathless, she points to the shop that has a sign over the display window: *Samuel Tompkins and Sons*. "There is his shop, Jean, and look, there is a side door with a knocker."

She lifts the heavy iron knocker and bangs it several times against the wooden door. The sound echoes within and she stands there shivering and looking anxiously at her friend.

Jean reassures her, "Don't worry, it will be fine, Amy." She puts her arm around her and they both huddle together, on tenterhooks lest she be turned away by Bobby's family. Then the door opens and Bobby himself is standing there.

"Amy! Whatever are you doing here?" He hugs her tenderly.

"I am so sorry Bobby, but I need your help. We have run away from Summerville House."

"But why? Whatever has happened?"

"It is because of Master Nathan. He saw us together, kissing the other day. That is not allowed and he threatened to sack me if I wasn't nice to him. To start with I just thought he wanted me to do extra domestic duties, but the other day he cornered me and forced me to kiss him and he put his hand up my skirt." She trembles at the memory, and then continues resolutely. "But he was interrupted by Apsey and I escaped. Then last night he came into my room and really frightened me."

"Did he hurt you, Amy?"

"No, I don't know what he was doing; I just woke up in time to see him sneaking out again. Jean said I had to leave because he is a dangerous man and she persuaded me to come and find you for help."

"Oh, Amy, you poor thing," Bobby kisses her on her forehead. "Thank you, Jean; you did right bringing her to me. Come inside and I will introduce you both to Mother."

Mrs Tompkins is dishing up breakfast for her boys as the girls enter. Their kitchen is gleaming and the bacon and eggs smell mouth watering. "Mother this is Amy, who I have told you about, and her friend Jean from Summerville House. Amy and Jean, this is my mother and my brother Harry."

They all greet each other warily and Bobby continues, "I am afraid the young master of the house has taken a shine to Amy and Jean has persuaded her, for her own safety, to leave their employ. Do you think we could find room for her to lodge here with us for a while?"

This is greeted with a shocked silence. "What has this master done that is a threat to Amy's safety?" Bobby's mother looks concerned.

Jean steps forward before Amy can say anything. "I am afraid that what he has done is so despicable that you would never believe it. I have to pluck up the courage to tell someone who is in a position to do something about it. I fear that all those who become involved in this may be at risk from this man and so it is safer for you that you do not know."

Amy notices Mrs Tompkins' raised eyebrows and wonders if she thinks this is all rather dramatic, but Jean continues resolutely. "Besides, I do not want this information to get back to him for my own safety. Amy has had a taste of what he is like, but she does not know everything. However, I can assure you she needs to be protected from him and I know that she and Bobby are sweet on each other. I beg you to let her stay secretly here with you, until this man is dealt with."

Mrs Tompkins deliberates for a few moments and then she decides. "Well, I suppose we can put her in the box room, Bobby, but you will have to clear it all out for her."

Amy rushes forward and tearfully grabs her hands with gratitude. "Thank you so much, Mrs Tompkins, I will help Bobby and please let me help you with the housework and cooking while I am here."

"Well, you will have to do something to earn

your keep, or Mr Tompkins will have something to say about it," she smiles good-naturedly, which takes the edge off her sharp words.

"Of course I will, I am so grateful. I was so afraid I would have to join the rest of my family in the poor house. I will keep looking for work in the meantime."

Jean gives a sigh of relief and then fixes her hat. "Well, I had better be on my way."

"Won't you stop and take some breakfast with us first, Jean?" asks Bobby kindly.

"Umm," she doesn't like to take advantage, but Harry has been tucking into it while they were talking and the food smells so especially good.

Mrs Tompkins intercedes, "Yes, child, you are welcome to eat with us. You have rescued my Bobby's sweetheart and I can see you are still traumatised. Come, both of you, sit down and I will put on some more bacon and eggs."

Bobby pulls out a chair for Amy. "If you stay here with Amy for now, Jean, I can take you home after I have finished my deliveries this morning. It will be safer for you with me in the wagon rather than walking unaccompanied."

"That is very kind of you, Bobby. Perhaps you could drop me off at Keeper's Cottage on Pound Lane, because I have a friend there who may be able to help us."

"I am sure Father will give me the time off, as Harry can cover for me this afternoon. You don't mind do you, Harry?"

"Of course not, I do most of the work anyway!" says his older brother with a grin.

Bobby ignores his cheeky insult. He has more important things on his mind. "Would you like to come as well, Amy, for the ride?"

"I would love to, as long as your mother does

not mind?" she looks at Mrs Tompkins for her approval.

"I don't mind, lass, as long as you both help me this morning to sort out the box room."

Later that day Amy and Jean are huddled together in their warm cloaks beside Bobby on the bench seat at the front of the butcher's wagon, covered in a soft woollen rug. As they set off it begins to snow and for Amy the journey is magical. She is extremely relieved to have left Summerville House and is so happy to know that she has a loving beau and a true friend sitting on each side of her. The gentle snowfall is very pretty, fluttering down around them. The flakes land on the dark background of the woollen blanket and the girls are delighted to see the many wonderful patterns that make up each snowflake.

The snow is settling as the wagon pulls up outside Keeper's Cottage. Before Jean gets down from the wagon she gives her friend her horseshoe for luck. "Keep it in your room, Amy." Then she jumps down into the snow and says farewell to her friends. "Good luck, Amy. Look after her, Bobby. I will call in and see you at the shop as soon as I can. It may be a while, if this keeps up." She smiles indicating the snowfall and then waves as the wagon continues on up Pound Lane, leaving track marks in its wake.

She knocks on the door of Keeper's Cottage and Toby answers immediately.

"Hello, young man, is your sister at home?"

"Yes, she is in the parlour."

"May I come in, please?"

"Yes." He stands to one side for her to enter and he closes the door behind her. Jean enters the parlour to find Lettie sitting by the fire, knitting.

"Hello, Lettie, I hope you don't mind me calling in, but I need to speak to you. There has been a development."

"Ah well, let's leave Toby in here in the warm and we can go into the scullery and get some tea and cake."

Lettie gets up and Jean follows her through into their scullery.

"What has happened, Jean?" asks Lettie as soon as the door closes behind them.

"Nathan Meakins has made a move on my friend Amy – I think I told you about her. Anyway, we both sneaked away last night. She has gone to Bobby Tompkins' family and, now that I know she will be safe, I too am going home, but I want to tell what I know to Lord Dryer. I know he is a Justice of the Peace now, because Raymond told me, and I wonder if he might be able to help us."

"I am glad you have come to me, because I know even more than you do about Nathan Meakins and I believe that Lord Dryer is the right man to go to for help." Lettie heats up the kettle and lays out the plates.

"Will you come with me, Lettie?"

"Of course I will, because he knows me and my family very well and he has been so good to our Raymond. I am sure he will give you reliable advice." She opens the caddy and spoons some tea into the teapot.

"You said that you know more than I do about Nathan Meakins. Can you tell me what has happened in the past?"

"I can do and as we are going to see Lord Dryer I think you ought to be aware of the whole story before hand. I expect you remember another young maid who used to work with you at Summerville House. She drowned herself about three years ago."

Lettie cuts three slices from a sponge cake.

"Yes, I remember, Millie Bonfield. I always thought the master had a hand in it somewhere."

"Well, you are right. Millie was made pregnant by him and was naïve enough to believe that he loved her. Of course she was devastated when he told her to get rid of the baby and she left her job because of it."

"Oh, poor Millie, she was such a fool to be taken in so."

"The thing is, she had the baby secretly before she died, without her parents or Meakins knowing. Her sister took the child and left her outside Alvington Manor, where she was found and taken in. She is still living there today. I am sure Raymond has told you about Aurora."

"No, he hasn't actually, but I don't see him very often."

"Well, she is living there as part of the family. All the staff care for her, but apparently Lord Dryer is worried lest Meakins finds out about her."

"Well, I can see now why he might want to help us."

The door opens and Toby walks in. "Is there any cake for me?"

"Of course, Toby, I was just about to bring some in for you. Here, sit down." She pours Toby a glass of milk and two cups of tea for herself and Jean and they sit down together at the table.

"If we are going to see Lord Dryer we ought to be going soon, before the snow gets any deeper."

"Yes, I think we should go as soon as we have finished our tea and cake."

There is then a sound outside their back door and Jean jumps nervously. "It is all right, Jean, it is just Pa scraping off his boots."

John Boucher then enters. "Ah! I thought I could smell tea."

Lettie fetches another cup and plate for her father as he washes his hands at the sink. "It is coming down quite hard now and it is small dry flakes, not the watery big ones. I think it is going to drift too, as the wind is getting up."

"We had better get going, Jean."

"Where are you two going in this weather?"

"I am going with Jean to see Lord Dryer, Pa; she has some important information for him."

"Well you had better make it quick, Lettie, I don't want you out still after dark."

"Don't worry, Pa, I will be back before then. I expect Lord Dryer will ask Billy to take Jean home anyway."

At Alvington Manor the girls go up the steps and Lettie bangs the knocker.

Gareth answers the door. "Good day, Lettie, can I help you?"

"Yes please, we would like to speak urgently with Lord Dryer, if possible."

"Please step inside the hall out of the cold, and I will see if he is available. Who shall I say is calling, Lettie?"

"Tell him it is me, and Jean Hawkins, Raymond's sister."

"Do take a seat, ladies." He indicates a large wooden carved settle and the two girls sit down gratefully. Jean is feeling anxious about facing this important man, whom she has never seen before.

Gareth knocks on the study door and enters. Joshua is sitting at his desk going over the estate accounts.

"Excuse me, my Lord, but young Lettie and Jean Hawkins, Raymond's sister, are requesting to see you urgently."

"Indeed Gareth, do you know what this is about?"

"No, my Lord."

"Well show them in Gareth, I am curious." Joshua closes his accounting book, replaces the quill pen on the ink stand that his sister gave to him last Christmas and tidies his desk absently.

Moments later Gareth returns with the two young women. "Lettie Boucher and Jean Hawkins, my Lord."

"Thank you, Gareth." His butler turns and leaves the room.

"Good afternoon, ladies, what can I do for you?"

Lettie says, "My friend Jean has something she wants to tell you, my Lord."

"Perhaps you had better both sit down." He gets up and brings forward two small, padded chairs and the girls sit down in front of his large desk.

When Joshua is again seated before them he says, "Please, go ahead."

Jean folds her hands in her lap. "Well, my Lord, it is a long story, but I wish to report a crime."

"I see, well in that case you must understand that I am required to take down all that you say in the form of an official deposition?"

"I understand, my Lord."

Joshua finds his ledger and picks up the quill pen, as Jean prepares to tell her horrific tale. "Well, my Lord, it is rather difficult to tell you everything, but I will do my best. It is about our master, Nathan Meakins, his sister Olivia and a satanic coven that meets in Newton Hollow."

Jean notes the look of increased interest pass across his features as he says, "I see. Well, please be assured that I will listen to all you have to say and do not be afraid to be quite frank."

Jean relaxes a little. "I will, my Lord. Well, it

must have been about three years hence on All Hallows Eve that I noticed the master and mistress and her ladies maid, Apsey, all dressed in their cloaks and leaving the house after midnight. Out of curiosity I followed them to the oak grove at Newton Hollow, where I find a meeting of a coven. Well, my Lord, I was scared of being discovered, but out of curiosity I hid behind some dense bushes to watch. There was a lot of chanting and circling around a star shaped area, within which there was a sort of stone slab set up like an altar. The master places his flaming torch into a point of the star and the high priestess raises up a sort of rams head with evil red glowing eyes."

"The mistress Olivia is wearing a red cloak and she lies down on the stone slab…" Here Jean hesitates, nervous and embarrassed about putting what happened into words.

"Please do go on, Miss Hawkins," encourages Joshua.

"Well, to be perfectly honest with you… and to cut the story short… she loses her maidenhead, in front of all the witches, with the warlock… who happens to be her brother, Nathan."

Joshua stops writing, his eyebrows raised. "Well, I am very glad you have found the courage to come and report this to me. It is a pity you did not do so at the time, however."

"I was too scared of being bewitched, my Lord… but that is the least of it, my Lord. The mistress Olivia, begat a child and she and Apsey kept it quiet from everyone, even after it was born. Then on the summer solstice I follow them again, for the mistress had been indisposed in her room for months and I see them all going off together into the night." She pauses a moment to collect her thoughts and her courage. "This time it was too dreadful, my Lord." Tears fill her eyes as she remembers every tiny detail. "They take the newborn baby with them and they sacrifice him to the Sun God, my Lord. They unwrap his swaddling bands and cut his tiny throat with the ceremonial sword."

There is a look of dismay on Joshua's face as he looks up at the distressed young woman, but he is concerned to take down every detail. "You say 'they' Jean, but did you see who it was that actually murdered the child?"

"I did, my Lord, it was the master... Nathan Meakins, my Lord."

"I see." Joshua gives a deep sigh. He cannot believe the depravity of this man. "Why have you not come to see me until now, Jean?"

"I did not know who to turn to, my Lord, or who I could trust. You see, I passed out when the deed was done and when I came round all trace of what had happened was gone, and I was not sure whether or not I had been seen. I was afraid I may have been bewitched. Besides, how could I go to the constable when there were so many complicit in the act and I was the only witness to challenge them?"

"So what has given you the courage to come and speak up now?"

"I have spoken to my brother, my Lord. He is going out with Lettie. I confided in them because I wanted an amulet for my protection and Ray said that Lettie's mother could make one for me. They also told me to be very careful because they knew what Nathan Meakins was capable of. When I went to see her today Lettie told me about the little girl you have living here and... about Millie Bonfield's... accident."

"I see." He turns to Lettie, his voice stern. "And have you spoken of these things to anyone else?"

Lettie looks guiltily back at him. "I have told no-one, my Lord, not until today when I entrusted Jean. I did so, my Lord, only to encourage her to confide in you."

"So what has happened to bring you to my door today?"

"I have left Summerville House with another young maid, Amy Proctor, because I believe she was his next victim, my Lord."

"What makes you think that?"

"Well, I could see the master had taken a shine to her and was always ogling her, but it all got out of hand after he caught her kissing her beau, Bobby, a couple of months back. He threatened to dismiss her unless she was especially nice to him. She told me that he trapped her on one occasion in the passageway and forced her to kiss him. He was trying to put his hand up her skirt when he was interrupted by Apsey coming along just in time. I fear he would have raped her there and then, but for the interruption, my Lord."

"I am sure your fears are quite justified," says Joshua with resignation.

"Then last night Amy was sleeping when she was awoken by a noise in her room and she opened her eyes in time to see Mr Meakins leaving. We could not think what pleasure he would have got from observing her sleeping, but she was terrified that he would return. Eventually she plucked up the courage to venture outside and creep into my room to tell me what had happened, and that is why we both decided to leave the house under the cover of darkness – to escape his evil ways, once and for all."

"We were then further troubled because, as we went along the woodland path, we could hear the witches up on Summer House Hill chanting and we could see their fire through the trees. We were terrified we would be captured before we reached the safety of the town." Then Jean seems to have another idea. "It had not occurred to me before, but perhaps he was going to take Amy there with him to join the coven, but decided against it in the end. He was biding his time, my Lord, but he planned to have his evil way with her one way or another," added Jean emphatically. "I was afeared he was there at night to bewitch her."

"Well, I can see that you and your friend have had a rather traumatic time, Jean. However, I have other reasons why I may be able to get this rogue into court. If I am successful, will you be prepared to stand witness against him?"

"I will, my Lord, if you will offer me some protection from him. I have already lost my job and I don't wish to suffer any further at his hands," says Jean hopefully. "Amy is staying with the Tompkins family, the butchers in the shambles in Ivell, and she has told me that she is also willing to make a statement, as to his treatment of her, my Lord, although it is not so serious."

"Every nail in his coffin is important to me, Jean. Will you now please read through what I have written and sign your name under oath to this recording of your statement."

"I would prefer it if you would read it back to me, my Lord. My reading is not so good as it should be."

Joshua reads back all he has recorded and Jean signs her name. Lettie signs as witness.

"Where will you be staying and what are you intending to do, Jean?"

"I am going home to my parents at Cobb Cottage, Dray Road, in Odcombe and I will be taking on some gloving like my ma, my Lord."

"Well, thank you for finding the courage to

come and confide in me, I will do my best to put an end to this man's wicked shenanigans once and for all. In the meantime, please keep all this information between ourselves."

"We will, my Lord, thank you for understanding."

Joshua gets up and shows the girls out to find the snow falling silently around them.

"My goodness, I had no idea it was settling so fast. It is quite deep, I will get Billy to take you home, Jean; Lettie, you may as well go with them.

Joshua watches thoughtfully as Billy flicks the reins and the gig rolls off towards Odcombe. Somehow he has to make this man pay for all the harm he has done and prevent him from perpetrating any more devastation.

To take this any further, however, he has to persuade Becky, as well as Jean, to testify in court against him. The only way they will feel safe enough to do that is if he already has a custodial sentence. To that end, he must make an impregnable plan.

CHAPTER 20 *(January – February 1854)*

PASSION, PRAYERS AND PRAGMATISM

Jean is feeling relieved and elated at finally making the decision to leave Summerville House. She stamps the snow off her boots and enters Cobb Cottage, eagerly looking forward to seeing her parents and Raymond. Her father is sleeping on the couch and breathing heavily. She decides not to disturb him, but goes through into their scullery to find her mother.

Her mother looks weary, her eyebrows furrowed, her hair hanging down from her clips and her worn pinny quite stained, but when she turns and sees Jean her face lights up, "Oh, Jean, I am so pleased to see you." She hugs her close and then her worries pour out in a torrent. "I have been really vexed about your Pa, Jean. He has taken a turn for the worse. He seems so terribly weak and I am doing everything I can to build him up, but he coughs until he is sick. It is as if his stomach just cannot take any more and I don't know what to do for the best." She is wringing her hands. "Don't get me wrong, love, I am really grateful that Raymond has a regular job at Alvington Manor, but it does mean I am here on my own all day and sometimes during the night, depending on what work Ray is doing. I am so anxious that the end might come while I am on my own with him."

Jean puts her arm round her mother's shoulders and leads her to a seat. "Well, I have decided to come home for good, Ma, so you will not be on your own any more. We will look after him together and I can take on more gloving to bring in a bit more money."

"Oh, Jean, I am so grateful, but I really don't think he is long for this world and I cannot bear the thought of it." She breaks down in tears and Jean comforts her.

"Come on, Ma, don't let Pa hear you crying. All we can do is make him as comfortable as possible and show him how much we love him. Will he drink a mug of hot chocolate?"

Her mother nods her head and brushes away her tears with her pinny. "He seems to manage liquid meals like soup better as well."

"Come on then, Ma, let's take him in a mug of cocoa and tell him that I am home for good. That might boost his spirits."

Later on when Raymond has returned home and they are all sitting around a roaring fire supping their broth, Jean tells her parents why she has decided to stay home. "It is a house shrouded in evil, Ma, because of Nathan and Olivia Meakins. They court the devil with their satanic ways and Master Nathan was after my friend, Amy. He knew about her beau Bobby and was trying to force her to be nice to him by blackmailing her about it. He trapped her in the service corridor and had his hands up her skirt. He expected her to just put up with treatment like that and we believe it would have led to him raping her eventually. Then last night she woke up just in time to find him leaving her room, which really distressed her and it was the last straw. So we both sneaked out together."

"Well, you have made the right decision, lass,

no-one has the right to treat another person like that and I am very glad that you are home, Jean," says her father hoarsely. "It is so lovely to see you and wonderful to have my family all together again."

"Well, it may have been good wages, but I could not be more relieved to have left that place. It was also more worrying not knowing how you all were, especially you, Pa, and so I am very pleased to be home at last."

However, their togetherness is short lived. Just over a week later, Gabriel Hawkins has such a prolonged coughing fit that his heart gives out and he dies in the arms of his wife. Jean is very dejected, but in one way she is relieved that at least she was able to see her father before his sad demise and that she is there to support her mother. She has to help her mother laying him out and with the organising of the funeral. In the meantime, they respectfully place pennies on his eyes, don their black clothes and lay straw on the road outside their cottage to dull the sound of passers by.

Albert Johnson is one of the ringleaders whom Joshua instructed to incarcerate in the house of correction at Ivell police station and he has asked to see Joshua before the trial. Joshua decides to take Mr Fairway with him as a witness to what is said and he is to take notes of their conversation. On arrival at the police station they are taken down a corridor to the cells and locked in with Albert Johnson.

"Right, Mr Johnson, how can I help you?"

"You said, my Lord, that if I was to give names of the venturers it would be taken into account when my sentence is decided upon."

"I did," says Joshua. "These names, however, will need to be corroborated by at least one other person."

"That won't be a problem, not if they also get a more lenient deal. Charlie will back me."

"Charlie?"

"Charlie Buchan, my Lord, he is in the next cell."

"Right then, let us hear what you have to say."

"There was five of 'em that I know of, Charlie may know more, but these are the ones that I am sure of: the landlord of the Pig in a Poke at Portesham, John Marchant Esquire from Toller Porcorum, Squire Brandon of Alvington, Sir Robert Mulligan from Wells and Simon Gregory of the George Inn at Midsomer Norton."

Joshua gives a huge sigh of satisfaction; he knows that Jack Hawkins will testify that Squire Brandon was the alias used by Nathan Meakins and so he can link him to the smugglers. "You are prepared to stand up in court and testify to this, Mr Johnson?"

"I am my Lord, but you will remember, won't you, that I have a large family at home and I badly need leniency when deciding on my sentence?"

"I cannot make any promises on what the other justices will decide, but I am a man of my word and I will ask them to take into account the evidence you have offered. I may be able to sway them in your favour, if what you say is true."

"It is, my Lord, I am basically an honest man. I only got involved with all this to make a bit more for my family and look where it has got me, my Lord."

"Have you got all that down, Mr Fairway?"

"I have indeed, my Lord."

"Right, Mr Johnson, we need your signature on this statement to be added to your deposition." Johnson signs his name. "We will see you shortly in court, Mr Johnson, and thank you for your cooperation." They bang on the cell door to be let out and ask to see Charlie Buchan. He corroborates what Albert Johnson has said and signs a statement to that effect.

On their way back to their carriage Joshua turns to Mr Fairway with shining eyes. "I do believe we have got him, Ambrose. Now we have to get a custodial sentence so that he does not slip through our fingers."

Joshua drops Mr Fairway off on his way home. The remainder of his journey is spent thinking out a plan to make sure that Nathan Meakins gets his comeuppance once and for all. He realises that he has to convince his sister to testify against him, now that he also has Jean's evidence about the coven and their satanic ways. He is not sure, however, if he will be able to persuade Becky to take the stand. What happened to her was so devastating, so intimate and tragic: is it right to influence her to make this public knowledge?

He decides to discuss this with Louisa, who knows better than anyone else what Becky went through as a result of Nathan Meakins' attack. On his return home Joshua asks Rosa to find Louisa and send her to him in the library. It is not long before he hears her gentle knock and her face appears around the library door.

Louisa is filled with nervous anticipation at being summoned to the library for an audience with her beloved employer. *Whatever does he want?* She knocks timidly and pops her head around the door.

"Ah, Louisa, do come in. I want to ask a favour of you. Please sit down a moment."

Louisa takes the seat by the window that Joshua

indicates and he pulls up a chair opposite her. "I wonder if you would accompany me on a trip to Portland to see Becky. I need your help to convince her to testify against Meakins."

She has to concentrate on what he is saying. He wants her to go all the way to Portland with him, alone, in the carriage. She is shocked. But what is he asking? He wants her to persuade his sister to testify. "I thought we had decided to keep it secret, my Lord?"

"Call me 'Joshua', please."

"I am sorry, Joshua. I really don't know what to say, I am not sure I want to collude in putting her through that indignity."

"The thing is, Louisa, there are further developments that you are unaware of, which throw an even more serious light on things. I am sure when you hear what I have to say you will see that she really has no choice. Last week Lettie came to me with Raymond Hawkins' sister Jean, to tell me that she was a witness to him committing infanticide during a pagan ceremony held before a coven of witches."

"My God! Does Meakins know he was seen? Is she safe from him and his evil ways?"

"I do believe so, for I am sure he would have acted by now if he was at all suspicious. This means that we have him for smuggling, rape, witchcraft and infanticide, but I need Jack and Raymond Hawkins to testify with regard to the smuggling, Jean Hawkins with regard to the witchcraft and infanticide and Becky with regard to the rape. Because of his family's high ranking, I think it will take all three to get a conviction."

Louisa considers this. "But the murder of an infant is a hanging offence, is it not?"

"Yes, Louisa, it is, and if he had his way it could

have been Aurora too. He certainly is responsible for the death of Millie, and for the child that Becky was carrying. Louisa, we have to put an end to his villainy once and for all. To this end I would even consider asking you to help by giving evidence about his treatment of Millie, but if we did that, Aurora's true parentage would be exposed and we cannot risk it."

Louisa feels the need to know more. "What exactly did Jean see?"

"She saw Nathan Meakins take up a sword and without the slightest hesitation, before the coven of witches, he cut the baby's throat. I will tell you everything on the way to Portland, if you agree to help me."

"My God, he is the very devil! Of course I will help you, now that I see how terrible the situation has become. I agree, he has to be stopped somehow and I will help Becky to be strong. She has nothing to be ashamed of, she was unfortunately one of his hapless victims."

"You had better go and prepare. Pack some warm clothes and we will leave first thing tomorrow morning."

She stands up to leave. "Very well, my Lord."

"Will you never get used to calling me Joshua?"

"I am sorry, Joshua, but it is difficult in my position to accept such an intimacy." Then she blushes at using such a word. *Whatever was she thinking?*

Joshua smiles as he stands up and leans forward to kiss her on her cheek. "This is intimacy, Louisa." Then he takes her in his arms and with great sensitivity he kisses her on her mouth.

She tingles from head to toe. Her brain is telling her she should push him away, as her sister Millie should have pushed Meakins away, but her heart wants her to put her arms around his neck and reciprocate tenderly. This time, her heart wins. The kiss seems to last an eternity, but Joshua finally pulls himself away. He kisses her lightly and lovingly on her forehead. "You know I am not like Meakins, don't you Louisa? I would not behave this way if I did not truly have strong feelings for you."

Louisa looks disappointed: *strong feelings are not love*, and she was hoping for love.

"I had better get on… Joshua. Please excuse me, for I need to pop home and get my best clothes ready for tomorrow." She leaves quickly, before he can stop her.

The following morning Louisa dresses in the leaf green costume that her mother made for her nineteenth birthday. She is filled with eager anticipation at her trip in the landau all the way to Portland. She has never been on such a long journey and every minute of it she will be alone with her wonderful Joshua. She wonders if he will kiss her again and if his strong feelings will ever turn to love.

Billy, swamped from head to toe in warm woollen clothing, arrives with the landau and Gareth straps on their travel bags. As Louisa climbs up into the carriage her heart is thumping and she is flushed and excited. Then Joshua comes down the steps; he looks very handsome dressed in a long frock coat, carrying his tall crowned top hat and gloves. In the crook of his arm he has a warm woollen rug and he climbs up beside Louisa and wraps the rug across her lap. "It will be very cold along the top road, there may even be some snow still lying around in places. This will help to keep you snug."

She smiles lovingly at him. "Thank you, Joshua," she says.

"My, my; intimacy already and we haven't even left Alvington yet," he says with a twinkle in his eyes.

They set off across the gravel and onto Pound Lane. As the carriage lurches across the muddy ruts of the lane Joshua takes one side of the woollen rug and folds it over his legs, so that they are sealed together cosily in its warmth. Then he removes the glove on his right hand and slides it under the rug to find her hand. At his touch her heart pounds a little stronger.

During the course of the journey Joshua tells Louisa all the details of the witches' coven that he learnt from Jean, explaining what Nathan did to Olivia at All Hallows; that he is the warlock and that Olivia's ladies maid, Apsey, is also involved.

"The witchcraft statutes were repealed in 1736, but it does not stop folk believing in witchcraft still. The existence of this coven will shock local people, some of whom may decide that a trial by water is the only answer, if the other members of the coven come to light."

"I have to say that I would like to try Nathan Meakins by water. It would be poetic justice after what happened to Millie."

"Well, one way or another I do believe that he will be brought to book. Jean also told me that his next victim was another young maid at Summerville House called Amy Proctor. She is safe now and secretly living with her beau's family, the butchers in the town. Amy and Jean both sneaked out of the house before dawn to escape his clutches forever."

"They must have been very afraid of being caught. I do believe that Jean Hawkins is a brave girl to tell you what has been going on and to be prepared to stand up in court to say so as well."

"I know. Thankfully she has a strong character; it must run in the family because her brother has turned out to be a loyal hard worker too. John

Boucher came to see me the other day and said that the lad had surprised him with how quickly he had picked up the work. He is really good with the young birds and the breeding programme and never shirks his duty, even if it means staying up all night."

Louisa smiles. "That should please Lettie, for she is very fond of him and her father was set against him at the start. I think they would make a good match."

Joshua nods his head in agreement, "Talking of good matches, it will be Malachi and Rosa's wedding soon. That will be something to look forward to, after we have dealt with Meakins and the court case."

"Are you worried about the outcome, Joshua?"

"Well, he is going to be a tricky customer to pin down, and I must admit to some anxiety lest we fail. But if nothing else, the bad press should put paid to his philandering ways. Rest assured, it is nothing for you to worry about."

He leans across and kisses her on the forehead. It is a kiss of reassurance, but she cannot help herself: she looks expectantly into his eyes and there is passion there. He kisses her on the tip of her nose, then on the mouth, gently at first, then with rising ardour. Louisa tingles all over with excitement. Could he really love her? He seems so sincere and she truly adores him. She responds passionately and feels his wandering hands searching her body. This is bliss; she does not want their journey ever to end. She enjoys being held in his strong arms, kissed by his soft lips and touched by his gentle hands. Then the horses are pulled to a standstill and they can hear Billy getting down to pay the toll. Joshua tears himself away from her and tidies the rug over their laps. Billy calls out to them, "Do you wish to take some refreshments, my Lord?"

Joshua looks at his timepiece. "We are making good time. Are you hungry, Louisa?"

"I would like a drink, please, and maybe a small bite to eat?"

"Come, let me help you down." Joshua opens the door of the carriage and steps down, holding out his hand for Louisa."

"Thank you, my Lord," she says, as Billy leads the way into the traveller's inn.

Sir Oliver Meakins is reading the front page of the *Western Flying Post* and is about to use a silver and bone page turner, when his son catches sight of the headline news: *'SMUGGLING GANG CAUGHT RED HANDED BY MILITIA.'*

"Papa, if you have finished with the front page may I please have a look?"

"Of course." His father holds the newspaper over the page turner and, removing the outer sheet, he passes it to him. "The militia did well by all accounts. No loss of life. They seem to have ambushed the smugglers last Friday in what they are calling 'The Battle of Hamdon Hill' and captured a whole lot of contraband into the bargain. They say it was a forced run and so, with the batmen as well, it was more than forty men. Depending on where they reside, they are being held at either Dorchester or Shepton Mallet prisons until the Easter quarter session in March," says his father conversationally.

"All right, Papa, I am reading it for myself," he snaps irritably.

It is a windy day in early February when the funeral takes place for Gabriel Hawkins. The snow has melted and the previously frozen ground is again soft enough for the preparation of the grave. Many of the villagers attend, because the family are well liked and Lettie walks up to Odcombe to stand beside Raymond during the ceremony. Reverend Phelps conducts a poignant service and afterwards, during the committal, Lettie is moved to tears by observing how upset and distraught Jean and her mother obviously are. Even Raymond is finding it hard to control his emotions and she takes his hand in hers to comfort him.

She glances up to observe the other mourners and suddenly notices, at the back of the crowd gathered sombrely around the grave, the figure of Nathan Meakins. She is astonished that he should be there among all the village folk; she is sure that he was not inside the church earlier. *Whatever could this mean?* She squeezes Raymond's hand to alert him.

After they have uttered the final amen, the villagers begin to disperse and Lettie and Raymond both turn to warn Jean of his presence. Jean and Mrs Hawkins are busy thanking people for their support. Before they have time to join them, Nathan Meakins seizes the opportunity to beckon Raymond to one side. Lettie watches them anxiously.

"I don't suppose you have read the *Western Flying Post* this week, Hawkins?" says Meakins sarcastically.

"Why? What is in there that might concern me?"

"Only that the smuggling gang, which you and your uncle had dealings with, has been captured up on Hamdon Hill."

"You mean that *you* had dealings with, don't you? It was nothing to do with us; we were just doing your bidding – under duress, if I remember rightly."

"That may be so, but you were both seen by the gang as being involved and I was not. So if I were you, I would keep my mouth shut tight, or you may have to suffer the consequences."

"I think you may be forgetting that you *were* seen, not only by Malachi and Jacob Warren, but by Lord Dryer himself. He is now my employer and I take my orders from him, not you."

"Well, that is up to you, Hawkins, but my family have power in this area and I am simply warning you. Keep your mouths shut about Squire Brandon, or you will rue the day."

Raymond is about to walk away when he feels Meakins grabbing his arm.

"By the by, who is the pretty little filly holding your hand earlier? I am sure you wouldn't want anything nasty to befall her, would you?"

Raymond can feel his lip curling in anger and he is about to punch this cruel man in the face when he spots the vicar looking in their direction and remembers that it is, after all, his father's funeral. He snarls back at him, "You can take your bully boy tactics and shove them where the sun don't shine for all I care, but if you go anywhere near her, you have my word that I will kill you." He says this with true menace, and then, with huge restraint, he adopts a more nonchalant attitude. "Otherwise, I am not unduly worried because I doubt you will be around much longer. I would put my money on Lord Dryer rather than you any day."

With that he strides off towards Lettie, leaving Meakins staring after him in frustration.

Lettie greets him with relief, "What was all that about?"

"Nothing for you to worry about, Lettie. Come, let us thank the vicar."

"He is still staring at us, Ray."

"Just ignore him, Lettie. Don't give him the satisfaction of seeing that you are concerned."

They turn their backs on him and do not therefore see him making towards Jean.

"Good afternoon, Hawkins."

Jean jumps at the sound of his voice. "Good afternoon, sir," she replies shakily.

"I am glad to see that you are hale and hearty, Hawkins," he says sarcastically. "But I am curious to know why you absconded from our employ, with another servant girl, without a bye-your-leave or thank you?"

Jean has rehearsed a response to this question many times over the past few days. "I had a dream about my father, sir, that he was failing fast and I was compelled to leave in haste to make sure that I should see him before it was too late, which turned out to be portentous in the light of us attending here today."

"But that does not account for Proctor."

"Proctor, sir?" She feigns surprise. "I know nothing of Proctor, sir."

Meakins laughs in her face. "Do not take me for a fool, Hawkins, for you are no match for me. If, for example, I should find any of the household valuables missing, I will know where to lay the blame."

"Not at my door, sir. I am completely innocent, you know that very well and Proctor too."

"That, my dear, is beside the point." He grins down at her, "You make sure that your reckless imbecile of a brother knows when to keep his trap shut and we will say no more about it."

Jean wants to argue with this arrogant man, but

she feels drained. She may be more confident now that she has told everything to Lord Dryer, but she is still very wary of his powers of witchcraft and so she bites her tongue. "I am sure I don't know what you are talking about, sir."

"That is good, Hawkins. Let's make sure it stays that way and no-one else does either." With that he saunters off down the church path to his waiting horse.

Whilst talking to the vicar, Raymond has noted Meakins' intimidation of his sister and his blood is up. Suddenly he cannot let this man leave without having the last word and he strides across the churchyard and grabs the reins of the horse before Meakins sets off.

"What did you say to my sister, Meakins?"

"I was simply telling her that we are about to do an inventory of the silver and I trust that there will be nothing amiss."

"Don't you dare threaten my innocent sister, not when you are such a vile devil. I have heard the rumours going around Stoford about the coven at Newton Hollow and the goings on there; I am sure I can find one of the loose tongued witches willing to point a finger at their warlock!"

Raymond watches Meakins' jaw drop with satisfaction. "No one listens to tales of witchcraft anymore, besides it is not against the law."

"No, I do realise that it is things like *smuggling*, *rape* and *murder* that are illegal, but people still take against witchcraft and some folk are prepared to take the law into their own hands. How would you stand up to a trial by water?"

Meakins for once is speechless. He flicks his whip angrily and the horse breaks away from

Raymond's grasp, and trots off down the lane.

Raymond is left shaking with fury and indignation at the church gate. But what has he done? He might as well have accused him of infanticide. Has he gone too far and alerted the villain to Lord Dryer's plans?

Violet is thrilled to see Joshua, especially as he is accompanied by Louisa. "Well, what a wonderful surprise. To what do we owe this pleasure, darling?"

"We need to have a chat to Becky about something rather important."

Violet's eyes light up. Could it be that they want Becky to be a hand-maiden? "She is upstairs, I will fetch her for you. I have just come home in my lunch break to prepare the evening meal; I had better pop out and get some more provisions, as we have such special guests."

"Don't go to any trouble, Ma, we only intend to stay for one night. Do you mind if Louisa has my room?"

"Of course not darling, your bed is already made up."

"I have sent Billy to book a couple of rooms at the Cove House Inn for him and myself. I don't think it would be appropriate for Louisa to stay there un-chaperoned."

Becky comes hurtling down the stairs. "Josh! And Louisa too, how astonishing to see you both. Come into the parlour, I will light the fire."

Violet comes downstairs in her outdoor clothing. "I have to go back to the shop to tell Molly that you are here and she will hold the fort for me; then I will pop to the butchers and be back as soon as I can. I cannot wait to have a chat with you both." She kisses each of them affectionately and then leaves hastily.

Becky takes the 'go to bed' from the mantelpiece and is immediately on her hands and knees lighting the driftwood fire with a Congreve match. She is so thrilled to see them, *how can he spoil her happiness by making her relive the past?* He does not know where best to start but he has to be hasty, he has no choice. "Becky, we have come all this way to see you, because I am determined to get Nathan Meakins to pay for his misdemeanours in court. I know what you went through was dreadful, but even worse has happened and he has to be stopped somehow. I am sorry to plunge straight into this, but we need to talk it over with you before Ma comes back."

"You want me to appear in court, don't you?"

"I wouldn't ask this of you, Becky, if it wasn't so important."

Becky's eyes brim with tears. "I cannot do it, Josh, it is too shameful. What would Ma and Pa think? They would be so upset that I have kept it from them all this time."

Louisa goes to her and puts her arm around her shoulders. "Becky, I was against it at first, but Josh needs your help. He needs you to be strong, darling. There are things you do not know."

"I am sure there are, Louisa, but I am not sure that I want to hear about them."

"I am afraid you have to, Becky, for you have to know what your brother is up against. Meakins and his sister Olivia are members of a coven and it is unbelievable what they are capable of. The arrogant man actually had sex with Olivia in a pagan witchcraft ceremony. She, like you, also conceived of a child and she secretly gave birth. It was a little boy, but they are so very wicked, they sacrificed the poor little mite at the summer solstice. They are both evil, Becky. He is a murderer and someone has to speak out against them. I will come with you, I promise."

"I believe I have him bang to rights with the smuggling, Becky, and we have a witness to the slaughter of his tiny son. I have her signed deposition and she is willing to speak against him under oath. If we had your testimony as well, I cannot see how he could possibly escape the noose."

Becky stands up from the fire and then sinks into the nearest armchair. "You have another witness?"

"Yes, Becky, it is Jean Hawkins. She was horrified when she followed them up to Newton Hollow where the coven met and she watched as they committed incest on the first occasion. Then she was even more traumatised when at the summer solstice she witnessed the murder of the baby. She is very brave; even though she is terrified of being bewitched herself, she has come forward with another maid, Amy Proctor, from Summerville House. Both are prepared to give evidence against him."

"What happened to the other maid?"

"She was being bullied and blackmailed by Meakins to 'be nice to him', or she would lose her position, because of her friendship with the butcher boy. It would mean her going into the workhouse with the rest of her family. In the end she was that scared of Meakins raping her that she and Jean ran away in the night to escape him."

"I am sorry, Josh, for being such a coward. If you really need me to do it, I will. You are right, Louisa; too many young women and their babies have suffered at his hands and I must try to be brave and stand up to him."

Louisa takes both of Rebecca's hands in hers. "Oh thank you, darling, I am so proud of you."

"When will it be?" she asks her brother anxiously.

"I am not sure yet, but there is no need for you to come back with us now if you could just write a statement in your own words of what happened. Louisa will witness your signature before me and I will take the deposition back to show the other magistrates."

"All right, but I may need your help, Joshua, to keep it unemotional."

"Of course we will help you to keep it relevant, but it must be in your own words."

They spend the next hour helping Rebecca to compile her statement.

"Thank you, Becky," says Joshua, putting his arm around his sister. "You can forget all about it for now. I will send Billy to collect you when the time is right, just put it out of your head in the meantime. I have a few loose ends to tie up first; I want this case to be watertight."

There is a knock at their front door and Joshua goes to answer it. Billy is back from the Cove House Inn and shortly afterwards their mother returns with the shopping. Feeling somewhat relieved Joshua spends a leisurely day with the ladies and Billy, until Matthew and Ben join them after work.

Louisa fits in so well with his family. He can see they all love her and every now and then he notices a knowing look passing between his mother and Becky. He knows, however, that he cannot rush her. Neither does he want to start speculation among the staff at Alvington Manor just yet. Little does he know that several of his staff have already put two and two together.

The following morning he leaves Billy at the inn to go and say his farewells to the family. Louisa is ready and waiting for him and after lots of hugs and kisses, Violet and Rebecca wave as the young couple go together to the end of the path to meet

Billy with the horse-drawn carriage. Joshua packs their bags on the landau and they set off on their long journey home.

CHAPTER 21 *(February 1854)*

THE BLACK PANTHER CLUB

As soon as they return to Alvington Manor, Raymond Hawkins arrives asking to see Joshua. Louisa takes her bag and goes to the Dower House to change and Raymond is shown into Joshua's study.

Immediately he blurts out his fears. "Thank heavens you are back, my Lord, I didn't sleep a wink last night. I am afraid I have done something rather foolish."

"Sometimes I think your middle name should be 'foolish', Hawkins! What have you been up to now?"

"I am so sorry, my Lord, but that Meakins showed up uninvited at our pa's funeral. I don't know how he heard about it, but he is a warlock after all. It was probably him responsible for Pa's death anyway."

"He is just a nasty specimen of mankind, Hawkins, have no fear, for he has no special powers, I can assure you. You had better tell me what happened."

"I have to admit, my Lord, I told him that the existence of a coven at Newton Hollow was common knowledge in Stoford and moreover that he was their warlock."

"Whatever made you tell him that, Raymond?"

"I am sorry, my Lord, he just got my blood up. He was bullying our Jean in the churchyard and threatening to accuse her of thieving. I just wanted to wipe that smug smile off his face."

"I do understand that he has that effect on folk, but the last thing we want is for him to do a runner."

"I know, my Lord. That was my fear and it is why I am here now, my Lord."

"My God, we passed a very smart carriage with a family crest on the side on our way along the Dorchester Road. I hope it was not him making for the coast; he could be away to America or Africa or anywhere, if he reaches the docks in time. Right, we need to act now Hawkins. Go with haste to find John Boucher and Malachi and bring them back here with their guns to the stables. Jacob will be busy with the lambing, so perhaps you would come with us too, in his place?"

"Of course, my Lord, if I can make amends I am more than willing." Raymond puts on his cap and leaves.

Joshua summons Gareth to go and find Billy, to organise the landau and to saddle his horse. When the men arrive back at the stables he instructs Malachi to go into town on Capricorn and summon the constable, then meet them at the end of the drive to Summerville House, whilst Billy conveys John, Raymond and himself in the landau to visit Lord Helyar at East Coker.

On reaching Coker Court, Joshua is quickly shown into Lord Helyar's sumptuous parlour.

"Good day, Joshua, to what do we owe this pleasure?"

"I am sorry to intrude uninvited, my Lord, but matters have come to a head with regard to the subject we discussed at my house, back in October. I have reason to believe that our fox may try to go aground if we do not act decisively now. I have sent my friend Malachi Warren to call out the constable in order to arrest the villain, but I feel I need the back up of the militia and I do not know where they are quartered."

"Is all this urgency called for, my dear chap? It is, after all, only a charge of venturing, not murder."

"Well, that is the problem, my Lord. Since our meeting more information has come to light and I believe I also have evidence that can convict him of both rape and murder. I trust you will understand that I cannot go into it with you now, for time is of the essence, but I want him safely under lock and key before we charge him with the more serious offences."

"I see. Well, I am afraid the militia are at present encamped near Wellington and obviously we do not have the luxury of waiting for their support. I do, however, have some ex-militiamen among my staff and I can muster them for your assistance if that would be helpful."

"It would indeed, my Lord. Thank you."

"If you would like to set off to meet the constable and your friend, I will organise for them to follow you shortly."

"I am grateful, my Lord. I plan to leave the constable and Malachi Warren in the landau so as not to arouse suspicion, whilst I ask to speak to our quarry. Then, once we have ascertained that he is present in the house, the two men can then join me to arrest him. I will post my gamekeeper, John Boucher, and Hawkins on guard at the back entrance in case he tries to evade capture and escape that way. I would appreciate it if your people could come, well armed, and split up to help guard both exits, as soon as they arrive."

"I understand your plan and will instruct my men accordingly. I wish you Godspeed."

"I am indebted to you for your help, my Lord."

"Don't mention it, my friend; I am glad to be of assistance." They shake hands and Joshua sets off again, feeling a mixture of anxiety, elation and determination.

The sun is setting as Joshua drops John and Raymond off in the estate hamlet at the back entrance to Summerville House. He continues down the lane to the outer end of the main driveway, where he finds the constable and Malachi patiently waiting for him. Malachi ties Capricorn and the constable's horse to a post at the main gate and both men get into the carriage.

Inside the manor, Wadman, the footman, is having a quiet smoke in the servants' hall with Morton the butler. With their employers all absent for a variety of reasons, they are taking advantage of the peace and tranquillity. At the sound of the doorbell ringing insistently, Wadman sends the new maid up to answer the door, while he puts out his pipe and puts his livery jacket back on.

When Joshua asks to see Nathan Meakins she stutters and stammers that the young master is not available. Joshua is suspicious that she is acting on his instructions, but she could merely be of a nervous disposition and he simply asks, "Could you please tell me, then, where I might find him?"

"I believe he went to his club earlier this afternoon, sir, at Catkin Mill." This sounds quite plausible to Joshua.

Wadman comes up behind her, scowling with annoyance, presumably because the maid should not have divulged the master's whereabouts.

"Can I be of any assistance, sir?" he says self-importantly.

"Well, I was hoping to speak to Mr Nathan Meakins, but I have been told he is not at home."

"That is correct, sir. Would you like me to pass on a message on his return?"

"No, thank you, that will not be necessary."

Joshua's instinct is that the maid was, after all, speaking the truth and it is fortunate that it was she who answered his knock. He does not believe that the footman would have given out this information.

He returns to the carriage and informs the constable of their conversation, who agrees that they should make haste to Catkin Mill. At the main gate they discuss whether or not to leave Malachi, John and Raymond behind, in case of it being a deception. "No, I am pretty sure the young maid guilelessly divulged his whereabouts. I think we would be wiser to go in strength to the club."

He and the constable both jump astride their mounts and they make their way back to the hamlet, where John and Raymond take their places inside the carriage beside Malachi. Joshua takes the lead, as he is hoping to meet up with the Coker men on their way. Sure enough, as they are going along the Dorchester Road, a party of six or seven men are seen approaching them. Joshua hails them, explains the situation and they are soon off in a large party to raid the Black Panther Club.

As they turn into the lane that leads to Catkin Mill they can see two carriages and a few horses tethered in the driveway, with a young lad minding them. Joshua dismounts, hands the lad Capricorn's reins and goes up the steps to the front entrance, accompanied by the constable and Malachi. The other men remain in the background.

The doorman asks him for a password. "I do not require a password, I am a Justice of the Peace and I have the constable with me. We wish to speak to Nathan Meakins immediately."

"I see, sir, and may I tell him what it is about?"

"No, I simply wish you to take us to him."

The doorman is aware of the posse of men on horseback, ready to back up the Justice of the Peace and constable, and does not want any trouble at his club. He decides he has no wish to come between Meakins and the law and he beckons them to follow him. "This way, gentlemen, please follow me."

The three men follow closely behind him. The main salon is opposite the front entrance but the doorman takes them along a scarlet-coloured passageway to the left. The décor is oriental in style and, off the passageway, doors lead to private rooms, where gentlemen are entertained by ladies of the night. This is made obvious when they pass an open doorway and witness a bed, the red satin sheets crumpled and recently occupied.

At the end of the corridor they are shown into a dimly lit room, where the sweet aroma of opium hangs oppressively in the smoke-filled, humid air. The room is divided by hand-painted oriental screens for each patron's privacy. Behind one of the screens they find Meakins alone, lying on a chaise longue in an opium-induced stupor, with a bottle of absinthe and the opium smoking paraphernalia bubbling away on a small table beside him. Joshua extinguishes the flame. He cannot wait to get out of this opium den, before the vaporised contents of the bowl has its effect on all of them.

"Help me to get him up, Malachi." Meakins is so deeply lost in his intoxication that he is easily lifted and manhandled out of the room and along the passageway. As they pass the entrance to the salon they are unfortunately spotted by the Seymour brothers, who untangle themselves from the arms of the women draped around them. One makes to follow them, whilst the other rushes off to enlist the help of the owner and his bouncers.

Joshua and Malachi are halfway down the front steps, with the constable bringing up the rear, when the indignant owner and his cronies rush around the side of the building, armed with a variety of improvised weapons and stand before them, blocking their path.

"What the devil is afoot here?" The owner asks belligerently.

The men begin to bang their weapons together threateningly and Joshua feels the hairs rise at the nape of his neck.

"This is not your concern, sir, we are here on court business," says the constable.

"Anything that takes place in this establishment is my business," he answers angrily.

Joshua goes for his weak spot: "We will bear that in mind, sir, when considering the illegal handling of smuggled alcoholic beverages, which this man is guilty of, and take into consideration those in receipt of it." Joshua sounds rather pompous, but it has the desired effect and the man changes tack immediately.

"Do you realise that you have disturbed the son of Sir Oliver Meakins?"

"Of course we do. He is the very man we are looking for and it is about time that people around here realise that status and power do not exempt them from paying the price, if they break the law." Joshua speaks with quiet authority. "Now, unless you are all prepared to suffer the consequences for interfering in police business, I suggest you lower your weapons and step aside to let us pass."

The owner looks behind him and sees the posse of mounted men, their horses standing steadfastly before him and he decides he has no choice but to back down.

"Stand aside men, this is not our concern."

The men turn away and leave them to it. Joshua and Malachi are finally able to manhandle Meakins into their waiting carriage.

Joshua walks over to the Coker men. "Thank you very much for your support gentlemen. I do not believe it would have been so straightforward without your backing, but I am glad that no force was necessary and no one was hurt. We can manage ourselves from now, but we are very grateful for your assistance. Here is something for your trouble." He tosses a pouch of coins up to their leader.

"You are welcome, Mr Dryer, my Lord. Thank you for this." He holds up the pouch. "Good night to you. I am glad the mission was a success." With that they all turn their horses and ride off back to their homes.

Meakins, although handcuffed, remains non compos mentis for the journey into Ivell town and does not show any sign of waking until they try to get him out of the carriage and into the police station.

"What the... devil... is going on here?" he splutters in confusion.

"Ah, you are back with us. Then let the constable explain," says Joshua, with a hint of satisfaction.

The constable takes his arm, "Nathan Meakins, you are under arrest for your involvement with smuggling."

"What! Was it really necessary to interrupt me... whilst I was happily 'chasing the dragon'?" He speaks slowly and with half-closed eyes. "It is my one vice... my dalliance with that enchanting potion... that intoxicating, mystifying, magical journey... enthralling me with illusions and hallucinations and pleasures unbound."

"Unfortunately, Mr Meakins, it is *not* your only

vice and that is what has led you here tonight."

Nathan Meakins is not prepared to put up a fight, but he is shocked at their audacity. It will be nothing that a hefty fine won't solve. He knows he is no match for both Malachi and Joshua and together they manhandle his lethargic body into the station and finally into a hammock in the police cell.

"I will wait until he sleeps it off before taking his statement, Mr Dryer."

"I think that is wise, Constable Gundry."

Joshua is jubilant when he joins his comrades in the carriage. "What a piece of good fortune, I cannot believe he was so compliant. It would not have been that easy if he had been at home under the noses of his parents and Olivia, I'll be bound."

"Raymond and I cannot wait to tell Jean and Lettie, my Lord. They will be so relieved," says John Boucher.

"I should like to be a fly on the wall in his cell tomorrow morning when the reality of his situation sinks in," says Malachi.

"Well, this is only phase one of the attack, we still have a long way to go before the battle is won. A lot depends on the testimony of the ladies he has wronged and our witnesses," says Joshua sagely.

Joshua is weary when finally they reach Alvington Manor. Having taken Raymond back to Odcombe, they drop John off at Keeper's Cottage and then he says goodnight to Billy and Malachi at the stables. In the hall he removes his boots and outdoor clothing. Michael Porter takes them from him. "Can I get you a nightcap, my Lord?"

"I must admit I am ready for a nightcap, but there is no need for you to stay any longer, Michael, go home to your wife. Thank you for waiting up for me."

He leaves his footman in the hall and goes through to the Oak. He pours himself a generous glass of brandy and sinks into an armchair beside the fire. Moments later there is a tap at the door. "Come in," he calls out distractedly.

Louisa enters, still wrapped in her cloak. "I am sorry to bother you, my Lord," she says timidly, "but I could not retire for the night, I was too concerned. Did you manage to find him?"

He is thrilled to see her and to be able to tell her the good news. "Yes, we did, Louisa, and he is at this moment incarcerated in the Ivell House of Correction."

"Oh! Thank the Lord for small mercies, what a relief."

"Here, let me take your cloak and please join me for a nightcap."

"I really shouldn't, my Lord, 'tis rather late."

He is already removing her cloak. "Oh poppycock, who cares? We are entitled to celebrate after all that has happened today. Please, sit here opposite me beside the fire. What would you like?"

She sits down and nervously places her hands in her lap. "May I have a small glass of Madeira wine then please, my Lord?"

"Of course you may," then wickedly he adds, "but Louisa, what has happened to our intimacy all of a sudden?"

Joshua watches intently as Louisa smiles enchantingly. "I am sorry, Joshua, it takes a bit of getting used to."

He pours out the Madeira and places it on a small table beside her. As he does so he bends and kisses her lightly on the top of her head, closing his eyes and inhaling the sweet scent of her luxuriously abundant auburn hair.

Louisa looks up into his tired face. "Thank you,

Joshua. You must be exhausted, for it has been a long day. After all, we were on Portland this morning and just look at what you have achieved."

He sits back down in the armchair and puts his feet upon the fender, sighing with satisfaction. "It is actually all thanks to Raymond Hawkins, for he rather forced our hand by alerting Meakins to the fact that some folk were aware of the coven and its goings on."

"He never did!"

"Yes, he did and I was afraid that the devil would escape punishment by leaving the country before we could get to him, so I decided to make our move without further delay."

"I did wonder what all the commotion was about, but I thought it unwise to broach the subject until I had spoken to you. I was really worried from the moment I saw you leaving." Louisa takes a sip of Madeira and enjoys the strong, sweet taste as it slips deliciously down her throat.

"Well, the reason it all went so easily was because Meakins was in the realms of fantasy, high on opium, and he put up no resistance whatsoever."

"No wonder he is so volatile, I heard that dope is very destructive."

"It is indeed, it causes paranoia, hallucinations and is extremely addictive."

"What an idiot! He has more money than sense."

"I agree, Louisa. Anyway, I have instructed the constable to ignore any applications from his family to pay a bond to procure his release, for when he comes down from his high he is going to be a very angry and demanding prisoner indeed. I am not sure when exactly to have him charged for the more serious crimes. Both offences carry the capital punishment and will definitely have to go before a judge in the Court of Assize at the New Shire Hall in Taunton."

She takes another sip of the Madeira, thinking ahead to the court case and its implications. "Do you not think we will need more proof of the murder than simply Jean's witness statement?"

"Well, ideally we should present some physical evidence. According to Jean the child was cremated, but there was only a thin layer of ash left behind on the sacrificial altar."

"But you said to me that Jean passed out and so it is possible that the small corpse was buried. Even if it was burnt, surely there must have been something left? Isn't it possible that the child's remains are buried nearby?"

"Louisa, you are a marvel! If we could find the remains, they would have to proceed with the case. We owe it to that poor little mite to catch and convict his murderer. First thing tomorrow I will send Billy to collect Jean and Raymond from Odcombe. Jean can take us to the murder site. John Boucher can come along with Honey. It will be relatively safe to go there, now that Meakins is under lock and key."

"What about Olivia?"

"Well, if we go there in broad daylight it is unlikely any of the witches will be in the vicinity. They only show up under cover of darkness, I'll be bound."

Their conversation is then interrupted by a huge clap of thunder and a lightning flash brightens the night sky.

"Oh dear, I had better make a run for home. I don't like thunderstorms and would prefer to be tucked up safely in my bed." She quickly downs the remainder of her wine and stands up to leave.

Joshua is smiling, thinking how wonderful it would

be to take her upstairs and tuck her up safely into his own bed. He walks with her to the front porch and watches as she makes a dash for it across the driveway to the Dower House. As she enters their front door the heavens open and the downpour descends. However, both are now fortunately under shelter. Louisa made it just in time and she waves happily. Joshua blows her a kiss goodnight. With providence, it should be another eventful day tomorrow.

Joshua sleeps fitfully, listening to the rain lashing the windows and the wind howling down the chimneys in between his dreams. He awakes to the dawn chorus the following day and as he stretches drowsily he remembers with dread the horrific task they have to undergo in order to put paid to Meakins once and for all. They could well be wasting their time, but if they can find any evidence of this appalling crime then they must put in their best efforts.

Once his ablutions are completed and he is dressed, he goes downstairs and instructs Billy to go and fetch Jean and Raymond in the carriage. Then he strolls up to Keeper's Cottage to find John Boucher. He explains to John what is required and he suggests they take Honey with them. Together they stroll up to the top of Pound Lane to meet Billy on his return from Odcombe. It is a mild, sunny morning and the wet foliage glistens in the morning sunlight. Honey is wagging her tail and weaving in and out of the hedgerow, sniffing interesting scents and causing the odd shower of raindrops to cascade down onto her head. Her shaggy coat has been touching the long wet grass and she shakes herself dry as she steps back onto the track.

When Billy arrives with the carriage, Honey

jumps in and leaps up affectionately to greet and lick Raymond, making him protest that she is making him all muddy and wet. Everyone laughs and it goes some way to dispel the shadow of horror associated with the task they have yet to face.

As they near Newton Woods, Jean points out a lane that leads up to Summer House Hill. "I think, my Lord, if you take the carriage up that way we will be able to approach the hollow from above and we will be out of sight from the Ivell Road."

Joshua hails Billy and instructs him to take the track on the left. The carriage lurches over the rutted track until they find a place for it to pull in and wait. The woodland to their right descends steeply down to the Ivell Road below them.

Billy steers the horses onto a shallow verge on their left, pulls the brake on the carriage and gets down to put a safety block behind the wheels. Honey leaps down with John Boucher behind her.

"You stay and look after the horses, Billy. Right then, Jean, you had better lead the way."

"Please bear with me, my Lord, we are coming at it from a different angle and I may have to go down the hill and try to retrace my steps."

"Well, let us do that right now Jean. I don't want to waste any more time than absolutely necessary."

Joshua, John, Raymond and Jean all go back down the lane to the Ivell Road and several hundred yards down the road Jean finds the footpath. As she slowly climbs the hill underneath the dripping trees, she is holding her petticoats up in front of her to avoid the damp ground and tripping over any bare tree roots. The men follow patiently behind her. They are near the summit when they reach a clearing in the centre of a ring of ancient oak trees. A pheasant cries out its alarm call from deeper within the wood. The ground here is level and in the centre is a large stone slab.

"This is the place," says Jean, her voice low. "We need to keep out of sight of the Round House, for that is the home of the high priestess."

Joshua can see the stone built Round House through the trees and realises that they have come a very long way round, for Billy is waiting with the carriage not far from that sinister building. However, he can see that Jean has gone pale at the dreadful memory. "Here, sit down, Jean, and rest," he says kindly. "You have done your job. It is up to us now."

He leads her to a sizeable fallen tree trunk on the outer edge of the clearing and she sits down gratefully. Honey is sniffing around the area excitedly, as the men carefully comb the leafy dell for any signs of evidence. They are all bent double, conducting a fingertip search around the makeshift altar and its periphery, disturbing all manner of insects. The crows caw macabrely above them, but as time goes on Joshua despairs of discovering anything at all.

The ground is very wet and spongy from the storm the previous night and the air is full of the scent of rotting leaves, fungi and wet foliage. Rivulets of water run from the edge of the clearing, where the ground slopes away down the hill, and there some of the fallen leaves have been washed away, revealing bare earth and exposed tree roots. It is here that Honey is concentrating her attention. John goes over to see what she is after and immediately calls Joshua to go and see what she has uncovered.

"It looks like a small piece of charred bone, my Lord," he says sadly.

"Right John, hold Honey back. We need to get the constable here to record the discovery officially and exhume the remains, for I am sure that it will be the remains of that poor little boy. Come on everyone; if we all go back to the carriage now, Billy can drop me off at the Ivell House of Correction and I can bring the constable back here with me."

They are an extremely solemn group of people, as they climb to the top of the hill and walk back down the short distance to the carriage.

Joshua returns some time later with the constable. Together they carefully exhume the remains, with the constable meticulously noting and sketching each stage of the process.

"This is very serious, Mr Dryer, I think we should go straight back to the lock up and charge Nathan Meakins with infanticide."

"I agree absolutely, Constable Gundry. It is important to charge him before anyone can post bail for the smuggling incident, by going over our heads."

"Do you also want to press charges for the rape of your young sister as well?"

"Yes, I think so. I have her signed deposition and she has said to me that she is prepared to give evidence in court. I believe the more we have to throw at him, the more likely we are to get a conviction. We are, after all, up against a powerful and influential family." Joshua thinks about his poor sister and, although he knows she would find it less of an ordeal if her case was dealt with at the Ivell Town Quarter Session, because rape is also a capital offence he feels that both the rape and the murder should be tried at the assize court. Meakins will then already have a conviction for smuggling to be taken into account when sentencing for the more serious crimes. "Meakins is due to stand trial for the venturing in two weeks time. I think we should consider all three charges at that session and indict him to appear at the Taunton assize for the two most serious charges of rape and infanticide."

"So be it, Mr Dryer, my Lord."

"Let us go back now and set the ball rolling. I cannot wait to see the expression on his face when he realises that we have him."

CHAPTER 22 *(March-April 1854)*

IVELL TOWN QUARTER SESSIONS

The Easter Quarter Sessions take place on Monday 14th March. The public gallery is more crowded than normal, as word is out that the accused is someone of stature in the community. The jury of twelve men are seated together on the left of the room and a reporter from the *Western Flying Post* is seated in his usual spot on the press bench.

Jack Hawkins is sitting in the front pew and feeling anxious about being called as a witness. He is staring reverently at the royal coat of arms positioned high on the wall behind the magistrates long table, when the clerk of the court announces, "The court will now rise."

Everyone stands as Joshua, the Reverend David Phelps and Lord Helyar all take their seats on the bench. The clerk of the court instructs the usher, "Please bring in the prisoner."

The usher leaves the court to collect Nathan Meakins and he enters, handcuffed to Constable Gundry plus another escort. He looks angry and belligerent as he takes his place in the dock alongside the policemen.

The clerk of the court reads out the charges against him. "The prisoner in the dock is facing three separate unconnected charges; one of smuggling, one of rape and the third the most heinous crime of infanticide." There is a gasp of shock from the public gallery.

"My Lords, have you had sufficient time to make a decision based on the evidence available to you?"

Lord Helyar is the most senior magistrate and as such he is their spokesperson. "We have indeed, Mr Boswell. This bench is unanimously agreed that, given the witness statements, there is a *prima facia* case for the accused to answer on all counts. However, considering the most serious charges of rape and the murder of an infant, the prisoner is indicted to appear before the judge and grand jury at the county assize in the New Shire Hall in Taunton. We will, therefore, deal only with the charge of smuggling today in this quarter session. Do you understand these charges Mr Meakins?"

"I do, my Lord."

"With regard to the charge of smuggling, does the prisoner plead guilty, or not guilty?"

"Not guilty, my Lord," says Nathan Meakins indignantly.

"The plea of not guilty is recorded and you may be seated."

Meakins sits down in the dock, as Mr Jonathan Birch, the prosecutor, states his case for the jury. "The prosecution claims that the accused, using a false name, is one of several men of means who collaborated to regularly fund the purchase, importation and conveyance of illicit cargoes into the country, avoiding the government tax duties. To make the case for the prosecution, I should like to call my first witness: Mr John Hawkins of Camp Road, Odcombe."

The usher indicates for John to take the stand.

"Mr Hawkins please would you raise your right hand, place your left hand on the bible and repeat after me – I do solemnly, sincerely and truly declare and affirm that the evidence I shall give shall be the truth, the whole truth and nothing but the truth, so help me God."

Hawkins repeats the oath nervously. He knows he is going to have to admit to having an affair as evidence that he was blackmailed, and he does not want this reported in the *Western Flying Post*.

"Mr Hawkins, do you recognise the man in the dock?"

"Yes, sir, it is Mr Nathan Meakins of Summerville House."

"Am I correct in understanding that Mr Meakins approached you and your nephew some time ago and requested that you fulfil an errand for him?"

"Yes, sir."

"What did this task involve?"

"Well, I thought the job would be something to do with beating for the shoot, because that was what my nephew Raymond usually did for Mr Meakins, and a bit of extra cash is always handy. But he wanted us to meet the smuggler's mule train and lead off the animal loaded up with the crop intended for a Squire Brandon."

"And who did you understand Squire Brandon to be, Mr Hawkins?"

"It was Mr Meakins himself using an assumed name, sir. Although he told us he had put up some money for the venture, he did not want to be recognised."

"And did you agree to this arrangement?"

"No, sir, I told him I didn't want to get involved with any shady dealings and that he should do his own dirty work."

"And was that an end to the matter?"

"No, sir, he told me that he had seen me canoodling with the wife of a neighbour at the Alvington Summer Ball and that he would expose me as an adulterer if I did not do as he asked."

"And is that what persuaded you to go along with his plan?"

"Yes, sir. I did not want to hurt my wife, or my neighbour and I did not want a Skimmington neither, sir." There are sniggers from the gallery at this comment.

"So in consequence you and your nephew committed a crime?"

"Well, all we had to do was lead the animal away from the mule train, down off the road and across the Alvington estate, where we met up with Meakins and handed him over."

"Do you think the accused was wise in choosing to trespass on Lord Dryer's land, considering he is a Justice of the Peace and a magistrate to boot?"

"No, sir, I do not, but being born with a silver spoon in your mouth don't necessarily make you wise do it, sir?" There is an outburst of laughter from the gallery at this bravado and the prosecutor smiles.

"Did you continue with this arrangement with future consignments, Mr Hawkins?"

"No, sir. We were seen in the act and recognised by Lord Dryer, and me and Raymond was brought before him the following day. We gave our word that we would no longer do his bidding and I promised to finish my affair, for I had been given a shock. I realised that I had been very foolish and it would hurt too many people to continue. I love my family very much, sir. Besides, we would have lost our jobs and the tied cottage if we did not comply with Lord Dryer's wishes."

Mr Boswell then looks in the direction of the newspaper reporter. "I would appreciate it, Mr Rowlands, if Mr Hawkins' private life could be kept out of the newspapers. It is not him who is on trial today and infidelity is not against the law."

"Of course, Your Honour."

"So, Mr Hawkins, at that time no charges were brought against either of you?"

"No, sir. Lord Dryer realised we weren't actually smuggling, we was just duped by the accused and, with assurances that we would have nothing else to do with him, he let us off."

"Thank you, Mr Hawkins. I have no further questions for you."

The prosecutor sits down and the clerk of the court asks the accused, "Do you wish to cross examine the witness, Mr Meakins?"

Meakins shakes his head as if in disbelief. "Yes I do, my Lord." He turns to the witness. "I put it to you that you are a liar, John Hawkins, for I know nothing of what you are accusing. If this had happened, as you say, then why was I not charged with smuggling at the time?"

"Maybe Lord Dryer was after more evidence. Your family are influential in this area and with a good brief you may have been able to wriggle out of it."

Meakins looks up at Joshua sitting in judgement over him and suddenly he loses his temper and points in his direction. "That man is leading a vendetta against me, an innocent man. He is fabricating stories to instigate my demise. He will not be happy until he sees me dead. He is supposed to be a religious man, a Justice of the Peace, a pillar of the community, but he has swindled his only brother out of his share of his inheritance and he is only attacking me in an attempt to silence me forever."

There is a crescendo of noise from the public gallery and Lord Helyar bangs his gavel and cries: "Order! Order! Sit down, Mr Meakins."

Joshua speaks quietly to Lord Helyar and then

stands. "I wish to address the court, Mr Boswell."

"Silence in court," shouts the clerk authoritatively. The background chatter diminishes. "Go ahead, my Lord."

Joshua clears his throat and speaks clearly. "Gentlemen of the jury, as I am sure you are aware, my personal business is not a matter for the court this afternoon. It is Nathan Meakins in the dock and not me. However, I do feel it is necessary to answer these allegations before we are able to proceed. It is true that I have a younger half brother, although this information has only recently come to light. The fact of the matter is that my half brother, whom I always took to be my cousin, is younger than me and is also illegitimate. As such, he is not legally entitled to any part of my father's estate. I have discussed this recently with his mother and she has begged me to keep this matter to myself and not divulge the truth to her son, for fear it will spoil their relationship. It is for this reason that the facts have not, until now, been in the public domain. I have done nothing underhand and my reasons for bringing this man into court are purely due to his own illegal and dreadful actions." Joshua then faces the newspaper reporter. "I would be very grateful, Mr Rowlands, if this information could also be kept out of the papers. It is no one else's business but that of my family and it will hurt more people than it will help."

The press reporter nods his head in agreement. "Of course, my Lord."

"Thank you, Mr Boswell." Joshua resumes his seat.

"Do you have any more questions for the witness, Mr Meakins?"

"No, my Lord, but I would like an answer from the *honourable* Lord Dryer," he says sarcastically. "He still has not answered my question: why did he not have me charged immediately if he caught me smuggling on his land?"

"I will answer his question, Mr Boswell. Mr Hawkins was correct, I believe you to be a habitual offender and I wanted further evidence of this, Mr Meakins."

"Where is this evidence then, Dryer?"

"I suggest you should be a little more patient and all will be revealed."

Mr Boswell then intercedes. "Do you have any additional questions, Mr Meakins?"

"No, my Lord," he says morosely.

"You may step down, Mr Hawkins." John Hawkins steps down from the witness box with a sigh of relief and he takes his seat back in the gallery.

Mr Boswell then addresses the prosecutor. "Do you have any further witnesses, Mr Birch?"

"Yes, my Lord, I would like to call Mr Albert Johnson of Church Street, Weymouth."

Meakins looks taken aback at this development.

The usher opens the door to the court and calls, "Albert Johnson." Mr Johnson follows him in, also handcuffed to a constable and they stand together in the witness box.

"Mr Johnson, please would you raise your right hand, place your left hand on the bible and repeat after me – I do solemnly, sincerely and truly declare and affirm that the evidence I shall give shall be the truth, the whole truth and nothing but the truth, so help me God."

Mr Johnson swears the oath and crosses himself at the end of it.

"Mr Johnson, would you please confirm your full name for the court."

"It is Albert William Josiah Johnson, sir."

"Thank you, Mr Johnson. I understand you are still awaiting trial for your part in the smuggling venture that took place on 27th January this year, known in the press as The Battle of Hamdon Hill."

"Yes, sir."

"In your statement for the court, after the capture of the smuggling gang on that eventful night, you were able to name a number of gentlemen who were instrumental in funding the venture with you. Do you stand by that statement?"

"I do, sir."

"One of the names was that of a Squire Brandon. Did you ever come across this man in your dealings?

"I saw him only once, sir. It was in Weymouth one night at the Old Sea Cow public house with the other men who were planning the venture. They didn't know me at the time, but I was sitting at the next table with my mate."

"What were you doing there?"

"It is my local hostelry, sir."

"Do you see this man here in court today?"

"Yes, sir… I do, sir."

"Would you please indicate which person bears that name in this court?"

Albert Johnson points to the man in the dock. "That is the man before you there, sir."

Mr Birch smiles and says simply to the bench, "I rest my case, my Lords."

The clerk of the court looks contemptuously at Nathan Meakins. "Do you have any questions for this witness, Mr Meakins?"

"Yes, my Lord. I put it to you that you are a part of a conspiracy and that you are making all this up in return for leniency, Mr Johnson."

"I am not a liar, sir, I am a religious man. I am not really a smuggler, I only got involved to try and make ends meet and feed my family. As true as I am stood here before you all, that is the man that I saw, who helped fund the runs and called himself Squire Brandon."

There is a long silence, while Meakins looks perplexed.

"If you have no further questions for this witness, Mr Meakins, then Mr Birch should do his summing up."

"I have no further questions, my Lord."

Mr Birch then stands and addresses the jury directly. "Gentlemen of the jury, you have heard the testimony of both Mr Hawkins and Mr Johnson, who swear under oath that Nathan Meakins used the *nom de plume* of Squire Brandon in his dealings with the smuggling gang now incarcerated at Shepton Mallet Prison. Apart from claiming that 'it is a conspiracy', he has offered no evidence to establish his innocence and I therefore suggest you have no option but to offer up a verdict of guilty as charged." He then turns towards the bench. "I rest my case, my Lords."

Mr Boswell then turns to the dock. "Will the prisoner please stand." Meakins gets to his feet. "The defendant also has the right to make a closing speech. Have you anything further to say Mr Meakins?"

"I have, my Lord." It is Meakins' turn to address the jury. "Gentlemen of the jury, I am sure that you all know myself and my family, if not personally then by reputation and therefore you will be aware that I have never been accused of any misdemeanours in the past. It is quite preposterous that these charges should be laid against me in this vindictive manner; I trust that you will see sense and find me not guilty."

"You may be seated, Mr Meakins, while the jury make their deliberations."

The jury huddle together and discuss the case quietly among themselves and it is not long before the foreman stands up.

Mr Boswell asks, "Have you reached a verdict on which you are all agreed?"

"We have, my Lord."

"Do you find the prisoner guilty, or not guilty?"

"We find him guilty, my Lord."

Joshua gives a small sigh of relief and the three magistrates confer for only a few minutes. Lord Helyar indicates to the clerk of the court that they are ready to pronounce the sentence.

The clerk of the court cries, "Will the prisoner please stand." Meakins and the constable stand once more in the dock.

Lord Helyar reads out the sentence. "The prisoner is convicted for the offence of smuggling and is ordered to pay the maximum fine of £100, plus a custodial sentence of six months. The prisoner is, in any case, to be remanded in custody to answer for the two more serious charges of rape and the murder of an infant child at the Court of Assize in Taunton, on a date yet to be decided upon. Take him down."

Meakins looks angrily at Joshua and yells over his shoulder, "You might have won this round, Dryer, but I will have the best lawyer money can buy for the next trial and you won't have your cronies backing you." He is led away by Constable Gundry and one of his colleagues, to be taken back to the police cell in Ivell and thence under escort to Taunton Prison.

"The court is adjourned. All rise!"

Joshua says his farewells to Lord Helyar and David Phelps and the other court officials before going to find John Hawkins to give him a lift home in the gig.

"Well done, John, and thank you. I know it was

hard for you admitting the affair, but it is not against the law and I am sure it will soon be forgotten. I doubt your wife will even get to hear of it, as it will not be reported in the newspapers. Meakins will try any dirty tricks to protect himself, hence his attack on me. Nevertheless, we have the upper hand whilst he is safely under lock and key."

Joshua realises that his staff and Louisa in particular will all be waiting anxiously for any news of the trial. On reaching Alvington Manor he eagerly rushes up the front steps to tell them all the good tidings.

Louisa is hovering in the hallway as he enters and he grabs hold of her excitedly. "It is good news, Louisa, the jury found him guilty and we sentenced him to six months in gaol with a £100 fine. He is remanded in custody until the assizes in Taunton."

"Thank heavens for that! Well done, Joshua."

Rosa has just entered the hallway and she witnesses the master holding Louisa happily and hears Louisa call the master by his first name. She smiles to herself, for she has suspected for some time now that her friend is in love with the master and he must have encouraged this familiarity.

"Please tell all the staff the news; I have to rush back now for the second sitting this afternoon." He smiles at Rosa. "I will see you all later." He is obviously in high spirits.

Rosa approaches and Louisa turns and sees her. "Rosa, it is good news; Meakins is to be in prison for at least six months and he is going to be tried for rape and murder at the Taunton assizes."

"I can see it is good news, Louisa." She raises her eyebrows and smiles knowingly. Louisa, realising that Rosa must have caught them together, blushes guiltily.

"Lord Dryer was just relieved and excited that

he had won the first stage, Rosa, nothing more than that. But we had better go and tell the others."

Although things settle down to normal everyone is aware of the impending court case; it is like a dark cloud looming on the horizon and casting its shadow over Alvington Manor. With Easter approaching, Joshua tries his hardest to keep everyone's spirits up. He encourages Louisa to help Aurora make and decorate a large papier mâché egg and, in addition to the Easter cakes that Flora and Elsie were planning, to cook some hard boiled eggs ready for dyeing and decorating, hiding and using in the egg rolling competition. He also encourages the ladies to titivate their Sunday hats by awarding a prize for the best Easter bonnet.

However, as the Easter Sunday family Communion Service is about to begin and they are all assembled in the appropriately decorated chapel, he is shocked when the old oak door opens and the Bridewell sisters enter. They look wonderfully glamorous compared to the amateur efforts of the estate ladies and Joshua feels very aware of an aura of disappointment among the women, as the three girls sit down together at the back of the chapel in the pew beside the font.

Joshua smiles to welcome the ladies as David Phelps starts the service. "Good morning everyone, how wonderful the chapel looks this Easter morning. Thank you, ladies, for all your hard work with the flowers." He smiles at Rosa and Louisa, who he found earlier doing the finishing touches. "I would also like to thank Beatrice and Toby for the wonderful depiction of the Garden of Gethsemane, with the tomb decorated in moss and flowers and the huge stone cast aside for the resurrection of

Jesus Christ. It is a wonderful idea and a lot of hard work went into creating it. Well done, children.

"Now, down to church business. Can I please have your attention as I hereby publish the banns of marriage on this day, 20th April 1854, between Malachi Joseph Warren of Home Farm, Alvington Manor and Rosa May Price of the Dower House, Alvington Manor, both of this parish."

"Hooray!" cries Toby excitedly and everyone laughs.

David Phelps clears his throat. "This is the first time of asking and if any of you know any cause or just impediment why these two persons should not be joined together in holy matrimony, you are to declare it now."

There is silence.

"In that case, please all rise to sing the Easter hymn, 'There is a green hill far away'." The congregation are definitely in the mood for singing now and the three soprano voices of the Bridewell sisters and Louisa's mellow contralto are sounding crystal clear among the other mixed ranges of the gathering.

Reverend Phelps reads the sermon and then they all kneel in prayer.

Aurora, who is sitting with Louisa, chatters throughout the ceremony and eventually gets down from the pew and goes to join Luke. They are obviously excited because there is to be an Easter egg hunt on the way to the Orangery later and an egg rolling competition for the older children up on the hill by Camp Road.

However, it is at this point in the service when the congregation all, in turn, take Communion. This takes some time and Louisa is thankful that she is not queuing alongside the three elegant Bridewell ladies. When everyone is again seated,

David Phelps announces the next hymn, number eighty-four, 'Christ the Lord is Risen Today' and the little chapel is filled with the sound of joyful singing. The service ends with the parishioners reverently repeating the Lord's Prayer.

Louisa takes hold of Aurora's hand and as they all spill out into the fresh April air she is very aware of Joshua going hastily to greet the young ladies from Clifton Maybank. She cannot help the feeling of jealousy engulfing her. Whatever is it that has brought them here today? She uses the Easter egg hunt as an excuse to dawdle with Aurora and Luke, in order to eavesdrop on their conversation.

Serena Bridewell is saying, "I hope you didn't mind us joining you in your Easter service, Joshua, only Keziah wanted to come and say goodbye to you before she goes off to St Thomas' Hospital in London to train to be a nurse with Florence Nightingale."

"Really? Is this true, Keziah?"

"Yes, Joshua, I am leaving on Wednesday."

"That is incredibly benevolent of you, I am most impressed. I am sure it will be extremely rewarding."

Keziah smiles. "Well, we have been hearing such dreadful things about the unsanitary conditions in our hospitals; I simply felt I wanted to do something more useful than what I am doing at present."

"I do understand and I think it is very commendable, but I suspect that you and Alicia will miss her, Serena?"

"We will indeed," says Serena.

"I won't miss her pinching my hairbrush, or borrowing my best shawl, however," says Alicia, laughing, as her sister pokes her indignantly.

Louisa gives a small sigh of relief and, smiling

happily, she wanders off towards the Orangery, with the children still hunting for the elusive eggs. When they have both found a couple of eggs each, they go on to join everyone else inside the beautifully glazed building.

The table at one end of the room is spread with brightly decorated food. There are Easter biscuits, hot cross buns and simnel cake, plus tiny chocolate eggs and sandwiches. Unsurprisingly, Aurora and Luke make a beeline for the chocolate eggs. They are soon smeared with dark chocolate, around their mouths, melting on their hands and covering their clothes. "What a sight you do look, both of you," says Louisa laughing.

Elsie is in charge of the samovar and Louisa goes to ask her for a cup of tea. While they are chatting, Rosa and Malachi join them.

"Not long now Rosa before he makes an honest woman of you," says Elsie.

"I know; 18th May, it is only a month away. The time is going by so quickly, but things are all coming together nicely. My trousseau is nearly completed, thanks to Lucy and Malachi's mother, and everyone else from the manor who has contributed something. Lord Dryer has agreed that we can have the cottage in the hamlet, so Malachi and Jacob have been cleaning and painting the cottage, and tidying and planting up the garden ready for the summer. It is so exciting Lou Lou."

"I don't know about exciting, I'm exhausted," complains Malachi good-naturedly.

"He has been working so hard, I could not wish for a better future husband."

"I think you are both very lucky to have found love within such a small proximity of each other, don't you?"

"It is rather magical, I must admit," says Rosa,

all smiles as she links her arm through Malachi's.

Louisa then spots Alicia entering the Orangery. Joshua has obviously persuaded the sisters to stay for refreshments. Alicia turns to their host as he follows the girls through the doorway. "We read in the *Western Flying Post* that my ex-fiancé has been convicted of smuggling and is to be tried for rape and murder. What is all that about?"

"Well, I cannot really go into that before the trial Alicia, but I did warn Serena that he is a nasty piece of work. He is a wolf in sheep's clothing, I am afraid."

"It sounds as though I had a narrow escape and although rather upsetting at the time, I am grateful to you for your forewarning me. Thank you, Joshua."

"You are most welcome, Alicia. I hope you can see now that I was simply worried on your behalf."

"Of course."

After everyone has eaten their fill of the fine fare, Joshua bids farewell to the Bridewell sisters and returns to the Orangery to announce the winner of the Easter bonnet competition.

"Right, ladies and gentlemen, I am now ready to award the prize for the best Easter bonnet, although congratulations must go to everyone, for you all look very charming and gay in your wonderfully imaginative creations. The winner, however, is Miss Emily Potts. Would you please come forward, Emily, to receive your prize?"

Emily, who has made her bonnet herself from the farm straw and has decorated it with primroses and some purple periwinkle flowers, steps forward shyly.

"This is very professional, Emily, how did you learn to do this?"

She smiles coyly. "My Aunty Mabel showed me, my Lord."

"Well, you definitely deserve the prize and well done for all your hard work. My sister makes these to sell in my mother's shop on Portland and she could not do a better job than you have here. I am very pleased to award you this year's prize for the best Easter bonnet at Alvington."

Joshua passes her a basket of goodies and all present cheer and clap. Emily blushes and smiles. "This is the first time I have ever won anything and it is the happiest day of my life," she says and then she adds, "so far," and everyone laughs.

"In the junior category I think that Bunny Warren's bonnet, decorated with paper ducklings, is also exceptional. Bunny come up and get your prize of an Easter egg."

Bunny skips up to Joshua and eagerly holds out her hands for the chocolate egg.

"Well done Bunny," says Joshua and gives her a kiss on her cheek. "Right, let us all set off up the hill to see who is going to win the Easter egg rolling competition." Joshua picks up Aurora and puts her onto his shoulders and she squeals with delight, as all the boys and young men race ahead of the older folk. Jean Hawkins is walking with her mother and her Aunty Molly, enjoying the unusually mild and sunny spring afternoon.

Isaac Warren, John Boucher and Jack Hawkins are joined by Raymond and Lettie as they walk more slowly up to the top of the hill. "Thank goodness that rogue Meakins is finally behind bars, I always thought he would come to a bad end," says Jack Hawkins.

"I couldn't agree more," says John Boucher, but as he speaks he catches Raymond and Lettie exchanging a knowing look. Immediately suspicious, he says, "What's going on with you two?"

"It's nothing Pa."

"What do you mean it is nothing, Lettie? I saw the look that passed between the two of you."

"But we have promised his lordship to keep it to ourselves."

John Boucher stops in his tracks and looks severely at his young daughter. "I am your father, Lettie. There is nothing that you should be keeping from me. Now I will ask you again, what is going on?"

Lettie looks again at Raymond, who avoids eye contact, but she cannot help thinking that maybe it is safe to confide in them, now that Meakins is behind bars. "It is just that there is still more shocking things about Nathan and Olivia Meakins that folk around here don't realise and me and Raymond, we know it all."

"Well, as I say, I am your father Lettie and Jack is Raymond's uncle, now standing in for his sadly departed father. You need to tell us what is going on."

Lettie feels she has no choice but to tell all, with her father looking sternly and expectantly down at her and she feels almost relieved to unburden herself. She gives a small sigh and lowers her voice. "It is about the coven. That is why he is being tried for murder. There is a coven that meets up on Summer House Hill and they make sacrifices up there. They murdered Olivia's baby. Raymond's sister Jean saw them, and Olivia's ladies maid, Apsey, was with them. She recognised the high priestess too, but the other folk she was unable to identify, all with their faces partially hidden by their hooded cloaks."

Isaac Warren is exasperated. "I knew there was witchcraft still going on hereabouts, and the law is powerless to deal with it. We have to make a plan to fight these pagans ourselves. We need to enlist help from the other good Christian folk hereabout. That is what we need to do. Will you help me lads, to rally some folk to go with us on a witch hunt?"

"I will," Jack agrees, "and my boys will join us."

"Mine too," says Isaac. "If we get enough folk to stand against them, we should be able to put a stop to this. I know a few farmers who will want to put a stop to this too. Are you with us Ray? Do you think that Jean will stand with us too?"

"I cannot speak for my sister, but I am with you. What they have done is despicable, but Jean has to stay safe for the trial. That is why Lord Dryer wants this kept secret, to protect his witnesses."

"In that case we will wait until the trial is over to make sure his goose is well and truly cooked, but then we can deal with the rest of them," says John Boucher. "My Flora can work on her remedies in the meantime."

Isaac nods in agreement. "Then let us put it out of our minds until then, for it is disheartening when everyone else around us are trying to enjoy themselves."

They all gather at the top of the hill and John Boucher, putting aside his worries, fires his gun to set off the race. There is a lot of shouting and tumbling before Billy Riddick reaches the bottom of the hill and is declared the winner. Joshua awards him a flagon of cider and when Toby is the first among the younger ones, he is also given a prize of an Easter egg.

Overall, everyone enjoys the day and the younger ones are particularly weary, as they all wend their way home after the festivities. Joshua is glad to have been able to lift the spirits of all those connected with the coming trial and he waves merrily to Jean and Raymond as they go off with Lettie, following the Hawkins family back up the hill towards Odcombe.

Aurora has not stopped chattering all day and Joshua can see that Louisa is looking very fatigued as she carries the child on her hip back to the house.

"Have you enjoyed today, Louisa?" he asks, coming up behind them.

"Yes indeed, it has been enormous fun and the children particularly have loved all the merriment. At least for one day we have been able to put the horrors of the forthcoming trial to one side."

"It will soon be over, Louisa, and don't forget we have Malachi and Rosa's wedding to look forward to afterwards."

"I know, but I will not rest easy until that evil man gets his comeuppance."

CHAPTER 23 *(May 1854)*

LIFE SENTENCES

Joshua has arranged for all those involved in the court case to join him in the drawing room, in order that he might allay their fears by explaining to them the legal procedures and formalities they will face at Meakins' trial commencing on Tuesday 6th May. Rebecca arrived from Portland at about two of the clock. She has brought with her an extra hat and two straw bonnets from her mother's shop for the girls to try on. She has chosen a leaf green hat with a gold feather trim for Louisa, because she had already seen her outfit at the harvest service. For herself, her mother has given her a French navy, stylish hat decorated with gold braid. For Jean to choose between, she has two spare bonnets, each trimmed and tied with different coloured ribbons. She has taken some refreshments with Joshua and they are now seated in his study with Louisa, Jean and Amy.

Joshua is reading aloud from the *Western Flying Post.*

"'The High Court Circuit Judge, Lord Harvey-Goldsmith, is due to arrive in Taunton on 5th May 1854. He is to be escorted to the New Shire Hall by the high sheriff and the chaplain in the ceremonial carriage, four javelin-men on horseback…'" He explains, "these are men who are armed with pikes and are there to keep order," and then continues to read, "'plus the superintendent and two trumpeters, also on horseback, and other town dignitaries. His lordship will then officially open the commission at the Shire Hall, where the court will be held. After this, Judge Harvey-Goldsmith is due to attend a church service with the mayor, the sheriff and other members of the corporation. The following morning the judge is to take his seat at the crown court at around ten of the clock, when the grand jury will be sworn in.'"

He looks up from the paper. "That is, when the judge delivers the charges and makes any comments he feels necessary regarding the cases to the grand jury. Then they will retire to the chambers to review the bills laid before them, study all the witness depositions and consider the indictments, before returning these to the clerk of the court. The high sheriff will be sitting in attendance. Then those prisoners whose indictments are found to be a true bill will be brought to the court, charged and then tried."

"What if they don't find it to be a true bill, Joshua?" asks Rebecca nervously.

"Don't you worry about that, Becky, they have no choice, not with the evidence we now have. Anyway, after that the trial follows a set pattern. The petty jury will then be sworn in, the prosecution will outline details of the case and the witnesses for the prosecution, such as yourselves, will be called and sworn in to give their evidence. In this case you will also probably be cross-examined by his defence lawyer, as one of the last things Meakins said to me was that he was going to get the best lawyer money could buy."

"Oh no!"

"Don't worry, Becky, they have your statement and you only have to tell the truth. You also have Louisa's testimony to back you up."

"It is just so humiliating!"

Louisa puts her arm around Rebecca. "You are not the one who will be humiliated Becky, you have done nothing to be ashamed of. But he has and we have to prove it."

Joshua looks encouragingly at his sister. "You know that Louisa is right, Becky, so you must be brave, all of you. It may be rather nerve-racking but you must try to relax and simply tell the court what you know. They are human beings just like us and if it helps try imagining them all sitting before you stark naked."

They all laugh at this idea.

"Anyway where was I? Ah! I remember. Following the cross-examination of all *our* witnesses for the prosecution, will be the witnesses for the defence, but I doubt he will have any. However, if he has, they can be questioned by the defendant, or in this case his lawyer, and cross-examined by the prosecution. The prosecution will then make his closing speech and the defence lawyer will do the same, before the jury retire to consider their verdict." He looks from one to another. "Is that all clear to you?"

"Yes, my Lord," they say in unison, apart from Rebecca, who says despondently, "Yes Josh."

Joshua sighs, they are all so young. Has he made the right decision to put them through this? He clears his throat; it is no time to back-track now and he has to inspire them with confidence. "I have arranged accommodation for us all at the Octon Lodge Coaching House on the Shoreditch Road just outside Taunton. I am not sure how long the trial will take, but you must look on it as an adventure. You have done nothing wrong. All you have to do is answer their questions honestly and truthfully."

Tuesday the 6th May turns out to be a mild and

sunny day. John Moore drops them all off outside the Shire Hall and returns to the Coaching House. Joshua is to take them all out to lunch between sessions and John Moore is to return to collect them at six of the clock that evening.

The Shire Hall is a new building and the place still carries the aroma of the freshly sawn wood of the wainscoting. Joshua reluctantly leaves the three witnesses sitting together in a row, on a pew in the outer witness waiting area. His sister looks very smart in her blue and gold plaid skirt, her French navy jacket and gloves and the matching hat with the gold braid, fixed with a hat pin through her black hair. He knows she is very nervous, as she is playing abstractedly with the chain on the reticule in her lap.

Louisa is looking beautiful as always in her best leaf-green costume, with Rebecca's green hat and its pretty gold feathers perched among her luxuriant auburn curls, tied under her chin with a gold ribbon. Jean, bless her, is wearing her red Sunday-best frock with her green woollen shawl, grey kid gloves, plus one of the straw bonnets that Rebecca brought for her, trimmed and tied with dark green ribbon. They all make a pretty picture sitting there together and Joshua is aware of them all watching him anxiously, as he leaves to enter the courtroom.

He hopes that he too looks smart and stylish in his moleskin trousers, long burgundy frock coat and matching waistcoat, with a navy blue floppy cravat and a crisp, clean, white wing-collar shirt. For their reassurance, he finds a pew where they will easily see him when giving their evidence.

The twelve men of the petty jury file in and sit down in a special section on the left of the courtroom. Then the usher cries "All rise!" and Judge Harvey-Goldsmith enters, dressed in his scarlet robe with white fur mantle and cuffs, his chain of office and a long, horsehair white wig. He takes his place at the large desk, in front of the royal standard.

The clerk of the court instructs the usher, "Please bring in the prisoner."

Moments later Nathan Meakins is standing before them, handcuffed to his guard.

The judge reads out the charges against him. "The prisoner in the dock is charged on two counts, the first is for rape and the second charge is for infanticide." There are cries of 'shameful' and 'barbaric' from the public gallery and the clerk of the court calls for order. When it is quiet again he continues, "The grand jury have deliberated and the indictment has been declared to be a true bill. Do you have any representation, Mr Meakins?"

"No, Your Honour, I have decided to defend myself and to save my guinea."

More likely his father has stopped his allowance, thinks Joshua wryly.

"I think we should deal first with the charge of rape. Would you care to call your first witness, Mr Morrison?"

"Thank you, Your Honour; I should like to call the alleged victim, Miss Rebecca Stone, to the stand please."

Joshua sighs anxiously as the usher goes to the door of the courtroom and calls, "Rebecca Stone!"

Rebecca looks at her two friends nervously and then stands. She follows the usher, dressed in his long, black robe, through into the courtroom and he leads her to the witness box. Avoiding eye contact with the accused she takes her place in the stand and repeats the oath without any hesitation. "I do solemnly, sincerely and truly declare and affirm that the evidence I shall give shall be the truth, the whole truth and nothing but the truth, so help me God." Her voice is quiet but controlled.

"Would you please confirm your full name and address for the court?"

"I am Rebecca Stone of Coastguard Cottage, Chiswell, Portland, Dorset."

"I understand from your deposition, Rebecca, that you were staying with your brother on the night of 21st June for the occasion of a summer ball at Alvington Manor."

"That is correct, sir."

"How old were you at that time, Rebecca?"

"I was fifteen, sir."

"Please would you tell us from the beginning, in your own, words what happened?"

She starts hesitantly. "Well, sir… I was upstairs on the gallery with my friend, Lettie. We were looking down on the spectacle… enjoying the music and the dancing and observing all the pretty attire, when Lettie was called away to the kitchen. She was helping the maids, sir." She pauses as she recalls the sequence of what happened and her voice begins to waver.

"I stayed a few moments longer, until I saw… the accused… making towards the stairs to the gallery. He was striding away from the dance floor with a very angry expression on his face and, because I had encountered him in the past and did not like him, I decided to turn along the passageway towards the bedrooms to avoid him, sir. Unfortunately, I was too late, for he had spotted me." Rebecca pauses again; for months she has buried the horrific memory of what happened to her, into the deepest recess of her mind.

She looks at Joshua, who smiles encouragement. She must do it for his sake. Feeling nauseous she recalls her terror in the seconds just before Meakins reaches her. Hot tears fill her eyes as she takes a deep breath and forces herself to re-live the nightmare. "He grabbed me from behind and pushed me into one of the bedrooms, sir. I try to dodge him, but he pushes me onto the bed." Her tears are now falling and her voice is more hesitant. "I try to fight him off… kicking and scratching him… but I am not strong enough and… the more I struggle the more he seems to like it." Her throat is hurting, as she tries her hardest to tell her story without crying. "He laughs at me, sir… then he puts his hand over my mouth… he pulls down my drawers… and… and he rapes me." She takes her handkerchief from her pocket to wipe away her tears and blow her nose.

"Just take your time, Rebecca; I know this is difficult for you."

"I was intact, sir… I was a virgin and he hurt me dreadfully. He pinned me down by my hair… and his knees dug into my legs… and he bit me." She is aware that her voice has become more and more high-pitched.

"Did he say anything to you?"

"Yes, sir." She takes a deep breath. "He said… 'You know you like it, so why fight me'… he was absolutely vile. He also said… I'd never had 'the honour of a gentleman before'. Oh, and something I'll never forget, he said that he liked his… tarts… virginal, sir."

"Thank you, Rebecca, you have done very well." He pats her hand kindly and turns to the judge, "I have no further questions, Your Honour."

Rebecca casts an apprehensive glance at the jury of twelve men and her heart sinks to see them all, without exception, looking so impassive. Have they no sympathy at all for her situation?

"Do you have any questions for the witness, Mr Meakins?"

"Yes, I do, your honour," says Meakins. "Why was it, Miss Stone, that you were all alone up on the gallery? It looked to me as if you were up there waiting for me."

She looks at him face to face now. "I was not waiting for you; I was trying to escape from you," she replies angrily.

"Come now, Miss Stone, we both know that that is not the case. You turned back and smiled at me, enticing me along the passageway, wiggling your bottom seductively. It looked to me as if you were begging for it."

"Objection, Your Honour!"

"Objection sustained, you will please keep to the facts, Mr Meakins!"

"I am sorry, my Lord, but Miss Stone might exhibit a heart cold as stone in the courtroom today, but she was far from stony on the night in question."

"You, Nathan Meakins, are a contemptible liar and I despise you," says Rebecca spiritedly. "I have given my oath before God and all that I have said is the whole truth and nothing but the truth. You, on the other hand, worship the devil and your oath before God can be taken with a pinch of salt." Rebecca is aware of mutterings among the people in the gallery. He has made her lose her temper.

Meakins smiles annoyingly. "I really seem to be able to get under your skin, don't I, Miss Stone. I have no further questions, my Lord."

"You may stand down, Miss Stone," says the clerk. He turns to the prosecutor. "Do you have any further witnesses, Mr Morrison?"

"Yes, my Lord, I should like to call Miss Louisa Bonfield to the stand."

The usher escorts Rebecca out and calls for Louisa.

She follows him into the courtroom, takes her place in the witness box and repeats the oath. Her eyes scan the courtroom until she finds Joshua. He is smiling at her reassuringly.

"Would you please confirm your full name and address for the court?"

"I am Louisa Elizabeth Bonfield of the Dower House, Alvington Manor, Ivell, Somerset."

"I understand from your deposition, Miss Bonfield, that you were at the summer ball on the night in question?"

"I was, sir."

"Would you please tell the court, in your own words, what happened in relation to this incident?"

"Well, my Lord, my friends and I had missed seeing Rebecca, Lord Dryer's sister, for some time. Although she was not dressed for the ball, she had been helping her friends behind the scenes and enjoying the spectacle from the gallery. Her brother had invited her to attend, but she is quite shy and preferred to stay in the background. I went up to the gallery to look for her and I heard someone weeping. It was, of course, Becky; she was in a terrible state and she told me that Nathan Meakins had raped her, but she begged me to tell no-one as she was so humiliated. I helped her to go to her own bedroom and put her to bed, for she was still suffering from shock. Then, because of my promise, I went down to the kitchen to tell Lettie and the others that Becky was unwell with a headache, and that she had retired for the night. I went back upstairs with a ewer of hot water for her to wash and a mug of hot chocolate. She was very distressed, tearful and embarrassed, sir."

"Did you intend to keep this a secret, Miss Bonfield?"

"I didn't want to, I was so worried about her, but I gave Becky my word, sir."

"If this is the case, then how did this unhappy situation come to light?"

"Unfortunately, Becky was made pregnant from the rape." Louisa pauses; she does not want to say that her friend deliberately tried to lose her baby. Then she continues, "But she lost the baby when she fell from a horse. This was an added trauma for her to suffer, all due to this man's villainy."

"Was she attended to by a physician?"

"Yes, my Lord, she was very ill and nearly died. Lord Dryer called for Dr Gillingham. It was during this time that Becky confessed to her brother what had happened to her."

"Thank you, Miss Bonfield, I have no further questions."

"Does the defendant have any questions for this witness?" asks the clerk of the court.

"Yes, my Lord, I do." Meakins turns to Louisa. "I put it to you, Miss Bonfield, that you are making up this pack of lies in revenge for the untimely death of your sister?"

"I may despise you, Nathan Meakins, because you seduced my sister and I believe you were responsible for her death, but that does not mean that I would lie under oath."

"It was not my fault your sister was besotted with me; she should not have got herself in the pudden club."

"You seduced her while she was working as a maid at your parents' home and you know the child was yours. She went to you for help and you callously cast her aside. She was only just seventeen and she was so distraught... she drowned herself."

"I cannot be held responsible for maids who get above themselves. I didn't know that the other girl was Dryer's sister; I thought she was just a maid. What did she expect dressed like a commoner? She should have had better sense."

Again there is a muttering wave of disapproval from the gallery.

The judge is getting impatient. "Do you have any further questions for this witness, pertaining to the case in hand, Mr Meakins?"

"No, my Lord, I have no further questions."

"In that case, the court will adjourn until two post-meridian, when we will deal with the extremely serious matter of infanticide."

The clerk of the court then cries, "The court will now rise." The judge takes his leave and a general hubbub ensues.

Meakins is led away, still handcuffed to the constable.

Joshua finds the girls and immediately hugs his sister. "Becky, you did really well! You must feel so relieved that you have stood up to him. I am very proud of you."

"Me too, Becky, you were splendid," says Louisa.

"You were too, Louisa," says Joshua with a big smile. "You should have seen them, Jean; they really made Meakins look like a real heel."

"It did not seem to irk him though, Josh; it was like it was just a game for him," says Rebecca bitterly.

"That may be so, but the jury were taking all that in and the folk in the gallery showed their disapproval, so I think maybe Meakins is only fooling himself."

"You must be so thankful it is all over for you," says Jean. "Just a matter of waiting for the verdict, but I am still having kittens."

"Don't you fret, Jean, it will soon be finished and it is not half as bad as you might imagine," says Louisa kindly.

"Besides, I think we might have him on the ropes, however invincible he might believe himself to be," says Joshua.

"Just think how wonderful it will be when the guilty verdict is reached and he is sentenced, Jean," says Rebecca trying to be as encouraging as the other two.

Joshua takes the girls to a nearby hostelry where they are served their victuals, before returning to the court just before two of the clock.

The preliminaries over, Meakins takes his place once more in the dock.

Mr Morrison outlines the case for the prosecution. "The defendant is accused, in addition to the charge of rape, of the murder of an infant child. It is the case of the prosecution that this man dabbled in witchcraft and paganism and when he discovered that his sister was pregnant with his child, they decided between them that they would sacrifice the baby to the Sun God. To substantiate this charge I should like to call my first witness, Miss Jean Hawkins, to the stand."

The usher calls, "Jean Hawkins." Moments later Jean takes her place and repeats the oath solemnly.

"Would you please state your name and address for the court?"

"I am Jean Hawkins, of Cobb Cottage, Dray Road, Odcombe, near Ivell, Somerset, my Lord."

"Please would you tell the court, in your own words, exactly what you witnessed, Miss Hawkins."

Jean looks straight ahead, avoiding any eye contact with Meakins, but Joshua does not take his eyes off him.

"Well, sir, I was working as a maid for the Meakins family at the time and I was woken on the Eve of All Hallows by the sound of footsteps on the gravel outside. I looked out of the window and saw three cloaked figures walking away from the house together. I thought they were the young master and mistress and another person, probably Apsey the ladies maid. Out of curiosity I decided to secretly follow them."

Joshua observes that Meakins has gone rather pale.

"I donned my cloak and rushed downstairs quietly. I could see the flaming torchlight ahead of me and soon caught up with them, although keeping well back to avoid being seen."

Suddenly, Jean's statement is interrupted by a commotion at the door to the courtroom as a large number of people enter and jostle for their seats in the public gallery.

Joshua turns his head to see what the hullabaloo is all about and is surprised to see David Phelps and a number of his parishioners, who must have learnt about the court case in the *Western Flying Post*. Then he spots Jean's brother, Raymond, with Lettie, and young Emily Potts proudly wearing her Easter bonnet among the crowd. They must have travelled together on the steam train from Hendford Station.

There is a hum of quiet chatter and the clerk calls, "Silence in court! Please continue, Miss Hawkins."

"Well sir, I was amazed to discover they were going to a meeting of a witch's coven near to the Round House at the top of Summer House Hill. I kept out of sight and secretly watched the coven's rituals and I soon realised that Nathan Meakins was their warlock. They were having some kind of fertility ceremony and I was very shocked to observe Mr Meakins and his sister removing their cloaks, for underneath they were both naked. Then, they actually had sex on a sort of altar in the centre of the pentacle."

There is a rumble of disapproval throughout the courthouse at this scandalous comment and Nathan Meakins colour has returned to his face in a deep, red hue.

"Are you saying that Nathan Meakins committed incest with his sister?"

"Yes, I am, sir, with all the witches chanting and dancing around them.

"Was the mistress willing?"

"She looked pretty willing to me."

There are sniggers throughout the courtroom.

"Please continue, Miss Hawkins."

"The worst of it was that it turned out she had conceived a baby."

"That must have been rather a tricky problem for them?"

"Well, sir, they managed to keep the baby a secret from the whole household. Of course, her ladies maid, Apsey, was in on it because she was also present in the coven. She managed to look after her mistress while she was indisposed and even after the child was born." Jean cannot help the tears from pricking her eyes at the memory of what happened next.

"Are you alright, Miss Hawkins?"

She clears her throat. "Yes, sir." She blinks away the tears and continues. "They managed to keep the child hidden right up until the summer solstice, then one night I heard them on the gravel again. I was suspicious, because the mistress had been indisposed for several months and yet she was outside with them, so I followed them again. I wish to God I had not, for I have had nightmares ever since."

"Could you simply tell us what happened to the child, Miss Hawkins?"

"They sacrificed him to the Sun God, my Lord.

Nathan Meakins himself took up the ceremonial sword and slit the poor babe's throat."

There are gasps of shock from the public gallery and angry cries of "Murderer!" and "Bastard!" Joshua looks back at David Phelps and his party who are shaking their fists at Meakins furiously. Some of them are holding up their crucifixes before him.

"And no-one tried to stop him?"

"No-one, sir."

"Do you know what they did with the child's corpse?"

"No, sir. Because it was such a horrific thing to witness, I passed out, sir."

"I have no further questions for this witness, Your Honour."

"Do you have any questions for the witness, Mr Meakins?"

"I do indeed, my Lord." Again there are jeers from the public gallery; Joshua recognises Raymond's voice among them. Ignoring them, Meakins turns towards the witness box. "Miss Hawkins, if what you have just said was true, how come you were happy to stay in our employ and not tell anyone until now?"

"It is true, and because of it I was terrified of having a hex put on me. I didn't want to alert anyone to the fact that I knew about the coven. However, because I lost consciousness I was not sure I hadn't been seen anyway; I lived in fear of being bewitched."

"I put it to you that this is all a figment of your imagination; a childish fantasy thought up to spite me for upsetting your friend, Amy Proctor."

"No, it is not, sir. I am telling everyone here before me, truly, what I saw."

"I know that your brother is now working for

Joshua Dryer and that man definitely has it in for me. This is all a concoction and a conspiracy to bring me down. I have no further questions for this liar, my Lord."

Raymond has had enough of his bullying and jumps up to defend his sister. "Don't you dare call my sister a liar! What she is saying is God's own truth and you know it, Meakins."

The judge then bangs down his gavel. "Order! Order! Silence in court! Usher, kindly expel that young man from my court."

The usher attempts to remove him, but Raymond cannot resist turning back and shouting, "You don't want to listen to that lying bastard, Your Honour, he wouldn't know the truth if it bit him on his arse."

"If I hear another word from you, young man, you will be charged with contempt of court."

The usher escorts Raymond out of the courtroom and he sits down in the outer area, waiting for his sister. Lettie is tempted to follow, but she is too nervous to move; besides, she doesn't want to miss anything. The clerk of the court directs Jean to stand down and, relieved it is all over, she quickly joins her brother.

"Do you wish to call any other witnesses, Mr Morrison?"

"I do, my Lord. I should like to call Constable Gundry to the stand."

The usher calls for the constable, who enters and takes the stand. He raises his hand and repeats the oath, then he states his name for the court.

"Mr Gundry, would you kindly tell the court your part in this investigation?"

"Yes sir." He clears his throat. "We already had Mr Meakins in custody on a charge of smuggling. We apprehended him at his gentleman's club, where he was heavily under the influence of opium." Constable Gundry looks at his notebook. "Anyway, on 14th March, Lord Dryer, the Justice of the Peace and magistrate at Ivell, came and asked me to accompany him to Newton Copse, where his gamekeeper's dog had unearthed a charred fragment of a tiny human bone. I went with him to the place and together we carefully exhumed the partial remains of what appeared to be a newly born baby, which had been burnt and buried in the undergrowth on the edge of the oak grove. The remains had been hidden there for some time, but a thunderstorm the previous night had washed away some of the top soil and mulch that had covered it."

"What do you have to say to this, Mr Meakins?"

Joshua and the girls watch with interest as Meakins decides to brazen it out. "It has nothing to do with me. It could be anyone's child; young wenches are always getting themselves into trouble. The child could have been born dead and the shameful hussy buried it, rather than face her parents' wrath."

"Strange that, Mr Meakins, but I don't believe in coincidences. We have an eye witness who places you in Newton Copse and who saw you murder an innocent chid. Do you really expect us to believe that there has been a rash of child deaths in that vicinity? What kind of devil are you, to stoop to such depths of depravity?"

Meakins looks panicked now. "I didn't do it. There must be some other answer, for you have the wrong man."

"I don't think so, Mr Meakins. Do you have any questions for the constable?"

"No, I do not," he says dejectedly.

"You may step down, Constable Gundry."

Mr Morrison then says, "I should like to call

Olivia Meakins to the stand." At this, Joshua notes with satisfaction that Nathan Meakins' jaw drops open.

The usher calls, "Olivia Meakins."

Olivia walks in, dressed up to the nines in a very stylish costume and fancy bonnet. She takes the stand, repeats the oath and states her full name, but her voice is shaky and she appears to be trembling.

"Is it right, Miss Meakins, that you are a member of the coven at Newton Hollow?"

She looks at the bible and answers truthfully. "It is, my Lord."

"Is it also true that you have had carnal relations with your own brother, the man standing before you in the dock?"

Keeping her eyes averted, she replies, "It is true, my Lord. I was thirty-nine years old and a spinster, having been jilted at the altar ten years earlier. As it was my birthday, I wanted to experience the joy of union with a man. It was my brother's gift to me."

"Is it a fact, Miss Meakins, that the result of this was the birth of a male child?"

She hangs her head, looking down at the bible on the shelf before her. "Yes, my Lord," she replies, her voice low.

"Did you keep your condition and the birth a secret from the rest of the household?"

"We did, my Lord."

Joshua can see tears welling up in her eyes.

"Why did you do this, Miss Meakins?"

"My parents would not have understood how this had happened and so we had no choice but to keep it a secret."

Suddenly, Mr Morrison's voice becomes louder and much sterner. "Is it correct then, Miss Meakins, that you and your brother conspired to murder the baby in cold blood?"

Joshua can see the pain of the memory etched on her face as she answers. "I did not want to, my Lord; in those few days I had grown to love him, but my brother would not allow me to keep him."

"Nevertheless, you were present at the sacrificial ceremony and did nothing to stop it?"

"That is true, my Lord. I was afraid to go against my brother; his addiction to opium altered his disposition and he had become aggressive and a bully. Besides, I could not see a way out of the situation we were in."

"You are therefore, in your own words, an accomplice in murder?"

"It was under duress, my Lord. I was not myself, sir. After the birth of Helios I was depressed, exhausted and unable to cope. Apsey, my maid, did everything for me and I let them take over, but I regret it now." Olivia bursts into uncontrollable floods of tears.

Judge Harvey-Goldsmith intercedes. "Am I to understand that you were suffering from post-natal insanity, Miss Meakins?"

She nods her head in the affirmative, and wipes away her tears. "I believe that must be so, Your Honour."

"I have no further questions for this witness," says Mr Morrison.

"Do you have any questions for this witness, Mr Meakins?" asks Judge Harvey- Goldsmith.

"No, I do not!" snaps Meakins defeated.

The judge then asks the prosecutor, "Do you have any more witnesses, Mr Morrison?"

"No Your Honour, I don't think I need any more."

"In that case I will sum up for the jury." He turns towards them. "Gentlemen of the jury, this man has been accused of raping a young girl and murdering an innocent baby. You have heard compelling testimony from the alleged victim of the rape and from several other witnesses, yet the prisoner's only defence seems to be that both charges against him are a great conspiracy. You as jurors have to decide whether or not you believe the testimony of the witnesses. Your job is to decide whether, beyond any reasonable doubt, the prisoner before you is guilty, or not guilty, bearing in mind that these are both capital offences and carry the death penalty. You may now retire to consider your verdict."

The clerk calls, "Please rise," as the judge stands and leaves his podium. Then the jury file out.

Joshua turns to Rebecca and Louisa. "That was a bit of a shock, seeing Olivia Meakins on the stand."

"Yes it was, but I cannot help wondering how genuine her tears were," says Louisa sagely.

"Let's go and see David. It was very good of him to arrange the hecklers; a Christian outcry can only reinforce our case."

They wait until other members of the public have left the gallery and then join their friends. Louisa greets Emily, "What are you doing here, Em? I didn't expect to see you."

"Well it was my afternoon off and I heard that Raymond and Lettie were going, so Mrs Abbott gave me the money for the ticket. She said I could go early with the others to catch the train with the reverend. It has been quite an adventure. I loved it on the train, seeing all the countryside flying by, it was very exciting."

Lettie asks Joshua if he thinks that Raymond and Jean will be allowed back in to hear the verdict.

"I am sure they will not even be noticed, Lettie."

"Shall we go and find them?"

"You don't want to miss the verdict. You stay with Becky and Louisa and I will go and fetch them back in," says Joshua. "I don't think they will be long deliberating."

He rushes off and, after a quick word with the usher, is soon returning with them. Less than thirty minutes have passed when the clerk calls, "Please rise." They all stand as the judge re-enters and the jurymen file back in.

Judge Harvey-Goldsmith asks the usher to bring back the prisoner and moments later Meakins enters the dock, still handcuffed to the policeman.

Judge Harvey-Goldsmith addresses the jury, "Foreman of the jury, with regard to the charge of rape, have you reached a verdict upon which you are all agreed?

"We have, Your Honour."

"Do you find the prisoner guilty, or not guilty, of rape?"

"Guilty, Your Honour."

Rebecca and her supporters give a collective sigh of relief.

"With regard to the iniquitous case of infanticide, have you reached a verdict upon which you are all agreed?"

"We have, Your Honour."

"Do you find the prisoner guilty, or not guilty, of infanticide?"

"We find the prisoner guilty, Your Honour."

Again there are jeers and cries from the public gallery and a middle-aged woman angrily throws a rotten tomato at Meakins. It splatters against the side of his face, the juice running through his sideburns, down his neck and onto his white shirt's wing-collar. He appears to crumble dejectedly before their eyes.

The clerk cries, "Order! Order!"

The judge bangs his gavel and shouts, "I will have silence in my court!" He turns to the prisoner. "Mr Meakins, before I sentence you, is there anything you wish to say in mitigation to the court?"

"I have nothing further to say, Your Honour."

"May I please speak on my brother's behalf, Your Honour?" Olivia stands meekly before him.

"I will grant your request, Miss Meakins, but please make it brief."

"The man who stands before you today bears no resemblance to the young brother I once knew, Your Honour. It is the drugs and drink that have changed him and I beg you to bear this in mind when deciding upon his sentence. If it was not for the opium, I assure you he would be a kinder man."

"That may be so, Miss Meakins, but you conspired in this crime together and your character reference is therefore hardly a good testimonial. These very serious crimes carry the capital punishment and your brother has been found guilty on both counts. I am afraid I have no choice but to hand down the most severe penalty." The judge dons the black cloth sentence cap and a hush falls throughout the court, as he turns toward Nathan Meakins.

"The court doth hereby order you to be taken hence to the place from whence you came, and thence to the place of execution, and that you be hanged by the neck until you are dead, and that your body be afterward buried within the precincts of the prison in which you shall be confined after your conviction. May the Lord have mercy upon your soul."

Olivia looks with anguish at the blanched face of her brother.

CHAPTER 24 *(May 1854)*

THE WITCH HUNT

Since the announcement of the impending wedding, Mrs Abbott has been busy helping the girls making their new costumes for the occasion. Louisa, Lucy and Beatrice Warren are to be Rosa's handmaidens and Jacob is, naturally, Malachi's best man.

Joshua has purchased an imported American Singer sewing machine for Mrs Abbott to use and she soon learns how to operate it by following the instruction manual. She is also their tutor, as they sit together by lamplight in the evenings when they are off duty, hand sewing, embroidering and making lace collars and cuffs in the parlour of the Dower House. Rosa has so much to do; Mrs Abbott volunteers to stitch all the curtains and soft furnishings for the hamlet cottage she will be sharing with Malachi. The girls take turns to watch her working and it causes much excitement to see how quickly the long seams of the curtains are stitched into place in perfect symmetry.

Now that the stress of the court case is over, everyone is more relaxed and Joshua has given permission for Louisa to go with Rosa to help with the cleaning and organising of the cottage. It is a furnished cottage, but Rosa is keen to put her own stamp on it. They are very happy working together, scrubbing, cleaning and polishing, then ferrying household items donated by Mrs Warren to fill up the kitchen cupboards. Finally they hang the new curtains and replace the old cushions.

"We have only the bed to sort out, now. It is so kind of Lord Dryer to buy us a new mattress and pillows."

"Yes, he is very thoughtful." Louisa can picture him doing his regular morning rowing across the lake as she says this and she shakes her head to dispel the image. "Rosa, shall I strip off the old bedding and put it with the laundry while you go and get your bottom drawer things from the Dower House?"

"Yes, that is a good idea, I won't be long."

Louisa is busy with the bedding when she hears someone entering the cottage. Rosa could not have been that quick. She goes nervously to the top of the stairs and calls out, "Who is there?"

Joshua's head appears around the doorway at the base of the stairs.

"Joshua; thank goodness it is you, I thought for a moment that the place was haunted!"

"No, Louisa, have no fear it is only me." He climbs the stairs slowly. "I come, however, as the bearer of bad news. I thought I ought to come and tell you in person that Sir Oliver Meakins has obtained a barrister and they are appealing against the death penalty for his son. It must have come as a great shock to him that his own son could actually be convicted of murder. He had no idea what Nathan was capable of, and they are appealing on the grounds of him being under the influence of opiates. Nevertheless, I am sure he will never be freed, but it is possible that his sentence may be reduced to transportation to Van Diemen's land."

"Oh no! I thought it was all over."

He puts his arm around her, comfortingly. "I am sorry, Louisa. The other thing is that Olivia is to be tried as an accomplice. However, she has been granted bail as her plea is one of post-natal insanity, but he will not be given bail and so we are safe from him. He will never get his hands on Aurora, you can rest assured about that, for if he escapes capital punishment then he will surely be transported."

Louisa is aware of her rapid heart rate as Joshua holds her close to him. She makes an effort to remain calm and pursues the subject of Millie's daughter. "I have been thinking about confiding in my mother and father about Aurora, now that he is under lock and key. I feel it is only right that they should know they have a granddaughter."

"I think you are right, Louisa. Would you like me to come with you to explain? We could take her with us to meet them."

She is aware of him looking down at her tenderly and feels as if he might be about to kiss her again. She turns her head away as she speaks. "That would be wonderful, but I think maybe we ought to break it to them first and give them some time to get used to the idea, before we take Aurora with us." Although she is eager for her parents to see Aurora, it will be such a shock for them and she would prefer it if they were calm and collected when they all met for the first time – for the child's sake more than anyone else's.

Joshua agrees. "Yes, perhaps you are right; it might be better to break the news first and take one step at a time. Let us go together tonight to explain to them that they have a beautiful granddaughter."

"Do you think that they might hate me for what I did?"

"No, Louisa, I am very sure they will both understand how scared you were and that you thought you were doing the best thing for your sister at the time. Besides, I will be there to support you."

She moves away to the window, nervous of his close proximity. He is her boss, the master of all around her and yet they are both alone, unchaperoned and, like Meakins, he could easily take advantage of her. She stares out at the back of Home Farm, trying to collect her thoughts and think of something to say. She is grateful that he is going to go with her to see her parents, but she is very worried that they will blame her for her sister's death.

"Louisa, don't worry; everything is going to be resolved shortly and you will never have to worry about Meakins again." He is standing close behind her and she can feel his breath on her neck. *Was that his lips lightly brushing her hair?* She turns to speak, but as she does so his lips meet hers and she is kissing him back ardently, passionately.

He has lifted her and she is now pressed against the bedroom wall, her heart thumping and her body responding, as she is entangled in his strong arms. Suddenly, Rosa walks in on them and the magic dissipates.

"Oh! I am so sorry. Please, I beg your pardon."

Joshua releases her. "Don't be sorry, Rosa. You should be pleased for your friend. We are only doing what you and Malachi have been doing for some time now," he grins. "I will leave you to your chores." He looks back at Louisa. "I will see you later, when we go and see your parents." He gives her a gentle smile and a cheeky wink and rushes off.

As she straightens her clothes and her hair she knows that Rosa can see how flushed she is, and she is embarrassed. Rosa is squealing with excitement and, having piled up her things on the bed, she is suddenly hugging Louisa. "You are going together to see your parents? Oh my! It is like a fairytale."

"Don't be silly, Rosa, we are going to tell them all about Aurora."

She watches her face drop. "Oh! For a moment there I thought he had proposed."

Louisa surreptitiously wipes away a tear. "Of course not, men in his position do not wed their maids."

That evening it is warm and dry and Joshua has decided that they will stroll around to her parent's cottage. He walks respectfully beside Louisa and she is trying her hardest to suppress her beating heart. She wants to enjoy his nearness and the fact that she has him all to herself for a short while, but she knows she is not worthy.

Louisa taps the front door as she enters, habitually calling out to her parents, "It is only me." This isn't strictly true and her parents are extremely surprised to see them together. They both jump up from their seats.

"Hello, Louisa." Her father holds out his hand in welcome and Joshua shakes it warmly. "My Lord."

"Is something wrong?" asks her mother.

"No, Ma, nothing is wrong, but we have something to tell you. I think you both ought to sit down."

"This sounds ominous," says her father in an aside to her mother.

Louisa takes a deep breath. "I know this will come as a shock to you, but I think it best to simply say it outright. I have been keeping a huge secret from you." Louisa pauses for a moment and looks at Joshua for reassurance, before continuing. "Aurora, the little foundling child who was left abandoned in the clock tower at Alvington Manor… is actually Millie's child. She is your granddaughter and my niece."

"Don't be daft, Lou Lou. How can that be? Our Millie was never pregnant."

"But she was, Ma. Nathan Meakins made her pregnant and then deserted her. Millie managed to hide it from you, but she had the baby here one night in September and she begged me to take her and leave her where she would be found and looked after. She was afraid of what you would think of her, but even more afraid of what Pa might do to Meakins. Now that he is finally locked away, I want you both to know the truth."

Her mother is astonished. "I cannot believe it! She had the baby here in this house and you were able to keep it from us? How can that be?"

"I was terrified, Ma, but we just had to cope as best we could, and Millie was so brave." She bursts into tears.

Joshua steps forward to further explain, noting the shock on the faces of Louisa's parents. "When we found the baby abandoned at Alvington I arranged for her to have a wet nurse and she has lived at the manor ever since. It is her home and she is well looked after and cared for. Louisa loves her like a daughter and we both want you to know her, as your own true granddaughter."

Louisa says, "She is our flesh and blood and we want you both to have the joy of her."

"So Millie really did drown herself," says Mrs Bonfield, sadly resigning herself to the truth. "She must have been absolutely heartbroken. How could you keep this a secret from us? You really should have told us Louisa, we would have cared for both of them. You know your pa is not a violent man."

Joshua then speaks to her father. "I am afraid that Nathan Meakins would have tried the patience of any man, Mr Bonfield, but Louisa thought she was helping her sister at the time. It must have been very traumatic for her, witnessing the birth of the baby and the pain and heartache her sister endured, but she has watched over the child ever since and has ensured she has a good home."

Mr Bonfield then says regretfully, "I am just sorry they did not confide in us, for we would have continued to care for all of them and it may have prevented Millie's death."

"I am truly sorry, Pa. Millie was so upset; I felt I had to do as she bid me."

"I do understand the anxiety and strain you must have been under… I am glad you have found the courage to come and tell us the truth after all." He beckons to Louisa and she goes to him for a reassuring hug.

"I was absolutely horrified when she drowned herself… filled with remorse for what I had done and I realised then I should have sought your help. It was just that Millie begged me not to." She is crying again now and her father holds her close.

"Hush child, don't blame yourself. It was not your doing that caused all this, but that nasty piece of work, Nathan Meakins."

"I know, Pa, and he is going to the devil one way or another, either by the noose or via Van Diemen's Land."

"Well, now we know the truth we must try to make amends. When are we going to meet our granddaughter?"

"I will bring her myself in the carriage one evening, Mrs Bonfield. Things are very hectic at Alvington at the moment in preparation for Malachi and Rosa's wedding, but we will fit it in one way or another."

"Thank you, my Lord. We are very grateful for your kindness for all this time in looking after Millie's baby. We will be forever in your debt."

"Think nothing of it, Mrs Bonfield. She has brightened life in the manor for all of us. She is a little ray of sunshine every day."

"Would you care to join us in some supper, my Lord?"

"That is very kind, Mrs Bonfield, thank you."

Over the past few weeks since Easter, Isaac Warren has been busy talking with his farming friends and neighbours about the coven on Summer House Hill and he has made a decision as to who he is going to involve in any action that is planned against the two other known witches, who seem to have got off lightly. They will raise their own hue and cry making them and the law realise this will not be tolerated in their locality.

Raymond has spoken to Jean about their plan and she is fearful that her brother will get himself into trouble. She has told him that she wants nothing to do with it and advised her brother to keep out of something that is sure to end badly.

Lettie has decided that she wants to go along on this adventure with her father and her beau. On the night in question Isaac and his sons, John and Lettie Boucher and the Hawkins men all make their way to meet the other folk involved under the folly, 'Jack the Treacle Eater'. They are armed, as if they are going wassailing, to make as much noise and mayhem as they can. At the very least they want to put the fear of God into their prey.

As they approach the folly Isaac is astounded to see the number of men and women gathered there milling around and leaning against the stone archway. There are at least three times as many as he expected. He is suddenly mindful that he is responsible for instigating this and he is worried that things could easily get out of hand. It is like an army of fustian jackets with a few long skirts among them.

A hush falls over the gathering as they recognise Isaac and his sons. All the faces are looking expectantly at him. "Hello everyone," Isaac smiles to those he recognises. "We are grateful for your support in this serious matter, but I did not expect so many and I must remind you that there is a need for stealth here. We do not want to alert our quarry to our plans and so I must ask you all to be quiet until we reach the vicinity of the Round House. At first I will knock the door to see if she will come out of her own free will, but if not then we can commence more menacing tactics. The idea is that we show her we are not afraid of her powers and we will not tolerate witchcraft in our parish. We want to frighten her, to stop her overlooking us, but not harm her. We do not want to end up in court ourselves."

"Well, I think we should set up a trial by water, that is the only way to deal with witches," shouts someone from the crowd, whom Isaac does not recognise.

Isaac responds amiably, "It would be well if she believes that those are our intentions, but I do not personally want to be responsible for drowning anyone. Anyway, let us set off quietly across the fields and see if we can entice her out of her own free will. When we get there keep back in the shadows and cover your lanterns, so as not to alert her."

They all turn northward towards the summit of Summer House Hill, following the light from the hurricane lanterns as Isaac, Malachi and Jacob lead them onwards.

That evening Jean sits anxiously at home worrying about Raymond and Lettie's father. She could not stomach her supper and she cannot concentrate on her gloving. She feels she should go and warn Lord Dryer of what is planned, but she does not want to get her brother into any more trouble, even though, according to him, most of the men on the estate are involved. If she leaves the cottage, however, what excuse is she to give to her mother? Besides, she does not relish the long walk to Alvington alone with darkness falling.

Her mother is concerned. "What ails you lassie? You have not said a word this last hour?"

Jean sighs, her brows pinched together. Finally she confesses her fears, "I am worried about Ray, Ma."

"Why is that child? He said he was going to be late because he and John Boucher are after that old fox that has been taking the young pheasants."

Jean sighs again, reluctant to betray her brother, but scared witless that he will come to harm. "I don't believe they are, Ma. I believe they have gone on a witch hunt."

"A witch hunt!" exclaims her shocked mother, spitting out her pins. "Whatever do you mean, Jean?"

"I think Ray and the men from the Alvington estate have all gone off to deal with two of the witches, known to be from the coven that meets on Summer House Hill. I am worried that things will go badly. I think I should go and tell Lord Dryer."

"My God, child, tell me all that you know, Jean!"

"Well, they were talking of a witch swimming trial."

"I don't like the sound of that, Jean. Whatever are these men thinking of? Where were they going?"

"They talked of going to the Round House first, to get the high priestess, then to Summerville House to get Miss Apsey."

"This is serious Jean; no good can come from it. Common folk like us have no business taking the law into their own hands. I agree with you, we should alert Lord Dryer, but you are not going alone. It will soon be dark and so I am coming with you." She puts down her gloving. "You are quite right, things are bound to go wrong and the blame will surely fall on the heads of Ray and the others."

"We'd best hurry, for there is no time to lose. If anyone can stop it, Lord Dryer can."

The moon is partly concealed behind a cloud as they approach the Round House, giving it an eerie silhouette in the half light. Lettie has an overwhelming feeling of foreboding. Isaac puts his fingers to his lips for them all to remain silent and Lettie, who is keeping to the back of the crowd, holds her breath as he knocks loudly on the heavy wooden door.

A subdued, nervous voice calls out, "Who is there?"

"It is a neighbour who needs some assistance. Our child has a raging fever and we need some potion to ease her suffering. Please ma'am we need your help."

There is a long silence and then a muffled reply, "I am not leaving the safety of my home at this hour; I don't know who you are from Adam. I am sorry, but you must fetch a doctor. I am but a poor woman living here alone."

Isaac beckons to a woman in their party. "My wife is afraid she will die," he continues and then he indicates to the woman to join in.

At Isaac's entreaty, with a note of desperation in her voice, she says, "Please ma'am, don't turn us away."

There is another long silence and then they hear heavy bolts being drawn back on the inside of the door: she has fallen for their subterfuge. The high priestess opens the door and stands there before them. She is dressed in a long, white, cotton nightgown with a mop cap on her head. Wrapped around her is a red woollen shawl.

Swiftly the woman, who had appealed to her to help them, grabs her arm and pulls her out into the crowd, which is now milling forward. They immediately commence the hue and cry with their improvised implements.

The high priestess appears terrified; her face matches the white of her gown as she struggles to free herself. The noise of the crowd is intimidating and chilling, echoing across the hills. All of a sudden flames and the smell of burning fills the air, as an effigy is thrust skywards on a long pole and waved around in a macabre dancing motion.

The crowd let up a cheer and someone shouts out, "This is what happens to witches in our parish!"

Then Isaac says, "You may have the ideal home for overlooking, set as it is upon this hill. We can see that you can overlook the whole of Ivell and the countryside for miles around, but we want you to understand that we will not stand for it in our neighbourhood."

The high priestess responds to the sound of his reasonable words. "You are right, I can see for miles from my home," she says shakily. "But I am a white witch; you should note that this is a round house and I choose this home because the devil cannot hide in the corners of a round house."

John Boucher then speaks up angrily. "That may be so, but a witch you confess to be and an infant child was sacrificed before you and the other old crones in your coven. You are all accomplices to infanticide and we intend to set an example to the remaining witches in the vicinity."

She cries out in pain as they drag her down the garden path and into the copse, down through the bushes and trees. They pull and slide her through the mulch and down towards the River Ivell, which runs through the grounds of Summerville House.

Lettie nervously picks up the muddy and trampled red shawl as she follows reluctantly behind them. She has had a change of heart and now wishes fervently that she was back at home with her mother. Fearful tears prick her eyes – tears of guilt, for she is responsible for this, because it was her who had betrayed Lord Dryer's trust and divulged the secret of the coven.

Lettie follows the light of the flaming effigy, observing the sparks tumbling off it, as it brushes against the overhanging boughs. Several folk make attempts to scratch and pierce the high priestess with their fingernails or a variety of pins and she squeals at each attempt. She is grabbing hold of random branches to try to pull free of them, but it is to no avail. They are calling her names like 'murdering witch' and 'witching old bitch', then, as they reach the roadway in the valley, they go silent again and the group splits into two.

Isaac, Malachi and Jacob lead one group off with the high priestess, now mute with fear, towards the boat house. The other group, led by John Boucher, approaches the big house. They go around to the back entrance and Isaac persuades Jack Hawkins to speak, as he is known to them at Summerville and therefore will not arouse suspicion.

The group stand to one side in the shadows as Jack knocks on the back door. A young maid answers the knock. "May I please speak with Miss Apsey?"

"Who shall I say is calling, sir?"

"It is Jack Hawkins, Jean's uncle."

"Just a moment, sir, I will go and get her."

At Alvington Manor, Gareth answers their insistent knocking.

"We need to speak urgently to Lord Dryer, please."

"Of course, ma'am, who shall I say is calling?"

"Raymond Hawkins' mother and sister," says Jean breathlessly.

"Please follow me, he is in his study." They follow Gareth and wait with agitation outside the door, while he informs Joshua of their request to see him urgently.

"Please go through, ladies." He steps aside for them to go in and closes the door behind them. They are both hot and flushed after their long walk.

"Good evening, ladies."

They both curtsey. "Good evening, my Lord. This is my mother."

"I am pleased to meet you, Mrs Hawkins."

Jean continues, "We are sorry to disturb you my Lord, but we are very worried about Raymond and the other men from the estate."

"Please do take a seat. What is troubling you? I am sure it cannot be that bad."

"But it is my Lord; there is no time to lose, for they have all gone off on a witch hunt, my Lord."

He looks stunned. "A witch hunt!" He rubs his hand across his forehead. "The damn fools! This is serious; where have they gone, Jean?"

"They have gone to the Round House to get the high priestess and then they are going to get Apsey at Summerville House. It is beside the river, my Lord... and there is talk of a trial by water."

"When did they leave?"

"I have no idea, my Lord, but they planned to do it under cover of darkness."

"I am sorry, but you are right Jean — I don't have any time to waste. Thank you, both of you, for coming all this way to let me know, you did the right thing. Billy will take you home shortly if you would be kind enough to wait in the hall for now, and please try not to worry. I will go post haste to put a stop to this." He is up and leaving the room hurriedly, ushering them out, calling for Gareth to fetch his riding clothes and asking Michael Proctor to get Billy to saddle Capricorn.

Jean sits down on the settle next to her exhausted mother and gives a worried sigh. She is glad to have unburdened herself, but is still apprehensive lest it might be all too late to prevent disaster.

Apsey, who was easily duped, is now standing nervously beside the high priestess on the boat house jetty. She is dressed in her maid's uniform and she too has blanched; they are both huddled together, shivering in the night air.

The men are arguing among themselves. Because they are not equipped with a ducking stool they have decided to bind the women's right thumbs to their left big toes and then, with a rope tied around their waists, to throw them each in turn into the fast flowing river. If they float then they will be deemed in league with the devil, but if they do not they will be proved innocent.

The high priestess is to go first. With difficulty they separate the two women and Apsey watches as they truss up her colleague and callously fling her into the river. The woman sinks immediately. Trussed as she is, she is unable to swim, even if she could. Apsey and the witch hunters observe the circular ripples of water where the women sank.

Isaac can bear it no longer. "She did not float and therefore she is innocent. Pull her up, now."

"Let the bitch drown!" cry several voices.

Isaac grabs the rope and begins to heave her in. John Boucher and Raymond lend a hand and they are soon pulling her limp body up onto the jetty. "We have drowned her!" says Isaac guiltily.

"Nevermind her, it is now the turn of the other one," says an elderly woman, and they commence trussing Apsey.

Isaac steps forward to stop them. "Don't you think we have done enough damage for one night?"

The high priestess then makes a choking sound and vomits.

"There you are, she is alive after all, the evil, witching bitch," says a young man with a beard.

"I am sure it is only by the grace of God that her life has been saved," says Isaac, with relief. "Under the law, if she had perished, we would be responsible for murder, just as we are accusing her. I say we have made our point."

"Then maybe you are the wrong person to lead us," says a large man with long, bushy sideburns and a ruddy face. "The other one has not suffered nearly enough. Come on, lads, let's toss her in quickly."

They are manhandling Apsey when Lettie plucks up the courage to step forward from the crowd. She begs them, "Please stop this, it is going too far. We do not want to be judged to be as bad as they were."

"Who are you, maid, to be telling us what to do?" asks the young man with the beard.

"I reckon she is one of them herself, coming to plead for them. Let's do her next," says the ruddy-faced man as he shoves Apsey unceremoniously into the river and grabs hold of Lettie.

Lettie screams in terror, "Let me go!"

"Take your hands off her," says John Boucher, pushing through the crowd onto the jetty, followed by Malachi. The large, ruddy-faced man elbows John aside, but Malachi pulls Lettie free and then picks him up and hurls him into the river. Lettie runs to her father as a fight breaks out among the different factions of the mob. They have forgotten Apsey at the end of the rope.

Suddenly a shot rings out and the brawling is interrupted. "Get that woman out of the water this instance."

Isaac recognises the voice of his lordship. He grabs the rope and with help they haul her back onto the shore of the river. She is shivering with fright and coughing up river water. The ruddy faced man is trying to drag his dripping body back onto the jetty.

Joshua can see that the two women are traumatised, but they have narrowly survived their trial by water. He grabs the remains of the charred effigy and hurls it angrily into the river and then waves his pistol around menacingly until the sullen crowd have dispersed, apart from those from his own estate. The ruddy-faced man goes off with the support of his comrades. Soft-hearted Lettie shakes the woodland debris from the woollen shawl and wraps it around the shoulders of the two women. She feels ashamed. *What if these folk took against her own mother like this for using her charms and potions?* She comforts the women as best she can, whispering to them, "You are safe now; Lord Dryer will not let any further harm come to you."

Joshua directs his annoyance at his workers. "Whatever were you men thinking of, taking the law into your own hands? There could be any number of mitigating circumstances why those two women became involved in the coven. Apart from anything else, they were both dependent on the Meakins for their livelihood and all this would have come out in a court of law. Under these circumstances, I believe they have both gone through enough traumas, as according to our old laws they did not float and are therefore innocent.

"Lettie, please take Olivia Meakins' maid back to the house and get help from the staff there to attend to all her needs. John, you and Raymond go with her and then you are all to go straight back home.

"Thomas and Frank, you are both young and strong so I want you to carry this lady back to the Round House. Jack and Isaac, I want you to go with them and make sure that she is safe. She will need a hot toddy and a fire lit to make sure that she suffers no physical ill effect; you have done enough damage to her peace of mind already.

"Malachi and Jacob, I want you to see that there is no more trouble from the rabble rousers and then get yourselves back home. I will see you all tomorrow."

The men look shamefaced as they do as he bids and the rest turn to home.

The following day Joshua has the perpetrators lined up outside on the terrace, where he berates them indignantly. "I am shocked and disappointed by your actions last night. Your behaviour was barbaric, forming a huge gang of rabble rousers to terrorise two simple women like you did. You are very fortunate that neither of the women drowned, for you would have had that on your consciences for ever." He pauses significantly, looking at each of the men, and then he continues, "I want your assurances that you will never act as judge and jury against your fellow countrymen or women ever again. I did not become a Justice of the Peace to find my own employees usurping the law in this uncivilised way."

Isaac looks crestfallen. "I am sorry, my Lord, it was me who started it. I have been overlooked so many times in the past and I was so angry when I thought of that innocent babe, but I was also frightened when the crowd became unruly and I realised I could not keep order. There were far more folk joined us than I expected."

"It is not fair to put all the blame on Isaac, for we were all keen to join in, my Lord," says Jack Hawkins.

"That is right, my Lord, but we did not allow for the possible consequences," says John Boucher, shame-facedly.

"Well, I hope you have learned a hard lesson. Don't, however, think you are getting away with this without some form of recompense; maybe a contribution to the church or the poor house. I will give some thought as to what that will be, but in the meantime I am going to ask each of you for your word of honour that this will never happen again."

Joshua goes to each of them in turn and they all respond, "You have my word, my Lord."

"Then, for now, let that be an end to it. I want no more talk of it here on the estate, for the fewer people who know about it the better. Please all go back about your work and I will come to you individually when I have decided upon your punishment."

CHAPTER 25 *(May 1854)*

ROSA AND MALACHI'S WEDDING

All those involved in the witch hunt are eager to put the trauma behind them and the Warren family are no exception. Jacob has been kept busy with the lambing and on the 15th May he is exhibiting some of his sheep and lambs at the Ivell Agricultural Show at Huish Field. Malachi is going along to help him and at dawn that morning they are out in the yard, hard at it washing and brushing the animals ready for the competition. They have had a few days of heavy rainfall and the mud is caked around their legs and bellies, but eventually they are all hosed down and looking spruce again. As the sun comes up, it promises to be a cloud-free day.

Jacob whistles for his two collie dogs, Hamish and Angus, who slink out of their kennel and stretch lazily, then they set off together into town. Jacob leads the flock off by rattling a bucket of feed and Malachi and the sheepdogs bring up the rear. The small lambs run alongside their mothers, occasionally jumping in the air for the sheer fun of it and Malachi enjoys watching their antics as they go along.

He is thinking of Rosa and their wedding ceremony on Sunday. It is to be the start of his new life as a husband, with responsibilities for providing for a wife. And what a wife! He really is very lucky to have found such a beautiful and talented girl, but it is still hard for him to imagine his carefree existence transforming into that of a family man like his father. Will they have many children? Will there be a boy to take over the farm, like he will someday? He tries to picture himself sitting with Rosa at his hearth, her with a child in her arms and another playing at her feet. It would be a dream come true and he wants to make her happy more than anything else in the world.

When they draw near to the new railway line, they can see in front of them a flock of geese, honking and posturing as they are herded through the stone bridge underpass by a neighbour, and they follow on through behind them. Up ahead they hear vendors shouting their wares, cattle lowing, more sheep bleating, chickens clucking and people greeting friends as they near the showground. The cacophony of sound grows louder when they enter the field and the steward shows them to their enclosure. The dogs herd the flock through into their corral and lie down on guard, whilst the men relax and look about them.

Interspersed among the livestock areas are various vendor's stalls selling anything from the latest agricultural implements to dairy food, hot refreshments, wickerwork, domestic ironmongery, haberdashery and sweet candies.

"Mal, I am going to go off to get myself some new blade shears, ready for shearing next month. Do you want to stay here or come along?"

"The dogs will look after the flock; I'll come along with you and have a look around."

They set off together, inspecting the livestock, especially the other sheep, and Jacob finds the ironmongery stall. He chooses some well made, robust blade shears and pays the man, looking with interest at all the other items on display. Malachi, however, has spotted the familiar pugilist's boxing booth and, when Jacob has finished perusing, they stroll over to see the proprietor. It is the same showman who hosted the match that Malachi won at the Saint Leonard's Day fair. He will never forget how invincible he had felt when he had won those ten guineas.

The showman sees Malachi and Jacob. "I recognise you two boys, don't I?"

"Yes sir, I took up a challenge once before."

"That's right, you were the 'Magnificent Something or Other', weren't you?"

"'Malachi the Magnificent', sir," he says with a grin.

"Well, I have the very man to challenge you here later today." He turns to Jacob. "You were his second, weren't you lad?"

"That is right, sir, and I am to be his second again this Sunday when he is to be wed." He looks at his brother as he adds, "So it would not be wise to go into combat before then and spoil his handsome face."

Malachi looks despondent, but his brother is right. Rosa would never forgive him if he turned up for his wedding bloodied and bruised. "My brother is right; although it vexes me, I will have to forgo the opportunity this time, sir."

"Even though it may mean another ten guineas for your marriage pot?"

"Even so, I am afraid. My fiancée has been planning this wedding for months; it will not do to upset her on her big day. I am sorry, but will you be here again at the Saint Bartholomew's Day fair in June?"

"I may well be, good sir."

"Then I will see you there, after my nuptials."

"I hope so lad, because I see a little of Jem Mace in you. I think you could be a champion."

They turn away and Jacob looks accusingly at

his brother. "You were actually prepared to take up the gauntlet, weren't you?"

"I was tempted, Jake; it is such a lot of money and it would really set us up. There is so much stuff we need in order to make that cottage into a home. I don't know where it is all going to come from."

"Ma and Pa won't let you struggle, they will surely give you some essentials. It will take years to build up all the additional comforts that we enjoy, a lot of which our parents inherited from our grandparents. Anyway, you only have to wait another month to satisfy your lust for blood and sweat, as it turns out."

As they wander on they can see the judges inspecting the shire horses; several splendid mares and stallions, their polished tackle glinting in the morning sunshine. In another enclosure are the colts, fillies, foals and geldings on sale for breeding, riding, driving and farm work. The lads enjoy walking around, meeting and greeting their neighbouring farmers and assessing all the animals on show and for sale. In the main, it is a man's world and they both feel completely at home.

They are enjoying some ham and a baked potato when Malachi is nudged from behind and nearly spills his lunch. He turns around, expecting an apology, but comes face to face with the Wessex Wonder, who he had knocked unconscious the last time he fought.

Malachi suspects that the nudge had been deliberate, but no apology is forthcoming.

"Ah, is it not the chap who had the lucky punch last time we met, Fred?" the pugilist comments to his colleague.

"That was no lucky punch, my friend; I fought you fair and square and won the purse," replies Malachi indignantly.

"In that case you will be happy to give me a sporting chance once more, to prove your point?"

"I think not. I have no need to prove anything. As I said, I won fair and square the last time we met." Malachi turns away.

"I do believe I see a yellow streak down this chap's back. Do you see it too, Fred?"

"That I do, Hubert."

Malachi turns back laughing, determined not to rise to their taunting, "Hubert! No wonder you call yourself the Wessex Wonder."

"Well, I don't see what is so damn 'Magnificent' about being too cowardly to take me on again."

Jacob, seeing the danger, steps forward. "My brother is no coward, sir. He is twice the man you will ever be."

"Ah! So your little brother has a voice, does he? How about you and me together in the ring instead?"

Malachi quickly intercedes. "There is no need for that, I don't take kindly to being called a coward and I will take you on myself, but in the proper ring where folk can place a bet if they wish."

Jacob pulls him aside. "Mal, I can stick up for myself, there is no need for you to fight him. No need at all."

However, it is too late; the Wessex Wonder jumps at the opportunity. "So be it, I will be waiting for you at the boxing booth in an hour."

Later that evening, back at Home Farm Isaac Warren has just finished milking his herd of cows. He is stiff and tired as he enters the farmhouse, to find his mother snoozing beside the range in the kitchen and his wife and daughters working together by lamplight in the parlour. Beth is sewing covered buttons and putting the finishing touches onto Lucy's bridesmaid's gown. Lucy has Bunny up on the table, turning around slowly, so that she can pin up the hem on her handmaiden's frock. They make a pretty scene and he sighs contentedly as he sinks wearily into his armchair. There will be no more witch hunts for him; he knows he will be a proud man in three days time, on his eldest son's wedding day, and he thanks the Lord that no permanent harm came to the two poor witches to jeopardise his happy family life.

"I'll just finish this button, dear, then I will make you some supper."

"No hurry Beth, I'm merely glad the day is over and I can put my feet up."

Moments later he hears the pump in the outhouse and then his lads entering. Jacob looks around the door first.

"I am warning you all, you had better brace yourselves for a bit of a shock."

Then Malachi enters; his face is a mass of cuts and bruises, one eye completely hidden by the swollen skin around it and his hands are battered and swollen.

"Oh Malachi, whatever have you done now?" says his mother pitifully.

"I am fine, Ma, 'tis just superficial."

"But what happened? Were you attacked?"

"No, Ma, I was challenged to fight in the ring. At first I said no, but then the chap I beat last time called me a coward, so I had no choice."

"But the wedding! Whatever will Rosa think when she sees you looking like this?" asks Lucy.

Bunny bursts into tears.

"Really, Ma, it will be all right. I heal quickly; it won't look so bad in three days time."

"I wouldn't bank on that my son; besides, you

"are bound to see Rosa before then."

"If I was Rosa, I might well call the whole thing off," says Lucy haughtily.

"Well, if I have my way she won't see me before our wedding day. I may need your help to endeavour to keep us apart until then. Jacob and I are both busy with the agricultural show, so it should not be a problem."

Beth puts down her sewing things and gets up. "Come into the kitchen and I'll find some balm for your cuts and bruises. Lucy, would you please make a start on the supper? Bunny, please stop crying, everything will be fine."

Isaac delays Malachi. "Before you go son, what was the outcome?"

"I won the purse again, Pa. Not only that, Jake backed me to win and he won five guineas for himself."

"Well done lads! At least it was all worthwhile in the end."

Malachi winces as he attempts a wry smile. "That is what I hope Rosa will say… eventually."

Malachi asks Lucy to confide in Louisa what has happened and for her to endeavour to keep Rosa and Malachi apart. This is not as easy as it sounds, because Rosa has many things she wants to discuss with her beau before the big day. She is disappointed that he is so involved with the agricultural show that he is not available, even during the evenings.

After Rosa has made several daily unsuccessful trips to Home Farm, Louisa finally persuades her that it is bad luck to see the groom on the eve of the wedding night. She can see that Rosa is upset and puzzled that Malachi has been avoiding her.

They are working together, decorating the little

estate chapel with flowers, when Rosa comments, "Maybe he has had second thoughts about us getting married?"

"No, of course he hasn't. He has just been very busy Rosa; besides, maybe he has been planning a surprise for you."

"What do you mean a surprise?"

"I don't know, do I? But I am sure that if you are patient things will come to light and all will be fine." She did not sound very convincing even to herself, but what else could she say? "This is supposed to be a time when you enjoy support from all your girlfriends and so Mrs Abbott has arranged for us all to have supper together. Forget about Malachi for now. I'll finish up here while you go and get yourself changed, for the others will be here soon."

The girls arrive one after the other, each with their own contributions to Rosa's bottom drawer and she is, for the time being, distracted from her worries. Mrs Abbott opens a bottle of elderflower wine from Flora's pantry and they all enjoy a happy, relaxed evening, looking forward to the celebrations the following day.

Malachi is pleased that the swelling has gone down around his eyes, although the purplish-yellow bruising still remains. He prays that Rosa will not be so angry with him that it spoils her wedding day. He smiles to himself as he watches his whole family, all in a state of excitement as they prepare for this momentous occasion. He and Jacob each dress formally in their ivory silk ruffled shirts and bow ties, deep purple waistcoats, black morning coats and moleskin trousers, while their father is wearing his Sunday best lounge suit. Mrs Warren is also in her Sunday best costume as she helps Lucy and Bunny to dress in their different shades of lilac bridesmaid's gowns. Everyone is filled with nervous anticipation; even Malachi's father cut himself shaving earlier, something he has not done for years.

Jacob has put the precious gold wedding ring in his waistcoat pocket and soon they are all leaving the farm house for the short walk to the chapel, his two sisters holding up their skirts to avoid the dirt. Lucy, as always, looks very demure and sophisticated, but it is strange to see Bunny, the baby of the family, also looking more like a young lady. Lucy takes Bunny into the Dower House to join Rosa and Louisa, while he continues on towards the chapel with Jacob and his parents, where they are greeted enthusiastically by the guests already milling about outside. They loiter there chatting until Reverend Phelps arrives and the congregation filter inside to take their seats, before the arrival of the bride.

Louisa is helping Rosa to dress in her wedding gown before she dons her own bridesmaid outfit. When she first enters Rosa's room, Rosa is in her robe. She has already washed and dressed in her undergarments, but she is waiting for Louisa to lace up her corset. This done, she dons her wedding chemise, which is of the finest tulle and has a high, round neckline with long sleeves edged with lace. Then Louisa helps her on with the beautiful wedding gown. It has an ivory tinted lace bodice, with a scooped neckline and layered lace capped sleeves, dipping down in a V shape at the waist and giving way to multiple layers of the softest tulle skirts. Her hair is pinned up and Louisa carefully places the floral band among her curls, arranging the delicate veil to hang mistily over her shoulders.

"Oh Rosa! You look like an angel!"

"Thank you, Lou Lou, but come on my dear friend, don't tarry – it is your turn now. Quickly, I can hear Lucy and Bunny coming."

"Lucy can help me, Rosa. You just make sure you don't get any rouge on that dress."

Louisa meets Lucy on the landing and they go into her room. Lucy ties Louisa's laces tightly and then helps her on with her gown. Like Lucy's, it is a deeper shade of lilac than Bunny's and it looks fabulous with her dark auburn hair, pinned up in her tortoiseshell comb. They are just completing the finishing touches when they hear Joshua calling up to them: "I am here ready to escort you young ladies to the chapel."

"Go and tell him we are just coming, Bunny," says Lucy.

Bunny goes to the top of the stairs and, holding up her skirts, she carefully descends. "They are just coming, Lord Dryer, sir." No sooner said, the girls all follow her down.

Bunny picks up her basket of flowers and Lucy passes the bouquet to Rosa.

"My word, Rosa, you really are a very beautiful bride. Malachi is a very lucky fellow and I think myself truly honoured to be giving you away to him today," says Joshua.

"Thank you, my Lord." Rosa blushes at the compliment.

Joshua then looks gently at Louisa. "You all look absolutely splendid. Come, let us not keep everyone waiting any longer." He holds out his arm for Rosa and they set off to the chapel, with the bridesmaids making a pretty procession behind them.

Louisa cannot help feeling a little melancholy as

she walks behind Joshua and Rosa, for they look like they are the wedding couple. Despite knowing such is not the case, she still feels bitter pangs of jealousy stabbing mercilessly at her heart. *I am a little fool, who will end up like my poor sister if I continue to follow this impossible dream.* She pushes away the taunting images and places a happy smile on her face for Rosa's sake.

Malachi and Jacob are sitting in the front pew, awaiting the arrival of Rosa and her entourage. The organist is playing incidental music, until the signal that the bride is about to walk down the aisle, when he begins to play the 'Wedding March' by Mendelssohn. Malachi does not turn to look at Rosa for fear he will frighten her, but stands looking towards the altar until she is standing beside him. Then he looks out of the corner of his eye to see her.

She looks so beautiful he wants to cry. Her skin is like the finest porcelain, her cheeks tinted with rouge. He has never felt so moved before. She has cream coloured blossom fixed in a band across her dark hair and a fragile veil falling delicately from it. Her gown has a fitted lace bodice over her rounded, wonderful breasts and is nipped in at her tiny waist, falling in layers of light-weight cream material. He has never felt so proud. Then she turns towards him and he sees the horror in her eyes.

Rosa cannot believe that Malachi is standing before her on their wedding day in such a dreadful state. Her handsome beau is sporting two black eyes, as well as other cuts and bruises. Whatever has he been doing! Her questions will have to wait because

Reverend Phelps is starting the ceremony, but her mind is wandering. Someone has done this to Malachi and he has been hiding from her because of this, she is sure.

"Let us sing together the hymn 'Praise my Soul the King of Heaven'."

Rosa sings along with the congregation until she comes to the line: *'rescues us from all our foes'*, when she looks across at Malachi meaningfully. He, realising she is looking at him, turns and smiles and winks at her. She cannot help but smile back at his cheeky, happy grin and she knows then that, despite sporting an eye that matches his purple waistcoat, he has come to no harm.

The hymn comes to an end and the congregation all sit down.

"Dearly beloved, we are gathered together here in the sight of God, and in the face of this congregation, to join together this man and this woman in holy matrimony; which is an honourable estate…"

Joshua is standing beside Rosa, feeling envious of their love and devotion. For the first time in his life he is yearning for the love and companionship of a wife. He imagines himself stood in Malachi's place and Louisa stood on his left. The sound of the ongoing ceremony is fading like a distant echo.

"Wilt though have this woman to thy wedded wife…"

His mind wanders to the time he comforted her beside the pond after Millie's body was found and how his heart ached for her; the time he gave her the Boxing Day fare for her family and they were alone together before she hurried away, as if she was frightened of him; the many times they have sat

421

in perfect harmony reading together in the library and how pleased she was when they made friends walking in the orchard, when he asked her to call him Joshua.

"… and, forsaking all others, keep thee only unto him, so long as ye both shall live?"

Rosa answers, "I will."

Joshua is brought back to reality when he suddenly hears David Phelps asking, "Who giveth this woman to be married to this man?"

He steps forward and places Rosa's hands in those of the vicar, then steps back into the pew behind him where he is able to observe Louisa, who is standing immediately behind the bride, beside Lucy. *She is everything a man could want in a wife: she is beautiful and clever, with an appealing face; wonderful, rich, dark red hair; hypnotic aquamarine eyes and a gorgeous figure. His family all adore her. Why has he not said something before now?*

"I take thee, Rosa Marie Price, to my wedded wife, to have and to hold from this day forward, for better for worse, for richer for poorer, in sickness and in health, to love and to cherish, till death us do part…"

It is such a solemn vow to love someone until parted by death, but he is ready to promise this to the woman he loves. He studies her carefully, trying to read her mind. He is definitely ready to plight his troth to Louisa, but will she accept his proposal?

Rosa is taking Malachi's right hand in hers and repeating after David Phelps, "I take thee, Malachi Isaac Warren, to my wedded husband, to have and to hold from this day forward, for better for worse, for richer for poorer, in sickness and in health, to love, cherish and to obey until death us do part, according to God's holy ordinance and thereto I plight thee my troth."

Jacob steps forward with the ring and it is placed on the bible held by David Phelps, who holds it out for Malachi to place on the fourth finger of Rosa's left hand. He holds it there and repeats after the vicar: "With this ring I thee wed, with my body I thee worship, and with all my worldly goods I thee endow, in the name of the Father, and of the Son and of the Holy Ghost. Amen."

They both kneel down and David Phelps says, "Let us pray."

The congregation all drop to their knees in prayer and Joshua has an overwhelming urge to hold out his hand to Louisa, as David Phelps continues, "Oh eternal God, Creator and Preserver of all mankind, Giver of all spiritual grace, the author of everlasting life…"

The prayers over, David Phelps joins their right hands together and says, "Those whom God has joined together, let no man put asunder."

Then he directs his words to the congregation. "For as much as Rosa and Malachi have consented together in holy wedlock, and have witnessed the same before God and this company, and thereto have given and pledged their troth either to other, and have declared the same by giving and receiving of a ring, and by the joining of hands; I pronounce that they be man and wife together. In the name of the Father, and of the Son, and of the Holy Ghost. Amen."

David Phelps then adds his blessing, but Joshua is not really listening; he is working out a plan in his head. His thoughts are interrupted again when he hears David Phelps saying: "Let us all sing together, 'Lead us, Heavenly Father, lead us'."

After the hymn the happy couple go off together to sign the register and the organist plays Bach's 'Air on a G string'. Louisa signs her name as Rosa's witness and Lucy signs for her brother. The ceremony is then concluded and the organist plays the 'Trumpet Voluntary' by Mendelssohn, as the bride and groom walk through the chapel, hand in hand as man and wife, Malachi beaming from ear to ear and Rosa smiling sweetly.

Joshua follows them out into the sunshine and the congregation spill out behind them. He watches Louisa joining the other maids and throwing rice over the couple, for good luck. She looks so carefree and happy, after the days of worry prior to the court case. He makes up his mind to act before it is too late and he loses his nerve, but first he needs to have a word with David Phelps.

CHAPTER 26 *(June 1854)*

A TOWERING PROPOSITION

The Alvington Manor staff are still buzzing with excitement the following day, even though the celebrations are all over. On Mrs Abbot's instructions, Louisa is ferrying some of the floral arrangements from the chapel to the manor for everyone's continued enjoyment.

Joshua catches her at the altar of St Andrew's, standing in a shaft of light from the stained glass window and looking quite angelic. He is determined to put his plan into operation as quickly as possible.

"Ah, Louisa, after you have finished your duties today, I wonder if you would accompany me on an errand this evening in Odcombe? I need your help with something very important."

"Of course, my Lord." He raises his eyebrows and watches her face suffuse with colour as she realises her mistake. "I mean, of course, Joshua... may I have a few moments at the end of the day, to change my clothes?"

"There is no need for that; your uniform will do splendidly. I will wait for you outside with the curricle."

Louisa is intrigued – what could he possibly want with her in Odcombe? Although she spends the whole day musing over it, she is none the wiser when her working day is over. She goes with a racing heart to find her master, as arranged. He is sitting waiting for her in the curricle and she feels the heat rise in her as he leans over to hand her up beside him, before they set off at a trot up Pound Lane.

Louisa is glad of the fresh breeze as it gently lifts her hair and cools her flushed cheeks. She really wants to be looking her best, seated as she is so close to her beloved. Looking out across the countryside she thinks how lovely it is, bathed in the evening sunlight as it casts its slanting shadows, with birds and butterflies flitting among the wild flowers and hedgerows. She is determined to enjoy this rare and precious moment spent alone with Joshua. It is not long before they pull up outside the Church of St Peter and St Paul, where he clambers down quickly in order to help her descend.

He takes her arm and leads her up the path to the church. She thinks back to yesterday when he was escorting Rosa to the church and flushes with pleasure, as she enjoys the feel of his manly strength supporting her this time. She can hear organ music wafting on the evening air and, as the church door opens, she recognises the melody as 'Jesu, Joy of Man's Desire'.

Joshua acknowledges the organist with a wave of his hand. "The organist is practising this evening," he explains to her. "Come, follow me."

She is quite mystified as he leads her to a small arched doorway, set on one side of the bell ringing chamber at the back of the knave. He takes out a key and unlocks it. "Come on," he says, holding out his hand.

Louisa takes his hand and follows him happily through the doorway and up some narrow, ancient, kite-shaped stone steps, the edges worn away by the many footsteps throughout the ages. The stairway is very narrow and dusty and she is glad she is wearing her uniform, for it would have been impossible with the wider skirts of her Sunday best outfits. The spiral stairway goes up and up and Louisa's legs are aching a little by the time they reach the belfry. As they reach the small door at the top she looks down at the belfry with its louvered windows and she can see the six graded bells with their ropes descending down into the ringing chamber far below them.

Joshua opens the door and they step out onto the rooftop of the church tower. Louisa is shaking as she steps gingerly towards the balustrade at the edge of the roof and gasps in wonder as she takes in the magnificent views for miles all around her. She can see over the rooftops of Ivell as far as Montacute and even Ilchester in the north, into the valleys of East and West Coker and as far as West Chinnock to the south west.

"Isn't it wonderful?" says Joshua, coming to stand immediately behind her.

"It is amazing, Joshua, I never imagined you would be able to see so far. It is panoramic." The organ music is drifting up to them and mingling with the birdsong. House martins are darting to and fro and a song thrush is perched high in the yew tree at the edge of the churchyard, serenading its mate.

"I wanted to bring you up here to show you the extent of the boundaries of the Alvington estate. You see Camp Road and the estate cottages?"

"Yes."

"Well, that is the boundary to the south; and you see the new railway, beyond Lease Farm?"

"Yes."

"Well, that is more or less the boundary to the north, apart from a few fields the other side of the underpass. On the west it is right up to the churchyard here, and on the east it ranges nearly as far as Nash Priory." Joshua points out the landmark, "You see over there?"

"Wow, how wonderful to be able to see the whole of your estate from up here." Louisa is looking at all the tiny cattle, sheep and pigs and all the miniature buildings. "Even the manor looks like a child's model, it is quite magical!" She sighs with satisfaction and wonder. "Look, I can see Elsie taking in the washing!"

They both laugh.

Joshua looks thrilled to see the awe and amazement on Louisa's face. "However, the magnificent view of the estate is not the only reason I have brought you up here."

She is absolutely stunned and amazed when he suddenly drops down on one knee and takes her right hand in his. She begins to shake nervously, unable to believe what she is seeing.

Joshua looks earnestly up into her anxious face; he must be able to feel her trembling. "The most important matter that I wanted to talk to you about is something I have been thinking of and longing for for some time now. I want to ask if you, Louisa Elizabeth Bonfield, will do me the great honour of accepting my proposal of marriage and becoming my wife? I promise to love, cherish and honour you, and I promise that all my worldly goods, which you see before you now –" he holds out his other hand and extends it around as far as Louisa is able to see, " – I thee endow."

He completely takes her breath away. *Marriage!* Louisa has gone weak at the knees. She looks down into his eager, upturned face. *Surely he cannot be jesting about such a serious matter?* She sees the gentle, loving look in his eyes and knows immediately that he is serious. "You really mean it, Joshua? You really love me?"

"Of course I do, you silly goose."

Tears of joy prick her eyes, as she softly replies, "I will... gladly, I will."

Joshua immediately stands and, taking her in his arms, he kisses her tenderly. She feels as if the tower is spinning, as she closes her eyes and kisses him back passionately. The organ music wafts up through the belfry. This is the most romantic thing that has ever happened to her. She feels that she must be the luckiest girl alive.

He leads her away from the edge of the tower, so that she is supported by the little doorway, kissing and caressing her in the most gentle loving way. She eventually pulls away from him for air. "I must be dizzy with love for you. I don't know how my shaking legs are going to carry me back down those stairs!" They both laugh happily.

"We have a lot to plan, my darling, but one of the very first things I should like for us to do is to go and tell your parents that we are to be a real family now, and that we will adopt Aurora as our own child."

"Oh Joshua, that would be wonderful! They will be so amazed." She looks out towards Preston Plucknett to find the little cluster of cottages, where she can just make out her family home and the Abbey Farm opposite. She can see a miniature carriage and horses travelling along the Preston Road into Ivell, but that is the only sign of life near to her home. She feels like waving, just in case her parents are looking in her direction. "Can we go and tell them tomorrow?"

"Of course we can."

Louisa smiles. "I feel like shouting out our news, so that the whole world can hear."

Joshua pulls her back towards the edge against the balustrade. "Come on, let's shout out that we are on top of the world!" He puts his arm around her. "Ready; one, two, three…"

They both shout in unison, "We are on top of the world!" then dissolve into happy giggles.

The following day, early in the evening, Louisa has put on her Sunday best costume, dressed little Aurora in her prettiest frock and pinafore and tied back the top layer of her hair with a matching ribbon, in readiness for their meeting with her parents. The child is two years and eight months old and is able to express herself well. She has not long been out of nappies and is very particular about what she wears. Today she is happy with her floral print, layered frock with the white, lace-edged pinafore and soft kid leather booties. She is running around in the driveway, watching her skirts swish to and fro with each turn. Joshua chases and catches her, making her squeal with delight as he lifts her up into the carriage and Louisa climbs in beside her.

The trip to her parents' home is short, but Joshua insists on the carriage. "I don't want my two ladies getting tired out," he says, knowing it is not long before Aurora would need her bed.

Even though Louisa is a little apprehensive about her parents' reaction to Aurora, she is incredibly excited to be going to tell them that Joshua has asked her to marry him. She will, after all, be Mistress of Alvington Manor and she still cannot believe how fortunate she is to have been chosen by Joshua, whom she loves with all her heart.

"I think we should introduce them to Aurora, before we tell them the good news about our engagement, Joshua." Her mind goes back to earlier in the day, when Joshua had taken her into town and she had chosen her engagement ring. She removes her glove and looks down at her dainty little diamond ring, glinting in the spring sunlight. Her mother is going to be so thrilled.

"Pretty ring, Lou Lou," says Aurora.

"Yes, my darling, it is my engagement ring." She looks up at Joshua and they both smile happily.

The carriage pulls up outside her old home and Joshua steps down. He lifts down Aurora and then hands down Louisa.

Louisa taps the front door as she opens it and walks in. Her parents are relaxing in their parlour and look up with pleasure on their faces as they realise it is Louisa.

"Hello, Mama, Papa; I have bought some visitors to see you both."

"Hello, my Lord. Welcome once more to our home; please sit down." Mr Bonfield jumps up to give his guest a comfortable seat.

"No thank you, Mr Bonfield, I would not dream of disturbing you, besides we have another little visitor for you." He opens the door wider to encourage the child to follow them in. Louisa can see that her mother is immediately captivated.

"And who is this little charmer?" asks her mother, smiling down at Aurora.

"This is Aurora, Mama."

"Hello, Aurora, you are a little sweetie, aren't you?"

Aurora has become shy and is hiding behind Louisa's skirts. "Say hello, darling, this is my mama."

"Hello," she whispers, peeping from behind Louisa.

"Would you like a piece of cake, poppet?"

"Yes please," she says coyly.

"Come and sit down next to our Louisa and I will fetch some cake for us all." Mrs Bonfield goes into the scullery to the larder and returns with a

Victoria sponge cake and some plates. She cuts off a piece for Aurora, who accepts it eagerly and sits eating happily while the adults talk.

"She is a lovely child and so like both you and Millie, Lou Lou."

"I know, Ma, she is happy and contented too."

Her mother engages the child in conversation. "I like your pretty frock, Aurora."

"Tank you." Aurora brushes away some crumbs and smoothes her skirt. "I have dot mashing hair ribbons too."

"I can see and you look lovely, darling."

Joshua clears his throat. "Our visit today is actually for two important reasons. The first, of course, is for you to meet your delightful little granddaughter Aurora, but the second reason is perhaps even more significant. You see, I wish to ask you, Mr Bonfield, for your daughter's hand in marriage?"

Louisa is amused by the look of shock on her father's face. "'Tis true Pa, and with your blessing, I have said yes."

Louisa's father looks meaningfully at her mother, then turns back to Joshua. "Well of course we would give our blessing. All we have ever wanted is for our Louisa to be safe and happy, and I can see that she looks happier than I have ever seen her." He holds out his hand to Joshua and they shake hands, as if to seal a bargain.

Louisa's mother jumps up to hug her daughter tearfully. "Oh Lou Lou, how truly wonderful!"

"Look at my engagement ring, Ma." Louisa removes her gloves.

"My love, it is beautiful."

Her father clears his throat emotionally. "Well, I think we should raise a glass and celebrate your happy engagement. Have we a drop of mead handy, Martha?"

"I am sure we have." She goes to the sideboard and brings out a bottle. "Get us some glasses, Lou Lou."

Louisa fetches some glasses from the kitchen and her father pours out the liquor. "I would like to raise a toast to welcome Lord Dryer into our family, and to bless your engagement to our Louisa. Congratulations to the both of you."

They all raise their glasses to toast Louisa and Joshua's futures together. Louisa enjoys the sugary warmth of the mead and the happiness radiating from all present.

Joshua, however, is keen to reassure them. "Now that you have given us your blessing, I want you to know that when Louisa and I are married, we plan to adopt Aurora as our daughter."

"That is very kind of you, my Lord. If it wasn't for the fact that she has already been brought up knowing Alvington to be her home, we would offer to take her in with us," says Mr Bonfield thoughtfully. "But, I can see she is completely content with both of you, so what more could we want for her?" He holds up his glass again. "Let us raise a glass to young Aurora: may her future be full of love and laughter, with worries few, and may she be fulfilled in all her hopes and dreams." They all raise their glasses and drink a toast to Aurora and her future happiness, before spending a cheery hour chatting together until it is time to take the child home to her bed.

On the short trip home to Alvington Manor, Joshua is reminded of the day he travelled this same route to his new home, accompanied by his good friend, Ambrose Fairway. Everything along the way was fascinating to him, but his abiding memory was the man sitting astride his dappled grey horse up on the hill, and the young red head who was so distressed and running for dear life away from him. *What a tragedy that had led to, but maybe between us, Louisa and I will now be able to make amends.*

He turns to Louisa. "I feel so optimistic that all our troubles are over now; together we will make a good, loving home for Aurora and make up for the poor start she had in life."

"Yes, Joshua, I feel just the same. Now that the villainous Meakins is out of the picture, whether he should hang or be transported, nothing should stand in our way. He will never be able to hurt us again, will he?"

ACKNOWLEDGEMENTS

I should like to take this opportunity to thank my husband, Barry, for his patience and support, and for his contribution of the thumbnail images for the map; my son, James, for taking the night-time photographs that were used for the cover and my daughter, Nicky, for reading the manuscript and for her crucial, insightful advice.

Also my gratitude goes to my other family members and friends who have kindly read my story and offered their encouragement (you know who you are).

Finally, thank you to all at Matador for their guidance in production of my books.